The Anuk Chronicles

The Ballad of Persephone

Abdur R Mohammed

Other Works by Abdur R Mohammed

<u>The Anuk Chronicles Series</u>

Rise of Villains, Vol 1

Rise of Prophecy, Vol. 2

The Anuk Chronicles

The Ballad of
Persephone

Abdur R Mohammed

Copyright

Cover design by Abdur R. Mohammed. Images courtesy Pixabay
Interior images courtesy Abdur R Mohammed & Pixabay
Editor: Jeff DeMarco
DeMarco Writing and Editing, LLC
Lexington, MI
(989-912-9011) https://demarcowriter.com

Abdur R. Mohammed

Visit my website at www.theanukchronicles.com

First Printed in the United States of America

First Printing: August 2019
Paperback :ISBN 13: 978-1-7324-7536-6
Digital Copy: ISBN 13: 978-1-7324-7537-3

Dedication

"To the One True Master of the Universe"

To the Men and Women of the Armed Forces around the world who sacrifice more than their average citizen counterpart will ever know.

To all who challenge the contemporary fallacies which plague the past, influence the present, and hamper the future.

To family, a reality transcending blood, space, and time.

Acknowledgements

Erich Von Daniken..................... www.daniken.com
Author/Researcher/Lecturer. Chariots of the gods

Andrew Collins................... www.andrewcollins.com
Author/Researcher/Lecturer. Gods of Eden

Jenna Moreci....................... www.jennamoreci.com
Author of The Saviors Champion & EVE the Awakening.

Meg LaTorre......................... https://iwriterly.com
Author/YouTuber/Fmr. Literary Agent.

Vivien Reis............................ www.vivienreis.com
Author of The Elysian Prophecy series.

Jeff DeMarco................... https://demarcowriter.com
Author of Once Upon a Wolfpack, Tread Fallen Nation, Into Armageddon, Born of Chaos.

Stuart Arbury.............. Ramo Law – Los Angeles ,CA
Entertainment Exec.

Preface

"The Ballad of Persephone" is the heart of "The Anuk Chronicles." This installment is a 'Stand-alone' story to Volume I & II, but it connects elements presented, and emboldens upcoming struggles.

If you enjoy this novel, please leave a review on amazon, goodreads, and/or storefront where you received your copy; doing so will be a tremendous help.

Please consider sharing this novel, i.e. spread the word, for it will help with our ultimate goal – securing interest to develop a script for the screen (Television or otherwise.)

Thank you for choosing "The Ballad of Persephone" and "The Anuk Chronicles." Visit our website at www.theanukchronicles.com for visuals, trailers, store links, and news of upcoming titles.

Enjoy,

Abdur R. Mohammed

TABLE OF CONTENTS

The World before the Great War

Circa The Age of Libra (15,000 BCE)
THE KINGDOM OF HYPERBORIA
a.k.a. Earth

Capital of Hyperboria

Illyria

Aryavan

Western Continent

pTah

Ulimoroa

Forbidden Southern Continent

CITADEL   PERSEPOLIS CAPPADOCIA REKKAM

CORINTH

ILLYRIA
Western Europe, Northern Europe, Balkans, Russia, Central Asia, Southern Europe, Middle-East, Arabian region, pTah.

ARYAVAN
Central Asia, West, East, & South Asia, Australia. Ulimoroa (ancient name for Australia,) Pacific Islands.

HYPERBORIA
Capital city, Western Continent (Including Central and South.)

FORBIDDEN SOUTHERN CONTINENT
Forbidden frozen wasteland. No Information in database.

Chapter 1: Time Lost, Time Regained.

Wind and sand blow without mercy against six faltering tents, posted along the desert road from Persepolis. Tonight is dark and evil, filled with omniscient forces gathered around a besieged party of rebels trapped in an oasis of death. Monstrous vehicles pelt out light, piercing the blackness; the malevolent enemy is waiting, seething. The rebels hold vigil with their masters. Gathered together, it is clear that few remain.

Shining through a dismal sky is the magnificent star, Vega. An old man braves the onset of a violent lightning storm to offer supplication on his knees. Outstretched palms reach for the glorious star in desperation. His eyes blaze with fire; his voice determined to be heard above howling phantoms.

"Almighty Creator, your humble servant Peki pleads for thy mercy. Help us oh Lord in our hour of need. Protect us from those who will do us harm – hasn't she suffered enough in her short years?"

Lightning bolts split the sky in brilliant splendor. Thunderclaps resonate through the man's wary chest. He wipes a flood of tears escaping down his brown cheeks. A bloodstained hand grips his shoulder. He peers at the soldier, an Anuk General beaten by the ravages of time, yet his visage remains large and intimidating. "General Markus, did you find water?" A sullen look instead of a parched voice answers the question.

"Three days under siege. We won't last much longer."

Peki accepts a helping hand off tired knees. They don dark scarves over blistered faces to stave off the sting of whipping sand, then trudge towards the largest tent at the camp's center, despair fermenting in empty stomachs. Peki pulls the warrior close. "Why haven't they finished us off? How many are left?"

Markus shrugs. "Scouts estimate 100. Curses on House Moira of ENlil. We will hold the line as long as we can, but…we are only 20."

"Thank you, General." Peki pulls the tent flaps in a slow, controlled manner, careful not to startle three women lamenting prayers near a 25-year-old girl in a bloody gown. Vacant blue eyes stare up at him. Flickers of light from a fire urn's calm embers distract his gaze. Eyes fall on a motionless bundle wrapped tight in cotton, absent any discernible features under its shroud. A wave of sadness washes over his body, the grip of despair choking every fiber of his being. His lungs empty with a silent, agonizing shriek.

The chanting ends abruptly as the girl rolls on bruised knees to crawl towards the crumpled man. Her long dirty-blonde hair drags as her head drops low, dusting the ground with each push forward. Peki straightens up to receive the broken creature he cared for all her life – loved her as his child. She climbs on him, holding on with a weak grip.

"Your Grace, you must rest. Regain your strength for I fear you are the only one who can protect us."

A long arm reaches for Peki's face. "My beloved will come. Oh Peki, my race is a violent one. Look at what we have done to the world. It is my fault."

"Nonsense. You speak of things you know nothing about."

"But I do. If I were born into the common human stock, none of it would have happened. You would be safe, and baby Kor…Koray would be safe." Heartbreak pours out in her trembling voice and shaking body. She closes her eyes at Peki's embrace. "I am the 'Destroyer-of-Worlds,' so proclaimed by my ancestors, Lord ENlil and ENki."

"There'll be no talk of that as long as I'm alive."

"What happens when you have passed? I'll go on for a thousand years without guidance. Not even my faithful advisor Samiri, can offer your wisdom."

"If he were here, what would he advise?"

She thinks for a moment. Her pale cheeks redden, pores on cold skin swell with heat radiating throughout her body. Bloodshot eyes darken as they travel to the innocent bundle near the fire. "He would say, 'Kill them all.'"

The silent women bow their heads with eyes shut tight, waiting on divine light to descend from heaven. But there will be no such thing. Instead, the girl's blood surges with her inherent nature. The power coursing through her veins runs more potent than any Anuk with claims of a direct line to the Forefathers from the Stars. Between the delicate drum of a heartbeat, she disappears, leaving the tent's flap rustling with howling wind. All eyes fall on the vacant spot near the urn.

Soldiers holding vigil are startled by a wraith darting towards the oasis' dry edge. A lightning flash illuminates the Anuk descending on the besiegers' encampment.

Enemy spot-lamps fall on the tall girl with a swaddled clump of dead flesh that was once baby Koray held high for all to see. A line of sentries train rifles on the haggard intruder. Some tremble, others strengthen their resolve.

"This is your legacy!" Her hateful gaze travels slowly from left to right. The enemy gathers quickly to bear witness to the proclamation. Markus and his soldiers struggle to reach a bluff to lend aid to their Queen.

"Forget this night for it deceives you about tomorrow. Forget the dead for they will turn away from your embrace. Remember my dead!" Her eyes glaze over with tears threatening to weaken her resolve. She tightens her grip on Koray to remind herself, *this ends now!* "Surrender your souls to what you will remember." She kisses her bundle on its way to the sand. "Tonight, I will taste blood like your pagan ancestors did…all of you, descendants of man. Why? Because the blood of the ancients burn in me; the light of Orion shines in me. The mysteries of Lyra are mine to herald, for I am Persephone – bringer of your doom!"

Fear covers the sentries' faces. She disappears between desperate blinks. Howls of death compete with thunder from above. Gun-fire erupts. Blasts of light crisscross in wild desperation to catch the attacker. Bodies fall with hot blood pouring on the sand. Internal organs spew out with crimson splatter as they are ripped out in a fury.

The wave of death encircles the oasis seven times in quick succession, eradicating every soul it encounters. Markus urges his soldiers to fire with extreme prejudice on anyone left.

Dust clouds in Persephone's wake dissipate at the end of the assault. Her blank stare cries out for relief. The living sees the Queen tumble to the bloody ground.

Markus darts off to her, pushing his mind past the gut-wrenching fear creeping up his spine. He drops hard, panicked at the weakened body before him. He stares into her fading eyes. "Majesty," he sobs, "you can't leave us."

"My protector – I remember…the girl of 12, saved by strong arms, these arms. I couldn't protect her…forgive me. Tell my husband, kill them all."

"You can't die. They can't win."

"They will never win, for the awakening will come. Markus, grieve not for in my life I've known true love, friendship, loyalty. Remember me, Markus. Remember Koray."

The light in Persephone's eyes goes out. Her body drops limp. Markus cries out to the sky with piercing rage. His waling brings all from the oasis into a circle. They fall on knees and bow their heads. Peki clutches the wrapped child and drops on his Queens cold lap.

Thunder rumbles down on the grief-stricken. Clouds let loose their stores in a torrential downpour – giving credit to the lie of Persephone's godhood. Bloodstained sand is washed clean as a testament to the eventual renewal of things. In this tragedy, both Markus and Peki fear, no such miracle will bless the departed.

8 The Ballad of Persephone

PART I

Before the Fall

"Forget what you know. Cast aside the burden of deceit for it shall drag you into oblivion." - Unnamed Watcher (circa 2,019-age of Libra)

All accounts contained herein have been processed through stringent quality control mechanics at the Library of Thoth.

A significant number of events are re-purposed into a palatable offering by scaling back the horrors of the period. Relevant 'time-jumps' take place to ensure a proper presentation of the facts, rather than stifle the seeker with unimportant happenings. Ambiguous interpretations have been composed into a logical adaptation of all personas involved in the rendition.

From "Library of Thoth User Manual" by the Grand Librarian

The materials presented are a recount of an ancestor whose existence was eradicated with malice from history, in an attempt to subjugate a global population consumed by a lie. Fate returned her to the halls of legend, spun her into myth, and in your time, downgraded her life into a story.

A brief picture shall be painted from the knowledge we possess, as provided by sacred texts decoded at the Library of Thoth. A rigorous treatment of genetic memory, soul-exposure, and factual accounting derived from credible sources have been employed. Understand this – what you call magic, we refer to as Anunnaki (Anuk) science. What has been lost to you was prevalent in my age.

Queen Persephone's plight transcends the barriers of space and time. Her descendants acting by proxy changed the very road humanity has traveled on since its reemergence. To understand why you departed from the ancient ways, you must first understand our beloved matriarch.

Reveal all of it or none of it.

- *Liviana Badur*

Chapter 2: The Creator

Almost one Sar has passed since the progenitors from the stars retreated to their hidden land of Lumeria. The world progressed as expected, but not without tumultuous pitfalls. The Anuk was never a race to bask in extravagant wonders or be driven by a need for technological advances. Over time their descendants reconciled warring hearts and settled for the social and technical infrastructure left by the Forefathers. Anything beyond the existing bordered on heresy.

Aversion to progress would not last. A renaissance exploded onto the world, enticing the creation of marvelous monuments and science, with a tentative balance between the physical and spiritual being struck.

Throughout city-realms exist high structures constructed from melted stone – an engineering fingerprint of the old ones. A unique feature of all civic buildings is their size. Sprawling promenades open up to megalithic buildings placed with precision to keep a visitor in awe. Streets are wide. Electric lights burn bright on towering poles, and in many towns, mobile units soar high enough to tell lies on the moon.

A technology of convenience brought from the realm of ANu, the father of Lord ENlil and ENki, was technology the ancients called 'Travel-by-Light.' Within moments one could leave temperate lands of Hyperboria to arrive at warmer climates in the middle of the Western continent. Portals dotted the Earth in countless numbers, with locations being common knowledge in the early days. War, disease, and social upheavals of the past brought a severe decline in portal demand. Usage today is limited to the order of Watchers and those pledged to the Keeper-of-Secrets.

To compensate, shuttles, heavy transports, and smaller passenger crafts populate the controlled skies. Menacing military ships of various designs keep a watchful eye on the affairs of each principality.

War is a tragedy of the past. The stain of conflict, however, still echoes in the mind of all humanity. While standing armies are not encouraged amongst the ruling Houses, having them is not forbidden. It is common for visiting Royalty and aristocracies to enjoy an armed escort during a journey to foreign lands. For the King of Hyperboria, the ultimate ruler of the realms, the local military of any territory is his escort.

King Shuru is the current ruling monarch. He considers himself a modest Anuk, devoid of frivolous inclinations of amassing wealth; a condition plaguing the kin of his House.

The structure of rule is an easy one – the King of Hyperboria is always a direct descendant of ENlil, ruling all banners of the Great and Lower Houses, which in turn rule over the realms of both Anuk and man.

The Great Houses are made up of the King's direct kin, all of whom can trace their bloodline to the seven Forefathers. Lower Houses comprise of cousins and their own bloodline, with a blended heritage of Royal and common Anuk. Primaries rule over their banners bearing allegiance to either ENlil or ENki. The Primary of ENlil controls its banners, so too does ENki's Primary. The King controls all. In the absence of a King, the Primary of ENki acts as Regent.

There are three realms with civilized life: Hyperboria the capital, the Principalities of Hyperboria called Illyria, and the lands of the east called Aryavan. In this age, the return of the Forefathers is believed to be a legend bordering myth. By all accounts, it has been 33,000 years since their departure from humanity. Many contend they left with their great ship in the forgotten past.

Watchers, the sub-race of humanity created during the time of the Forefathers still exist. Once great advisers to the Anuk, they have been downgraded to ranks of lesser servants, priests, honor guard, scientists. A Watcher's lifespan is shorter than a Royal Anuk's but longer than man; the longest-lived Watcher-priest boasted six-thousand years in service. These days conflict and disease have reduced the lives of the long-lived considerably.

Through the enormous length of time since the first arrival, it is almost impossible to point out one race from the other. The Royal Anuk is indistinguishable from the common Anuk and man, save a natural birthmark of the constellation Lyra appearing on random parts of a Royal's body. Anuk grow past six-feet in adolescence, are resilient to disease, exponentially stronger than man, and live longer. The Royals, however, enjoy a ripe old age in the 10,000's, while the commoner reaches a paltry 1,200. The 'Pure-Bloods' do possess greater strength and agility compared to the commoner.

Watchers resemble mankind in all physical facets, but their unique existence sets them apart. Disciplined, blessed with abilities of the common Anuk, intelligent, they possess their own culture stemming from the religion of 'the old ones.' Their demeanor, eloquent speech, and pristine traits allow them to stand out amongst the melting pot of society.

Ethnic diversity is common within the three races. Despite differences in genetic make-up, since the beginning, all fell under the umbrella label of Human, as the Forefathers were called.

"Why are we taking this long?" King Shuru complains to his well-dressed, slim aide. They are in the royal quarters of one of many of the king's shuttles. His excessive girth struggles to remain concealed under fitted robes of royal-blue silks. His square face still radiates strength in these twilight years, yet today it beams with anxiety.

The young aide, a Watcher, finds silent amusement in his flustered master fidgeting with a neatly wrapped box. "Your Grace, shuttle speeds are restricted within controlled airspace. The plague is yet to stop consuming portal engineers. Our inadequate infrastructure is being dealt a severe blow."

"Don't lecture me, Samiri," Shuru booms. "My nephew should have cleared the airspace."

"It was you, Majesty, who insisted no upheaval of normalcy should be undertaken on your account."

Shuru sends an accusative smirk Samiri's way. "Yes…an error on my part."

Samiri returns a crooked smile. "I only give good advice. You're the one who has to consider it."

Shuru ignores him in favor of stroking his well-kept gray beard. The color annoys him, for it was only two thousand years ago it started to turn from a dark reddish-brown to this miserable lack of color. At seven-and-a-half-thousand-years old, none of his remaining three consorts have ever accused him of lacking vigor as a result of gray hair. Vanity is a trait he is secretly a slave to.

"What is it?" Samiri asks, glancing at the King's present. The silk-wrapped square container appears comical in the Anuk's large hand.

"A seedling from the Lotai plant."

"Forgive me…maybe it's because I am relatively new, but I am struggling to grasp just how does part of a sacred plant serve as a gift to her Majesty?" Samiri stares at the box with genuine curiosity. "Shouldn't the birth of your first child in eons demand a grander affair?"

"Didn't they teach you anything at the academy?" Shuru asks. His casual tone with the Watcher is drawing curious glances from the nearby Lords and Ladies. The aristocracies are known to be snobs.

"The Lotai is sacred to all Anuk, as it was brought here by our ancestors." Shuru pantomimes, mimicking a teacher educating a student. "This gesture signifies the hope for a fruitful and blessed birth. Since presenting a flowering plant may be deadly to a newborn, a seedling is a much-preferred offering."

"Especially now with the plague infecting everyone…we cannot be too careful. Until we find a cure, all our lives are in danger."

Shuru regards him with a kind smile. Samiri's long dark shoulder-length hair falls smartly on his olive-colored garment; it reminds the King of his own flowing matte of gray. He rests his large palm on the Watcher's small shoulder. "We will survive this."

"Your Grace." Samiri speaks with hesitation in his voice. "Perhaps if you allowed the Watcher's Council access to the Amon-I, we might find a cure from its divine wisdom."

"Impossible," Shuru responds in a whisper. "Using the Amon-I for this purpose can be likened to using the ocean to fill a teapot."

"Your daughter will be at risk the moment she enters the world...Majesty. Will you not protect your sole heir?"

Shuru looks at him with sad eyes. "I will consider it."

An announcement crackles from the shuttle pilot informing the passengers they were minutes away from arrival. Samiri looks over his master before attending his own restraints. Shuru's eyes transfix on the bulkhead.

"One of the sacred tenants of religion is to trust in the Creator. If it is his will to take Persephone from me within moments of her first breath, then so be it. I am not one to challenge it, for the Creator's will is supreme." Samiri drops his head, assuming a dismissal. "If she is infected...then I will have The-Keeper-of-Secrets deliver the Amon-I to the Watcher-temple."

A wide promenade stretches across the front of the Temple-of-the-Sun. Here in this principality of Northern-Illyria, it is packed with citizens from all the realms. Crowds gather to honor King Shuru's visit, but more importantly, seventy-thousand made the pilgrimage to celebrate the birth of Princess Persephone – sole heir to the Hyperborian throne, and thus all the wealth of the Anuk.

It is not customary for a Queen to rule. For countless millennia, archaic mindsets remain rooted in practice traceable to Forefather ENlil himself. On the twenty-seventh day of Persephone's life, audacious campaigns for her hand in marriage will begin; If Shuru has a son later on, however, the throne will pass to him. War and disease have rendered the monarch childless for four-thousand years. This birth, by all accounts, is a miracle.

The grand temple is ancient, constructed by House ENki when the forefathers walked the Earth. Shaped like a pyramid, its height is 721.7847-feet, covering an area of 372,043.244-feet-square, it is a marvel to behold. Grand walkways lead to the dark-blue structure where multiple entrances welcome patrons and visitors alike. For eons, this has been a center for the healing arts. Today it welcomes a royal birth.

Inside is sterile and bright. On each level, there is a flurry of activity; research, health care and worship, space is allotted for everyone. A grand hall on the first level seats 30,000 attendees to any affair. Today, despite the King's insistence for privacy, assorted pageantry has made its way into the monarch's agenda.

Prince Vali, the Regent of House ENlil and Northern-Illyria, stands on a raised platform with arms outstretched towards the approaching King. His face is reminiscent of a lean pampered Royal who is concerned with grooming rather than public affairs. His effeminate mannerisms echo taboos publicly shunned in Hyperboria, but mere whispers do not perturb him; this age has seen many a departure from the old tenants of religion, and Vali considers himself to be a trendsetter.

With a broad smile, Shuru embraces his nephew for all to see. "Vali…I told you, no pomp."

The Prince smiles with mischief on his face. "Oh, come now uncle, it's more for me than you. Can't a loving child dote on his King?"

The Royals face a sea of applause. Silver spheres hover close, capturing the scene, buzzing with dim lights and pre-programmed instructions from newscasters below. Shuru shifts away from the cameras and throws a protective hand over his beard.

Vali gazes with love at his King. "I have a hair-technician who will do wonders with that mess."

Shuru steps to a podium, ready to deliver an unplanned address while Vali retreats under a magnificent banner.

"Citizens, I am humbled to see such a gathering. My family and I receive your good wishes with much gratitude and love. Thank you for your prayers and support. I understand feasts have been commissioned throughout the realms. When I raise my wine glass, I do so with pride and honor to you. It is because of your affections we live in an age of peace and prosperity. I love you all." Thundering applause join enthusiastic cheers.

Shuru offers a final wave. He anticipates Vali's approach after throwing a glance his way. *That smug little shit!* He hurries to an exit before his nephew reaches his back. His thoughts fall heavy with Queen Farah.

On the Pyramid's higher levels, a myriad of personnel rush about in a frenzy to cater to Lords and Ladies. His Majesty's travel companions enjoy the anxious pretense of the commoner to appear 'important.'

Trays of wine shuttled in from Aryavan fill cups. Fruit from the Western Continent overflow on plates. Musicians soothe the snobbery with eloquent classical tunes administered via stringed instruments. Quick sneers from the staff go unnoticed; the subservient class of Anuk and man carry on with their resentment bubbling in privacy.

Two levels above the chaos is the private birthing wing. Medical personnel draped in white gowns stroll through bright passageways, each locked in the sole task of attending the Royal family. Queen Farah has been in labor for 6-hours now. All eyes are on the physicians who are hopeful the princess will be born without a stain of the plague.

A century ago, the world emerged from a dark period of pestilence lasting 727-years. Humanity succumbed to a deadly flu-like virus running rampant without regard to race or social status. Religious adherents proclaimed it was judgment from the Creator for lives led in derogation of holy decrees. When the epidemic was subdued, thanks once offered were replaced by the decadent acts, held in blame. The reprieve was short-lived. Five years ago, a new viral strain emerged. The disease attacked at an alarming speed, killing the victims within days of contraction.

Efforts to eradicate the contagion were futile. The global population diminished, eliminating long-lived Anuk and Watcher scientists who contained the previous outbreak.

Extraordinary efforts have been undertaken to protect Shuru's heir from the invisible attacker. Only those cleared to interact with the Royals can do so, at least while here at the facilities. Further limitations reduced the birthing staff itself. In the past a host of priests would be present with the family; today only the King and his aide are present in the birthing station.

"Curious," Samiri blurts out while observing the physicians and the Queen from behind a wall of glass. Shuru stands beside him in a sterile blue gown, making ready to enter the chamber.

"Out with it," Shuru says, as he fumbles with the plastic garment.

Samiri shifts over to assist. "I have never witnessed a birth."

Shuru chuckles. "Lucky for me, I have participated in seventy-two; thirty-six my own offspring."

"I am sorry, Majesty," Samiri says with a sad look about him. "Sorry for the travesties which robbed you of family."

"The greatest tragedy any parent can endure is the loss of children." Shuru sends Samiri a thoughtful look. "Be thankful your race does not have to face such evil."

"There may be some advantage to being grown in a gestation pod after all." Samiri smiles in an attempt to lighten the mood. "Did you know my batch is the last to be blessed with long life?"

"I did not know."

Samiri returns his gaze to the Queen. "Yes, I am fortunate to have a shelf-life of five-thousand years. The new generations will have half that."

Shuru begins his entry to the room but stops midway. He stares at Samiri the way a father would. "You have been in my service for ten years…Samiri. You shall now be attached to Princess Persephone and rewarded handsomely with unheard-of privilege for a 'Doh-fan-ae.'"

"You honor me Majesty," he says humbly with a bow. The King hurries to his Queen.

A calm silence envelops the executive lounge below the birthing wing. Festivities on lower-levels remain a distant clamor for a few seeking refuge in the elegant abode of opulent appeal. Samiri sits on a comfortable leather chair, locked in quiet contemplation about his new-found favor within the royal household.

Hours ago, he was a Watcher, relegated to serve as an aide to a master – in his case the highest master of them all. Now, he is blessed with privilege once afforded the 'Doh-fan-ae' in eons past. His thoughts drift to musings on what a great teacher he will be to the Princess – protector, guide, friend. A pleasant feeling of accomplishment washes over him until his meditation is disturbed by a rude rustling in an attached seat.

"Samiri," the female Watcher says in her soothing tone.

At first, he is startled but finds calm in the brown eyes staring at him. "Aspasia. What are you doing here?"

Aspasia crosses her legs, draped in black leather and fashionable boots. She shifts her athletic body to face him, offering a calculated smile rather than a response. Her raven hair shines with the overhead light, giving her a devious appearance. She drops her hand on Samiri's arm, squeezing gently as he tries to move it from the armrest. "Are you avoiding me?"

"Don't be ridiculous. I have been busy with my duties."

"Nonsense. Does the King agree to send us the Amon-I?"

"I made the suggestion just as you asked. He will consider it."

Her grip tightens. Her teeth clench with delight. She drops her gaze to her peach-colored hand, squeezing her contemporary's pale appendage. "Not good enough." She relishes in her power over him.

She is much older than Samiri – where he is a mere 20 years since commissioning, she is 1,043, though the casual observer would think she is in her late twenties.

"What do you desire of me, Aspasia? What crooked affair has the High-Priest sent you trotting off with? I refuse to be a part of your schemes, whatever they are."

"Our numbers are dwindling brother. You are part of the last true 'Doh-fan-ae,' not this new generation of subservient slaves." She releases her grip as an Anuk Lord and Lady stroll through the lounge. Samiri begins to rise. "Wait!" Aspasia urges.

He slumps back down and leans for a whisper. "I worked my way up to aide as you instructed. I provided you with secrets known only to Anuk Royalty. I aided the Council with forbidden science at great risk. I have done everything you've asked of me."

"You have done more than that, brother. It was your science which provided the path to the plague."

"What!" He jumps off his chair, seething with disgust and loathing. His hateful stare does nothing to break Aspasia's resolve.

She stands in her casual way, pushing up close to him to exaggerate her five-foot-ten-inch stature; two inches taller than Samiri. "Yes, you are the ultimate creator. We intended to thin the herd of man for our kind to prosper once more. Inter-breeding between Anuk and man created the pandemic today, not us."

Samiri clenches his fist and growls, "And now it is not man that suffers, but all humanity."

Aspasia softens her gaze to one of plight. "We need the Amon-I to fix it. Help us."

"No," Samiri says, still aggravated. "You want the Amon-I for something more. I suspect this much. Remember I've seen the secret writings of the Anuk. I know what they fear and where their knowledge comes from. The relic may fix the travesty you let loose on the world, but it can do more…so much more."

"I assure you; we desire is to save 'Doh-fan-ae,' and humanity."

A moment passes to bring calm on both Watchers. Samiri relaxes. "The King will consider gracing the High-Priest with the Amon-I. Even if I object to such power being in the hands of imbeciles, I cannot block a path to end this madness. His Grace will not take a chance with the life of his heir. That alone is enough to sway him."

Aspasia clasps Samiri's shoulders. "Then you must ensure this brother." She reaches into her jacket, retrieving an object.

Instant horror overcomes him. "I cannot," he says with eyes fixed on her hand.

Aspasia pleads, "It is the only way. If the child is free from disease, then it's the only way. Save us, Samiri."

After a long night, the birthing wing is quiet. Dim corridors leading to a sterilized chamber are filled with armed sentries on watch. Princess Persephone is left to sleep in her small neonatal incubator, with one attending nurse perched in a corner. The room has a dark-blue glow to it. The air is cold, lowered to match the temperatures of a Hyperborian palace.

Exhaustion overcomes the nurse. An unnoticed blanket of green mist flowing through the room's ventilation encapsulates the woman. Her heavy eyes scream for sleep. Her body gives in without resistance to the nasty toxin.

Slipping in from the ventilation masked by shadows, Samiri approaches the incubator in the manner of an unwilling fiend in vehement opposition to his task. He taps an illuminated button on the enclosure.

A tray extends outward slowly from the incubator; the wait is brutal, testing his resolve. Latches snap into place; he chokes with doubt, his mind screaming with indecision – to act or to run? A bead of sweat rolls off his brow. "It's a path to the Amon-I," he whispers, then drops the syringe in the compartment. The tray retracts and he swallows hard. Now, the pathogen shares delicate space with the newborn.

Persephone is clean of the disease, bringing hope to the parents of their dynasty's continuity. In the past millennia, most Pure-Blood Anuk babies died soon after birth; only two from the higher echelon of royalty survived. Hours will prove if Persephone will be number three.

Samiri picks up the syringe through protective gloves waiting ominously inside the incubator. A moment of hesitation overwhelms him. *What am I doing? I am not a murderer for surely this will kill the child.*

"Do it!" a harsh whisper hisses behind him. He recognizes Aspasia's voice. "If you don't, all hopes to get the Amon-I is lost. Prove your loyalty to the cause."

Persephone's eyes open; she looks at Samiri, paralyzing him with hesitation. Her piercing blue eyes bring pause to the Watcher. She makes what he assumes is a smile, breaking his heart for what is about to be done.

He calls upon his training to assist his resolve. His heart pounds more laborious than a herd of mammoths in an open field. The sting of Aspasia's harsh whispers fades with his exhale. He breathes in deep then without further hesitation and pierces the infant's skin. She cringes with pain and her face sours, though she does not cry out.

Chapter 3: Graven Images

Hyperboria is a vast expanse of cold lands spanning the top of the planet; a frozen umbrella whose tips touch each land-mass at their northernmost edges. Sporadic ice sheets cover unpopulated areas year-round; however, patches of warmer areas exist closer to the globe's apex – this is where the capital of 'Hyperboria' sits; the city's founders did not care to make a distinction between land and city.

Here exists the seat of power for the Anuk Empire. Despite having their own lands outside Hyperboria, Greater Houses in Illyria and Aryavan all pay homage to the reigning monarchy. All being products of the homeland, with ultimate rule emanating from the capital.

Every five-year-old in Hyperboria endures what every five-year-old must throughout the realms – school. Four-hours of each weekday is spent in a congregation to learn the foundations of society. A sizable compound at the outskirts of the Royal Palace is set aside for this purpose. Students are not confined to an indoor prison but instead, are gathered outdoors to bask in the wonders of nature.

In front of the classroom are sprawling green hills. At the back are high cliffs with a majestic waterfall streaming into a misty river. A smaller, less powerful waterfall flows off a rocky mound sixty-feet up. The local temple designated for the aristocracies sits just to the right of the water's edge, creating an image of high-holiness enveloped in thick mist. A cool breeze carries sounds of birds and flowing water, soothing restless students, numbering 25.

Here they learn about their ancestry or rather, a sanitized version of the historical records. Tremendous care is exercised to keep the violent tales of humanity away from precious ears. Both Great and Lower Houses have children enrolled at the facility. It is a mix of humanity comprised of both Anuk and man. The distinction has disappeared over the years, with only strict prescriptions of marriage and breeding adhered to in the Greater Houses.

A fading constraint of civilized society once prohibited a marriage bond between Anuk and man. In those times relationships were tolerated, but union and childbearing remained a taboo. Age-old stipulations encouraged rebellion in the eastern lands of Aryavan, and in covert instances within Illyria, though in Illyria the ruling class turns a blind eye.

After the decline of the Watchers' dominance of high posts in government, mankind held desirable positions of nobility. The Forefathers viewed man as a naturally occurring species, just like their Anuk counterparts. Similarities between both races over time led to speculation of mankind being a satellite colony, long forgotten before the Forefathers' arrival.

Whatever the truth is, they remain the envy of the Watchers, who are viewed as a 'created' race.

For the Anuk bloodlines, it is simple – there are only ENlil and ENki. These Great Houses are bound to enjoy ultimate rule. The remaining five Forefathers are the collective cousins of the two brothers; their lineage comes from the maternal side of the father, ANu. Their descendants make up the Great Houses, and the children not commissioned to rule are relegated to the Lower Houses. Mingling between the Greater and Lower Houses happens all the time, however, strict adherence to keeping the lines of ENlil and ENki pure is maintained; those of ENlil stay in their House, as does ENki. No one knows why – it just is.

In this age House Vali is the only direct line to Lord ENlil after King Shuru. The King's deceased brother is Vali's father. Likewise, House Odin traces its lineage to Lord ENki.

Mid-morning is approaching. Children are becoming restless. The teacher stands tall in front of a giant square field of light, pointing to bright symbols with her rod. The lesson of the day is the ancient alphabet. In unison those paying attention sound off the names of each symbol. One little girl is distracted by a small box passed to her from an unknown sender.

"Persephone!" the teacher shouts, interrupting the Princess' stare. "Pay attention."

The child makes a face to express her boredom with today's torture. In her short life, the Princess has gained a reputation for mischief, mayhem, and vanity. School for her was just an interruption in a day filled with adventure. She was not brilliant by any measure, but she coerced others by flirtatious means to do her bidding, including schoolwork.

For today's lesson, she had a palace librarian give her a copy of the ancient alphabet, which she memorized. "I already know all this drivel. Can I go?" she shouts to the teacher. All eyes fall on her.

"You may be the heir apparent, but in my classroom, you are a disruptive little brat." The teacher fumes. "Very well, recite the sacred letters., on your own." With a gesture, the images in the light field disappear. Persephone closes her eyes and does as she is told successfully. To her relief, the day's session is over, as indicated by approaching guardians. She makes another face at the teacher before running off with her box.

At the edge of a small bush, Persephone opens her present. A giant toad leaps out, startling her to the point of falling on fresh mulch. She hears snickering at the edge of a nearby path. "Osiris, you little shit, I will get you for this!" She takes off after the boy and his band of jokers. She loses them around a bend at a parking lot. She huffs and decides it' time to go home. Her eyes lock on to the smiling face in the crowd, and she beams at the sight of her caretaker, Peki. She drops the box and runs off to complain about Osiris of House ENki.

"Who are they?" Persephone asks Samiri, while looking out the window of their vehicle. She is in awe of the line of marble statues along the path to a wide boulevard.

"Those are the Forefathers, my dear," Samiri answers. Peki interjects, "Princesses do not climb on doors inside moving cars…now come down from there."

Persephone slumps down on the leather seat, looking at the floor to avoid Peki's stern gaze. Unsatisfied with the answer, she is compelled to complain, "But those are stone, not the Forefathers."

Samiri smiles at the observation, "They are representations of them. To be adored by all."

"But they are stone," she says. "I do not understand."

"Soon, a statue of you will be put up in the square. The people adore you too," says Peki in his optimistic way.

"Why do they adore me? My teacher doesn't."

A moment of guilt passes through Samiri's soul. He swallows hard and holds his breath to hold off the tight feeling in his chest. The child doesn't shift her gaze from him as she patiently waits for an answer.

"When you were born," Samiri says. "the world was plunged into despair from a deadly plague. You were immune to the disease and hailed a miracle from the Creator. The doctors used your DNA to create the means to eradicate the virus. So, you see little one, some adoration is expected."

"I don't want a statue. The people should adore me, not a piece of stone."

Samiri forces a smile. He marvels at the arrogance, vanity, but also the truth of it. "We are meeting the Queen at the temple. So, best take your complaints to her."

The afternoon sun shines through open-air structures of the majestic temple, next to a waterfall. The roar of the water provides a therapeutic immersion to all who visit. Today, Queen

Farah soaks up the sun with her handmaidens, waiting for her daughter to arrive.

Farah is a fortunate woman. She is the third consort of King Shuru, the youngest, and as her title suggests, the favorite. She has contributed her share of jealousy and intrigue within the household, but when she bore the King an heir, her status as Queen was sealed.

Footsteps interrupt her daydreaming on a comfortable chair. Her handmaiden whispers news of a visitor. She looks at a nearby clock and decides it's time to end her lounging. She makes her elegant stride into a large rotunda, and sloshes a wine glass as she waits for the caller.

She is not as vain as the King and Persephone, but her station demands she straighten out lingering wrinkles in her short royal-blue dress. She pats her curly, auburn hair and dusts her cheeks to make them rosy.

Farah is not the prettiest of the consorts – she thinks she is. Since giving birth, she packed on a formidable couple of pounds, but not too much to distract from her oval face and voluptuous breasts. Her piercing hazel eyes are the only thing any recipient of her 'dress-downs' remember; those fierce, judgmental eyes are the scourge of her staff.

The visitor finishes his climb up wide stairs to enter the stone rotunda. Prince Vali's entourage joins him in a humble bow to the Queen. "Your Majesty," Vali purrs as he throws his outstretched hand in front of his head, in a mocking gesture.

"Well, this is a surprise," Farah says. Four fingers tap on her wine glass. "Up, you morons." She looks at the entourage. "Leave us." The group hustles to join the Queen's handmaidens.

"What brings you to Hyperboria cousin?" She pours Vali a glass of wine.

"Such harshness will only cause worry lines across that pretty forehead of yours."

She chuckles, "The only thing I worry about is what new scheme you are slithering in here with."

"You wound me Farah," He moves close, leaving an uncomfortable space between them. "I am here to oversee the dedication to our little miracle."

Farah gives him a polite smile; mental screams are manifesting in her reddening complexion. She grabs Vali's privates and squeezes like a vice-grip. Searing pain washes over the Prince's face, matching the high pitch in his voice, "Calm down cousin, I meant no disrespect."

"Sure you did. How dare you use my daughter in whatever sordid affair you're hatching?" She releases her grip violently, driving Vali back.

"Careful," he warns, "how quickly you forget. Persephone may be your and my uncle's spawn, but she is my miracle. It was my science that allowed you to conceive in the first place. Without me…my dear Queen…you would be nothing more than relegated to consort number three, playing the bitchy housewives of…"

"Shut up you imbecile!" Farah snaps. "Shuru is forgiving, he will understand."

"He will, but your unscrupulous behavior to mother an heir will leave you shunned in your own home. Laughed at in all Hyperboria. Neither of us wants that, now do we?"

"Alright Vali, what do you want?"

"Nothing. Everything. For now, simply to elevate Persephone to godhood."

"Blasphemy! Even I am appalled," Farah says with disgust. "Leave me."

"Blasphemy you say? That burden belongs to the masses. They cling to whatever we feed them by way of news and entertainment. Religion is shaped by the priests, not the divine word. If everyone followed the word we wouldn't be in perpetual chaos, would we? They're stupid, ignorant of the truth, believing what is prattled off. So, my dear Queen, it is too late. The spreading of my word began five years ago."

Pattering feet running up the stairs interrupts both adults. Vali spins around and drops down to meet Persephone. "Give your uncle Vali a big hug."

"What did you bring me?" the Princess demands. Vali dips in his pocket to reveal a bar of her favorite Illyrian candy. She takes it and hugs him once more.

"You see, cousin, this love affair is beyond your control."

In an instant, Vali's frightening intentions become clear in Farah's mind. Throughout Aryavan and Illyria, there has been a movement towards deifying the forefathers. Once Persephone joins the ranks of gods, her name will be unstoppable.

Samiri stares out at rolling hills on the temple's side. He stands with his hands behind his back, appearing to be meditating to any casual observer. His thoughts are jumping from carefree days at the Watcher academy, to the previous day's meeting with Prince Vali. *How far have I descended into oblivion?* he laments. A faint shift in the wind alerts him to someone's approach.

"Aspasia," he says calmly. She doesn't answer.

She joins him at the edge, planting a careful foot on a moss-filled rock. "It's a long way down," she jokes. "You will be pleased to know Prince Vali is following your plan to the letter…"

"And he still does not question our motives?"

"These Anuk are blinded by their immediate obsessions. Soon, my lover, our world will begin anew." Aspasia grabs hold of Samiri's arm and looks into his eyes as if bearing her soul. "The Chancellor summons you."

"What for?"

"It is time you understand the full scope of our agenda; time you take your rightful place in the journey forward."

"No, I want your words," he whispers. "Five years I have followed you, loved you, killed for you. Your words carry more weight than those of…a priest."

"Very well," Aspasia takes Samiri's hand. "In secret, our scientists have isolated the genes which will allow procreation. After years of research, we have found the way. Contained within the Amon-I is the knowledge to achieve this – to repair and regenerate what the Anuk stole from us. Engineered or not, it is our right to propagate, on our own."

"That is not all, is it?" Samiri smiles in malevolent splendor. "The Amon-I also has the secrets of the Anuk, the code to their long life, and their origins; in short, the mysteries of the universe. To possess such a thing is to have power beyond measure."

"We do not want such things," Aspasia whispers.

"I do."

Aspasia releases her hold. Her heart sinks with a miserable feeling, one of dread at his revelation.

"In all your thousand years, you have never once wanted such knowledge?" Samiri asks.

"Never. Not even the Anuk want such things. No one can control the Amon-I, not even you."

Aspasia's sudden aversion brings pause to Samiri's. Since giving in to that moment in Persephone's incubator five years ago, he has done unspeakable things on the path to possessing the Amon-I. Along the way, the relic's true nature revealed itself to Samiri, for which he deems the Watchers council unworthy of possessing. They were on a nominal path, but he wanted more.

"You are correct," he says, trying to appease her, then lets out a long sigh. "It is too much of a danger. If it were achievable, fate would have delivered it by now."

Aspasia puts her warm hand on Samiri's face, "We are blessed with time. When the Princess weds Prince Vali, the Amon-I will be delivered to us, as promised."

The last day of the week concludes with a gathering of the most influential members in the government, the 'Assembly of the Royal Comedians,' as King Shuru calls it. Though not in a particularly comedic mood, he forces himself to attend.

Governing members of each Great and Lower House assemble to conduct affairs of the realms. Those residing in Hyperboria sit in the grand chambers, while those in Illyria and far off Aryavan attended via a holographic representation of their live image. In total, a horde of 37 quarreling bodies makes up the council. Prince Vali is among the attendees, along with Prince Odin of House ENki.

Every session explodes in bickering, insults, and rude stare-downs during serious discussions. Today the chamber is living up to its expectations.

Shuru shouts as loud as he can to quiet the rowdy mob. In the past it was comical, now these traditional outbursts are shaving off the monarch's last nerve. "If there is nothing else, we are done for today."

Prince Odin stands to address the gathering. His cousins have not seen him for ten years in Congress, so all afford him the extra time in the day. The female cousins marvel at his warrior physique, along with the temporary eye-patch he wears – the product of conflict in the untamed lands to the south. "Your Majesty, royal cousins, Lords and Ladies, I am honored to be in your presence once more. I would like to bring your attention to the increasing departure from religion. The cults rising throughout-"

A cousin obscured in the back shouts out, "You bear the name of a Forefather, but you do not speak for that line!"

"There now, Cousin Odin," Vali interjects with a snicker, "we all know your son has been chosen for the 'Keeper-of-Secrets.' No need to spread gospel on his behalf."

"That's enough!" Shuru snaps. "Vali, Odin is the Primary of House ENki, as you are of ENlil...show some respect."

"Yes, uncle." Vali bows his head. "Apologies Cousin. Carry on."

Odin shrugs off Vali's outburst. "Worship of the Forefathers as gods is rampant! I decree all Houses of ENki stay clear of such perversions. We cannot allow this to fester so close to the awakening."

"The awakening?" Prince Atlas shouts. He is known to relish conflict. Atlas is Vali's elder brother, and was passed up from his birthright to be primary of ENlil; his demotion after that subjugated him to a Lower House under his brother. This sting remained with him, and at every instance, he makes as much noise as possible.

Atlas waits for the dramatic effect of his pause to wear off. "Anuk myth meant to scare humanity. The Forefathers have returned to whence they came. So, what if they are worshiped? It provides a tangible deterrence in the hearts of the governed."

Odin casts a sweeping gaze at members of his House. "Even so, do not let their legacy be one entrenched in fallacy." Vali's unusual silence prompts him to takes his seat.

Shuru stands, prompting the gathering to do the same. After some words bidding the group good intentions for the weekend, everyone rushes out to carry on with their evenings.

Odin remains with Shuru. He grabs his uncle's arm but is soon pulled into a warm embrace. "I've missed you Odin. You've been gone too long."

"You honor me, my King. It has been a difficult time in the wastelands. Thankfully, rebellion has been quelled, and life goes on as it should."

Shuru gestures to the empty chamber. "I am tired of all this. I want peace before the light of Orion is extinguished from my soul."

"Nonsense uncle, you have decades left. I'll hear no more morbid outbursts before dinner. By the Creator, one session here is enough to send me back to the badlands."

"If only there was a way to transfer rule to you permanently. The vultures have been gathering for five years, all wanting a piece of my precious 'Sephie. I fear this is the end of my dynasty."

"The Creator only makes his will known to those with the patience to receive it."

Before the King can start a sentence, Persephone rushes in with a stuffed toy in her grip. She jumps on her father and hugs him.

"Time to go, papa," she says, displaying her plush bunny wearing a white coat, as her father sets her down.

Odin kneels beside the girl, a kind glance breaking through his weathered exterior. "What's his name?"

Persephone peeks out sheepishly from behind her rabbit. "It's a girl. Her name is Polly."

"You take good care of her, and she will be with you for thousands of years," Shuru proclaims. Odin looks to the open chamber doors as his two sons approach. Beaming with pride, he urges them over.

Thoth is by Odin's second wife. He is lean, tall with vibrant dark skin like his mother. Osiris is Persephone's age and by Odin's first wife. He's a stout boy with a light shade of olive skin. Both children grew up in the Royal household and are comfortable with Shuru. In formal settings, they afford their monarch all the courtesy expected of them.

Odin holds his youngest hand and looks at him intently, "I believe you have something to say to the Princess?"

The five-year-old pout as he stares at the floor. "I'm sorry your Highness, for sending you a frog in class."

Shuru bursts out in uncontrollable laughter, much to his daughter's dismay. "Come here, Osiris." With Persephone set on his right thigh, he lifts Osiris on to his left. He hugs the boy and kisses him. "You two better be friends, understand?" Osiris nods in acknowledgment.

"Never," Persephone declares in her bratty voice. Shuru puts them on the ground like a pair of dolls – one squirmy and one well-behaved.

"Thoth, come here son," Shuru says warmly. "You're 15, aren't you?"

"Yes, Sire."

"Listen to me very carefully…being chosen as an indoctrinate to the Keeper means you will become the representative of the Forefathers themselves. An honor bestowed only to those worthy. Swear now your loyalty to your brother Osiris, heir to House ENki, and Persephone, heir to Hyperboria."

Thoth drops on one knee "I swear it, for you my King."

PART II

The Realization of Destiny

"Man cannot rule man." - Lord Xi-Wang-Mu, Queen Mother of the West (circa 2rd Sar)

- *Liviana Badur*

.

Chapter 4: Curse Not the Holy in Vain

Long ago during the great expansion, cousins from both Houses migrated to the south-eastern edge of Hyperboria to establish the Principality of Aryavan. Borders were cut along the edges of Illyria in the west, and continued down the continent, incorporating a vast island they named Ulimaroa. When a conflict between ENlil and ENki erupted eons ago, all from ENki were expelled from the realm. To date, none of their Greater Houses exist amongst the Aryans.

Aryavan is as diverse in culture as it is in climate. Here the taboos, which are shunned upon in Hyperboria, are exercised freely without fear. Codified Religion has been replaced by a fusion of mankind's old beliefs and cults given fresh life 18-years ago.

The landscape at the borders of Hyperboria, Illyria, and Aryavan boasts a comfortable resort-like setting for anyone with the means to indulge oneself. Nestled on the Aryan side, a modest palace complex cut out of bedrock overlooks a vast lake.

Here, visitors partake in a host of holiday activities, including discreet encounters not suitable for the public realm. The locals have a saying, 'The Creator won't see what you do because his back is turned.'

A frequent visitor to the decadent resort is Prince Vali. Here he can roam the streets freely with countless lovers hanging off his arms. His stays are always incognito, with only his Regent cousin having any knowledge of the escapades. In this winter month, he is here to indulge in a secret ceremony of a fire cult.

Large owls feathered in regal coats of white settle in their comfortable abodes, perched high on tall trees overlooking a thick outcrop of foliage. Their occasional 'hooting' is a cry of protest to the humans disturbing this part of their forest.

Hidden in a dark grove behind the resort is the sacred gathering place for the local chapter of the Aryan fire worshipers. Tonight, members pay homage to their deity by dancing around a giant pyre, naked, masked with the heads dressed as forest beasts. Generous servings of opium are consumed amongst the jubilant party. They chant a variety of nonsensical words and moaning, lacking origin or meaning.

Dancing, swaying, groaning, each participant lets inhibitions fade with burning ember rising in gusts of wicked breeze. The cold wind caresses their bare flesh in an intoxicating frenzy. The moaning becomes a rhythm; soon, it carries a beat flowing into a pitch, reaching for the sky. Hands stretch out to stars, peeking down with sparkling brilliance. Arms lock together for a collective-union. Feet kick up dirt in a hurried side-step, circling the fire to the right. In unison, the crazy-circle moves with determination to an end known only to them. Five minutes pass before the ritualistic performance dwindles to a quiet spectacle.

No one cares about a participant's identity; none except a silent observer peeking through a thick bush. Queen Farah pulls her hood tight. She stoops low with a renewed effort to avoid detection.

The pyre roars high when it's given new life via fist-sized fire-rocks, cast into the dying flames by a fat priestess with the oversized head of a bear. Farah is startled by the encroaching heat reaching her 30-feet away. *I've seen enough.*

The rooms at the resort are large, comfortable; high ceilings are adorned with paintings of scenes from Holy Scriptures, blending into columns ripe with overabundant depictions of taboo – a variety of scandalous sex scenes. Fire burns aromatic wood in a well-crafted fireplace. Gold ornaments line ivory shelves. Large beds with full posts are a staple afforded to each guest. The opulence of the place reflects the clientele.

Exhaustion overcomes Prince Vali, as he nestles himself under a plush feathered blanket. A deep inhale matches an accompanying smile; warm therapeutic scents encourage a tight grip on his lover's arms. The young man is fast asleep, tired from the activities at the grove and the post-ceremony lovemaking with his Anuk patrons. It is another quiet night until doors fling open, crashing violently onto the stone wall.

Outrage is overcome by surprise, shining through Vali's wide eyes. His lover cowers beneath the blanket as he grasps the fabric across his chest in a feminine fashion. "Your Majesty!" he blurts out.

Queen Farah is alone with her gaze of fury; she points a determined finger at the male-prostitute rolling over his patron's chest.

"You!" Farah grabs the boy of twenty-something. "Out!" She tosses him across the room without so much as a strain or thought.

Frightened out of his mind, the escort rushes out.

"We have matters to settle, you and I," the Queen says. The fleeting shock allows the Prince to regain his composure. He climbs out the bed, insolently strutting off to the adjacent bathroom. "Come back here!" she yells.

"You are welcomed to watch me piss if you can't wait…your Grace," he says in his arrogant tone. He returns casually, standing in full view of the Queen.

She glares at him, enraged. "Put some clothes on, you pervert."

Vali ignores the request, "Cousin, I do believe you are blushing. Trouble in the royal bedchamber?" He flashes a playful, yet mocking smile. Farah's cold gaze encourages him to don a robe, carelessly thrown on the floor.

"You will not have her," she snaps.

Vali smiles wider. "My Queen, how quickly one forgets promises. The time approaches for old communions to bear fruit. Or shall I bring to light the circumstances surrounding the death of two royal consorts?"

"Are you threatening me?"

"Nonsense; I am stating a fact. I bear you no ill will to you, cousin. Here, sit, let us discuss a compromise."

Against better judgment, Farah sits on the bed, shifting away from the Prince, as he plants himself next to her. "Persephone shall be my bride after her seventeenth birthday – in a week I believe?

"Eighteen, you imbecile, it's her eighteenth birthday."

"Really? She's practically a hag. In return…" he pauses when Farah springs off the bed, then grabs her hand to gently pull her back down. "Our previous interludes with the late wives of King Shuru shall be buried for all time."

"I can have you killed and be done with all this."

"Ah, but if you could, you would have already. No, your Grace, you won't dare for the knowledge I hold, like a hidden dagger pressed against your throat. Don't be stupid Farah. Once the crown shifts you will ascend with me."

Farah breaks out in uncontrollable laughter. She is at the point of tears, giving Vali enormous grief. "I'm already the Queen you fool."

"Not when Shuru is dancing to the eloquent tune of 'Hold me daddy' in the glorious beyond. Odin will be regent until Persephone is crowned. Who's the fool now?" The laughter dissipates into a void of silence.

"Never," says Farah. "Not at my daughter's expense."

"You misunderstand, my Queen. Let me lay this out as simply as I can. Persephone and I wed. I rule in her name. Her divine status is almost secured in the hearts and minds of the people, thus making me, her husband, a god. Shuru, thanks to my encouragement, is in his last cycle. So, when you, the grieving widow and devoted mother, are brought into our household as consort, well…the title of Queen shall be yours once more."

A horrified expression overcomes Farah.

"Oh," Vali continues, "not to worry. All these years, I've been caressing that innocent mind of Persephone's to pursue a more noble cause than that of rule." His eyes shift, nearly giving away his lie.

Farah softens her gaze with curiosity replacing suspicion.

"Trust me, she will abdicate the throne in favor of divinity."

"I don't like this, Vali."

"But you like being Queen more, don't you?"

A brief silence passes; Vali looks at her with a mask of curiosity, "Tell me, what are you doing here?"

Embarrassment washes over the Queen's face. She attempts to hide it.

"Ah," he sighs, "The young lord from lower Aryavan."

"Your spies serve you well, Vali."

"Not well enough, or I would have known you were following me. See dear cousin, we need each other to hold the dark secrets between us." Vali kisses Farah's hand. "Now on your way...your Grace. And do send in the boy I paid a small fortune for."

Farah opens the door and steps out.

"See?" Vali asks, a sly yet confident look on his face. "We will never have a loveless marriage, rather it will be one best suited to our perversions."

Grand Citadel – Western Continent

Located in the Western continent, across the sea from the edge of Illyria, at the very spot where the massive ships of ENlil and ENki first arrived, a Grand Citadel was created. Bordering the untamed lands to the south and Hyperboria, it is a place forgotten by all but the Anuk priests who reside there.

Rich red canyons with multi-layered strata of gray, orange, and burnt-umber colored rock weave through thousands of miles in the desolate landscape. Wild rivers roar past small cities with colossal buildings touching the clouds. Hidden beyond the modern is the ancient, locked behind a valley of rock, out of view from their technologically advanced neighbors.

The Citadel complex is not large by any means, but can if needed, accommodate a population of 10,000. Over time, modest structures have been built upon the sacred grounds, housing libraries, temples, and other facilities to mimic a settlement. Today, the population is only 100. Amongst them on this cold winter day is King Shuru and Thoth.

Constructed in the ancient style, a grand library houses literature, histories, artifacts – the sort of things no longer coveted. An effort by Thoth to move everything to a secure location is almost at an end. On this bleak evening, he and the King oversee the final movement of relics. They sit in a large room with windows cut through stone. The sun's brilliance streams in to fight off the cold winds on the seventh level of the structure.

Thoth took on the mantle of The-Keeper-of-Forbidden-Knowledge one year ago. Indoctrinated at age 15, it took 10 years to learn the necessary foundations of the appointment. He was groomed ever since one of the priests here at the citadel, proclaimed to Prince Odin that his son will be the greatest

Keeper to have lived. Thoth, at age 10, graciously agreed to renounce all claims to the title of Primary to House ENki, and passed the mantle to his half-brother, Osiris.

"Uncle, here is your tea," Thoth says humbly to Shuru. He sits next to the aging King.

'Nephew,' if you only knew I consider you a Grandson worthy of praise the likes of which have never been heard, Shuru muses with a smile. The colloquial references amongst the Anuk are confusing to the casual listener, with generational designations being thrown into a simplified pot; regardless of time's separation, all Anuk of the Royal bloodlines are family, after all.

With eyes full of pride, Shuru keeps his gaze on the Keeper, until Thoth reaches over to kiss his forehead. He has been ill for the past year. Many fear the monarch is at the end of his cycle of life.

"A shrub from pTah can bring the color back to this mess you have going on," Thoth says while stroking the King's beard. The old Anuk laughs.

"Of all the youth I have encountered within the family over…too many years to remember, you are my favorite."

"You only say that because I indulge your fancies. I see you are still with the Amon-I texts."

"Yes, quite a shitty read I'll say," Shuru jokes. "Why in the name of the Creator did our ancestors insist on writing such mysteries coated with more mystery? Couldn't they simply say what they needed to without resorting to parables?"

Thoth picks up one of three leather-bound volumes to examine it. "These were transcribed from the Amon-I itself. Just a sliver of teachings made its way on the pages. I am afraid the full knowledge of the Amon-I will perish with the old ones. This is why I am recording everything."

"pTah. Of all the places in the world, that's where you will keep your library?"

"You should see it, uncle," Thoth says with a wide grin. "The library is hidden away in the old ruins of ATun - in their metropolis long abandoned. The desert sands have covered the plateau, allowing all the wonderful structures of the old world to remain hidden."

"I envy you Thoth," Shuru grumbles between sips. "You continue to receive the wisdom of our forefathers. To continuously bask in the ages and wonders of a world long forgotten. With all the changes over the years, I'm afraid soon we won't recognize ourselves."

"It all started two thousand years ago when the calendar was reinvented-"

"Those priests insisted on it," Shuru interrupts in a mocking tone.

"Yes, they claimed it is easier to measure time in ages rather than Sars. 2160 per zodiacal procession they say." Thoth chuckles, as Shuru grumbles at a page. "Why did you allow them to do this?"

Shuru looks at Thoth somewhat annoyed, "Those watchers claimed it would be better for predicting the return of the forefathers. Little did I realize, too late I tell you, they were orchestrating a union between religion and economics."

"The more frequent the cause for celebration," Thoth says. "the more stimuli the economy receives."

"Harmless," the King points out. "Tell me, what is the best secret you have yet to learn?"

Thoth hesitates for a moment. Butterflies flurry inside his stomach; he can't contain his excitement to answer the question. "I only tell you this because you are my revered King, my protector. There is a way to access the essence to preserve it within a sacred space in the Amon-I."

"The soul?" Shuru's eyes open wide with wonder

"Yes. Have you ever wondered how it is the Forefathers were able to span such long periods? One-hundred-and-thirty-nine-thousand-years have passed since they first arrived; Two-hundred-thousand since the father ANu walked the Earth."

"You're tickling my memory, taking me back to the myths of my Grandfathers. They said ANu was a Prince, heir to all of Vega, a scientist too. He could have engineered some form of life-extending protocols for his family. Besides, the Forefathers were born in one of the worlds of Lyra. They're not like us, adapted to this world."

"No, they're not like us, but they are not immortal. We were never taught as much, but they retreated to Lumeria to sleep for a Sar, then return."

"Incredible. Alright, you have revealed enough. I fear any more would put fanciful ideas in my head."

"Tell me a story uncle. Share with me the words of your Grandfather's past. I want to hear a living account, not read ink on a page or absorb recorded energy."

Shuru's face lights up. His heart lightens with love, for no one cares to indulge an old Anuk and his silent musings. He straightens up, sips his tea, and looks out the stone window, peering back in time, in a way only he can.

"This is a tale from grandfather's grandfather, when the Earth cooled, and all manner of life exploded unto the shimmering blue pearl of a planet. A huge melting-pot, vibrant with diverse creatures locked in exponential evolution. Years passed, yet nothing of note registered with celestial scout vessels deployed from the realm of the Anuk, 25-light-years away.

"On a routine trek across the void, curiosity grasped a handful of scientists. A fever infected their bones. They had to visit the fertile globe. They basked in unique comforts the world offered, marveling at the similarities with their own home. The local species were devoid of human intelligence, save a primitive branch incapable of language. The adherents of science felt compelled to do what they do best – experiment.

"Meddling proved futile. Disappointment encouraged a hasty departure back to their realm. The star of nine-planets yielded nothing to offer the Crown Prince ANu – the heir blessed with dominion over the mighty system of Vega.

"After ANu became Supreme Monarch he escaped to the Earth for a reprieve from the chaos of rule. At this time the vast resources of the planet became apparent. Endless gold and other minerals coveted amongst the worlds of Lyra overflowed in scattered regions throughout. The Anuk practice of expansion would now be applied.

"For ten-thousand-years industry mined the planet. From each continent hordes of product left in veils of light. Collection crafts received bountiful cargo in orbit. Once full, the long journey to Vega commenced.

"As with any civilization endowed with a wealthy monarchy, their disenfranchised servants begged to be heard. A long and terrible war broke out in Vega, spilling across the vast expanse of space, and ultimately reached earth in a hail of fire. Rebels incited unrest; violence encouraged action. A purge order resonated in the Royal halls of Vega; a deadly battalion was sent to wipe out all Anuk life on the planet. Dark skies exploded with the destructive force of military might, turning night into day and fields into rivers of crimson.

"At this point in the Earth's cycle of life, primitives evolved into a semblance of humanity. Some historians believed Anuk scientists played a part in the rapid onset of evolution. Others claimed blasphemous cross-breeding occurred. It didn't matter after the war ended – for the Anunnaki, or 'Those from Heaven who came,' as the primitives called the Anuk, returned to Vega, not to be seen again for another seventeen-thousand-years when the sons of ANu and their cousins came." The King exhales his exhaustion. He grunts before resuming his browsing of the ancient text.

Thoth makes his way to a nearby window. A shimmering case catches his eye. He is lost viewing the relics contained in the three-foot-long box. Inside, two parts of the royal brothers sit on lighted stands – a lock of hair from ENlil, and a severed finger from ENki.

He shifts his gaze to the window, soaking in the view of the grand-canyon, draped in an abundance of green. "The land has come a long way since our ancestors abandoned it – pTah that is. The people are ruthless, wild, cannibals; much like the inhabitants of these lands. But they possess a passion for life – a trait lost with the adherents to civilization."

"Those lands used to be in the line of your House, did you know this?" Shuru asks.

Thoth shakes his head.

"Then it is time it returns to House ENki. When your brother becomes the Primary, it shall pass to him by my royal decree, as so commissioned…" Shuru smiled. "Well, tomorrow. Where is Osiris anyway?"

"He is gallivanting through Aryavan. The petulance of youth." Thoth laughs then returns to his seat. "Uncle, there is a prophecy I encountered in the emerald tablets."

"Prophecy? You know I put no stock in those things. We are the masters of our being."

"Yes, but it is interesting. I believe it speaks of our time, of events recent and to come." Thoth closes his eyes to access his memories, then recites a translation of old words as best as he can, "When darkness consumes the souls of humanity, a hand of hope shall seal the bridge of divide. Great sorrow for the few, then great joy for the many. The veil of mystery shall defy time to start life anew."

"Thoth, I know you indulge in the white powder from the south, but that makes no sense."

"The true meaning is lost in translation, Uncle. But it is interesting."

"You want to hear what's interesting?" Shuru chuckles. "What I have translated from this mess, what I can understand, is that my daughter is not destined to be a secondary to any husband. She is the heir to Hyperboria, damn it. She can assume all the powers of a king in her title."

"That is correct," Thoth says with his eyes lowered. "It was not my place to challenge the patriarchal designs of the forefathers, but from the knowledge of the Amon-I, both male and female are equal in all rights. It is but a culture that determines, then forces the worst course for any disenfranchised group."

"Alright, you're making my old ears hurt."

"Uncle...seeing that you are in a generous mood, I would like to ask a favor."

"Ask me anything, son," Shuru says with happy anticipation. Thoth has never made a request for himself, and this rare instance warms the King's heart.

"I humbly request that you restore Markus to his station; allow my father's most trusted general to regain his citizenship in the Greater House."

"Ask of me anything but that," Shuru grumbles. "It was your father who stripped him of titles and banished his insolence to the wastelands."

"A verdict made in haste and with bad counsel."

"No." Shuru lets his command sink in. Thoth's disappointed look breaks his heart, but the personal anguish he feels cannot override his decision as monarch. "Markus made his bed. He broke your father's heart with his scandalous indiscretion. He is lucky I didn't have his head on a spike."

"I suppose living the life of a desert rat in Rekam is a suitable sentence," Thoth says with some reflection.

"Is that where he is?"

Thoth stares out across the land. "I ran into him there last month."

"It figures he'd find refuge with those artsy buffoons. Thoth...are you moving the weapons to pTah as well?"

"I haven't thought about it."

"You have free rein over anything under my gaze, except those. Leave them here. Let the remnants of Vega remain hidden...forgotten if possible."

Thoth nods. He shivers inside at the reminder of terrible weapons of mass destruction hidden and dormant, not far from where they sit. The Western Continent is an afterthought in the cog of civilization. He wonders if things will ever change.

~ Royal Palace at 'The Abode of Snow,' Aryavan ~

It has been one week since Persephone traveled to Aryavan with her mother. She is a typical 17-year old girl, almost 18 – past the cusp of womanhood in Anuk culture. Unlike the average girl her age, she stands tall at five-foot-ten and still growing – this due entirely to her Anuk genes. She has always maintained a slender figure and long blonde hair – although there was one time, she shaved it all off in rebellion to something or the other; no one knows, except it involved the Queen.

By all hushed comparisons, she is no striking beauty. Plain in looks, called 'scrawny' by the other members of her family, brash, unintelligent, and plagued with nervous quirks. She doesn't care. Her sheltered life promotes the opportunity to protest.

Time spent with eastern cousins has been recorded in her journal under the title '*A monumental exercise in benign living, bordering a whisper of suicide for the adventurous.*' Her boredom intensified when Queen Farah abandoned her to travel to the borderlands for some unknown purpose. There was nothing to do in this snow-covered corner of the province – nothing that she will be allowed to do, anyway.

Snow-capped mountain peaks stare back at her through wide-open windows in her chambers. The sunlight streams in warmth, teasing of better things to do in the village far below.

She huffs. A crystal vase catches her eye. *I wonder just how far it will fall.* She grabs the object and cocks her arm back. A large cat assaulting her stuffed bunny distracts her. She finds a new target and hurls the vase, narrowly missing the feline. The crashing sound brings the ever-vigilant Samiri.

"Princess?" he says. His body is half-way across the threshold, trepidation in his voice.

"I'm tired of being a prisoner." she sighs, then walks around in a fit of frustration, grumbling under her breath.

"Perhaps I can arrange a tour of something..."

"No...I want to go home. I want papa."

"I'm sure the Queen shall return soon." He smiles painfully at her. "I'll send Koray up with food."

Samiri leaves the room to make his way to a lower level. He is intercepted by Aspasia. She joins him on a long descending corridor.

"Our dispatch indicates they are ready," she whispers. "Only in Illyria will they move."

"And the savages agree to our conditions?" he asks.

"They will wait at the port. Once there, Prince Vali can make his astounding rescue."

"I do not trust your master, Aspasia. He'd better deliver the Amon-I."

She halts, bringing Samiri to an abrupt stop. Her hand wraps around his and she stares deep into his eyes, words stuck on the tip of her tongue, struggling to pass her lips. "We do not need the Amon-I any longer."

The sting of her statement rings in his ear, reverberating through his soul. His flushed face betrays his anger.

For years he waited to gain possession of the powerful relic. Plans were made putting his beloved Princess in harm's way, all in the name of a greater cause – his cause. It was Aspasia's prompting that led him down a path of misery. Betrayal was never a condition he expected from her.

He snatches her arm with a malicious grip. "Explain yourself!"

"Let go of me. I could not tell you until I was sure."

"Tell me what?" he asks, nearly spitting the words.

She lowers her gaze as if expecting a terrible response. "There has been a breakthrough. I am the first test subject to achieve success – I am pregnant with your child."

A hurricane of thoughts swirls in Samiri's mind. Anger finds itself at the forefront. His part in a plot to kidnap the Princess is predicated upon a promise that will bring the Amon-I to him. "Then why are we continuing down this fruitless path?"

"Because my master wishes it," she says with some embarrassment. "Once he is declared Persephone's savior, receives her hand in marriage and ascends to the throne, you and I will be set upon posts beyond our greatest expectations."

"You and your Watchers are a mangy flock, resigned to a singular concept of living," he growls with anger seeping into his tone. "I will keep my part in this affair, so insured by my blood-oath. Their lack of vision will be their undoing…not mine." He storms off.

The morning is progressing at a crawl. Aryans are a casual lot, devoted to a leisurely pace in all things. Thirty-minutes pass before Koray, Persephone's trusted handmaiden, receives the Princess' lavish food platter.

Koray doesn't mind the wait. There are enough young men worthy of flirtatious pursuits to keep her occupied. Always carrying a smile and a pleasant demeanor, she captures the attention of every eye straying her way. Her slender frame, flaming red hair and bedazzling appearance elicit confusion as to her status in the court; many assume she is Anuk – they are half-right.

Koray has been with Persephone for almost five-years. Her father is the once esteemed General Markus, who lost favor with Prince Odin and House ENki. Her late mother was a 'regular' human woman, born into a Lower House. She was never looked down upon, even though offspring from Anuk and man was discouraged. As Markus is from common Anuk lineage, the stigma of an interracial union did not sting.

When Koray was 12, she was instrumental in the recovery of twelve-year-old Persephone, who had gone missing while on a family retreat in Persepolis. Her bravery saved the Princess' dignity. Since then, they have been inseparable.

Everyone knocks before entering Persephone's chambers, well not Samiri, or Koray. With a wine jug in hand and three servants trailing, the handmaiden enters with her usual happy disposition; what she sees gives her pause. "'Sephie!" Immediately Koray orders the servants to leave their trays on the ground. She closes the door to begin an interrogation.

"Don't start." Persephone's eyes plead for Koray's silence. "It's not what it seems," she says, grasping a thin stretched out length of rope.

"So, you're not going to climb out the window without me?"

"Alright, it's exactly like it seems."

The girls peer out the window to look at the steep drop to a far-off platform. Koray lists more than a dozen reasons to dissuade Persephone, though she knows they will fall on deaf ears.

"You know I love you, right?" Persephone says. "But I have to do this on my own."

"I don't get it one bit. You've been acting strange these past months. I didn't want to say anything, but I feel as if I have to now."

"Koray, my only friend, I am stifling you. Instead of running around doing fun things, you're stuck in a desolate prison my mother designed for me."

"Then come explore the place, flirt with boys and destroy their fragile egos…"

"If only it were that simple," Persephone says. I know you're eager for the ball tonight. Why not go see what the town has to offer?"

"'Sephie, you know I won't go without you."

"You must. It's the only way we can act like two girls, without an entourage judging our every move."

Koray shrugs her concern. "I'm not going to like this am I?"

"Hush. After the chaos dies down, come meet me in town."

"What chaos?" Koray asks. "Meet you where?"

"Remember where the locals were flocking to? The drinking place?"

"Yeah." Koray grips a loose portion of the rope. "It doesn't seem terribly secure. You sure?"

"Yeah." The corners of Persephone's mouth curl up into a wicked smile. "We'll get drunk and spend mother's money."

"Alright. Samiri will have both our asses for this."

"Let me worry about him. Now secure the rope, I'm certain I didn't do it right."

Chapter 5: Covet Not that which is Forbidden

Aryan castles are almost always high up above the landscape. Since the movement to deify the Forefathers and Persephone began years ago, the abode of the ruling House in Aryavan has become known as 'Home of the gods.' The majestic mountain of Kailasa has a large town at the base, looking up at the Anuk structures embedded into the rock. Not much can be seen from below. Not even an escaping Princess climbing down jagged rock walls.

Persephone couldn't descend far with the meager length of rope she stole from a servant. Thirty-feet remains between her feet and the hard surface of a hanger platform. The plan was to 'borrow' a transport, but that seemed improbable now with the drop.

Clutching the rope tight her heart skips a beat. Koray looks down with a worried look. Below is a 30-foot drop. Her heart feels heavy with fear and doubt. *The fall will hurt.* With eyes closed, she releases the rope.

Her body slams on to hard concrete, knocking the wind out of her. She grits her teeth at imagined pain, but there isn't any. The cold ground vibrates with creeping intensity. A sudden sputter of engines demands immediate attention.

Fifty-feet behind her a craft rumbles to life, making ready its taxi to the forward edge for takeoff. With a desperate roll, Persephone anchors herself on the edge of the platform. She peers down the side, wishing she had not done so – screaming wind gusts intensify the reality of the enormous drop.

The sleek craft shoots out, into the sky. She rips her body upward and rolls onto the platform. "Damn it," she whispers, staring down at the oil spot on her blue tunic. Such trivial matters shouldn't concern her after the harrowing escape; it troubles her nonetheless.

The ground-crew are busy fueling, maintaining, and even lounging. A perfect opportunity to sneak onboard a dual-seater craft. *Time to use those lessons I hated.*

The glass canopy is rolled back. The cockpit is narrow, allowing a quick climb in. She ducks down, holding her breath in anticipation of getting caught. This is not Princess Persephone's first time engaging in grand larceny.

She looks for the battery grid. A panel light blinks at the flip of a switch. *Next, the auxiliary-power-unit.* She hesitates for once this switch is initiated, the hum will alert the crew. She scans for the engine starter. *It's now or never.* Her heart races. Quick hands accomplish the task before the ground staff catches on. The single afterburner ignites sending a powerful blue flame out the exhaust. In seconds the craft shoots out of the hanger, rising away from the mountain as the short wings expand.

Persephone screams with delight. "Such behavior is unbecoming of a queen," she says in a mocking tone, imitating her mother. "Well, I was bored and wanted to explore," she answers herself. "You cannot do-"

Alarms blare on a panel. She snaps her head back. *Damn it. I am not going back!*

Two aircraft engines roar behind the escaping craft. One fires a warning shot. Demands blare through Persephone's headset. She pushes her craft into a steep dive, relishing in the g-forces assaulting her body. She slams the stick to the left initiating a spin. Several revolutions later she recovers control, cutting thrust to let the pursuers accelerate past her.

The trick worked. The disruption in the rear airflow caused slight wind intake variations in the other crafts, causing their pilots to shift concentration to avoid a potential stall. They pull their sticks hard to break free from the rockface quickly approaching. Screaming curses erupt over the intercoms.

"Control tower, this is Princess Persephone," she transmits, with a slight giggle of excitement in her voice. "Call off your aircraft. I don't want your pilots getting hurt." She pulls back on the stick, sending her craft into a near-vertical ascent. *What the hell do we do?* she imagines them saying. She waits.

"Copy that, your highness." It's the smooth voice of an air-traffic controller. If he's nervous, he isn't showing it. "Disengaging pursuit."

"Princess Persephone." It's Samiri's voice over the intercom. "Perhaps next time, just ask."

She smiles wide thinking of the day's events. "But that wouldn't be any fun."

Crunching snow under her boots puts a smile on Persephone's face. The joy of walking around the dingy town amongst the common folk is overwhelming. Her cloaked visage incites a few onlookers to regard her with curious sneers. Her demeanor screams 'foreigner' to the locals. Her luxurious clothing stands out amongst the folks sloshing about in slush, carrying heavy sacks of simple food like grain and cheese. Fat pigs trot about through mud, infusing the air with their stink. *The smell of freedom.*

A vendor beckons the Anuk with enthusiastic hand gestures. The old man smiles with enthusiasm and missing teeth. His graying mustache curves upwards at both ends, complimenting his kind eyes, wrinkled face, and matches his gray fur hat. On his counter is an assortment of handcrafted beads, silver armbands, and other jewelry. Next to his stall, smoke billows from a baker's brick oven, enticing pedestrians with the aroma of fresh-baked bread. The old man rattles off in his native dialect.

"I do not understand," Persephone says. "The common tongue?" she asks with a poor attempt at gesturing her request.

"Ah," the man says with a smile and a nod. "For you." He holds up a multicolored necklace.

The Princess retrieves a gold coin but the man refuses.

"For you," he repeats with his humble smile.

"You remind me of my Peki…an old Peki," she chuckles and drops her coin in the baker's box. She grabs a large loaf, gives the old man two-thirds, then bites into the warm bread, filled with cheese infused with local herbs. She bids both vendors goodbye with a cheerful wave then gets on her way. *The simple life of these people. So humble and endearing; my people.*

A familiar voice sounding off curses in the local dialect breaks the Princess' musing. She darts behind a wall to peek at the source. Her curious stare is met with funny faces from pedestrians prattling off jokes at her expense. Her eyes twitch with her grimace. *What is he doing here!?*

Prince Osiris is dressed like a common street urchin, drenched in mud-stains. He looks up at the bouncer, shouting obscenities in a fruitless attempt to gain entry to the local tavern. He lets out a long sigh and reaches into his pocket, then slips a gold coin in the bouncer's hand.

The bouncer uncrosses his arms and smiles, allowing Osiris inside.

Curiosity encourages Persephone to investigate. She stops a woman trudging by. "What is this place?" Persephone asks, gesturing towards the building.

The peasant wrinkles her face before touching the tips of her left index finger and thumb to form a circle. She thrusts her right index finger through the hole several times before walking off.

Persephone huffs in outrage.

Patrons stomp along the dance floor, in tune with the spirited fiddler, spicing up the smoke-filled, raunchy tavern atmosphere, or brothel – it is unclear which of the two it is. Travelers to the Aryan province fill the cozy wooden walls, drinking together and making merry with the working girls.

Persephone holds the edge of a shaky bar-stool and climbs on with a nervous glare at the barman. Anxious wraiths wrench her stomach. Quick glances at the husky Anuk behind the thick burgundy counter brings on a terrible reaction. Her palms are sweaty, her heart races to an uncomfortable pounding. Nausea is setting in. *Why are you scared?* "Ale, please." Her lips tremble as she orders.

The barkeep looks her over with mild annoyance. He delivers a cold mug with an abundance of froth overflowing the top of golden nectar.

She sips the top like any Princess would – calculated. The barman sends a dismissive huff. "Seems you're out of your element."

Persephone winces; he's right. She gazes around, attempting to stifle her misplaced fears. The reveler's joyous and carefree spirit provides a welcomed distraction. Mugs are attended to, spilling ale without caution. Some patrons let out exasperated exhales after a single gulp. Others choke, eliciting riotous laughter from onlookers. Persephone decides to give the gulp a try. She plants her mouth on the mug's rim before making her tilt.

"Open your throat," the barkeep advises.

His smile under an otherwise menacing face relaxes her. She sends him a polite nod, grateful for the advice. Strong fermented wheat blended with exotic spices enters her mouth. Bitter herbs hit her taste buds, forcing her throat muscles to close. A wasted mouthful erupts on the floor. Persephone's cringing face brings an eruption of enthusiastic cheers from the crowd.

She bows in good spirit and takes another drink, throwing up less this try. The bartender tosses a towel and gives her and solid slap on the shoulder. The crowd returns to their business.

A rough hand grabs the Princess' shoulder from behind. "What are you doing here?" Osiris growls.

"Having a drink. What are you…never mind. You're here for a piece of ass." Persephone rolls her eyes with a grunt.

Osiris gets in her face. "You can't be here."

"Leave me alone. Go back to the whores, they look lonely."

"Shut up you spoiled brat," he snaps, and tugs at her expensive jacket. "Do you have any idea what will happen if anyone finds out who you are?"

"They will love me."

"Really?" he asks with an obnoxious smile. "Where's your entourage? Your kiss ass sycophants?"

"I'm alone, just so you know…but Koray will be here soon."

He shakes his head. "You're a test on that poor girl's soul."

"Oh, shut up. I know you've always had a thing for her."

"She's like my sister."

She rolls her eyes and takes a long drink. She drops the mug to protest when he grabs her hand. "Hey!"

"Come on then." He grabs her arm, spilling ale down her neck.

She rips her arm from his grasp. "I'm not going anywhere with you."

"Believe me, I don't want you going anywhere with me either. You want to mingle? There's something you need to see first."

She points her finger in his face "This better not be a trick."

Osiris leans over to the bartender and whispers a request. The bartender nods. Osiris pulls Persephone through a dark hallway behind the bar. Her protesting continues until they exit a back door.

The wind kicks up the invigorating stench from a muddy pigpen on their left. Persephone pinches her nose shut, staring suspiciously at Osiris. *Why is he smiling?*

Osiris lunges, striking Persephone square in the chest. The forceful shove sends her crashing between frightened pigs, parting the way to a cushion of filth. Mud splashes all over her expensive clothing, along with exposed skin and hair. Her surprise turns into anger at Osiris' uncontrolled laughter. She springs up, determined to knock him down.

"Hold on, now," he insists with palms out. "That was for your own good."

"What?" she shouts at the brink of tears. She looks at her body, sickened at the nasty covering. Brushing off the thick layers of pig-shit aggravates her even more.

"You can't go around looking like a palace princess. Now you look, and smell, like the common folk." Osiris teases her with pig grunts. He spins her around to slice off the mud on her back. His hands swipe down to her butt, igniting on further rage.

"You insult me, throw me in filth, and feel me up…boy this better be good."

"Be quiet. Save your 'Boo-Hooin' for later."

She throws her arms down at her sides, flinging shit and mud down to the ground. "I do not 'Boo-Hoo' you scamp."

"Yes, you do. It's just there's no one here to entertain it. Stop your whining and follow me."

The firm grip on Persephone's hand causes a tingle inside. She smiles inside, oddly excited to be dragged around by the Prince through the mud-filled streets, although she stifles any joy from showing on her face.

They avoid several bison-drawn carts, a mule, and barking dogs to cross a seedy-looking avenue. "There's danger everywhere," he whispers. "Pickpockets, hustlers… even monkeys." The journey ends at a corner with a welcoming view of a mud-brick straw-covered shed. A pair of pedestrians duck inside an adjacent butcher's shop.

Osiris pulls Persephone out of view behind a wall, the mid-day sun upon them. "We'll wait here for the shop to close for lunch. Won't be long."

She ignores burning questions about their venture. For the first time since arriving in Aryavan, she admits silently, *This is the most fun I've had.* She studies Osiris' blank stare on the ground. "Why did you leave me?"

"What?" he asks with an annoyed tone.

"Why did you leave…everyone? Hyperboria. Home."

He cocks his head in surprise. "You wait one year to ask me this?"

Her wide eyes beg for a response.

"We had fun growing up, didn't we? You, me, Koray." He waits for her nod. "After Persepolis…when you got sick, everything changed."

"I don't see the connection."

"You turned into a cold-hearted bitch, Persephone."

"I did not!" she yells. "I was 13."

"Please… that's when you stopped being a lovable brat and turned into a mean attention whore."

Osiris' words sting Persephone. She gasps at his accusations. "Oh really? You're just sore because I didn't entertain you and the tramp on your arm at my 15th birthday bash."

"Get over yourself. You were busy receiving praise from uncle Vali and his crowd adoring your fingernails…and anything else you cared to shit out for them." His hands rise to match a silly, mocking face. "Look at me, I'm Persephone…worship the dust under my feet."

She leans in close and slams her palms on his chest, snickering at each strike. He snatches her arms and pins them to her sides.

"It's not just then," he says in a severe tone. "I went from best friend to casual acquaintance overnight. You couldn't stand to be around me. You became self-absorbed in trivial things. Yes, we were children, but you turned into a stranger, and I can't apologize for something I don't know I did."

Osiris shoves her away to peer at the butcher's shop. She fumes in silence with her arms folded. Movement under the shed draws her attention. She scowls at the thought of continuing with whatever Osiris dragged her into, yet she does not want to leave. She softens her glare. "It all came back to bite me in the ass."

Osiris sighs in regret for undertaking the venture. "What are you talking about?"

"I live in a prison…I guess after I recovered, things changed. Mother keeps me under her thumb. Papa gives me whatever I want. They suffocate me. All of a sudden, I had to be Princess of Hyperboria, learning all the responsibilities required of me; cater to a multitude of others wanting my attention. How you deal with it, I don't know. Now, all I want is to run in the rain, roam the countryside without an escort, visit my friends unannounced…like you do." She settles herself on the wall near his side without complaint. "I still don't know why I was angry with you…or if I ever really was."

"Apology not accepted. Now be quiet." He hears the muffled insult as her nose goes up in the air – a trait he finds 'cute' but refuses to acknowledge it. "Look, I didn't mean…"

"I've heard enough," she says, with a dismissive hand shooting up to demand silence. "What are we looking at?"

"The butcher locked up. Come on."

They run under the shed. Osiris ducks behind the short mud wall and pulls Persephone down with him. "Shit! It's too late."

"Late for what?" she whispers.

"I wanted to show you something."

Forty-feet ahead in a square, people stroll by a copper statue of a robed woman. Candles flicker on the ground. Abundant streamers of yellow flowers litter the stone base and adorn the statue's neck. Copper bowls filled with milk surround smoking urns.

A bell rings out marking mid-morning. Snowflakes descend from the cold dark sky as if on cue. Foot-traffic diverts from muddy streets to the stone promenade. Within moments the crowd grows to almost fifty chattering heads.

Pushing through the crowd, a chunky woman in yellow robes makes for the statue. Her garb is accentuated with flowers and religious ornaments around her thick neck. Her bright lipstick is frightening – this is the priestess of a local cult. Two acolytes stumble through to reach the statue's feet.

"A comedy," Persephone announces with joy.

"Oh, it's a big one," Osiris agrees with anticipation. He barely contains his amusement, which she anticipates is a sign of excellent theater.

The mud-covered royals settle on a large bag of straw. They crouch together, thankful to be out of the accumulating snowfall. Their bodies move intimately closer, as the sharp wind slices through.

"Gather round my flock." The fat priestess motions with her hands and speaks in the common tongue. "Receive the blessings of the goddess." One acolyte translates while the other lifts a copper bowl of ash near her breasts. She passes her hands over the container, whispering words only she understands.

She closes her eyes. Her arms reach for the sky, grabbing an invisible power lost on the spectators. Her body shakes, her eyes roll back to reveal the white. She blurts out gibberish for all to hear. The acolytes chant in unison to the alleged torment; it lasts a full minute.

"Our goddess has revealed her displeasure," the priestess proclaims. She points an accusatory finger at the heads of the flock. "Her mighty wrath shall descend upon you like the plagues of old, destruction of the unfaithful…the unbelievers. You have seen her past vengeance. The wicked perished with the innocent. Why must we suffer so?"

"What can we do, holy one?" a voice screams out.

"Repent!" the priestess yells. "Repent to the holy mother. Ask her for wisdom in the coming days. She will send protection if you show reverence!" An acolyte moves about the gathering with a tray to collect offerings. "Come, be blessed with the ashes of the holy mother. Join our church, and you shall be saved. Be free from the wretchedness of disease that will rid the world of apostates. Let her save you from death, like she did before. Blessed art thou, our mother…Persephone."

"What?" the Princess blurts out. Osiris is stifling laughter. Persephone shoves the Prince aside to march out to the crowd.

"'Sephie wait!" he screams. He reaches her at the edge of the flock.

Before he can grab her, she spins around and points. "I only want to know what this is about…that's all."

"Fine. I warned you."

The Princess opens her arms as if ready to embrace the crowd. She looks at the priestess, "Good people!" she yells at the top of her lungs. The priestess hushes the crowd, confused at the sight of Persephone – the real one, not the statue. "What do you want, child?"

"Fear no longer, for I am amongst you."

Osiris drops his head. He plants a palm on his forehead, expecting the worst possible outcome from Persephone's naiveté.

"And who is this skinny little thing among us?" the priestess asks, rolling her eyes.

"I…" the Princess starts off with a glowing smile and muddy outstretched hands, "…am Persephone."

Widespread laughter erupts from the gathering. The priestess is horrified. "Blasphemy!"

Shock overcomes Persephone. She pouts without trying. *Do they not recognize me?* She looks at the statue, "Eh?" The face is of an old woman with round features. There is a pronounced belly, with sandals on the feet not even the poorest human in Hyperboria would dare wear. She starts to protest. A soggy heap of lettuce explodes on her head. More vegetables follow with remarkable accuracy. At this point, Osiris drags her off towards a back alley.

"Help me!" Persephone pleads to Osiris behind a mound of manure. She picks at residual tomato sludge lodged in her hair.

"You got yourself in that mess," Osiris says. "so clean up on your own."

"You're a horrible little boy who has no respect."

"Well, you're a nasty little girl who smells like pig-shit."

After all her years getting whatever she wanted, Osiris' blatant disregard for her feelings brings on an eruption of tears. She slumps down on the ground hiding her face with shame.

Osiris grumbles to himself, silently admitting it was he who brought Persephone to the gathering in the first place. He slouches down beside her, moves her hands with a gentle touch, and offers a smile to ease the sobbing. "I smell like pig-shit too."

Persephone looks over, then breaths in and out slowly, trying to calm herself.

"We can't stay here," he whispers. "How did you get here anyway?"

"I stole a ship," she says in a childish voice.

"Let's get back to it then. Come on." He extends a hand.

Persephone pouts but still takes it. "I've got to meet Koray."

Thirty minutes pass before the pair reaches the vicinity of the stolen ship. Persephone and Koray's meeting place is nearby. They hurry alongside a stable, hoping they are not noticed by stragglers from the gathering.

"What is wrong with them?" Persephone asks. She grips Osiris' hand tighter.

He gives her a quick look over his shoulder. "You really do live in a box. Didn't you know? You're a god."

"I don't understand. They were praising a statue."

"Exactly." He stops abruptly, and she rams into the back of him. "The religion of our Forefathers is no more. Practiced in Hyperboria yes, but out here…in the rest of the world, this is what you have."

"I'm not a god, that's blasphemy. Yet you would think they would love me if I were one."

"There isn't much going on in that pretty head of yours, is there?"

He thinks I'm pretty. Persephone blushes inside.

Osiris tugs on her hood to get a snugger fit. "Look here, stupid," he says, "Real people suffer at the hands of those who influence their lives and beliefs. It is just the way of things."

"And what are you doing about it?" she asks.

He ignores the question, yet the truth of it begins to fester. Between heartbeats, he darts towards a building 50-feet away. He stops mid-way to wave the Princess over.

She huffs with her slow run.

"You're joking." He looks down at her legs. "You still haven't gotten your abilities?"

She throws him a sarcastic look. "I'm less than a common Anuk…a common woman."

They run at regular speed to a corner. Pedestrians ignore them. They catch sight of Koray, investigating hanging fabrics. They waste no time in reaching her.

"Oh no…" Koray says with a chuckle at Persephone, "someone's going to kill you." She wraps her arm around Osiris. "I was wondering when you'd get here." They get a questioning glare from Persephone.

"You knew he was here?" Persephone asks

"What?" Koray shrugs. "It's not like you two ever talk."

Osiris fidgets with a wristwatch. "Alright you two, time to get lost. Go on with your business."

Both girls look at him with a questioning glare.

"Why in such a hurry?" Persephone asks. "Going back to the whore house?"

"No," he says sarcastically. His heart yearns for their nostalgic company. He takes a deep breath. "I'm in dire need of a church."

"What church?" Koray asks. They ignore her.

"Payback?" Persephone asks with a smile. Osiris nods.

"Koray, meet you in one hour." Osiris grabs Persephone's hand. They take off running.

Chapter 6: Religion of the Damned

Running to the docks takes a toll on Persephone. Each desperate gasp for air forces a crushing pain on her side; a reminder of her impotent Anuk abilities. Osiris shows her no mercy. He urges her on with grumbles and harsh prompts to hurry along. The abuse seems unnecessary when they reach the local chapter of the fire goddess' temple.

The modest building is hardly worthy of being called a church. Plain mud bricks make up the walls on the single-level structure. A thatched roof violates any fire code in existence if there are any. Sad windows scream of neglect. There is nothing holy around this insult.

Inside is bland, with rows of seating to hold fifty parishioners. Ugly statues line wooden shelves on the side walls. Pictures of the resident priestess hang high, showing off her gold teeth and wrinkled cleavage. Osiris leaves Persephone to catch her breath while he rummages through a back room.

"I found something!" he yells. Persephone peels herself off a bench with reluctance to join him.

"We should burn the place down and leave," she says, still catching her breath.

Wine boxes are tossed to the side of a wooden floor door with a padlock. "Care to open it?" Osiris asks. His face is serious.

Persephone sneers at him. "Very funny. You know I can't."

"Yes, you can," he says with an outstretched hand. His wiggling fingers draws her in. "Humor me."

She puts her hand on the thick lock. "See? I can't."

Osiris plunks down next to her, intimately close. His hand clasps hers with a gentle squeeze.

She meets his gaze, feeling the heat radiating from his skin, warm breath caressing her senses. Her heart takes off in a race she knows not where to. His grasp tightens.

"Your strength is in your blood, dormant, waiting to be energized. Light upon light captured in the plasma. Each thought solicits a reaction. The right thought activates power."

"I don't understand," she whispers.

"Shhhh. Close your eyes. Clear your mind. Pull."

She pulls with no result. Her scowling face screams of her failure.

"Pull," Osiris says. "Pull." His tone grows harsher. His hand fires off on the back of her head.

"Hey!" Her cheeks flush with anger.

"Pull!" he screams at her. "Pull!"

She voices her angst. A louder scream from Osiris compounds her anger. She rips the lock off in one swoop, sending the metal block shooting to the ceiling. The force it hits the brick with creates a gaping hole.

Persephone calms herself. She looks at Osiris with disbelief. Uncomfortable soreness infects the side of her right calf, mid-way below the knee. A desperate hand fires off to subdue the irritation.

"If I told you to get angry, it wouldn't have worked. Sorry for screaming in your ear."

"And for slapping my head!" She relaxes her shoulders and furious gaze. "Is that the trick to it?"

"No. It's a shortcut, not a very good one. Remember the sensations beneath the anger. The flow, heat. Using rage to enhance abilities will cloud your judgment. When I run, I'm not angry. I simply want to run. The thoughts linking the flow, calling energy up for use becomes second nature. Knowing it's there and how it feels is a step to unlocking it."

"It seems so easy." She laughs. "A joke. How is it I couldn't do this before?"

"My brother calls it the Light of Orion. It exists in every living being, Anuk and man. Our race can tap into the power, our genes are adapted for it. When an Anuk turns 13 a switch is turned on you can say. For us 'Pure-Bloods,' our genetics generate and absorb the power in far greater quantities. Your 'Light' collected into a powder keg…waiting for the match. The slightest spark would do."

He slips her hand off the itchy leg. "There's your stamp."

She lifts her pant leg, revealing a reddened pattern of dots formed like the constellation Lyra.

"Burns doesn't it?"

Persephone hugs Osiris as if it's the first time sharing an embrace. She lets go after an awkward look covers both their faces.

The door lifts with ease. Lights switch on automatically, showing off a wooden stairwell and concrete flooring beneath. Each descending footstep creaks from rotting boards.

Faint shifting in the wind alerts them to movement behind a far wall. Muffled shrieks flow in the stale, foul air. They approach with caution. On either side of a narrow path are boxes overflowing with gold coins, artwork, merchandise amassed from the Creator alone knows where. The corner comes upon them. Together they peer down a dark hallway.

Iron cages line a short wall, sectioned off in three compartments. Frightened people huddle in tattered clothes, pulling each other into darker corners of their cells. Cries from children ring out.

"Slavers," Osiris mutters under his breath. He gestures to the far cell. Persephone nods.

She grabs a steel padlock. Frightened faces stare back at her, bodies waiting to be lashed, hungry children at the point of collapse. Emotions tingle, boiling over into rage. She keeps the thoughts but channels the sensation to her hands. A subtle pull is all she needs. The lock breaks off without effort.

Osiris breaks the middle lock. No one leaves the cells. "It's not a trick," he says, motioning the slaves towards freedom. "Go quickly. Take as much treasure as you can carry."

"Hurry," Persephone says. "We're burning the place down. Get out. Now!"

The slaves rush out. The stampede clears within moments. Persephone and Osiris head back the way they came. Most of the treasure remains. They hurry to the stairs. A console catches Osiris' eyes. He breaks off to investigate.

"What are you doing? We have to go." Persephone starts to follow him.

He stops her. "Find anything that will burn. Cloth, a stick…make a torch. I'm right behind you." She complies and runs off.

He breaks open a draw. A fusion-cutter, logbooks and magazines bear no fruit until a data tube no larger than a little finger rolls out. On the bottom, the dark green seal of House Octavia of ENki shines in the overhead light. Osiris pockets his find. He flips through a palm-sized notebook. The script is unfamiliar, except for notations at the back, 'Dardanii.' "Finally, something I recognize." He takes it, as well

Intense flame burst out from the fusion-cutter's tip, ready to set fire to anything flammable. Osiris eyes the golden shimmer from a shallow box of coins. His pockets feel light. *Oh, what the hell.*

Topside, three slaves bunch up sections of dry bush on the roof. They jump down as Osiris makes his exit, and ignites Persephone's torch. Bowing, the slaves prattle off thanks in a tongue native to the Aryan coast.

Flaming embers drop from Persephone's torch. She grips tight, holds her breath and throws. The thatched roof ignites into a roaring pyre within moments. Black smoke crackles in a fury, the heat pushes on them from the river breeze.

"I'm thirsty," Osiris says with a smile.

Persephone looks at him with pride. She feels a tingle inside for her renewed friendship with her once lost friend. Reuniting with Koray will be the seal to a blessed day.

Returning to the village center is slow and pleasant. Osiris regales Persephone with tales of his travels. Past slights are forgotten. Plans made in pre-teen years were reignited, with images of climbing mountains, swimming in sacred Hyperborian pools and riding mammoths. It all sounds wonderful for children, but now into adulthood, the allure once felt disappeared, along with their innocence.

Ahead, a full marketplace under covered stands comes into view. Pleasant music draws in listeners to a short building with a half door and barman waiting at the counter. The sign brings warm thoughts on a cold day – it's an outdoor bar.

Osiris scowls at the pedestrian appeal. "There? What were you two going to do anyway?"

"Get drunk and spend money," Persephone says.

"Right…" Osiris rolls his eyes. "This way then."

Patrons are directed on to a narrow outdoor deck. Molded wooden floor planks contrast with white-washed posts touching dark roofing. Twelve square tables with four chairs each are spread out evenly on the noisy flooring.

Several patrons have begun late afternoon indulgence in the much-desired drink 'Boza.' Fermented wheat in a milk-like concoction; warms the body with its intriguing flavor and intimate burn. It is a perfect delight in the miserable cold. Koray relishes her second cup when she spots her friends.

"You caused a terrible uproar," Koray says with a slur. "Everyone is livid, except Samiri, which is strange. The Kitchen boys just told me."

Persephone shoves Osiris towards the ordering counter. She ignores the accusative smirk the handmaiden is sending her, however, silently delighting in the mystery swirling in Koray's head.

"Go over there, you stink of burnt rubbish and pig shit. Don't worry." Koray winks. "I won't ask...yet." Smiles break out.

Forced to sit next to Osiris, Persephone tries in earnest to resume the role of Princess, despite her disgusting appearance. "Typical," Osiris jokes under his breath.

Their greedy hands' press cups to lips. Patrons sitting downwind scowl and fire off insults, which is met with laughter. A couple of cups each diminish any semblance of social decorum.

Whispered recounts of the day's happenings are told, with exaggerated twists to induce excitement.

"Where do you suppose the slaves... I mean the people came from?" Koray asks.

A knot forms in Osiris' stomach. His hand feels for the data tube, rattling ill-gotten coins in his search. "Somewhere in Aryavan. They're free, that's what matters."

"But why were they kept in such horrid condition?" Persephone whispers.

"How do you think slaves come to be?" Osiris looks into her eyes, ignoring the confused expression. He chokes on his unfriendly tone; it burns his throat much like the Boza. His stomach turns as guilt creeps up his spine, for the seal burning his pocket.

"I don't know. They volunteer?" She feels the ridiculousness of her statement but does not have an answer. She turns to Koray who looks away with a mouthful of Boza.

"All slaves lose their freedom at some point," Osiris says in a friendlier tone. "Even the servants in your household. No matter how clean and pretty they look, they are slaves."

Persephone shoots Koray a glance. Tears glaze over her eyes.

Koray's eyes open wide. "I'm not a slave. Never was." "Not Koray," Osiris says, smiling. "She's nobility. I asked my father once about slavery in the banners of ENki. He told me it's not a subject I should concern myself with. No sense in worrying about an ancient practice, he warned."

Persephone wriggles her body and shoulders. Her grim look changes to joy. "Well…more important subject. This is the best day I've had in years. It's what I want, to do unexpected things, see the world." She nudges Osiris' shoulder.

"The world may not be ready for you," he jokes.

"You're lucky," she says with envy.

"Queen Farah keeps her on a short leash, ever since…" Koray begins but stops as a secret memory intrudes. An awkward silence prompts more drinking.

)●(

~ Five Years Ago ~

Childhood was a happy indulgence for Princess Persephone. Each year she looked forward to spending six weeks during summer months visiting the realms. Time was spent with families of Greater Houses, except Northern Illyria. Her holidaying with Prince Vali came to an abrupt end at age five.

In her twelfth year, the family stayed with Princess Dahlia, Osiris' mother, at an estate overlooking lush meadows and a small lake in Persepolis. Prince Odin's campaign in the wastelands continued with aggressive fervor, encouraging King Shuru to defer his visit in favor of lending support. This year only the girls were on holiday.

It promised to be a thrilling vacation because Koray would be there. She was Persephone's age and part of Dahlia's household.

These days Persephone's obnoxious behavior was considered a phase, and for the most part, ignored by her mother. She roamed free anywhere she liked with minimal supervision. On one of her defiant days, she slipped past the Royal-Guard and venture to a public lakefront.

The sweet smell of independence invigorated her. Being able to mingle with the common folk without prescribed fanfare was heaven. She made friends without any effort.

Koray was absent this day. Persephone wasted the afternoon basking in golden sunshine. After a quick swim, she invaded a meadow to nap amongst bright flowers.

Evil inclinations of man reared its ugly head. Dashe, a town's blacksmith, became enthralled with the Princess, ever since he laid eyes upon her during a visit to the city. He struggled for days with dark specters, inducing unnatural lust. It didn't matter who Persephone was or what she represented. The unthinkable burden of suicide crept into his soul; a preferred alternative if he couldn't possess her. Self-pity gave way to indulgence. He waited. He watched.

In the bushes, Dashe readied a dilapidated chariot, liberated from a broken theater at the city's outskirts. His dementia landed him in a grand epic within his mind, once sang about a heroic rescue of a maiden from the clutches of a warlord – a tale familiar to man a hundred years past. He lashed his steed as the sun sparkled above a watery abyss. On he rode with malicious thoughts stirring in his mind.

Under the guise of a friendly face, he encouraged the trusting Princess into his vehicle of despair. On they rode to unfamiliar grounds, descending beneath the earth into a labyrinth of darkness. Helpless, afraid, she retreated into a protective shell any mortal would cower into.

At first, he played simple games by dressing her up into the doll he wished he had. The next night brought on sinful touching. The third night, starved, beaten, afraid, Persephone succumbed to the most heinous violations of all.

A day prior, the heavens trembled when King Shuru descended on Persepolis with vengeful warriors, intent on razing every building until his precious daughter was returned. They searched in vain, until Koray prompted her father, General Marcus, to investigate the broken theater, where she often played as a child. In the meadow, she recognized a piece of the chariot's emblem, felled from the wooden relic.

Without time to return word, Marcus ventured with Koray into the bowels of the earth. Torches flickered in desperation inside damp caverns. Frustration ended when the seasoned General faced off with the terrible creature of a man.

Koray found Persephone crumpled in a destroyed state, bleeding, frightened, absent her senses.

The Villain endured a slow death at the hands of Shuru. A public spectacle done with purpose, to show off the wrath a parent will let loose on the world for their child. The entire affair was covered up; the victim's identity kept amongst those concerned.

Months of treatment restored Persephone to a recognizable state, but it was a secret exposure to the Holy Amon-I that brought her out from the depths of hell. She returned oblivious to a cloudy past.

Persephone's return to the 'Mountain of the gods' brought down an entourage of medical staff, priests, and an overabundant scolding by her uncle, the Regent. Once the ordeal finished, she expected the wrath of disappointment from her Watcher. To her surprise, a calm, collected air of reason greeted her. Samiri inquired on her state of mind and all that. Unknown to the Princess, during her escapade, spies from the Watchers local chapter observed her every move.

With the Watcher's counsel no longer requiring the sacred Amon-I, Samiri tasks himself to find a new road to the relic. *Allowing Persephone to roam free in the world could provide the right stimuli for a new approach.* He did not anticipate Prince Osiris interacting with the Princess, but this fortunate encounter opened the door to a yet unknown solution. He imparts his constructed version of wisdom – 'Safety is paramount in foreign lands,' before sending the Princess off to a well-needed bath.

A host of servant's fuss over Persephone in a large bathing area. Waiting patiently in the main chamber is her caretaker, Peki. He and his wife received a prestigious assignment to the Princess on the day of her birth. The couple is without children, so they treat their royal charge with as much love and consideration as they would their own child.

Servants escort the Princess to the main chamber for grooming. Persephone has her evening gown on for a banquet later. She cringes with the hair brushing, wishing to be out in the slums with Osiris. She swats the servant's hand before turning to Peki. "How is Shireen?"

"Much better, Highness." He tries to hide a sadness encroaching on his voice. Sad eyes give away the harsh reality of concern for his beloved.

"You should be in Hyperboria with her, not here with me."

"This is where I need to be, Princess. If it is the Creator's will to take my wife, it will happen, no matter where I am."

"It is not right. I will tell Samiri to arrange your return straight away." A loud clap summons a palace aide, perched at the door. The girl runs to the Princess. The moment she receives her handwritten note, she takes off with haste. "There…it will be arranged."

"You are too kind, Highness, but I am afraid it is your Watcher who secured me for this trip."

There is a lot Persephone does not understand. Her protected life created an imbalance with the version of reality she is taught and the real way of things. Despite the enormous affection she has for Peki, he is simply a slave. In her mind, he is a beloved servant, free to conduct his affairs as he wants, like Koray. This disparity in the social strata within her household is something she unintentionally ignores. Osiris' glaring point of her ignorance rings in her mind.

"Peki, have you ever returned to the place of your birth?" she asks with genuine curiosity, wanting to hear about a faraway place, foreign to her.

"No, it has been many years since I have seen my homeland." The old man sits near the Princess with a broad smile, causing her to reciprocate in anticipation. "I was born in pTah-"

"The Underworld?" she interrupts.

"Yes, on a small farm outside the Giza plateau. We could see the pyramid from there. Everything was as green then as it is now, full of wildlife and easy living. There weren't many people in the town, so everyone knew everybody. I had three brothers and two sisters…I am in the middle. The nearby lake flowed with cool clear water. We swam there in the warm months. For me, it was a paradise."

"What made you go to Hyperboria? It is always cold there. The opposite of pTah, isn't it?"

"I did not have a choice, Princess. I was taken by marauders from Aryavan."

"But why would they take you?"

Peki lowers his eyes. "It is the way of things, Highness.".

She leans closer to whisper, "Peki, are you a slave?"

Telling the truth is a trait the old man instills into the Princess through wisdom and deeds; he hesitates to offer this truth, which may shatter her view of him. *She must wake up one day.* He smiles warmly, "Yes. I am grateful that I have been fortunate. Many are not as I am, serving the Royal family, but this is the way of things."

"I don't like it. The people in the town here, is it like that everywhere?"

"Not everywhere," Peki says, and it's the only response he cares to offer. He stands, as the other servant finishes her brushing. "I beg your leave, Highness. I have duties to attend to before the banquet."

"Alright." She sighs. Peki bows reverently.

As he makes his way out, she regards the slave she's known all her life. *Such a humble man.* The experience in the town echoes in her head; the priestess with her flock is at the forefront of her memory. *Is this the direction we are headed? The elevation to godhood is but a descent into insanity.*

Chapter 7: Justice is But a One-Sided Affair

For one week, up until her departure from Aryavan, Persephone remained under the watchful eye of Samiri and her mother. Queen Farah returned one day after the Princess' gallivanting through the mud. Persephone bombarded Farah with questions about her place in the world, all of which fell on deaf ears, as they always do.

The Royal entourage made its way to a new city called Corinth in Southern Illyria; 'new' being relative to the surrounding cities, for Corinth is already 200 years old.

Queen Farah insisted the party travel the ocean, instead of the scenic but long journey by land from the airport in Mari. This past month has been a vacation for her and Persephone, so the conventional air transportation was passed up as much as could be tolerated, in favor of a sight-seeing tour of the world – anything to avoid Vali.

Warm blue ocean waters crash on mossy rocks near the harbor. The sun is bright. Birds are flying. A large sailing ship is anchored after its short journey from Anatolia.

The principality of Corinth falls within the territories belonging to House ENki. The Great House Octavia rules these lands; the Primary being a first cousin of Prince Odin – Princess Octavia. She holds the attention of any fortunate enough to be in her company.

Flowing dresses are a standard for this elaborate display, mixed with sparkling jewelry and styled red hair, done in the fashion of an expensive dancing girl. The elegant way she walks dazzles men, with rising anticipation of discreet conversation stimulating imaginations. Her pretty face always has what Persephone calls 'War-paint' plastered over age lines.

Opulence is an understatement when one attempts to describe the lavish lifestyle of Octavia. She is fortunate to control sea-lanes passing through her region, bringing much wealth to her House. A lesser-known source of her income comes from illegal temple activities.

Prince Odin banned all Houses of ENki from participating in popular heresies plaguing the civilized world. When enacted, he inadvertently encouraged the rise of secret cults within principalities under his rule. In Corinth, Octavia popularized a new phenomenon called 'sacred prostitution,' a growing attraction in the underbelly of society.

Devotees from all over come to be inducted on a roster blessed by the gods. The 'Line-up' is limited to 20 'sacred-prostitutes' per month, keeping the price of admittance high. Initiates are offered to suitors in search of a spouse, male or female. Episodes of debauchery and decadence are the norm. This is not an affair for the shallow pocket – another control set by Octavia to ensure secrecy.

The evening sun is low. Soft rolling waves crash on rocks at the back of Octavia's residence on the top of a hill. She refuses to call her dwellings a palace, although the decor, abundance of slaves in expensive dress, along with an endless supply of food and drink says otherwise.

Princess Octavia is a lean, well-proportioned Anuk of medium height; no one knows her actual hair color as it changes with the new moon. This evening she insists on wearing her hair in a nest of curls, adorned with blue flowers attached to strings of gold.

She looks ridiculous, Persephone muses with a slight chuckle escaping unnoticed. It's the 'lounging time before dinner,' as Octavia puts it. Everyone gathered are sitting on cushions, eating grapes, and indulging in lies. The chatter is a mix of pretentious laughter resulting from scandalous banter – foul yet entertaining.

"You poor dear," Octavia opens her arms wide in a gesture mostly for show. "Come, give your Thia a hug. We are fortunate you weren't attacked by those village people."

Persephone cringes slightly in her Thia Octavia's embrace.

"Shuru would have had a fit," Farah says before Persephone can get a response out. "You know how he loves his daughter. I swear Octavia, how you tolerate living this far south is beyond comprehension…the humidity is terrible."

"I think it's refreshing," Persephone says with a wide smile. "I noticed a shuttle from Hyperboria came in an hour ago."

Octavia's fires off a sneer. "It's only Thoth," she says with slight disdain. "They are here for the night."

Persephone's eyes widen to match her smile. "They?"

"Odin's sons, Thoth and Osiris."

"What are you grinning about, you silly child?" Farah asks.

"Nothing…just good to have people my age to converse with…unlike you old…"

"Persephone!" Farah yells. "Watch your mouth. Don't mind her, Octavia. She excels at being rude."

Persephone stands to brush off grape stems from her long cream-colored dress. "Since everyone is on the wrong side of 500…" she smiles at the crowd, "…no offense, except to my mother, I'll be off exploring."

At the onset of Farah's protest, Octavia grabs her arm, "Let her go, cousin…there aren't any villages nearby." They watch the Princess run off to a nearby hallway.

Octavia scowls at her handful of grapes. "My doors have been jarred open to visitors of late…first Markus and now my nephews." She catches Farah's questioning glare. "Not you dove. You practically own the place." She stuffs a grape in her mouth and mutters, "In name."

"So, you dislike Thoth?" Farah asks. "Shuru adores him, treats him like a son."

Octavia's face sours. "If he weren't close to the King, I'd consider an experiment in seduction. I'd only be wasting my time."

"How so?" Farah asks.

"Thoth is devoted to his duties as Keeper-of-Secrets...or is it Keeper-of-Forbidden-Knowledge. Bloody Anuk language can't even be translated right." Everyone laughs. "I love my nephew. I don't trust someone who possesses so many secrets...or a virile Anuk who withstands my charms."

"Octavia, you tramp," Farah bursts out.

Octavia throws her a devilish smirk. "Don't forget, you have your share of secrets too, hypocrite."

"Weren't your daughter and Osiris supposed to be matched?"

"They were, but the little shit wanted to explore the world. He claims he was not ready for marriage. Poor girl was devastated. She's quite young, only 300...she will be alright."

"An adventurer like his father." Farah chuckles. "I like him."

"And Persephone, is there a match coming soon?" Octavia's question stirs an internal revulsion in Farah. Nausea forces wine back up from her gut. Prince Vali's purring voice assaults her imagination.

It reminds her of his plans to be executed the moment the royal entourage arrives in Northern Illyria. She harbors misgivings about the affair; this is why she insisted on sailing for Corinth – her guilty way of delaying the inevitable.

"No," the Queen says. "She refuses any mention of a match or marriage. Her father only plays into her childish avoidance." Bitter bile settles in her throat.

Away from everyone, Persephone finds much-desired solitude in a large rotunda facing the sea. The real source for her anxious departure resides somewhere on the grounds. She peers at the shuttle parked in an open space. *Maybe they are in the city.* Footsteps entering the enclosure startle her displaced thoughts, but calm subdues her tension at the sight of Thoth. She jumps up and hugs her cousin with joy.

"I've missed you," she says with love in her voice.

Thoth smiles and greets her with a kiss on her forehead. "It's been too long. Three years is it?"

"Feels longer. In the meantime, I've had to put up with your rotten brother. Did you know what he was doing in Aryavan?"

Thoth bursts out laughing. "What my little brother does is his concern, unless it puts you in danger. He told me what happened."

"A whore and a snitch. Thoth, is the whole world like that? The Aryan village I mean."

"Thankfully, no." He looks at her with pride and a smile. "The world is a big place, made up of wonders and culture you are yet to experience."

"If my mother has her way, I'd see none of it on my own. Not to mention papa. I love him more than life, but he has his share of blame in locking me away from the world."

Thoth takes a step back. "I take no side in things beyond my station."

"Don't patronize me with calculated avoidance. We may have different parents but you are my brother. Speak your mind."

Pleasant shock shows on his face at Persephone's boldness; he finds it refreshing. "Alright… protecting you from the world is tantamount to lying, no matter the troubles of the past. There is a balance of good with bad in the world, or there used to be. Avoiding realities which will one day be your inheritance is a handicap they will regret."

She makes a sarcastic face. "Did you know I am a god? I did not realize the extent to which this blasphemy had taken shape."

"I've seen what's happening to your name, and the Forefathers."

"Uncle Vali says I have a spark of the divine in me. I did not realize it would amount to this."

"Divinity is reserved for the Creator," Thoth says. "What you are told is well-placed deception; this I have come to realize in the past months."

Persephone looks at him intently. "What can we do about it?"

"Nothing. We are a tolerant society now – this is a good thing, 'Sephie. It allows a version of freedom to those who lack it. Intolerance breeds disastrous outcomes in one way or another."

"I don't like it," she whispers. "Is there a way to avoid all the bad?"

"I don't know. I fear forces are plotting against you by propping up the new religions. Be vigilant in your interactions with everyone from now on, even those closest to you."

"Surely, not my parents." Her tension returns.

"Yes," he whispers, leaning in close. "Even though they may not be involved with…anything, they may be susceptible to external influences."

Seagull calls echo from above, breaking the uncomfortable silence, like the 'Meow' of hungry cats or the cackling of disobedient children. Wings gliding on soft wind pulls the Princess into deep thought. She exhales a comforting breath, the way Thoth taught her long ago. She grabs his bracelet to flick the beads like she did as a child. "I've heard that you commune with the Forefathers themselves. Is it true?"

"I heard you got a taste of your abilities. Is it true?"

"Shhhh. It's a secret." She looks at Thoth's smile, realizing the nature of her question.

"What are they like? Scary with lightning bolts shooting out their asses?" They chuckle.

"They are as human as the rest of us. Well, their souls anyway. Yet, the two times I have encountered them, my very essence was shaken. Do you remember their names?"

"Dragoi, the warrior. Odin, the peacekeeper. Shiva the bearer of wisdom. Xi-Wang-Mu, the healer. Sekhmet the powerful. And, ENlil lord of the sky and ENki lord of the plains."

"Good. But there is a multitude of other attributes, most proclaiming terrible things."

A brief silence passes. Persephone inquiries about Osiris, who has disappeared from the compound. Thoughts of running off on another adventure slip into the conversation. It ends when Samiri enters the rotunda.

"Forgive my intrusion, Highness," Samiri says with a bow, dropping lower than usual for Thoth's benefit. "The Queen demands your presence at dinner."

Persephone huffs, hugs her cousin, then hurries off to, as she puts it – 'The den of cackling hens.'

"My Lord, it is an honor to once more be in your presence," Samiri says.

"It has been some time since we last spoke. I hear rumors, Samiri. Talk of secret undertakings amongst the Watchers."

"This is but part of a concern. I seek humble counsel." Samiri sits at Thoth's insistence. He lowers his voice to a whisper. "I am of the opinion the Watcher's counsel can no longer be trusted. There are breaks in the ranks – separatists and loyalists-"

"Which one are you?" Thoth interrupts.

"I am neither, my Prince. I serve the Princess."

"I hear good things about you, Samiri. His Majesty praises you, Princess Persephone complains about you, in good light of course. I will ask her Highness to release you from service to join my order, but I caution you. Serving my order is also serving the Princess by proxy."

Samiri struggles to hide joy escaping through his smile. To be at the side of the Keeper-of-Forbidden-Knowledge is the closest he has yet come to see the sacred Amon-I. He knows it will be years before he can achieve his goal – time as it were, is something Samiri is blessed with. "It is a tremendous honor you bestow on me, my Lord."

He listens to Thoth ramble on, yet his mind wanders on the impending dilemma Persephone will face. Queen Farah can avoid fulfilling her promise to Prince Vali for so long.

Dinner at Octavia's is, as one expects, a lavish affair. Twenty of her closest friends gather with the Royal guests to dine on seafood, a multitude of fowls, exotic meats, exquisite fruit, and lots of wine. Accentuating the experience is an orchestra playing in an adjacent room. Melodies from old Hyperborian masters compete with 'the den of cackling hens.'.

"Persephone dear, do stop drinking…have some manners at the table." Queen Farah scowls at the Princess.

"Do shut up, mother. I'll drink as much as I want."

Outbursts such as this do not shock Farah. She nods at Peki. The devoted servant knows the request all too well. He approaches his charge with determination to save her dignity; it's tumbling faster than the wine spilling on her gown.

"My Peki," Persephone says with a drunken smile. "Or it should be *our* beloved Peki."

"Your Highness, it may be time to retire," the old man says in his soft yet firm way.

"No!" she bursts out for all to take notice. "Mother, I demand you grant Peki his freedom."

Embarrassment flushes on Farah's face. "This is not the time or place... stop it!"

"Very well. Persephone waves her hand around as if providing a blessing. "You are now free, my loyal servant."

Peki ignores the gesture, in favor of removing her from vile glares coming their way.

"Pay her no mind Farah...it's a phase," Octavia says. She sees the tension on the Queen's face. Her clenched teeth and twitching eyelids.

"I've had enough of it. She has been a petulant child all her life."

Octavia, in her nonchalant way, jokes, "Time to marry her off then." Laughter erupts from the table.

Farah slumps into a realization that she may very well see the departure of her daughter all too soon. "Excuse me," she announces as she leaves her seat.

Farah marches off to the exit doors. To her right is a hallway leading to the bedchambers. Hesitation overcomes her. She turns left to traverse a long passageway. She does not notice a passerby stop to observe her. A slim man, or youth, dressed in dark clothing. The figure immediately throws over his hood as he skirts around corners at the far end of the hallway.

After several flights of stairs, she stops at a grand garden illuminated by hovering lighting pods. She makes her way through a labyrinth of hedges to find a quiet spot. Satisfied she is alone; she opens a palm-sized device.

The figure following her stops a safe distance away, behind a shrub.

"Come on you swine," Farah says after touching a button. She crouches on the ground.

Prince Vali's face appears in the air above her pad. The arrogant smile is aggravating her. "Call it off, Vali!"

Behind the shrub, Osiris removes his hood. He strains to hear the Queen's conversation. A barrage of rain from sprinklers shower down on him. *Better leave this alone*, he advises himself before retreating.

"You know that tune you used to hum to my betrothed?" Vali asks. "I'll bet you don't know its origins."

"I do not have time for this you snake. She will not be yours."

"Humor me, then decide," Vali says.

Farah continues to stare at the image with rage building up.

Vali ignores her. "Long ago in the mountains of Aryavan, there was a kind maiden who lived atop a waterfall – the highest in all the land. She fell in love with a handsome stranger, had two beautiful children, and lived a happy life.

"One day, her husband fell ill after temple, causing fear to overcome the woman. She sought help from the village. A kind priestess would lend aid. In exchange, the priestess demanded a small sacrifice – the family's one milking cow, their only source of income. The woman agreed. The husband was cured, yet the woman did not give what was promised.

"Facing potential hardship, she offered other forms of payment in her desperate attempt to avoid the dreaded sacrifice. With a grandmother's smile, the priestess promised ruin. Months passed before the husband collapsed and died.

"The woman worked twice as hard. She made a trip to another village to trade, returning at the brink of collapse from hunger. Left in the brick oven was a scrumptious meat pie, delicious, savory. She devoured a portion, saving a serving for the children. Where are the children?

"She rushed in to check on the babes. 'They're not there! Where are they?' In a fit, the woman runs outside, screaming their names. She falls to her knees in front of the milking cow with tears pouring out tired eyes. She bites down with rage. Something troubles her. Caught between her teeth was a thin membrane with an unusual texture.

"She picked the object from her teeth. It was a slice of eyeball, with a hint of brown, like her daughter's gaze. Struck with horror, the woman rushed to the waterfall's edge. In a wail of regret, she hurled her body into the misty abyss. Moments too late, a neighbor reaches the water's edge to see the woman's body disappear. She screamed, 'Your children are safe…your children are safe!' The next day the priestess came, collected the children and the milking cow." Vali sighs deeply.

"Are you threatening me, Vali?"

"No, my Queen…just relaying to you, the Ballad of Persephone."

Farah's rage gives way to fear. A tear leaves her cheek and falls on the smiling hologram.

"The moral of this tale, dear Queen is to never, ever upset the order of things already in motion. Keep your promise." The image disappears.

Two hours before midnight brings silence throughout Octavia's residence. Everyone is asleep after the post-dinner festivities. Persephone is bundled up under a thin blanket in her comfortable bedchamber. Her guttural snores drown out crackling from the fireplace. Suddenly, a ripe tomato hits the window. It takes a barrage of vegetable assault before the Princess wakes.

Annoyed at the loud splattering sound, Persephone slips out of bed, stumbling by the wall to catch a glimpse of the perpetrator. She huffs at the sight of Prince Osiris hurling leafy projectiles. He points to her balcony. She scowls as she lies to herself, *He is getting on my last nerve.*

Cold wind blasts the Princess when she opens the double-doors. She is startled when Osiris appears rising in the air – a hum from the hover-bike becomes noticeable when it lifts into view.

"What are you doing here?" she snaps.

"I'm going into town…are you coming?" he asks in an arrogant tone. "And fix yourself, you look a mess."

"Why, you insolent shit…if you think I'm going anywhere with you in the middle of the night…"

"Alright. Stay here with a bunch of old hags or come with me on a small errand." He fusses with his jacket, ignoring Persephone's false look of outrage.

Her face sours. "I'll be right back."

Chapter 8: A Crack in the Chain of Antiquity

Corinth is a lively place at night. All manner of establishments are open for business up until sunrise. During the daytime citizens carry on with routines, adhering to strict codes of behavior. At night, the more unscrupulous activities take place under cover of darkness. This city is a tourist haven, and as such it caters to all sorts of depraved inclinations.

Nighttime travel on the highway on hover-bike is exhilarating. Two-miles of open road is devoid of traffic, encouraging Osiris to push the sleek two-seater beyond posted speed limits. Persephone holds on for dear life. Defying her mother's strict rules is more in-line with the Princess' behavior; she never broke these rules, however, while outside the protective borders of Hyperboria.

The Royals arrive at a packed parking lot in one of the city's seediest corners. A three-level building rumbles with pounding bass echoing beyond the walls. The door opens and the music reverberates out into the street. A large bouncer holds a miserable looking man by the back of his pants and collar. The bouncer heaves, throwing the man out onto the curb.

Osiris gestures to the entrance, "Afraid?"

"Don't be ridiculous," Persephone says. She fusses with her hood.

Osiris smiles at her. "You'll be fine, no one will recognize us."

"What sort of errand needs attention in this place?"

"I thought Thia would've had her claws in you by now."

"Well, your Thia can kiss my ass. And what is up with her hair?"

They chuckle, walking up a short flight of stairs. The doorman looks at their youthful appearance, issuing a judgmental grunt before allowing entry.

Plumes of smoke rise freely in the air. Sounds of revelry compete with loud music. Grumbling from angry couples in a corner goes unnoticed. Waitresses deliver beverages to thirsty patrons in dingy booths. A door at the far end opens.

The doorman leans on a large antique wine case. His snarling smile shows off one row of gold-plated teeth. He stands tall dressed in casual attire. A silk shirt hugs a generous belly. Bulging out on his waistband, a large pistol promises a careless accident. He makes sure it's noticed.

Persephone and Osiris pretend to be juvenile delinquents from the town in search of sordid 'back-room' affairs. Osiris wraps his arm around Persephone's waist, letting his palm caress her butt. The doorman's face lights up. "Enter if you dare," his mouth of gold purrs.

Unafraid, they enter a dim passageway to an unseen section. Ominous stairs to a basement level creak from years of rotting. At the bottom, there is a faint glow of yellow light and noise. A card game it sounds like.

Osiris gets settled at one of the eight poker tables.

Persephone sticks by his side, showing a hint of nervousness when prompted to join a game. Osiris encourages her to sit. She scans the room for signs of trouble brewing.

Complimentary drinks arrive. Osiris throws out a coin he stole in Aryavan. A high stakes game begins with the lighting of cigars.

Assorted card games ended after hours of play, leaving spectators to gather around one active table in the smoky room. A cloud of bad luck descended on Osiris after a lucrative winning streak; a seasoned observer would surmise he lost on purpose.

Six rough-looking Illyrian tribesmen took his winnings. Conversation revealed they were from the Dardanii tribe of northern Illyria. Excessive drinking and more questioning stirred up concerns their employer had for a recent loss of profits. Osiris felt it was time to leave, but Persephone would not have it. She insisted on trying her luck in a game.

First game, she barely recovered the initial investment. The men were jubilant to play with the female; such a thing is not common in Corinth. Their high-spirits disintegrated into heaps when Persephone won three games in a row, shaming the losers in front of their comrades.

One game remains. The Princess has all her winnings in the pot. Osiris stifles a smile at her losing hand. "Come on 'Sephie, it's getting late." His eyes freeze with horror. Tucked under Persephone's sleeve is a faint, suspicious outline of a card. His heart takes off when she makes a quick switch close to her chest.

"Time to run off to mommy," one man laughs. He drops his hand with a broad smile. The other player slams his fist in aggravation.

Osiris grabs Persephone's shoulder, affording the man a sneer.

Persephone grimaces at the ecstatic man. "I don't think so."

The defeated Illyrian pauses for a moment. "You cheated!" His companions gather behind him. They flash sharp blades stuffed in their waistbands.

"Tell the people you're sorry and let's go," Osiris whispers. Persephone throws him a crooked smile.

"My mistake," she tells the Illyrians. "Keep it."

They snarl at the pair. Gold-teeth appears at the foot of the stairs brandishing his pistol.

"Time to go." Osiris yanks Persephone towards Gold-teeth.

Illyrians rush behind them. Gold-teeth clicks his pistol's safety off. A shot fires over everyone's heads. Osiris launches a table at Gold-teeth. Persephone swings a heavy chair at the closest tribesman. The charging group stumbles on the falling man.

Osiris latches on to Persephone's hand and pulls her hard. They clear the lower level. He pushes her out the basement door then pulls a heavy cabinet across the cavity.

Startled patrons look at them with annoyance. They ignore curious glances in favor of a quick retreat.

Outside, they waste no time in firing up the hover-bike. It rumbles to life. One angry tribesman leaps down the stairs, screaming obscenities. In seconds they speed away from danger.

Two streets away Osiris pulls into an alleyway. Persephone's heart races with excitement rather than panic. A minute passes, and the thrill turns into worry. "They're going to find us," she says under her helmet.

Osiris doesn't answer. He attaches a device on his dashboard. It lights up with a map of the area. A solid red dot blinks then begins to move. He revs the engine and takes off to intercept the dot.

"Great, more docks," Persephone says, as the hoverbike stops.

Unlike in Aryavan, an ocean opened up in front of them rather than a river. Spotlights from across the channel shimmer on dark waters. Threatening air horns from approaching vessels announce the start of morning activities. The pair scramble behind a stack of barrels.

"Osiris…I think it's time you take me home."

"What? Just a few more minutes," he whispers.

"I don't like this. What are you up to?"

"The coin I lost is from Aryavan, from the church."

Persephone's eyes widen. Her aggravation slips out in her tone. "This was a ploy? Here I thought you were being nice!"

"Keep your voice down." He relaxes his tense gaze on a warehouse and lets out a defeated sigh. "I suspect Octavia is mixed up with the tribesmen and their operation. I need proof to expose her."

"Maybe she's innocent, Osiris."

"Then I'll expose the true criminals. And I thought you could use a night away from routine," he says, trying to sound altruistic. "I thought you wanted adventure."

Persephone slouches with fatigue and indecision. "I do, but…this is not my world. I had a good time tonight. Take me home…please."

Her pleading eyes force him to comply. The realization of his recklessness suddenly dawns on him. No matter whether he is the heir to House ENki and all it encompassed; Persephone is the heir to Hyperboria, the ultimate heir to everything. In his selfish desire to keep her company, he is putting her in danger. "Come on, let's go."

Speeding down the empty highway was not as thrilling as the first time. The pair remains frozen in their thoughts during the 15-minute ride back to Octavia's.

Tinges of red clouds peek out on the horizon, announcing sunrise and the lateness of the hour. Fortunately, Corinthians are almost as bad as Aryans to start the day. Not a soul is stirring in the villa's compound, except a few cats roaming. Osiris returns Persephone to her balcony without a word.

"Thanks for the interesting night," she says in an apologetic tone.

He softens his sturdy gaze on the dashboard, removes his helmet then receives hers. "You've got to stop cheating people that are bigger than you."

"Really?" she chuckles. Her chest suddenly feels lighter.

"'Sephie…there's something I should tell you." His intense stare returns, starting at the ground far below then into her waiting eyes. "Be careful on your way home, alright. Don't trust anyone…"

"I don't understand what are you saying?"

"Best to just say it," he mumbles to himself, strengthening his resolve. "I overheard your mother talking with Vali. She was hiding out in the garden, upset and being secretive."

Persephone moves back a few steps, scowling with disbelief. "How dare you?" she yells. "My mother is no saint, but she will never do anything to hurt me. And uncle Vali has nothing but my best interest at heart."

"Forget it." Osiris dons his helmet.

"No, you forget it. Get out, you miserable wretch!"

Osiris shakes his head. "Don't say I didn't warn you."

The bike drops out of view, then darts out the compound. Persephone remains staring at him with her mouth wide open.

~ Royal Palace, Hyperboria ~

Water tumbles down a steep fall near King Shuru's private bedchambers, sending a therapeutic hymn of power reverberating through the walls. Morning sunshine streams across a massive window with an invisible shield separating the sickly King from the elements.

After returning from the Citadel in the Western-Continent, Shuru descended into the grips of an unknown illness. Doctors panicked over symptoms pointing to a viral outbreak, but their concerns were calmed when all indications pointed to a common case of 'old age.'

Shuru moves around his spacious chamber like an old-man seeking a reminder of days past. He finds a picture-book with images of Persephone from birth up to one month ago. He smiles, wishing his one reason for living could be at his side. *The end is near, my Angel.*

A servant enters with quick steps to an aide posted near the chamber's entrance. "What is it?" Shuru asks, without breaking his stare at the picture-book.

"Prince Odin is here, your Grace."

Shuru grumbles his permission. A minute passes before Odin enters.

"Majesty," Odin says respectfully. He helps Shuru to a sitting area.

"You've looked better," Shuru jokes.

"What happened? All but a week ago you were well."

"Hyperboria doesn't agree with me anymore I'm afraid. It's all that bloody good living your son exposed me to at the Citadel."

"Yes." Odin Laughs. "If you call cataloging old books and prancing around with monks an appealing holiday."

"I am glad you are here. I don't see you as much as I would like. Didn't have time to tell you my wishes for the future; I do not know how much longer I have-"

"Nonsense," Odin interrupts. "No more talk of this. There is something wrong with you and we will figure it out."

"I have always considered you a son. My father and yours rose above their confinement of being cousins to become brothers, just as our forefathers ENlil and ENki were brothers,"

Shuru says. He raises a hand to quiet incoming concern. "As the law requires, you shall become Regent, to rule in my stead until Persephone comes of age. I am not waiting for my death. My declaration has already been logged with the registrar."

"The council will not receive this in good faith. Majesty, I fear your decision will stir up a hornet's nest."

"My aide has my full wishes," Shuru says with a smile brewing on his lips. "I want all lands once belonging to House ENki to be returned to you. The territories of pTah shall be given to Osiris on his wedding day. And, you, not the Primary of ENlil, shall be responsible for finding a suitable husband for Persephone. But only if she wants a union."

Odin's words get lodged in his throat. His heart sinks with despair on hearing Shuru's wishes as if signaling the monarchs entry into the beyond. His head feels heavy, shoulders weighed down by a hefty burden. Faces of House ENlil's Greater House Primaries infect his mind. Each screaming their legitimacy to marry the Princess.

"Your Majesty, this will anger all the houses of ENlil and ENki. A King must rule."

"So, what?" Shuru bursts out. "Let them stew in their failure to see the reality unfolding before their greedy eyes. Archaic traditions set for a culture that demanded it thousands of years ago have no place in the present. I have interpreted that much from the sacred texts of the Amon-I."

"We can't go against the mandate of Lord ENlil so close to the awakening," Odin says.

"Because a younger brother was given rule over the elder, does not make his example a case for all generations, despite what the line of ENlil thinks. Lord ENki allowed female Primaries, didn't he?"

"Majesty…Uncle, this goes beyond the progression of culture and civilization; it breaks from traditions rooted deep inside every Anuk, commoner and Pure-Blood."

"These are my wishes," Shuru says calmly. "A toothache hurts, does it not? Doesn't mean you have to destroy your mouth to get rid of the pain. That's what I will say to those insufferable asses."

Odin gives him an earnest look with a nod. "Your will shall be done, Sire."

"Osiris is a good boy. Pity the bloodlines cannot be joined. One more thing, send word for Farah to return home immediately."

"At once, your Grace."

~ *Watchers Counsil Headquarters* ~

"What is wrong with you Aspasia? Calm yourself," Prince Vali orders his Watcher. His eyes fall on her blank stare, lips held tight; she swallows intensely. Watchers' attire consists of light fitted fabrics; Aspasia's blouse left room for a casual breeze to flow through her bosom.

Vali gestures her into a circular glass elevator. The ride up the steep side of the 60-level pyramid is less than a minute; enough time for Aspasia to experience a severe case of nausea. "Compose yourself," Vali orders in a stern voice.

Her sprint to the bathroom is suspicious: Vali raises an eyebrow curiously

"Your Highness," an approaching voice says. Vali shifts his gaze to a watcher in a black gown. Chancellor Gaius bows with reverence. "Welcome."

"Have you been keeping secrets from me?" Vali asks coyly.

Gaius looks past small devices on the ceiling tiles, making sure he notices.

"Secrets can never be kept in these halls, Highness. I have Illyrian wine waiting."

A short trip ends at an inviting chamber, with large windows at the back. Once in, Gaius dismisses his aides. They hurry out, making sure to bow to the Prince. The doors close, initiating a heavy tint to envelop the windows. The Chancellor pulls a book partway out from a long shelf, initiating a soft hiss of air. The wall swings back. Blackness in a hidden room illuminates, the conversations will be held in secret.

"Shall we wait for your watcher?" Gaius asks.

"Yes." Vali nods. "Pregnancy can be a brutal condition, especially for one unfamiliar with its symptoms. Don't look surprised Chancellor...the wine?"

Shaking hands, trembling lips, and a furrowed brow betray Gaius' anxiety. "I cannot deny it; she is with offspring."

Vali crosses his legs, offers a villainous smirk, then regards his wine. "What sort of unholy venture has the counsel undertaken?"

"I assure you, Highness, our intentions are innocent; dare I say reasonable."

"Oh? And what are your intentions? Have you considered the repercussions this will have on society?"

"It is our right to seed our race. For generations, we have tried to regain what your ancestors took from us-"

"You cannot regain what you never possessed," Vali interrupts. "It is a simple matter of genetic manipulation. When your race was created, that ability remained absent for a reason."

"What might that be?" Gaius asks boldly.

"You are the product of Anuk and man; superior to the natural occurrence of offspring between the two races. Strength, intellect, loyalty; all traits infused into your DNA, absent the random chance of fate assigning you a less than desirable outcome."

"But are we human? Over time we have slipped from the pinnacle of honored service into one of lesser prestige."

"So, you're despondent of the status man occupies in the strata of things?"

"Yes," Gaius says. "We fear our extinction. So, dear Prince, you asked of our intentions. It is simply one of survival."

Vali remains silent for a moment. The thought of a mighty race able to breed without controls frightens him. "Chancellor, if you pledge me your support in the days to come, I promise you, your race shall return to the glory it once held. Additionally, I will use my resources to ensure a successful birth rate."

Shock overwhelms Gaius. His defensive tone melts into a welcoming one. "You shall have our support, my Prince. Dare I ask what venture it is you are embarking on?"

Vali's eyes glare at him with a wicked smile. "Nothing I dare discuss at the moment. I assure you it is nothing sinister, merely a desire to see our civilization progress into the next age." He holds his glass up. "To the spirit of progress."

The hidden wall swings with a quiet rumble. Aspasia lowers her head before presenting herself. Vali stares at her stomach, sending a shudder up her spine. "Highness, I…"

"No need," Vali says. "The Chancellor and I are in an agreeable state over your condition."

"On to other matters then…sit Aspasia." Gaius smiles warmly.

"Chancellor," Vali says. "I require a small service from Watchers in southern Illyria. You see, the King has fallen ill. Dare I say his condition is deteriorating rapidly. I am of mind he may pass in the coming week. Queen Farah is held up in Corinth, but I suspect when word gets to her, she will return with haste."

"Then all is as it should be, is it not?"

"I'm afraid the Queen refuses to use the Travel portals," Aspasia says. "She insists they are contaminated."

"Chancellor, you and I both know portals are unstable and unusable. I require discretion in escorting the Queen and Princess to Hyperboria. Neither the military nor the masses need to know of Shuru's condition. Aspasia shall be my proxy in this affair."

"I will send word immediately-"

"Just a decree in your handwriting will do," Vali interrupts. "A transmission can be intercepted. Rumors started. Let's keep it within the privy of this company, shall we?"

Gaius agrees. "Is Prince Odin involved? He will, after all, be the regent if the King passes."

"There is no need to involve my cousin in this. The Queen must travel today; she must arrive before...well, see that it is done. Courier your orders to the palace, will you?" Vali stands and motions that it is time to leave. "Aspasia..."

Prince Vali and Aspasia leave the Chancellor's office. They wait until they are inside the safety of their vehicle to break the uncomfortable silence. "Who is the father?"

"I do not know," she lies.

"It doesn't matter I suppose," Vali says, masking his concern with a fatherly smile. "You shall have my full support and discretion; however, this does not preclude your coming duties." *These offspring cannot be!* he screams in his mind.

"Thank you, Highness."

"Time is against us. I am hoping Shuru doesn't die before the council meeting – if all goes as planned, I shall rescue the Princess just in time for him to announce our union."

"What if he does pass?"

"Then Farah will make the declaration. It will be subject to debate of course, possibly opposition...this is why I need Shuru alive – his voice credits the marriage without question."

"Shall I send word to the others of the Watchers involvement?"

"No," Vali says. "Your role is to eliminate all traces of our hand. Let the wild men have their fun for a day or two. Our retaliation for their villainy will bear multiple fruit - one being the elevation of the Watchers standing in the court. See? We enjoy dual accomplishments in this undertaking."

~ Corinth Airport ~

Desperation is something Queen Farah does her best to conceal from Persephone. Her inner turmoil for plans about to transpire sends her into erratic thoughts of avoidance. Her panicked behavior is misunderstood as concern for her husband; no one but Samiri knows the real horrors which lie in wait.

"Your Grace, you cannot delay much longer," Samiri advises the Queen.

Farah hurries Persephone up the shuttle's ramp. Once her daughter is out of view, she hands Samiri a data tube. "Have this transmitted to Thoth immediately."

"What may I ask is its contents?"

"A private concern I fear only he can help resolve. Now, do as I say."

"At once your Grace," Samiri says with a bow. He steps back to allow the ramp to retract. Before it does, he catches sight of Persephone gazing down at him with a smile. He returns her wave. *You poor child. The wheels of fate are in motion.*

Whining engines increase in tempo. Exhaust burns white with a neon blue outline, joining soft blue hues from the shuttle's underbelly. Ion drives engage, lifting the craft 15-feet off the tarmac. The nose pitches 20-degrees above the horizon. Engines erupt into a roar sending the shuttle off towards the North.

Samiri enters a waiting car; he wastes no time in examining the Queen's private message on a monitor. *So, you hope*

Lord Thoth can avert the inevitable? My condolences dear Queen, but no one can save you now. "Drive on," he orders.

Thirty minutes of flight time puts the shuttle over the Dalmatian coast. A barrage of rockets launch from a large ship, targeting the Queen's craft. Erratic maneuvers are no match for the incoming projectiles, aimed with precision at the shuttle's wings. A direct hit sends the aircraft plummeting into the ocean.

Within moments small recovery boats swarm around the wreckage. Armed tribesmen waste no time plucking dead pilots and three passengers out of the water. Once the prisoners are safely on board, the crafts dart off to the attacking vessel under the guise of a cargo ship.

Northern Illyrian wild-men observe their incoming prize, particularly the Captain. Dardanes is a beast of a man with long dark hair braided in his tribe's style. He clutches a pair of binoculars with a smile showing off teeth stained from excessive tobacco use. He grunts with victory.

A tribesman similar in girth steps up to his side. Balaites, or Bal as the others call him, is the son of a chief, whose tribe was eradicated by the Dardanii's – the Captain's tribe. Now he serves as second in command in this pirating brotherhood.

The Dardanii are notorious for raiding unsuspecting villages throughout the Illyrian principalities. Not much is done to curb their activities; in fact, a blind eye is turned in favor of stimulating the black-market trade. *'Well, we're not going to catch slaves ourselves'* is what an Anuk Prince declared years ago. Once a modest fee is paid, the tribesmen are allowed their pillaging without repercussions.

"Secure the prisoners with the rest," Dardanes orders Bal. "They are important. No harm must come to them, understood?"

Bal scowls as he leaves the Captain.

On the lower decks, Farah receives the backhand of an irate deckhand. She connects her fist with the man's jaw, breaking it with ease.

Persephone snatches a dagger from another man, trying to subdue Koray. She presses the sharp blade on his neck.

Farah darts towards an attacking group, jumps high and plunges her body into the line. An intense beam hits Persephone's prisoner on his chest. She panics, *from where?*

Farah gets hit with a dart, dropping her with intense pain. Persephone lets her dead pirate slump to the ground. She looks around for the shooter and spots him on a high catwalk. *If he wanted to kill me, he would have,* she tells herself and rushes to her mother. Farah's eyelids slide shut. An impulse of fear creeps into Persephone's soul. She notices a thick royal-blue line forming at the needle's entry point.

The remaining pirates back away from the prisoners. Farah's display of strength and speed brings caution to the men. They all scream in their minds, *She's Anuk.*

Unafraid, Bal strides forward past Koray, glancing curiously at her. He smiles at Persephone as he pulls the dart from Farah. "No trouble and no antidote."

Persephone's blood burns with rage. She remembers Osiris' words of caution, yet the subtle hint of power courses through her muscles. Farah grabs her hand. With an intense look, she shakes her head to encourage compliance.

"Promise me," Farah demands in a weak voice, "Do nothing."

Persephone nods.

Bal grabs the Princess. Two pirates lift the Queen off the dirty ground.

Persephone tenses up her jaw. "Where are you taking us?"

Bal gives her a wicked smirk. "You'll see."

Chapter 9: The Cruelty of Man

"Outrageous!" Prince Odin screams in the royal council chambers. In the special session, a handful of attendees, members who live within the palace's precincts, gather after receiving word of the Queen's abduction. Three royals are present via holo-screens, including Prince Vali. "I want every last one of them killed!" Odin says.

"Calm yourself cousin. A rational mind will solve this," Vali says. "I am almost in my Capital. Soon I will gather resources for a viable plan."

"I will join you," Odin says. Protest erupting from the council members does not change his resolve. Vali's image smiles.

"I welcome the help. How soon can you arrive?"

"Father," Thoth interrupts. "This is unwise. His Majesty needs you here."

Vali's expression turns into one of concern. "I would heed the Keeper's advice if I were you, Odin. You will be called upon as Regent if our Majesty is returned to the Creator. Hyperboria needs you there. We will find them."

The council agrees.

"Very well," Odin concedes. "I want the criminals brought here."

"What is the mantra?" Vali asks rhetorically. "Man cannot rule man…that's the one. I will remind them of this." His image disappears.

A half-hour is spent debating strategy. Amid the clamor of outrage and complaint about Lower Houses' exercising 'a loose hand' in managing affairs, Odin breaks away to peer out the large window behind the King's seat. Memories of Persephone's last abduction assault his mind until sickening nausea churns deep.

Two things fell into an abyss on that dreaded season – Persephone's innocence and his marriage. His mind snaps back to the present at Thoth's call. He dismisses the members and their repetitive chatter. The room clears with a rumble of noise moving out of the chamber.

"I fear something hidden may be at play here," Thoth says with a grim expression.

"Tell me," Odin says, breathing deep, forcing calm.

"I am not certain of it, but I suspect the King has been poisoned."

"Can you help him?" Odin asks.

"We can try. I need to move him to pTah, to the Hall-of-Records."

At full sprint, Osiris slides to a halt next to Odin. "I'll go with Thoth, Father."

"Sorry, little brother. I need the ordained Primary of House ENki to unlock the vaults of ATun."

Odin puts his arms around his sons. "Things are about to change. Shuru has set in motion changes to the fabric of society. We need him to buffer the storm."

~ *Pirate Ship, on Corinthian Sea Lane* ~

Ships loaded with all manner of goods traverse dark-blue waters on the sea-route, stretching between two continents. At the north is the vast expanse of Illyria, spreading into the borders of Aryavan; in the south, the wildlands of pTah dissolve into a much-ignored continent. Making a right turn from the north, a hulking gray ship enters a heavily patrolled sea lane – destination unknown.

Rumbling bulkheads vibrate through every corner in the vessel's higher levels, indicating the ship is steaming at increasing speed. Narrow passageways barely fit two pedestrians walking side-by-side, even less so with the sizable tribesmen trying to push through to their stations. Two escort Persephone to a lower deck, filled with red light scantly illuminating the darkness. They descend metal stairs to a catwalk overlooking an assortment of crates. Each footstep clangs metal on metal. They arrive at a closed hatch with a small antechamber.

One tribesman spins the Princess around. "Remember me now?" he asks with a mouthful of tobacco sludge falling down his lips.

The other grabs her chin. His disgusting breath smells of fish. "You played your nasty game. Tried to steal our money."

The first pirate gets in her face. "Word is, you stole the gold from Aryavan. Caused a big loss, you did." His face gestures to the ante-chamber with a terrible smile. "Bal will take care of you." He pushes her in the metal room.

Muffled groans behind the bulkhead frighten Persephone. Muffled voices groan behind cold steel; images of apparition's long-dead fill her head. Frigid air accentuates the depressing nature of the surroundings.

"Leave," Bal grunts to his men. He holds up a rolled-up garment, a tattered heap of brown cut from dingy fabric. Delight gleams in his eyes, the corners of his mouth rise.

"No!" Persephone grumbles in defiance.

Before she can react, Bal slaps his broad palm on her neck, sticking her with a short needle attached to a ring. The tip is laced with a sedative similar to the one Farah received. "You may be Anuk…you may not. Can't take a chance if you are. Don't worry, it will make you drowsy. I sip it with my tea. You won't feel a thing." He holds up the tattered rags once more, insisting with his demeaning grunts.

She is disoriented. Her limbs are weakening, but she tries her best to fight off the poison's effects. Bal slaps her face hard, throwing her against the bulkhead.

"Change!" he screams.

"I will cut that hand off if you touch me." Persephone snarls. Another slap leaves its mark on her face. Tears well up; not from the burning on her cheeks, but rather for the building fear of Bal's lusting eyes.

She strips off her clothes in slow controlled motions. Clouded memories buried deep seep through a fragile mental fog she doesn't understand. Shame stings her thoughts, shame for something she cannot recall.

Bal swats her arms as she covers up her nakedness. Beyond any conscious reasoning on her part, she screams out.

A steady hand yanks Bal out of the chamber. Dardanes shoves him on the cold bulkhead, slamming his head several times to reinforce his displeasure. "You lay one finger on that girl, and I swear by my mother I will cut off your cock."

"Only trying to have some fun Captain," Bal says. He gives Persephone a dirty look before storming off.

Dardanes picks up the dirty clothing. "Do as you're told and it will be over soon." Alarms blare, resonating on steel and marrying up to flashing lights.

Two pirates rush to Dardanes, out of breath. "Captain," one of them says, "Corinthian blockade."

"Put her with the rest," Dardanes orders before leaving. One man grabs Persephone's arm while the other opens the main room's hatch.

Inside the space are 50 people huddled together; men, women, and children. The air is a foul mix of body odor and urine. Towards a corner, the pungent smell of feces compels the Princess to vomit. Without compassion, she is shoved on an old woman wearing similar garb. The door shuts with a loud 'bang,' dampening the alarms outside.

"'Sephie!" Koray's frightened voice calls out. She hugs Persephone tight, erupting in tears.

The old woman shifts her body to make room. "Calm yourselves, children. It is the only way to survive. What's your name?"

The Princess composes herself. "This is Koray. I am Persephone." Her head is spinning, limbs going numb. Her gaze falls on a girl, bruises covering her face. *She must be no older than twelve.* Persephone's breathing becomes labored. An invisible hand chokes her heart. The mental cloud returns.

"You're named after a god," the old woman says softly, pulling Persephone back to the present.

She scowls. "She's not a god. Just a silly girl who does not know how the world works."

The old woman looks beyond the walls of her confinement, up towards the sky. "I pray for her to save us."

"Don't waste your breath. There is no god but the Creator." Persephone closes her eyes and shakes her head, wishing the nightmare to end. "Praying to an Anuk Princess is a foolish endeavor."

The woman forces a smile, "I know she's not like the god. But there's no word to describe our thanks for her miracle years ago. It is because of her I survived the plague."

The words seem distorted in Persephone's ears. *What's happening?* she wonders. Her lips and tongue being to weigh heavy. She takes Koray's hand into hers. "What happened?" she asks the woman.

"They attacked our village. We are all that survived. When they come again, don't let them see your fear."

"Be quiet," an old man interrupts. "They are listening." he points to a small dark device on the ceiling.

Persephone lowers her voice to a whisper, "Not to worry. The Corinthian navy has put up a blockade. They will rescue us."

The sleek gray hull of a Corinthian destroyer rises and dips alongside the pirate vessel. Ocean spray hisses on steel. Metal planks drop in an unwelcoming fashion. Soldiers rush across the makeshift gangway, rifles at the ready, dominating the upper deck.

Dardanes waits for the officer in charge to approach. "Don't do anything stupid," he grumbles to Balaites.

"Never," Bal says with a cocky smile.

"Who is the Captain?" the naval Commander asks.

"I am," Dardanes shouts.

"Your credentials at once. We are searching this vessel."

"You are mistaken," Dardanes says offering a rolled-up piece of parchment.

The Commander snatches it. "It is you who are mistaken. Search the ship!"

"We have done nothing wrong," Bal says.

The Commander displays the unrolled parchment with a mild annoyance in his tone, "I do not care for your forgeries. Comply or you will be chained. Speak to me again, and I will sink this ship."

Dardanes smiles. *Arrogant Anuk pricks.* He activates a communicator. Within seconds Princess Octavia's image appears.

The Commander bows. "Your Highness."

"This vessel is under my protection," Octavia says. "Disembark at once!"

Without question, the soldiers promptly begin their retreat. Bal glances at his Captain with an uneasy, suspicious stare. "Is there something you are not telling me?"

"No concern of yours. Leave the prisoners alone; this is my last warning, Bal."

The last of the boarding party departs the gangway. Dardanes walks off to a tight corner with his communicator recalling Octavia. "Your Highness, you failed to mention I would be abducting Anuk!"

"Don't you dare take that tone with me!" Octavia shouts. "Discretion has always been your admirable trait Dardanes of the Dardanii. Never forget who facilitated your tribe's miraculous rise amongst the wild-men. Question my orders again and I will have you impaled with the pedestal you sit on, through your ass!"

"Who are they?" Dardanes asks. "A Royal and her handmaidens? My men accuse one of the females for our losses at Aryavan."

"I don't know about that. You lay a finger on those women, and it will be the end of the Dardanii." The image disappears.

"Bal!" Dardanes calls out. "Change of plans."

"Captain?"

"When we disembark at the Black Sea. We will journey south from there."

Bal looks at him cockeyed. "Destination?"

"Our hideout in pTah. Ready the cargo. How long do you estimate before port?"

"Without issues…six hours. Why not go directly to pTah, Captain?"

"The moment Octavia realizes we are off course, she will blow us out of the water. We have a two-day interval before turning over the prisoners. That should be enough time to get lost in the wilderness."

A worried look creeps over Bal's face. "I will alert our man to ready transports."

"Good." Dardanes puts a cigar to his lips. "Insist on clean transponders. With some luck, we can reach pTah in 24 hours."

Chapter 10: Sacrilege and Cruelty

Four-thousand years ago the ruling family from a House of ENki occupied a grand palace complex on the Giza plateau of pTah. It was abandoned when the monarchs returned to Hyperboria for a more luxurious lifestyle. They were purveyors of the sciences, pushing the allowed limits of innovation over established lines of heresy. If the House existed today, they would be heralded as geniuses, with humanity's divergence from religion in favor of what can be seen and proved.

Ironically, the real cause for the former House to abandon their region came from an edict issued by King Shuru to stop technological dabbling; the same Shuru lies on their marbled slab in a small chamber adorned with colorful depictions and blazing urns – dependent on the science contained there.

"Hold this," Thoth says to Osiris. He passes a golden goblet to his brother.

"What is it?" he asks, noticing the archaic inscriptions on the cup's body, matching the ancient language engraved in gold on the walls. Torch flames dance on the surface of familiar words. He strains to see finer details etched around symbols -

marks forming vowels and guttural inferences in pronunciations long forgotten.

"Our ancestors perfected a technique of drawing out elements from the body with sound," Thoth says.

"Can you do this?" Osiris asks.

"Yes." Thoth nods, proudly. "I can. Bring me that staff." He applies a lubricant with a consistency of thick syrup on Shuru's head. He grips the staff midway. The top emanates a bright blue light around its edges. As he starts his low, almost inaudible chanting, the tip explodes with a shimmer. A thick blue beam connects to Shuru's hair, traveling around his body to form a bright cocoon.

Osiris looks on in awe. He steps back against the wall. Curiosity mixes with a healthy dose of fear. He strains to make out what his brother is chanting – words in a low tone with lots of bass coming from his chest.

A pattern in the rhythm becomes evident, as it synchronizes with the deepening of the blue hue around the King. Thoth waves his father in.

Odin enters with careful steps, holding a shorter staff than Thoth, and not as thick. He looks to the Keeper to receive a nod and fights vibrations rattling his arms. A forceful thrust pushes his staff's tip to the light encasing Shuru's head.

A secondary beam erupts, directing a run-off light stream from the body into the golden goblet; it appears as puss flowing out a sore, turning into liquid inside the receptacle.

As the draw increases Shuru's body shakes. Osiris clamps his arms around the King as he thrashes about. Brightness increases three-fold. A droning sound reverberates from the walls. The golden symbols light up in splendor.

The ordeal lasts one minute, ending with a disorienting flash affecting both Odin and Osiris. They drop their hands just below their eyes to gaze in wonder at the Keeper.

Thoth grips his staff, chanting in the initial inaudible tone, lowering down into a whisper. His eyes are rolled back to show the whites. With a deep breath, he returns to a healthy state. "It is done," he says.

Osiris notices Shuru's complexion turning into a pale shade with a texture of oatmeal. "Is he alright? He looks dead."

"Not dead." A look of relief washes over Thoth. "Sleeping. Look."

Odin picks up the cup. "It's heavy, like molten lead," he says, swirling the contents with a gentle shake.

"My fears are realized, father," Thoth says. "Poison derived from the Lotai; the thickness gives it away. This attack reeks of science from one of two sources."

"Vali or the Watchers." Odin nods in agreement. "It can't all be a coincidence. This, or the abduction."

"Father," Osiris says. "I suggest we keep an eye on House Octavia."

Both Odin and Thoth drop their heads. Odin sighs. "Son, best stay clear of Octavia and her pursuits."

Osiris' eye twitches. He feels an awkward burning in his gut. "You know of her villainy?" His voice rises in pitch and aggravation. "Her corruption and disgrace to our name?"

"Osiris!" Odin shouts. He calms himself at Thoth's disapproving gaze. "Osiris...outside of myself, Octavia is the most powerful House in all the banners of ENki. She even holds sway with the King..."

"Yes, we all know of their past indiscretions," says Osiris.

"Without proof of her misdeeds, we cannot move on her," Thoth says. "Unfortunately, she remains free of stain."

Odin looks on Osiris with a sad benevolence. "When you are Primary you will understand."

"Maybe I don't want to be Primary. The system is broken." Osiris looks at his father's unhappy expression. "Father, a not so wise person asked me, 'What am I doing about it?' Well, I am. Here." He hands Odin his data tube with Octavia's stamp on the bottom. "I decrypted a ledger and vague references to activities in Aryavan. Yes, two Regents of ENlil are in her circle. I couldn't break through the rest."

Odin rolls the data tube around in his hand. "I'll take care of that." His hand drops on Osiris' shoulder. Uncertain feelings turn to pride. "You'll make a much better Primary than I, son."

"With your permission, father, I'd like to search for Persephone…on my own."

Odin nods. "You'll have support from us, anyways we can deliver it. Be careful, and trust no one."

"I will." Osiris embraces his family, then kisses his fingers and rests them on Shuru's forehead. "Be well, my King," he says lovingly.

Several minutes pass after Osiris' departure. Odin grabs the shorter of the two staffs. "Son, can I have this?"

~ Octavia's Residence, Corinth ~

"Come out Vali! I know it's you skulking around in there," Princess Octavia shouts to a hooded figure rummaging inside her private office. "I won't do you the favor of coming in."

Wearing an innocent smile Vali appears in the main room, clutching a palm-sized box. He offers it to Octavia.

"For me?" She blushes. Her expression returns to aggravation. "What were you doing in there?"

"Trying to hide your gift of course. Open it."

Like all Princesses, the shiny necklace intrigues her. "It's made of Lapis Lazuli." He takes the oval pendant and dangles it from a fine gold chain. "Go on, it begs for your neckline."

"A bit early for gifts, wouldn't you say?" she purrs coyly, accepting Vali's assistance with attaching a delicate gold chain. She blushes again at the wet kiss on her neck.

"You wouldn't expect me to visit empty-handed?" he asks rhetorically.

"But seriously cousin, why are you here?"

"Oh, very well...I am thirsty. Have that lovely kitchen boy bring us wine, before I lose my mind."

Octavia claps to catch the servant's attention. After the refreshment is ordered, she leads Vali into a rotunda overlooking the ocean. "Well? The truth."

"We are days away from phase three. I thought it prudent to review our plots before I am betrothed." A wicked smile falls on Octavia's stern gaze.

She huffs. "It's not like you're going to enjoy the pangs of marriage. The girl is an unruly creature; I suspect she is a half-wit."

"Yes, she is rather peculiar, isn't she? All evidence of my skillful influence on her, my dear."

"You've done such a good job filling her head with nonsense, it's a wonder she has any sense of reality."

A faint sound of cups rattling on a serving platter distracts Vali. He peers down the cobblestone walkway, waiting for the kitchen-boy to appear. "That nonsense has taken on a life of its own," he says dryly, then jumps up with glee at the sight of the approaching servant.

The Prince gushes over the lad in skimpy clothing as the wine is poured. Octavia plucks a handful of grapes and amuses herself over Vali's behavior. "Poor girl is going to have one cold marital bed." She laughs as Vali finishes his patting of the boy's arm, allowing him to leave.

"It's just as well," he says, pouting. "After this affair, it may be years before I'm allowed to put a prince in her belly. Who knows what can happen to a young maiden while in the company of savages? Defilement, rape, I imagine. Why do you think it takes a full day before I retrieve my bride?"

"You're a cruel bastard."

"I know."

Octavia swirls her fingers on the rim of her cup. She knew of the Prince's ambitions since they were children. Vali's father, Seth, was passed up for rule despite being the monarch's eldest son. Although this happened long before Vali's birth, it remains a burning insult to his family – at least in the Prince's soul. "Is Persephone yours?" Octavia boldly asks.

The accusation causes Vali to spit up wine. "You have to be the most disturbing woman I know Octavia. No…she isn't."

"Well, you are notoriously devious."

He composes himself. "I admit, the thought did cross my mind to plant my seed in Farah's wretched belly, but that did not sit well with future plans." He scowls at Octavia's sarcastic expression. "No, you cheap twat, I wouldn't marry my own daughter for the throne. Even I have boundaries."

"How did you do it then? I've always been curious. How did you fertilize our dear Farah with the King's spawn? Shuru's fertility rate was nil for thousands of years."

An uncomfortable silence overcomes the Prince. He hesitates to answer. His hand covers trembling lips as if a terrible secret is about to be divulged. Vali knows Octavia will pursue her questions to extreme ends if not satisfied. *It's easier to tell her.* He looks at the Princess, sighs before revealing his secret. "You know the relics of ENlil at the Citadel I assume?"

Octavia nods impatiently.

"I convinced the then Keeper-of-Secrets to use the Amon-I for…a union between a sampling of ENlil's genetic material and a fertility gene I concocted."

"That's sacrilege," Octavia snaps; her expression screams outrage for the violation of the most sacred Forefather.

"Let me finish," Vali says. "The DNA sequence seemed promising. Several tests on volunteers bore limited success with fusion, but the gene would not stabilize. Only after I introduced material from ENki did a path to success open. Sadly, there was only enough serum for one – Farah. For forty years, nothing happened. Then one day Persephone was born, immune to the plague – the miracle baby that cured the world. It was then I realized my hand was responsible for the miracle…not divine intervention."

"What if Thoth learned of this secret? He is, after all, privy to his predecessor's knowledge."

"If it were so, then Thoth would have already acted upon such knowledge. No, I believe this is a secret contained only to us."

A sickening thought crosses Octavia's mind. *This is dangerous.* She looks at her wine with suspicion brewing. *It's from your kitchen you fool* she chides herself. "Vali, I now share the burden with you. Allow me to help with its load."

"Please, Octavia, you need not worry about an untimely death by my hand. You and I have done far worse, won't you say?" He waits for her subtle sigh of relief. "By my calculation your confederates-"

"Our confederates," she cuts in with accusation in her voice.

"Yes." His eye twitches with annoyance. "They should be at the Black-Sea port right about now; having their victory celebrations no doubt."

"What of Farah?"

The Prince swoops in elegantly next to her, sitting close as two lovers would. He caresses her new necklace down to her cleavage. "A loose-end I am sure our confederates will be more than happy to dispose of. I've dispatched an antidote; Shuru will make a remarkable recovery, albeit short-lived. Our dear mother-bird cannot be trusted, I'm afraid; her actions of late telling as much." He holds the pendant close to Octavia's lips, "Kiss it."

"Vali, don't vex me with your silly quirks."

"Kiss it," he says, grinding his teeth. "Like this." He puts the back end of the pendant to his lips then offers Octavia the front. She reluctantly obliges him with a scowl and a chaste peck. "There, happy?"

"A mere gesture of our bond, and a promise to fulfill all matters in this affair; we are a symbolic race, are we not?"

"What happened to your volunteers after the fusion?" she asks.

He gives her a solemn look. "Their life force accelerated to the point of burning out. Within months they were dead." He peers out to the ocean with a look of wonder. "I had the staff killed. One technician escaped…Maya. Never heard from again."

~ *Port-Of-The Black-Sea*~

Dardanes' pirate ship occupies an inconspicuous berth on the eastern end of the docks. The vessel's cargo, including captured slaves, are moved into a port building with curved roofing tiles. Despair shows on each prisoner's face, echoing their loss of dignity and hope.

In droves, the people with tattered clothing are marched to a corner. They gather alongside tables set up with nourishment. They may be slaves, but they are still people. Dardanes acknowledges this with a decent spread of bread and meats. Jugs of water are scattered across the wooden table. A hungry man attempts to grab an apple. The crack of a whip across his back rings through the souls of the rest, reminding all of their desperate circumstance.

Sandwiched between a pair of youths, Persephone struggles to stand, using the kind shoulder of the boy to her right as a post. The sedatives in her system are almost diminished, but residual effects compounded with fatigue forces a struggle to remain coherent.

Koray puts together a small plate for her. "'Sephie…sit.'"

Her surroundings are blurred, hearing muffled, muscles weakened. All she knows is that Koray is with her.

"Hold her," an older man grumbles at the boy. "Don't let her fall or they will whip you both." On cue, a tribesman strolls up with a grim look.

Entering the building with Bal striding behind him, Dardanes stops in front of the prisoners and waits for a crate to be secured as a pedestal. Once on the box, he shouts, "Eat as if it is your last meal, for in two hours we leave for another location. Make any attempt to escape, and you will be shot." Dardanes looks at Persephone, "Make any attempt to alert outsiders, and you will be shot." He leaves for a corner.

"Captain," Bal says with worry in his voice. "Five shuttles came. Not enough for slaves and us."

"Double up passengers."

"The ships are old with limited fuel as it is. I am afraid we will not get very far with weight."

Dardanes ponders for a moment. "We will stop at Cappadocia. There is a weigh station, long abandoned on the outskirts. It's crude but may serve as a rest-stop. I will arrange fuel to be sent."

"What about the ship?" Bal asks.

"Half the crew will stay behind to give the illusion of our presence."

"And our guests?"

Both men look at the gathering at the tables. The hungry people cautiously eat their meal, glancing suspiciously at the guards. "Take the girls to the room. Keep them separated."

"As you wish," Bal says. He waits for Dardanes to disappear through the wide bay doors, then strides over to the table, calling on two men to join him. They stop next to Persephone.

The Princess struggles to eat a piece of dry bread dipped in a thick sauce. Her appearance is haggard. Her weak arm struggles to lift the food into her mouth.

"Get up!" Bal yells.

"I can't," she says.

The tribesmen pull her off the table. Koray receives a swift hand to her face for protesting. Bal's men drag both girls to a door at the side of the building.

The loud 'bang' from the closing door sends a fit of fear through Persephone's soul. She musters up enough strength to ask, "Where are you taking us?" No one answers. The dark passageway smells of urine and fish. A door at the far open is open; light spills out on to the walkway. Another open door next to it has a similar effect. She looks at Koray with terror in her eyes.

Bal stops just forward of the first door, allowing Persephone to peer inside. Small crates are littered around a small cot with restraints tied to a barred window. The men shove Koray inside; one enters and slams the door shut.

Without sympathy, the other drags the Princess to the adjacent room, dropping her on the ground before exiting.

Persephone doesn't move. She cries, watching her blood and saliva stream to the dirty ground. She keeps her gaze fixed on the floor; fearful to look at the bed she knows is there. Slowly she looks at the space beneath the cot. *I should hide.* She crawls into the dark area.

Silence brings momentary peace. Tension inflicting her body begins to dissolve, forcing her into the abyss of sleep. She forgets hunger in her belly. A muffled yelp through the thin wall snaps her back from the edge. Struggle turns to crying, pleading, and then a crescendo of screams.

The horror of Koray's rape plays out in Persephone's head. She clasps her ears, attempting to block out the violent destruction of innocence. Her blood begins to boil with rage, infusing her veins with the strength to overcome remnants of the poison in her system. She crawls out of the space, intent on ripping the attacker's head off. The screaming stops.

Approaching footsteps brings a new fear. She retreats into the farthest corner under the cot. She sees three men enter and holds her breath. A large hand grips the edge of the frame, lifting it with ease.

Close to the door, Dardanes stares at her with Farah in his arms. "Get her out," he orders.

As best as she could, Persephone claws at the tribesman who yanks her out into the open. The cot drops, promising a similar beginning to the despair in the other room. Persephone looks around for a weapon. She stops when Dardanes drops Farah on the cot then dismisses his men.

"I'm not going to hurt you!" the Captain says. "Tend to your mistress."

The door opens once more. A female pirate brings a tray of food and drink. Persephone crawls up to the Queen. "What have you done to her?"

"An unfortunate reaction to the poison," he explains, pointing to the purple vein-like lines streaming up Farah's neck. "Out!" he yells at the other pirate.

"Do you know who she is?" Persephone yells, finding strength once more with the encroaching rage.

"A Royal, I gather, making her a 'Pure-Blood.' Now do as you're told. Be thankful I show pity on you because of Bal's carelessness." He points to Persephone's puncture mark on her neck.

"Make them stop!" Persephone yells with hate in her voice, pointing to the wall. "Set us free."

"I cannot. If I do, my employers will kill us all."

"I will kill you," she whispers.

"I don't think so, little one." Dardanes chuckles. "If you want to escape, listen. I gave her an antidote, but I fear it may do more harm; we weren't expecting Anuk or a 'Pure-Blood.' The poison will be out of her system by the time we reach Cappadocia. I arranged to have a shuttle hidden for you. I have yet to meet a Royal handmaiden who hasn't been taught to fly."

"Everyone leaves," Persephone says through clenched teeth.

"No." His face is cold, unforgiving. "The longer the charade continues, the further away you can get. I'll send in your companion."

The small concession calms the Princess. "Why should I trust you?"

"You shouldn't. Trust in my instincts to survive."

Persephone's fleeting strength diminishes as she calms the storm in her soul.

Dardanes leaves the room. Persephone soaks a rag. As she reaches for her mother, Farah grabs her hand with a weakened grip. "I am sorry, my daughter." Her voice is faint.

"Mother, it will be alright. Rest and it will pass."

"No. There are vipers in the nest. Do not give in."

"You're making no sense. Rest, soon we will leave and be back with papa."

"My end is near, child. Forgive me for my trespasses. 'Sephie…I am sorry."

Confusion overcomes Persephone. She dismisses it in favor of tending to the build-up of sweat on her mother's forehead. Footsteps from outside startle her.

Dardanes shoves Koray in the room. "The order has been given. No one will touch her, or you."

Persephone glares at him. "The slate is still not clean between us."

"I should expect not," Dardanes says. "Before you start firing shots, ask your mistress who my employer is; I suspect she knows." He shuts the door.

The next click on the lock brings a slight sense of security. Farah slips back into her sleep before any questions can be asked.

Chapter 11: Not So Innocent Games

The return trip to Hyperboria for Samiri is quick. He uses the only known 'clean' portal from Corinth, instead of traveling with Farah's court via a shuttle. Time is proving to be an adversary he no longer seeks comfort in. Word reaches him of Aspasia's mission to the Black-Sea-Port, with a contingent of Watchers, for one purpose – eliminate all traces of her master's hand in the kidnapping plot. An order requiring his brethren to aid such a venture requires, a hard directive from none other than the Chancellor.

Inside the Keeper's Temple is a lavish display of a rich heritage going back eons. Giant polished tiles match 100-foot high ceilings propped up with columns, shooting up in magnificent splendor. Unlike many structures in the populous regions of Hyperboria, the temple is illuminated by blazing urns and hanging torches. The ambiance is ancient – purposely kept in such a condition to incite feelings of holiness in the devout. The quiet halls are bare, leading to dungeon-like rooms that serve as office spaces. Upon entering an area, the illusion of antiquity dissolves into the modern world.

Posted at the heavy oak door to Thoth's office, Samiri waits patiently for his new master to return. Amaya, Thoth's receptionist, sits behind a comfortable station lit with dim artificial lighting. She glances at him stealthily. The female Watcher is no older than one year since commissioning, 21-human-years in appearance – Samiri deduced this from her casual nature. Her delivery of short, poorly thought out answers regarding the Keeper's location gives away her lack of training. *It has been the end of the Watchers for years*, he complains in silence.

He suspects the wait shall be extended; the explanation for Thoth's delay is 'Our Lord is conducting affairs at the Royal Palace with Prince Odin.' Being a proper Watcher means always knowing the spirit of an answer before asking the question. Samiri's cohorts already hinted that Thoth's spiriting away King Shuru in the dead of night – destination unknown. With no indication as to when he will receive an audience, Samiri shuffles off to a private area designated for distinguished visitors. He makes a call on his communicator. An uncomfortable moment passes before his counterpart appears.

"I urge you once more, Aspasia, leave this terrible design to its doomed fate."

"You know I cannot disobey my master. Samiri, a new world awaits us at the end of this ordeal. Our kind will finally be free to forge our own path."

"I forge my own path," he whispers."

"What?" Aspasia asks surprised. "Our child means nothing to you…"

"Incorrect," Samiri says. "I am embracing the concept. For you it is made easy by the life you carry; it is a part of you…"

"Our son is a part of you, too."

"A son?" Samiri's heart skips a beat. A burning elation electrifies his body. Joy takes over his being. For a moment he forgets the Amon-I, Persephone, and grumblings from Thoth's order against Watcher procreation. "Send me your location. I desire a meeting."

"Very well. There is a clean portal at my intended location. Wait for me there and do not announce yourself. I look forward to your arrival." Aspasia's image disappears.

Minutes go by before Samiri accesses the data-tube Farah had entrusted to him in Corinth. He erases all its information, then composes a new one.

'*My Master, I am embarking on an effort to retrieve Queen Farah and Princess Persephone. Contained herein is the first location of the villains whom I hope to confront. I know not how deep the conspiracy goes, but caution must be paramount when dealing with Chancellor Gaius and the Watchers Council. I fear an unsanctioned undertaking has left an initiate in a compromised situation. I plead mercy and sanctuary for her; it is through her help that I will be successful in this endeavor.*'

Satisfied with his composition, Samiri hurries to the receiving area to entrust the data-tube to Amaya.

~ Black-Sea-Port, Illyria ~

A contingent of 12 Watchers arrive in a single shuttle near a secluded wharf; twelve is all that's needed to subdue 100 tribesmen on any given day. In addition to their primary function, Watchers possess a secondary skill which includes combat. This particular team is trained for assassination, espionage, and other unspeakable skills the counsel declares as myth.

Dressed in form-fitting black clothes and a small sigil of House ENki on the right shoulder, the group disperses around the premises of the berth, where a vessel sits motionless in the water. Aspasia clutches her weapon as she jumps 30-feet up from the docks to the ship's deck. She signals the rest to follow. One by one, the Watchers land softly on steel-plated flooring. Darkness masks their incursion on the unsuspecting occupants.

A rhythmic droning from generators deep in the hull flows through narrow passageways. Lights shine red inside. In groups of three, infiltrators search for the pirates. Aspasia comes upon the Captain's cabin. She attaches a device over the keypad. Seconds pass before a soft 'click' confirms the door is unlocked. Weapons ready, three assassins burst into the quarters.

Lounging on a modest bed are two female escorts and the ship's captain. The bearded man jumps to a shelf for his weapon. Between heartbeats, Aspasia clears 20-feet between them to rest a blade on her victim's neck. "Where are they?"

The Captain breaks out in panic. "Who are you looking for?"

An uneasy feeling creeps up Aspasia's neck. The Captain does not match the description her master provided. *This is not a tribesman.* "Don't play games with me. I want your prisoners."

"Prisoners? This is a cargo vessel bound for Aryavan." The Captain does not bother asking for the intruder's credentials. He knows immediately from the clothing and sigil these are watchers. "I offer any help you wish." Aspasia releases her weapon, much to his relief. He grasps his bleeding neck, feeling the sting of the blade on lightly pierced flesh. "I received gold to move into this berth two hours ago."

Two more watchers enter the cabin. Aspasia leans in close. "This is a decoy," she whispers. "They're here, somewhere. Search the adjacent building."

All indications of a gathering are evident around the port building – tables with remnants of meals for 50 people, crude restraints in several rooms, and a gravel field outside with indentations left by shuttles.

A Watcher strides up to Aspasia with a grim look. "What now?" he asks.

She points to spots of hydraulic fluid staining the white gravel. "They left by transport."

"They could be anywhere," the young Watcher says.

"Five shuttles," she says. "From the mess inside, I'd say they were moving slaves, and in quite a hurry."

The younger watcher observes his superior examine the fluid spills. He marvels at the intelligence of these elders, although one would mistake Aspasia for his younger sister. "How did you come to this conclusion?"

"Apart from the distinctive marks, the spills indicate they left in a hurry – they didn't bother cleaning up after themselves. Meaning their hurried departure was unplanned. Something changed." She gestures for the young Watcher to follow. "If you want to catch a bird, you should shake the tree."

"Mistress?"

"The slaves were meant for this port; therefore, a trader would be logged for a visit at daylight. Find out who he is and what he knows. Find the new location of his meeting. One more thing, look into fuel movements and depots within a 500-mile radius - large air shipments included."

He nods. "By your command."

When the young watcher disappears, Aspasia notices a figure step out from behind a wall; she recognizes Samiri. "I told you to wait!"

"What did you find?"

Arguing with him is not a task she is willing to take on at this moment. She decides to enlist his help rather than alienate him from the search. "Well, what do you think?"

He scans along the ground. "They are heading south."

"How can you tell?"

Samiri points to a heap of seating gutted from at least five shuttles; next to the pile are torn off labels from one-gallon water containers – ten by the looks of it. "See the straps? Grooves cut in the metal connectors are fresh, and they tore off the labels to keep a watch on water consumption. But why load extra weight if you're leaking fuel?"

"They're going somewhere dry, without a known source." Aspasia's admiration for Samiri's intelligence swells. A spark returns to a dead pyre she keeps locked away under layers of mistrust for her former lover. His new stance on her pregnancy returns a resolve to look towards a hopeful future together. It shows in her smile.

They make their way into the rooms, grimacing at the cruelty inflicted on the prisoners. Samiri immediately recognizes the space where Persephone was kept. He does not divulge this, opting instead to spend an additional moment looking around. Aspasia sees his attempt at deception. She lets it play out, knowing she can win whatever game he is playing. She knows and respects his connection to Persephone.

A blood-soaked rag catches his eye. He moves the mattress to investigate the ground, sniffing like an animal for a lingering scent. Aspasia moves a serving tray and utensils around. She pretends not to notice as Samiri finds a message written in red under the mattress. She strains to make out the word 'Cappadocia.'

"There's nothing here," he says.

"Are you playing games with me?"

"If I am, know it's only to protect you."

"Protect me?" Aspasia yells. "How quickly you forget your part in this conspiracy. I am a servant like you."

"Yes, protect you. Play your part for Vali, and I will play my part for our son. It is the only way we can adhere to our oaths without compromising each other."

The mention of her unborn child sends a flood of emotion through Aspasia. She feels a slight kick inside her belly. She gets closer to Samiri, grabs his hand and allows him to feel the miracle. "That's life," she says. "Ours."

"It is... amazing."

The parents forget their dilemma for a moment. They smile as anyone would.

Samiri clasps Aspasia's hand. "There will be no blame on you if I find the Princess first. When this is over, you may gain sanctuary with me. Thoth will make sure of this."

"And our child?"

"We will take our leave and raise our son away from the entire world...in peace."

His words ease Aspasia's concerns. "Go then. Find the Princess." She smiles warmly, but she fumes inside. She knows her oath will be unbroken, and confident she will reach

Cappadocia long before Samiri does. She kisses his hand.

~ *Outskirts of Rekkam* ~

Flowing red hues cover the vast landscape on the approach to Rekkam – a principality of a Greater House of ENki. Large swaths of luxurious fruit-trees tower over rich vegetation, leading up to a serene river. Sailboats make their way towards the edge of the city, a pursuit common with tourists visiting the infamous cultural epicenter.

Five miles from the sprawling city exists the most significant fuel depot in the region. Massive underground processing plants refine abundant fuel for most of the world's vehicles. There is a strong military presence here to deter sporadic attacks from dissidents in pTah. A large industrial airport sits at the edge of the complex, hosting ground vehicles and airships. A thick haze overshadows all, like an apparition piercing the veil of industry.

Skulking around a giant air-tanker, Osiris attempts to blend in with a multitude of laborers. Dressed in oversized royal-blue coveralls stained with generous helpings of grease, he observes the workers scurrying off to perform their duties in this loud place.

He was fortunate to learn of an unusual delivery headed for an abandoned depot in Cappadocia. His father's spy network confirmed suspicious transactions between fictitious entities, pointing to the fuel order. He didn't have much to go on, but this trip he hoped would take him closer to Persephone.

"Hey! Who are you?" a rough-looking pilot shouts.

"I'm the new guy," Osiris yells, pointing to his name tag he didn't bother to check. His wide smile distracts a muscular woman making her way to the ship's ramp.

"You've got nice teeth for a fuel-ee." She winks at him. "Come-on then, times ah wastin'."

They walk up the short ramp to the tanker's cabin. The engines rumble, igniting a soft-blue glow at the rear afterburners. Five minutes pass before the behemoth rises off the tarmac. The craft lumbers on with a trajectory 20 degrees above the horizon. It pushes hard with a volatile cargo of liquid and solid fuel mix. Blue flames spew out a trailing gray smoke tail, joining the whine of engines struggling to achieve lift. The hulking mass moves slow, looking relatively smaller the further away it gets, disappearing into the open expanse of sky.

Like all tankers, the crew cabin is bleak, bare, slick with an oily residue on every surface. Twelve Fuel-ees make up the bare minimum of a detachment on a tanker this size; on this trip, the roster is six - another check-mark on the list of suspicious things.

Violent rattling on the airframe eases once power is reduced on level flight at 15,000 feet. The grizzly female fuel-ee stuffs a sandwich in her mouth while staring at Osiris like a piece of meat.

Is she flirting with me, he wonders, and immediately shudders at the thought.

Another crew member retrieves his meal from a bag, grimacing at the grizzly woman glaring at the young man. "What are you doin'?" he asks his counterpart.

The fourth crew member looks aggravated as he huddles in a corner, trying to fall asleep. His face is wrapped in a rich burgundy scarf, showing off a pair of bloodshot eyes closing from fatigue.

"How old are you?" the woman asks. She strains at Osiris' name tag, "Asir?"

"Old enough," the Prince says.

"I don't like him." She stares up and down the length of him. "He's too clean."

"Do shut up, the lot of ya," the aggravated man in the corner shouts. He pulls a blanket over his cloaked head.

"Don't mind Erich; he sleeps a lot, or Ruia, she's just rude. I'm Tymaeus, people call me Tim. First time on a tanker?"

Osiris nods.

"It's going to be an easy job this one."

"Really?" Osiris asks. "I noticed we're short on people."

"Don't worry," Tim says. "The clients have manpower…a quick getaway if you know what I mean."

Osiris looks at him cockeyed. "Who are they?"

"They're much scarier than him," Tim says gesturing to Erich. "More like her." He scowls at Ruia.

Ruia purses her lips.

Tim pinches Osiris' collar, "Where's your safety vest?"

"I didn't get one. This is my first job."

Ruia grumbles as she pulls a package from under her seat. She tosses a red vest in clear packaging at Osiris. "Put that on," she snaps. She waits for him to don the garment over his coveralls. "It goes inside, idiot; close to the skin to protect from absorption."

Like a pervert, Ruia watches every move Osiris makes as he exposes his bare chest. She ignores the pattern of dots beneath the left side of his chest; though, Erich notices it.

~ Abandoned Fuel Depot, Cappadocia ~

"Five miles in, there's a village ripe for the picking," Bal says with greedy eyes to his Captain. He lifts a rusted covering on a water barrel of similar condition, expecting to find at least a swallow – the receptacle is dry. "Where is that tanker?" He licks his dry, crusty lips.

"They're in the middle of nowhere," Dardanes says. "But they could have protection from the Principality – this one doesn't take kindly to slavers. The banner of Moira controls the region, House ENlil."

"I curse the House that got us in this mess. I say we ransom the Royal to whichever house they crawled out of and be done with it."

Dardanes does not respond. He looks past Bal at the canyon walls on either side. They are in a narrow valley leading towards conical mountain stacks of Cappadocia. This gap is the only direct route into the village, with a roaring river on the other side. The pirate sighs with thoughts of better days on the open seas. He leaves his companion without a word.

Bal looks at him with suspicion crawling up his back.

All the prisoners are herded into a bleak building. They crowd together like a collection of human baggage waiting for transport. Huddled in a corner away from the gathering, Koray hugs her knees with terrifying thoughts showing on her face. Farah is propped up next to her, weakened, yet more coherent than she has been in the last 12-hours.

The Queen's appearance is haggard like the others, with only her original travel clothes making her stand out from the rest. Residual marks on her neck are not prominent as before, indicating Dardanes' antidote is working. Her strength is still diminished. She looks around the dusty room for her daughter.

Still, in a poor state from her dose of poison, Persephone makes her way towards a sectioned-off kitchenette. She fumbles with dirty bowls on a rusted sink. She sighs with relief when water spurts out from the faucet, albeit at a trickle. The running water distracts her from the discomfort and fatigue. Satisfied with her collection, she ignores the footsteps behind her in favor of a hasty retreat.

"Where are you going?" Bal whispers with a hint of delight. He slams his weight against her back, clasping her body with his giant arms. He smells her hair. His hand grabs her waist then makes its intrusive descent. He feels the fear manifesting in her trembling body - it excites him.

No matter how immune to the terror Persephone is convinced she is, the impending moments locks her mind into a perpetual cycle of fear. Her feeble attempt to recall adrenaline-fueled rage cracks in favor of tears and shallow breaths. Her body solidifies into a weakened statue. Her grip on the bowl intensifies – this distracts Bal. He shoves her aside for water.

Thirst quenched, he grabs Persephone's face. His repulsive hand shifts her head from left to right.

Persephone is frozen with fear.

He rips her tattered clothing down before bending her over the counter to admire her bare skin. He spins her around to gaze at her naked front. Thoughts of his Captain's orders are fleeting. His groin burns. His solid fist smashes her jaw

She falls hard on the floor.

Bal throws himself on her, clamping her wriggling body to the ground. His foul tongue licks the sweat on her chest, hot breath assaults her skin. It violates her delicate nipples. He hits her again, this time spinning her around.

She claws the ground, screaming for anyone who would hear.

Bal's firm grasp on her waist sends shock waves through her mind. Everything is going black. Her head buzzes, muscles tense. Then, piercing pain enters her body. Her palms curls, clenching into petrified fists. Each thrust slams hard into her, until only shallow gasps remain.

Her eyes flood with tears. Hate tries to burst out, but is subdued with grunts from behind. Again, and again, the tribesman's disgusting flesh violates her innocence. Persephone can't breathe.

Bal pulls away. He kicks her legs down, fixes himself, ending with a victory spit. "I prefer redheads."

The door creaks open. A tribesman looks in.

"What?" Bal yells.

"A message for the Captain," the thin pirate mumbles, his eyes fixed on Persephone crumpled on the floor. He licks his lips and his hand drops on his crotch; his gait becomes anxious. "The shuttle is here is all it said." He moves forward.

Bal grasps his throat. "What shuttle?" He lets the man wriggle his ignorance then turns to Persephone. "She's mine." He pulls his comrade out the door.

Still frozen, Persephone waits for the evil man to reappear; minutes pass – he doesn't. Feeling returns to her arms and legs, prompting movement towards bunched up rags. She grabs the heap and dresses as best as she can. Pain in her groin burns. Her face is sore, yet a warming sensation pushes back discomfort.

Knots fester in her stomach, loosening with each breath. Swirling juices seep up from her stomach, souring her mouth. She rocks her head back then forward in nauseum, throwing up bitter contents from within. Spasms in her stomach continue to spew bile. Tears roll down on spit leaking to the ground.

A violent scream wants to burst out, but can't. She struggles to appear as if nothing happened, but really, she is overwhelmed and embarrassed, as if she had done something wrong. A trolley catches her wandering gaze. The half-dozen bowls are *ideal for carrying water*, she decides. She spends the next 10-mins filling drinking water for her companions.

Creaking wheels capture Farah's broken thoughts into the singular focus she was severely lacking. She sees her daughter emerging from a room, rolling a trolley with water splashing to the ground. After a slow blink, the image changes to Persephone distributing bowls to the people. *A common house slave*, Farah thinks. She closes her eyes once more – after an eternity it seems, the gentle touch of a hand presses her chin. "Drink, mother," Persephone says, with the rim of a bowl on her lips.

Koray sees dry blood on Persephone's upper thigh. Thoughts of her own suffering disappear. A fit of tears overwhelms her, flowing for her 'Sephie; Koray's trembling lips giving form to her rage at the evil. She closes her arms around

Persephone, tightening her embrace with any solace she can provide.

"I won't let anything happen to you," Persephone says in a sharp tone. A slamming door plunges both girls' hearts to oblivion. They dare not look up to greet their fear. Three tribesmen hurry over to them. Without remorse, they pull Farah and the girls out of the building.

"How much further?" Samiri asks his stout shuttle pilot.

"Not far," the pilot yells over the roaring engine.

The trip is an uncomfortable one; Samiri is strapped in the rear seat of a small craft designed to move livestock. Putrid scents of animal feces assault his senses, yet there is no discernible reaction on his face. "Is there any traffic in the area?"

"No," the pilot yells. "I'll let you out at the outskirts."

The shuttle lands in a clearing surrounded by a thick tree-line. Afterburners kick up dust on a strip, used as a common drop-off point. The side door swings open the moment the landing struts hit the dirt. Samiri jumps out, happy to be away from the smell.

He looks around for a path. A narrow one catches his eye on the far right. The departing shuttle rumbles away, returning the area to a perpetual stillness.

A gentle wind entices the flutter of leaves. Samiri stops walking. He cranes his neck towards the sounds around him. His heightened Watcher senses pick up subtle hints of stale engine fluid in the air – quite distinct from the exhaust. *A craft was leaking*, he remembers. This is enough for him to change direction to a ledge beyond the tree-line.

Ninety miles out from Cappadocia, Aspasia's shuttle races to intercept Samiri. She types in a sequence on a screen, calling up Prince Vali.

"Report," he says in an official voice.

"We are ten-minutes out," Aspasia says. "If they are there, then the area will be cleared in twenty."

"No, Scout the area first; I want conditions to warrant my rescue. Don't be a blunt instrument, Aspasia. I've taught you better."

"Of course, Highness."

"What of the other location?"

"The trail ends in pTah, Sire. An Illyrian slave merchant provided the intelligence."

"Then it's simple. Send your team to pTah where I shall meet them. Handle Cappadocia personally – if the Princess is there, then we shall return to take care of matters. pTah right now is the more solid lead."

"Yes, your Highness." Vali's image disappears. She relays orders to drop her off near the river Hyles, behind Cappadocia.

Chapter 12: Hope Stifled

One street across from the prisoner building is a line of storefront-sized rooms, long since abandoned. A wooden path separates two structures leading to the rear of a lengthy "L-shaped" wall. Inside the last room, Persephone, Koray, and Farah lay crumpled in a corner. Three menacing tribesmen watch them with malicious intent as they wait impatiently for their Captain.

Pounding boots move along the creaky floorboards outside; each step brings terror into the girls' minds. Farah, regaining a fraction of her mental focus, pulls herself up to stand on shaky legs. *It is time to end this* she repeats silently. Footsteps stop at the wooden door. Through the dirt-encrusted glass, the silhouette of Dardanes appears. Several seconds pass before he enters.

"The tanker is almost here, tend to the transfer," he says, stepping inside the room. Without questions, the men depart. A mask of regret covers the Captain's face. Each passing second, he sinks further into the pit of realization – this unprofitable endeavor will cost more than just money. It may well cost him his life, and he feels the noose tighten around his neck. "I- "

"Whatever Vali is paying you," Farah interrupts, spitting the words with as much contempt as she can muster. "Is your head worth it?"

Dardanes eyes reveal a hint of remorse. "Not in the slightest. But it is Octavia who commissioned this affair. We don't have much time."

"Octavia?" Persephone asks. Her questioning gaze digs into her mother's resolve.

Farah drapes her arms around Koray to begin moving. She gives the handmaiden a warm look of concern.

"I'm ok, Your Grace," Koray says, smiling through the pain.

Farah stops to gaze at her daughter. *I may not get another chance.*

Your Grace? The truth dawns on Dardanes. His heart nearly stops. "Queen Farah," he whispers, then looks down. "Persephone."

"This is my fault, my daughter," Farah says solemnly.

Farah's gaze is heavy on Persephone. "I did unspeakable things to bring you into this world – to give your father an heir. I was naive, blinded by ambition, blind to the evil that transpired."

"Mother, what is going on?"

"When we are safe, I will reveal all." Her head hangs, shame overcoming her. "In the event of my death, I want you to promise to seek sanctuary with Thoth, both of you…promise me!"

Persephone nods.

A thunderous noise rumbles overhead, the crew ushering in the tanker's arrival.

Dardanes grabs the Queen's hands. "I had no idea." He drops on his knees at Persephone's feet. His eyes fall on her bruises, his eyes strain at a guess for what happened. "A thousand pardons Highness."

He receives a hateful stare in place of an answer.

Koray grabs hold of Farah's arm, tightening her grip as fear courses through her. Bal's silhouette covers the door's pane.

Persephone feels her stomach plunge at the precipice of uncontrollable fear. A glance at Koray pulls her back into overwhelming hate. The frightened handmaiden trembles, as the door cracks; Bal enters brandishing a dagger. He lunges at Dardanes.

There is not enough time to reach a weapon. He barely avoids the blade to his back. A head-butt sends Bal staggering back two paces. The tribesmen square up for a brawl. They slam into each other, pounding, slashing.

Persephone swings at Bal connecting with exposed ribs. There is a sharp snap, she's broken at least two. – .

Hate builds in her mind, of earlier desperation for what they've done to her mother, and Koray, and her; it floods her senses. She imagines a warm glow under her skin, yet it is real. Electric sparks tingle damaged tissue on her face, muscles in her legs, ruptured vessels in her cervix. *It's real,* she thinks, smiling inside. Hate is subdued, yet the power remains.

Bal shakes off his pain to focus on the girl. He doesn't see his Captain wielding a heavy wooden beam, nor the beam swinging down on him. Bal crashes on to empty crates in a corner, knocked out, or dead – there is no time to check.

Dardanes clasps Persephone's hands. "Half a mile north in a cave blocked with a red bush. It's the only one." He stares deep into Persephone's eyes. In that split-second, a plea for mercy shines; Persephone nods her forgiveness. Dardanes smiles. Koray screams.

Dardanes' expression turns to a painful gasp for air as his body convulses from the murderous blade entering soft-tissue. Bal rips across his back with enough force to sever his spine. His body drops like a stone.

Koray struggles with Farah's weight, trying to make it outside.

Persephone has Bal's full attention. She swings with frightening power, connecting with his jaw. A surge courses inside her – the inhibited strength she's subdued for so long. Clenched fists match a roar of hate descends on Bal.

He shifts his wounded head in time to avoid the killing blow, swings his leg to trip the unskilled Princess, sending her crashing to the ground. Before she moves, he positions himself with his hand aiming for her neck – the poisoned ring is made ready in anticipation of trouble. He thrusts his fist down. She catches his wrist with both hands. Her arms begin to buckle under the pressure.

Regret burns her mind, regret for avoiding her Anuk strength after the incomprehensible tragedy she barely remembers. She tries to trigger a burst of power, failing miserably.

Bal's hand's inch closer to her neck. He is on top of her, pushing, grunting. His face is red with vengeful desire.

I can't give in! she screams inside.

A thin plank cracks the side of Bal's head, breaking across his ear. Koray steps back with vacant eyes and trembling body, expecting an attack she will not survive.

The momentary distraction is enough for Persephone to smash her knee into his groin. She slips out from under him, strength returning. A pistol catches Koray's eye, dropped during the fighting. She grabs it with murder in her heart.

Persephone snatches Bal's arm. She wrenches his 220-pound body over hers, hurling him against a deteriorating concrete wall 12-feet away; the impact breaks the surface and flimsy beams behind it

Koray fires her pistol. Concentrated shots of light fire off towards the fallen tribesman. The careless aim destroys the surrounding area, bringing the ceiling down on top of him.

Still burning with hate, both girls hold each other's hand for comfort. They contemplate pulling the body out to remove his head, but the need for escape supersedes want for vengeance.

They rush out of the room to join Farah. "We have to go, now!" Persephone tells her mother. They slip across the walkway to a covered area.

Koray spots a bush behind a building, "There!" They support Farah on wary shoulders, pushing forward as best as they can, hoping to find the transport Dardanes promised.

Rumbling engines from the parked tanker resonate on the canyon walls. Fueling of the depot's long-empty stores is underway. One Pilot settles in the cockpit, the other monitor's crucial gages inside the crafts pumping-station. The crew is outside manning hoses. Two dozen tribesmen join in the work, eager to refuel their shuttles for a quick departure out of desolation.

Osiris notices Ruia head off on her own. "Where's she going?"

Tim spits a wad of tobacco. "She's on her own business. No worries now. Keep watching that gauge. I'm off to take a piss, yeah?"

Hairs on Osiris' neck rise with his nagging feeling. "Tim, I really have to take a shit!"

"Well, go on then…be quick about it. We're not spending all day here." Osiris runs off to pick up Ruia's trail.

Crossing a narrow street, Ruia greets a tribesman. From a distance, her words cannot be made out, but guttural inflections mixed with laughter give away her familiarity with both the man and his language. She blows out a thick glob of mucus, as expected from her degenerate manners, then disappears inside the rundown building.

What is she up to? Osiris moves closer.

Jubilant laughter erupts among the collection of heavily armed pirates. Ruia's distinct voice calls out, "Where is me brother?" Drink in hand, she storms off with four companions in the direction Bal traversed, not 17-minutes ago.

Back at the tanker pumping stops, engines continue to rumble, but the pilot is slumped on the cockpit floor with his jugular severed. The second aircrew suffers a similar fate – his neck is broken. Refueling of the smaller shuttles is underway.

"That haul should put wine in the belly." Ruia laughs, rounding the 'L-shaped' structures. The caved-in roofing at the corner raises her curiosity – small rubble rolls down the side as if it recently caved in. She ignores it. "Time to get rid of my lot then we can be on our way. Balaites, you sour bastard. Come out you mangy dog!"

Silence.

Ruia's escorts enter the vacant space. Horror destroys their enthusiasm. Bal shifts his body under a mix of concrete and wooden beams, eyes opening with a stare of death; blood streaming down his arm. The shock wears off. "Who did this?" she asks with her jaw and fists clenched.

"The girl and her people," a skinny pirate says. "Had to be."

Dardanes' dead body tells Ruia all she needs to know. She urges her comrades to dig Bal out from the crippling rubble.

Osiris hears enough. He darts under a covered space, ready to attack, and waits for the group to exit. As he plants his feet on the dirt, ready to speed off in a blink, Erich's secure grip forces his shoulder back in the shadow. "Where is it you think you're going?"

Surprise gives way to shock. Osiris' eyes widen as the man removes his face scarf. "I don't believe it. That was you on the tanker?" He nudges his shoulder free only to be pulled back by the former General Markus.

"I may be just a common Anuk, but I know I can drop you; don't give me cause, Highness."

"Tell me you're not with them, Markus. It would be a shame if I'd have to kill you."

"Relax…I'm not with them."

Osiris looks up and down the old General, part suspicious, part thankful. "Then-"

"Hush, boy," Markus says. "Save your interrogation for later. Put your energies to better use, like saving the prisoners."

There was not enough time to scout the area – Osiris followed Ruia and missed the building with the slaves. "Are Queen Farah and Persephone with them?"

"What?" Markus asks, surprised. "They're here?"

Osiris' questioning glare remains unchanged. "It's not like I went in to say hello."

Markus' face darkens. "Come on."

They dart off, away from Ruia and her goons. Markus is not a "Pure-Blood,' but he is faster than the regular human stock. Despite his speed, he cannot keep up with Osiris. Under a minute they reach the other occupied building.

Six tribesmen have the unfortunate detail of keeping watch on the 50 slaves. Relaxed hands grip weapons, without any thought of having to mount a defense in this barren canyon.

"Stay here," Markus says, and immediately slaps Osiris' protesting hand, reaching for his jacket. "Do as I say. You'll know when to attack."

Osiris reluctantly pulls back out of sight. Markus strolls out to the yawning pirates. The first to see him point a weapon on the dusty figure.

"I don't suppose you can spare a fella some water?" Markus asks. "Fueling…its thirsty business."

"Stop, maggot. You're supposed to be dead."

"Really? I'm on your side friend." Markus pushes his chest up on the rifle's muzzle. "Yeah, I'm with Ruia's…people."

The men laugh. The rifleman resumes his threatening pose. "We're her people." His finger starts its pull on the trigger. His ugly grin shows off stained teeth. He shoulders the rifle, expecting kick-back from the jolt of energy. Within a moment, Markus pushes the weapon to the side, slams his palm on the startled man's chin, and disarms him. – Osiris notes 0.37-seconds.

A quick shot burns through the closest tribesman's face. Another one hits him in the leg. It's too close for gunfire. Markus strikes his attackers without remorse.

The commotion alerts approaching pirates. Osiris calculates an unfavorable outcome for Markus. He leaps high in the air out of view and drops in front of the approaching men. The pirates freeze with shock – fighting ensues. Osiris breaks jaws and cracks skulls, smashing heads on the dusty ground. A pile of groaning tribesmen lay twisted on the dirt.

Markus' fight shows the same under the covered space. "You done?" he yells.

They hurry inside. Frightened prisoners huddle on each other, expecting the newcomers to bring a fresh wave of torment. "Don't be afraid," Osiris says with hands up. "We're here to help you." He looks around with hope. "Persephone!" No answer. "Come out!"

"They took her, son," an old man says.

"They're not here," Osiris grumbles to himself. "Where did they take them?" No one knows.

The doors slam shut; everyone gasps. Tim enters, frantic and out of breath from running. "What happened? The pilots are dead!"

Markus pulls Tim close. "Help get the people on the tanker."

Osiris grabs Markus with an anxious glare. "We have to find them."

"They escaped," says Tim. "Yeah, I saw it when I went to piss."

Markus swats Osiris' hand off his jacket. "I can't fly that thing on my own, and I know you have flight training. We can spot them in the air. Hurry, Tim, get them on board." He throws Osiris a stern look. "You're a Prince; these are your people. The Queen and Persephone can take care of themselves for now. We get airborne, we'll call for help."

No more words are needed. Tim helps them shuffle the people out the door, in a desperate attempt to reach the tanker unnoticed.

Back on the other street, Ruia and her comrades finish digging Bal out from under the rubble. His condition is bad, yet he is alive. He blinks at his sister. Ruia stuffs powdered painkillers in his mouth. "Find them!" she orders the men.

Tucked away in a shallow cave, a broken-down shuttle struggles to start. Sickening plumes of gray smoke sputter out from rear exhausts, after an unsuccessful rumble of starter-coils. The rolling whine settles down to a whisper. It tumbles again, wheezing to a disappointing stall.

"Hurry… they're coming!" Koray panics to Persephone in the cockpit. From her vantage point, he spots nine hairy tribesmen hunting for tracks left by their prey.

Tired of futile attempts, Persephone leaves the controls. A tornado swirls inside her mind and body. *Is this what it feels like to be a 'Pure-Blood?'* Farah's groaning interrupts her thoughts. She throws her mother a concerned look – the Queen recovered ever so shortly, but now her deteriorated state is begging for medicine. "I have to face them," Persephone whispers. "You still have the pistol?"

"No," Koray says with an apologetic look. "Show me how to start this."

The controls are simple – turn the battery on, wait for the light, engage the starter, then push the throttle. This correct combination failed the Princess on each try. *Maybe Koray will have better luck.* "Bleed-air," Persephone says in a moment of clarity. "That's what I forgot. Turn that knob, wait five minutes, then do like I showed you."

She leaves Koray to stare at the multitude of switches, forcing her memory to recall two lessons she intentionally forgot. Farah's groaning intensifies.

What sort of pain is she in? "Mother, I will return." Persephone kisses Farah then runs out the dented hatchway.

Rustling bushes in the distance mean one thing – they're here. Nine tribesmen, built like beasts, spread out to cover the cave within sight. One brute sniffs the air, catching the scent of exhaust, still stinking from failure. He points to the dark cavity, grunting his order with excitement. The others smile as though they've already won, confident their extraction will be quick.

The shuttle bleeds air in preparation for ignition – A gust of wind slicing through the enclosed space startles the tribesmen. Their worried look changes to bewilderment as Persephone appears in a flash, stopping with an awkward fall in front of the lead man. The secret is out – they have been holding 'Pure-Bloods' hostage. They know the retaliation from Hyperboria will be swift and without mercy. Kill or be killed takes on powerful meaning in their resolve. The lead tribesman fires his weapon.

Shot after shot of thick green pellets pepper Persephone's back and exposed legs, as she lays face-down on dry grass. The barrage stops.

Curiosity overcomes the man. He looks at her body heaving with labored breaths. Smoldering holes in her rags reveal welts instead of deadly burns. In one motion she springs up, grabs her attacker's throat, rips out his wind-pipe, then holds up the bleeding trachea for the rest to see.

Fire from the left pounds her hard. She ducks down to roll away.

The tribesmen tactic works to their perceived advantage. Attacking from the right, three of the nine swing daggers, while three on the left shoot without mercy. Two in the middle keep watch for any movement outside the kill box they created.

A tribesman's blade scratches Persephone's arm. She gasps and grips the wound tight, fearing the weapon is laced with poison. She lunges forward, locking the man's arm into a twist, breaking it with ease, as if it were a dry twig. Incoming fire on both Persephone and her victim forces her to fling the man towards the rest. She rushes the group.

A slight flicker in the wind brings Samiri into the fight. He plants himself next to Persephone, giving her a quick smile. Seven targets rush them. In bursts of speed the Watcher and 'Pure-Blood' dispatch the pirates. The men scream as arms are torn from sockets, bone is broken through thick flesh, heads are crushed in thunderous claps.

One dying tribesman fires off a shot at Persephone, hitting his mark above her left chest – the scorching on soft tissue burns, unlike previous hits she took on. Samiri brings death to the man with his boot smashing down on his waiting skull. The fight is won – no more remain. The rumble from a successful engine start adds to their victory. The wind carries a choking mist of exhaust rushing out from the warm cave.

Words fail Persephone. Tears flow uncontrollably at Samiri's hurried approach. He clasps his arms around her. She grabs him tight. "You came," she whispers. The unbreakable bond they share reinforces its power in the embrace. *Everything will be alright.*

The shuttle's engine increases in roaring splendor – a sign Koray is ready to relinquish control. Both Persephone and Samiri reach the craft between heartbeats.

Farah's condition demands attention straightaway. Samiri removes the Queen's upper clothing to trace the course of fading royal-blue lines. The marks converge on her heart, collecting into a painful sore no bigger than a grape. "She doesn't have much time," he shouts over the craft's hum.

"Can you fly this?" Koray asks Persephone, as she climbs into the pilot's seat. She looks at 'Sephie's painful expression. Her gaze falls on the bleeding wound. As in all shuttles, a medical kit is secured under the co-pilot's seat. Koray finds the small box and doesn't waste time rummaging through for a bandage. She slaps a square dressing on Persephone's shoulder.

The stink from green gel inside the dressing breaks Persephone's concentration. Seconds pass, the substance fizzles into a white powder, bringing rapid relief. The view outside is clear, the engine temperatures are stable. A push on the throttle clears the craft low into the sky.

Struggling to gain altitude, the shuttle shudders as it soars; they get no more than 1,500-feet before leveling off. The massive tanker still on the ground becomes apparent on the left. Straight ahead are the rising conical stacks of Cappadocia. The blue river Hayles flows uninterrupted behind a large village on the right.

Samiri hurries to the cockpit. "We have to put down in the town. Her Grace needs help immediately."

Persephone complies without argument. She points the nose towards the village and pitches it down awkwardly for a rapid descent.

"Hurry!" Tim screams at people stumbling into the Tanker's interior. Without aiming, he returns fire at approaching pirates.

Several former slaves fall victim to desperate shots aimed at the ship's hull.

Ignorant as they are, the tribesmen do not consider the vessel contains enough stored fuel, if ignited, will decimate a five-mile-radius, or perhaps they consider 'If we can't have it, no one can.'

The last survivor climbs in, the ramp retracts. "Go!" Tim yells into an intercom.

Alarms blare on panels flashing red. Osiris fumbles with a secondary panel trying to find whatever Marcus demanded. Unsure with his selection, he pulls back three switches, his heart beating out of his chest. — the symbols on the board are not familiar to him. A thin outline of the ship on an overhead monochrome monitor lights up. A border thickens around the seam. Yellow lights on a panel turn green. "The hull is polarized," Osiris says with a deep sigh.

Markus shrugs acknowledgment. His focus is on pushing up from the ground. He pulls hard on the control stick, sweating profusely from stress and the warm cabin. Clenched teeth rattle with the enormous rumble from engines blasting away at the surface beneath.

"Turn, turn, turn!" Osiris shouts in his ear. He points to the right, at the spec of a descending shuttle.

"What? Are you mad?"

"It's them…I feel it. Just do as I say, Markus!"

Frustrated with the order, Markus complies. He points the nose level with the horizon. "I'll make the call over the radio."

"No." Osiris glares at him. "The Queen and heir to Hyperboria were kidnapped. What are the chances the true villains won't be listening in?"

"Well, we can't put down near the village. There's no place for this beast."

"Closer to the river, then."

The airframe settles, reducing the pressure on the stick. Marcus feels the Prince is on the edge of a question, or questions built up over years of wondering. "Go ahead," Markus says. "Ask me whatever it is churning inside your royal head."

"Please…like I have time to waste on you."

"Fine… Highness. Better not let misguided anger flare up when we're down there, because we'll need our wits to avoid the tribesmen when they come looking for this little tanker."

"What were you doing with these criminals, Markus?"

"Glad you asked. Since your father stripped my life away, I've resorted to questionable things; often finding myself mixed up in sub-contracting."

"Sub-contracting?"

"Yes…it's a deplorable concept where an employer hires me to be a part of whatever sordid venture they are too timid to be a part of. In this instance, my job was to keep an eye on the crew with this transfer. The fuel was a 'back-channel' deal procured by questionable clients. I knew nothing else. Is that it? That's your only question that's got the vein on your forehead throbbing."

"Alright…you're a bastard." Osiris tries to maintain a calm demeanor. He feels his attempt slipping with Markus' chuckle.

"A bastard…that's all you've got? You can drop the act; we both know you're not as Princely as your father wants you to be."

"I looked up to you, and you returned my reverence by destroying my parents."

"Oh? You think I am the cause of your mommy-daddy problems? That started long before you were born. Your mother-"

"Don't talk about my mother," Osiris says.

"Your mother and I fell in love, simple as that. Our stations prevented a union so we settled for what we could get.

Don't be fooled by ideas of a perfect life because you're a 'Pure-Blood.' If anything, your lot is doomed to a miserable existence."

"Words will not take away what you did."

"I know. I've paid for my deeds ever since…" His voice trails off into a stifling memory of Persephone's abduction. Images of the crumpled-up little girl sink his heart into a void of despair.

"Ever since that day in Persepolis? I don't know what happened; no one talks about it. All I remember is that's when your indiscretions betrayed you."

"Be quiet, boy. I pray you find love in someone ideally matched for your station," Markus says calmly. "Start the landing cycle."

Boots pounding on metal stairs bring a welcomed distraction. Tim holds up a bag of water. "Thirsty? You two know each other?"

"No," Markus insists.

Tim's eyes light up. "Hey, I've got a spot to put down if you like?"

"After a quick stop, Tim." Osiris selects several switches causing the craft to shudder.

"Landing flaps?" Tim scowls. "We goin' down there?"

Markus keeps his gaze on the rising horizon. "Shut up, worm. Get everyone ready for landing."

"Well?" Ruia grunts at a tribesman strolling in with a grim look.

"Nine dead in the fields; ten more outside."

She looks at Bal. He finishes gulping wine from a leather pouch. "Leave them." There's an unusually calm look about him. His bloodied left arm is wrapped tightly, matching his abdomen and leg. Scorch marks dot his exposed back. Burnt flesh is covered with scant bandages.

Ruia's face flares with anger. "Cost me a lot of trouble to arrange that load, and you want to throw it away?"

"Forget the fuel, forget the slaves. Dardanes got us mixed up with kidnapping Royals. You want to receive their troubles sister?"

Ruia huffs on her way to the exit. "That kind of trouble is not worth it. But all is not lost." She grins obnoxiously; Bal glares at her back. "So, Captain, where be our destination?"

"pTah" Bal says. "We regroup, then it's back to a welcoming sea. The sweet stink of ocean breeze and helpless villages, ripe for plunder."

"So, that's it. Stick your tail firmly between your arse and run away?"

"Shut up, you insolent woman," Bal yells. "Do as I say!"

Chapter 13: Cappadocia

Midday sun shines bright overhead, with little cloud cover. Cold winds howl across valleys, marked by conical stacks typical to the region. Rushing waves from the river Hayles is a faint echo at the edge of the large village of Cappadocia.

Sandstone buildings are scattered between modern structures built in a contemporary style. Towering behind dusty alleys, held in trust by roaming cats, is a natural pointed outcrop of rock. Many of these volcanic protrusions provide crude residence for transients choosing to bask in the abundant and free accommodations.

Narrow streets start at the boundaries by the river, snaking their way to the village center. The haphazard layout of homes, tea-shops, and other laborious endeavors showcase the lack of planning invested in this township. A stranger may conclude it is a jumbled symphony, composed by an orchestra of slaves – they will be correct.

Founded one-thousand years ago by an Anuk farmer relishing a reprieve from polite society, the town grew at a snails' pace after necessary documents were filed with the Great House Moira of ENlil. Arid land proved difficult to cultivate any sustainable crop. Harsh winters followed, and by intense summer's heat, the sane-minded were dissuaded from investing in a doomed venture. The farmer relinquished land rites back to the ruling Principality.

Over time, all sorts made their way to the abandoned retreat. Runaway slaves, bandits, disenfranchised souls – all built up the village into an ignored piece of real-estate they squat in without oversight. Merchants from surrounding cities engaged in lucrative trade over the years, energizing the once careless residents into a settled identity. For a thousand years, Cappadocia existed in peace, unaware of the ancient world beneath their feet.

When the village was yet small, a ministry dispatched by the Watchers-Counsel attempted to establish a temple devoted to the Creator. One winter's day, surveyors ventured into a cavity discovered beneath a hollowed-out volcanic stack. What they found were tunnels beneath the Earth, dug out for refuge by Anuk dissidents of a forgotten age.

Exploration proved futile, halting after miles of searching for artifacts. The ministry packed up their Watchers and never returned. Cappadocia remained in the hands of runaways.

Samiri mentions the land's history to Persephone before they part ways on dusty streets. He goes in search of medical supplies for the Queen, leaving the Princess to seek out town-elders; 'Every town has them,' she insists - she is wrong. This place holds no allegiance to any government. On an individual level, the people manage themselves.

Harsh looks, suspicious grumblings, an aggravated dog, chases away all hope of success in the Princess' mind. At the end of her wandering, a line of stone buildings butts up against a short conical stack, blocking further travel.

An old-woman spots Persephone's wretched limping silhouette from inside a tea shop. Her heart wrenches out of her body at the girl's feet dragging along the dirt, hair stained with blood, bruised skin showing through tattered clothing. "Come here, child!"

Persephone forgets caution. The smiling woman beckons her to a sanctuary. She hobbles under an awning without words. Her dry lips attempt to open, but the kind woman pulls her inside the warm interior. "Thank you," she whispers. She sets down on a wooden chair, oblivious to the collection of grim faces staring at her.

Rattling cups on a serving tray reach her table. "I have no money," she says to the woman.

"No money needed, poor child. Drink. It's herb tea. It will give you energy. My name is Maya, and you are?"

Alarms ring out in Persephone's head. The kind woman does not look like the rest of the people she encountered, or the faces she just now notices. Maya may be in her 80's, dressed in old washed out Illyrian garb. Her weathered look accentuates vibrant blue eyes, much like her own. Her teeth are all accounted for, unlike every other resident. "Koray…"

"Koray?" Maya asks.

"No, Cora. Koray is my sister."

"Are you a slave?"

The question reminds the Princess of her question to Peki. *Oh, Peki…I need you.*

"My family and I were taken by tribesmen. We escaped but there are many more at a depot. Can you help? Is there a civil patrol?"

Maya puts a reassuring hand on hers. "No, child, there is no such thing here. We are all runaways, slaves, people wanting to be left alone. We can offer you and your family sanctuary if you wish it."

"We can't stay. They will come looking for us. They are terrible men."

Maya smiles. "All men are terrible at some point."

A rough-looking patron slams his cup. "We don't want trouble, Maya. She has to go. Go back to where you came from!"

"Please," Persephone pleads. "We're in danger. I fear you all may be too."

The man pushes up on Maya. "You come in that ship by the river? Maya, more strangers."

"No...I didn't," Persephone says with worry. "They're here. Slavers. You must fight."

"Time you leave!" The man points at the door.

"No," Maya says. "We never turn away anyone."

"I should get back to my family." Persephone backs away from the table. "Thank you for the tea."

Maya gestures her back on the seat and pushes the man. She waves over a boy behind a counter carrying a sheepskin bag. "Take this...it's some food, water, and candles. You'll find shelter in the mountain stacks."

"Can you get a message to Hyperboria?"

The faces look at one another. The man drops a box of matches in Persephone's bag. "We don't have a relay station. Go...we never saw you."

Chapter 14: Ghosts of the Past

Sixty-miles off the coast of pTah is the island of Thonis. Twelve-miles in diameter, it serves as a rest stop for merchant vessels before entering the mainland – it's really a haven for pirates and smugglers, but no one cares to investigate the rumors. It is a simple place without a big government. The one residing in the civic halls is as powerful as a dying squid.

Port buildings are the best attraction a visitor can hope for. Streets are dusty with foot traffic, competing for space alongside slow-moving oxen. A host of bars and restaurants provide refuge for the weary traveler, intent on meeting unscrupulous clientele. When night falls, those with deep pockets hustle off to the single brothel in the center of the island.

Built in the holy fashion of a Corinthian temple, the decadence transpiring here carries no worship or reverence to the divine. Instead, all sorts of perversions intoxicate participants with enough money to pay for it. Unlike the secret sacred prostitution establishments in the Greater House Octavia, this place is a common whore-house.

The property bears the seal of the Dardanii tribe, as do many of the port facilities. In secret, Princess Octavia owns all of it – the island, the infrastructure, and the whore-house. It is a flourishing part of her illegal empire she and her late husband established a thousand years ago.

On the northern coast where the port sits, Dardanes' pirate vessel is anchored in its usual berth. The crew is scattered about the island, doing what they always do after a round of pillaging and pirating. They were not present to witness Prince Vali's armed contingent of Watchers arrive several hours ago, nor were they privy to Octavia's separate arrival on the southern side.

Five small shuttles touchdown on a gravel stretch outside the town. The scant remnants of the late Captain's crew, involved in the sordid affair, mourn their loss with the new leader, Bal. Both he and his sister stroll into a villa serving as their headquarters on the island.

"You stupid ox, you never listen to me," Ruia says.

A slave-girl trembles at a doorway, clutching an amphora of wine. Bal grabs the container, slaps the slave, then walks into a full courtyard.

"One day is all I need," Ruia says, aggravated at the intrusion. Both pirates stop at a silhouette stepping out from behind a column.

"You need one day, I need one moment," Prince Vali says coyly. The Pirates drop to their knees, lowering their heads in frightened reverence. They've never encountered the Prince before, but they've seen his image. More important, he is one of the highest 'Pure-Blood's' in the monarchy. "You may rise."

"Your Highness, it is an honor," Bal says. Ruia trembles, afraid to look the Prince in the eye. Bal glares at her from the corner of his eye, encouraging compliance. "You meet us in unfortunate times."

"Oh?" Vali asks. "How so? Where is your Captain?"

"Dead."

"Unfortunate. I assume you are the leader?"

"Yes, Highness."

From the corner of Bal's eye, he spots two figures standing behind each of the six pillars across from one another. Instincts beg him to draw a pistol and seek cover, but he knows better. "Is there a problem, mighty one?"

Vali makes a slight head movement, which brings eleven armed Watchers into view. "That is a complicated question."

Bal realizes there is no point in resisting. He limps forward to meet Vali, with Ruia trailing behind. They are promptly relieved of weapons and communicators.

"Where are your prisoners?" Vali asks.

"Highness, there were complications." As the last syllable leaves Bal's lips, Vali's swift hand pounds his face, throwing him across the tiled floor.

In a split second the Prince is on him, gripping his throat. "If it is games you desire, then we shall play one – the crucifixion game. Only my version cuts off every dangling part before mounting you on a cross!"

"Vali!" Octavia screams out from the entrance. Her anger is apparent, manifesting in a reddening complexion, heaving chest, and a stance the Prince knows sets up for a sprint between human thought.

"Octavia, darling, I was making your confederate aware of who his employer is."

Accepting Vali's relaxed tone and demeanor as an apology, she strolls forward with hips swaying in distracting fashion. High-heels tap on the tile, stirring an echo in her march to the sub-servant tribesman. She thrusts her exposed toes in Bal's face. "If anyone will be doing the crucifying, it shall be me."

A lead Watcher drags Ruia next to her brother. Fear humbles her wretched soul.

Octavia stares at the pair with contempt. "Who killed Dardanes?" Her voice booms.

A bead of sweat forms across Bal's brow. His racing heart competes with overwhelming nausea forming in his guts. A metal cross erected in the port's square consumes the flicker of thoughts between his answer. "The 'Pure-Blood' girl did it," he lies.

Octavia throws Vali a questioning stare.

"How unusual," the Prince responds to the silent query. "Where are they?"

"We do not know Highness. The girl left me in this condition; killed half our crew. They couldn't have gone far."

"And you just left them?" says Octavia. "An unfortunate development for your future, Balaties."

Vali wrenches the tribesman to his feet with an effortless swoop. "You'd better pray they are still in Cappadocia. Take them away!"

Three Watchers hover over Bal's body when it falls next to Ruia. They hustle the pair away from earshot of the royals.

"All is not lost," says Vali.

"You have quite a hopeful nature." Octavia spits the words sarcastically. Her glare screams both concern and miserable failure.

"I always make it my business to engage is lucrative contracts – the kind to ensure success. Oh, very well, Aspasia is on site." Vali holds up Ruia's communicator for Octavia to see. "And apparently another," he says with a smirk.

Asking questions in a town where a mantra of 'Give shelter to all who enter' proves to be challenging. Osiris makes his way through a dismal alley, towards the last row of dwellings in the quarter. Not far off, Markus roams a broader street with similar results.

"Excuse me, miss?" Osiris says to a young woman clutching a baby and leading two youngsters. "Have you seen strangers today?"

The woman looks him over with an accusative smirk. "No one here today but you lot." She hurries to her front door, throwing a cautious glance at the Prince before disappearing into her warm abode. "This is hopeless," Osiris whispers to himself. He makes his way to Markus wearing a mask of defeat. "I've knocked on a hundred doors, and it's the same answer."

"What did you expect to hear?" Markus asks, sarcastically. "'Oh yes, laddy, we saw some strangers today that aren't you. Come, I'll show you where they are hiding.' This is Cappadocia, son."

"Where are we going?" Osiris grumbles with his head down.

"Up there in the cones. There are rooms cut out for people like us. We can get some rest and resume the search in the morning."

"I should have called my father."

"You said it yourself – no telling who's listening. Besides, I'd much prefer if you call his Highness when I am long gone."

Osiris moves closer to Markus. "When did you and my mother, you know?"

The question puts a pit in Markus' stomach. "You're really asking me that?" Osiris' quick nod turns the pit into an acidic bubble.

"Markus, I order you to tell me."

"We got involved a year before you were born."

Distasteful anger gives way to curiosity. Behind Osiris' clenched teeth is a fear he dares not give life to, yet it is nagging his soul. "When you returned from the badlands with his Majesty, to Persepolis, you didn't do so for noble reasons, did you?"

"Of course, I did…sort of. Your father was at a crucial point of negotiations and could not leave. I offered to join the King in his stead; to lend aid and to see Dahlia."

"And if you weren't found out?"

Markus looks up at the stars with a thoughtful glance. His mind strays into a realm of 'What-if's' for a few seconds of imagination, which hinges on an eternity. "Best not to wonder. You know, to this day it never occurred to anyone to ask why Dahlia insisted on vacationing at my estate." He looks at Osiris' glare. "You sure you want to ask that question?"

Words form in the Prince's mind – they struggle to reach his vocal cords in an uncomfortable heap of violent emotion. "Are you my father?"

Silence follows the question. Crunching sound from gravel beneath collective footsteps sours the dead air between the two Anuk. Suddenly, Markus bursts out laughing. His distinct pleasure at the discomfort he brought shines on his face. "No, you dumb twat. How could I be?"

"I don't know; it is possible."

"No, it isn't. I am a common Anuk; you're a 'Pure-Blood.' You bear the marks of Lyra on your body, don't you?" He doesn't wait for Osiris to answer. "That mark only graces a 'Pure-Blood.' A common line like me will never bring its stamp, no matter who the other party is."

Osiris' relief washes over his mind, calming any upsetting words ready to lash out at Markus. The burning question is answered. Forgiveness, however, is far off from being achieved. Brisk wind threatens to reach colder temperatures. One half-mile up a winding hill are the welcoming stacks of Cappadocia. Scattered pins of flickering light promise warmth inside comfortable dwellings.

Dark skies blanket volcanic stacks at the edge of the town below. Fireplaces carved inside caves hewn from the cone-shaped hills burn with brilliance. Many live in these make-shift dwellings, staying for no longer than several months at a time. Transients do their part to integrate into the village, engaging in work afforded them by the welcoming residents. After a proper house is constructed for those who remain, they are accepted into a society wishing to stay removed from the chaos of their homelands.

One such cave hosts three females and a Watcher, huddled around a crackling fire. At first glance, one may take them to be slaves attending to a sick mistress; this is the cover-story agreed upon by the Royal fugitives. Persephone jokes about her new persona – Cora, sister to Koray, a pair of slaves who ran away with their mother, Demeter.

Farah's strength continues to diminish, but her mind is recovering thanks to Samiri's intervention. Koray feeds her Grace a delicious serving of porridge with a wooden spoon. Persephone giggles at her mother's scowling face on each delivery; she cannot decide whether it's from the steaming grains or the 'common-folk' utensil. She ignores the disapproving glare shooting her way, and instead removes the blood-soaked bandage on her shoulder.

"You have to be more vigilant." Samiri points a stern finger. "Have you forgotten everything you were taught?"

"No. I am not used to the speed, that's all."

"You should have mastered your skills at 13…"

"But I didn't," Persephone snaps. "I had nothing to master. Now I'm supposed to be adept in abilities I should have received years ago?"

"Of course not. What I should have said was to remember the vulnerable points that bring death." Samiri's calmer demeanor encourages reception of forgotten lessons. "You may be invincible to a great number of things – wounds any other human will surely fall from, but there are two points any 'Pure-Blood' will meet death from. What are they?"

"The center of the neck where the spine meets the head, and the chest above the heart. Satisfied?"

Samiri smiles. "Use your body and speed to protect these areas next time, alright?"

"Is it the same for Watchers?" Persephone's question throws an unsettling knot in Samiri's stomach.

"No. We are blessed with your speed and some strength, but we die like any other human – Anuk or man." He checks a small pouch of herbs. "I have to get more. Her Grace will recover by morning, but only with a stronger dose. Be vigilant until I get back." He gives the Princess a stern look before scurrying down the hill.

She watches him go, feeling a renewed sense of security at the turning tides.

The horrors of the past days are still fresh in her mind, yet she manages to block out the undesirable memories. A side effect of the treatment from the Amon-I, after her torment years ago, balances her mental state to the point of inducing selective amnesia.

It was hoped this condition would disappear in time, but after the Princess recovered without the stain of her tragedy, efforts to rehabilitate her mind fell to the wayside. She remained a naive girl who expected the best in people, heard no lies, or passed up any occasion with excessive alcohol.

"We would've been back by now, in Hyperboria," Koray says in frustration. A bruise on her face catches the light.

Koray's constant shifting on the ground reminds Persephone of her own discomfort, inside and out. A pounding in her head changes into a hot knife slicing into her trauma. She plants her dirty palm on her forehead to beat off the pain. Koray jumps to her side, resting comforting hands on her trembling shoulders. "Have some food, you'll feel better."

"No," Persephone snaps. She realizes her harsh tone falls on her friend maliciously. She grabs Koray, pulls her tight, locks her body in an emotional embrace. "I am sorry, my sister. I wish I could take back everything."

"No one can." Koray throws three thick logs into the fire. "That should last several hours." She grabs a dusty blanket to cover herself and Farah.

Persephone steps out at the cave's mouth. She plops down, then peers up at the star-filled sky, inhales the fresh air, and puts her body and mind into a meditative state – a technique Thoth taught her to combat the onset of unsettling feelings. Worry for her father's reported condition occupies her thoughts.

She escapes to a vivid plane deep within, a familiar place she inhabits when soul-choking demons rise to assault her sanity. Soft waves crash on a sandy shore. The air is crisp, yet carries a hint of warmth reminiscent of a comfortable blanket on a midwinter's night. In front is a vast lake reflecting bright morning blue. The scenery is vivid, tingling with real sensations as if the world had dropped away into this nirvana.

Wind caresses all it encounters. A new wave brings a distinct fragrance. At once it takes hold of Persephone's senses. *Amberly woods, wet violet leaf, grapefruit granite. Reminds me of Papa.* The scent intensifies, bringing on concern with mounting fear. A rustle in nearby bushes reveals two significant figures wearing colors from pennants raised high in the royal halls of Hyperboria. *They're Anuk… how could this be?*

Persephone's heart ignites into a rapid throbbing, joining her inflating diaphragm, pulling in desperate air to stave off encroaching fear. Her limbs freeze into place. She clenches her fists, desperate to break free from the invisible hands enveloping her consciousness. The figures are close. They are tall, too tall to be Anuk. The light is swallowed up by their massive physique. They are close. A free-flowing build-up of tears betrays her fleeting courage. She closes her eyes, grinds her teeth, and waits for the worst possible torment.

A giant warm hand clasps hers. A feeling of love overwhelms her. An intoxicating blast of serenity filled with a solid reassurance of safety dispels the lurking chaos of darkness. She opens her eyes. Bright faces stare down at her. The two figures drop to meet her gaze.

Words aren't uttered. To her left is Lord ENlil - lightly bronzed skin, powerful shoulders, and a muscular jaw, with light curly hair fluttering past his neck. To her left is his brother, Lord ENki – similar build, a darker skin tone, matching hair and striking fiery hazel eyes.

"Fear not, daughter," Lord ENlil begins in a soothing voice. "You are of us as we are of you."

Persephone musters up her building courage to push words out her trembling lips. "Forefathers," she says with reverence. "Are you real?"

Lord ENki smiles warmly. "We are part of you, an echo of genetic memory living in your DNA."

"How?" she whispers.

ENlil answers. "The power of the Amon-I. You embraced your gifts, giving life to that which was broken."

She gasps in silent terror at the subtle blue light flowing from her ancestor's arms into hers. The dim glow from the snake-like helix is painless, yet worrying. "What do you want?"

In unison, the brothers answer, "To mend the path we set the world upon."

"I am just a girl. Powerless, afraid…broken."

ENlil releases his grasp. "Embrace the horrors infecting you."

"Set aside your rage," ENki says. "It gives you strength, yet weakens your soul. This is the demon which doomed our unity."

"I will try, Fathers. What should I do?"

The mighty sons of ANu stand, towering over the awestruck girl. Lord ENki points to the stars. A portion of the sky cuts away; it grows with six heavenly bodies, sparkling in the pattern of a lyre – the star Vega shines above the rest in brilliant splendor. "Home," he says, with yearning evident in his voice.

They leave the confused Princess where she stands, walking with smooth strides to the water's edge. Lord ENki looks at her with a smile. "You are the Destroyer-of-Worlds, little one."

A strong wind blows through their bodies, starting a brilliant cascade of light disintegrating their corporeal form. In a wash of ember, their presence floats up to the constellation Lyra, increasing speed midway then disappearing with a flash.

In the cave, Persephone wakes with a sharp inhale of cold air flooding her lungs. Her hands grasp her chest; retreating pressure tricked her senses to feel pain. The blur around her comes back into focus. Sounds of a gentle fire dying from starvation defy her measure of time. A fleeting memory pushes her mental encounter to the corners of her imagination. *I am the destroyer of worlds?*

Chapter 15: Mercy Dwells in the Heart of the Insane

Light illuminates the dwellings of a helpful villager; Aspasia crouches behind a bush, straining to catch sight of Samiri making his exit. Her cramping legs serve as a forceful reminder of the time wasted lurking. Her master's timeline demanded a quick resolution to the current problem – locate Princess Persephone. Yet her instincts screamed caution when she realized Samiri's rejuvenated role in preventing her mission's success.

In her soul, however, she suspects a deeper reason bears responsibility for her restraint. The life in her womb of late creates conflicting feelings about pursuing Prince Vali's agenda. Thoughts of this nature quickly disappear with fears of her blood oath taking a toll on her baby.

Watchers in high positions under Royal masters take a literal blood oath. There isn't any blood-letting involved in small ceremonies, rather it's a customary consumption of a peculiar concoction. Derived from the sacred Lotai plant, a chemically altered potion is introduced into a Watcher's system, taking hold of their genetic tailoring to ensure compliance. Failure to obey results in excruciating consequences, most often causing death.

No matter how much Aspasia desires to depart from her current orders, she knows both her and Samiri are bound to their commitments. A lingering sense of sadness prompts a hand to caress her bulging stomach. She loses herself with the touch, imagining her son's smile radiating through swollen flesh. A closing door snaps her attention back to less important affairs.

She notices Samiri's raised head sniff the air. He steps off the covered porch. In the blink of an eye, he appears looming over her. She smiles. "It took you long enough."

"You smell different," he says.

"Our child is bringing much change to my body – aches, unsightly marks, and a desperate hunger that demands the strangest things." A soft ping from her communicator announces a proper signal is established. A determined swallow and tightening jaw join a twitch in her left eye.

Samiri offers her a helping hand. "Why don't we find comfort for your appetite?" She accepts the gesture. "There are food stores in a warehouse on the other side." *A signal should be absent there.*

Aspasia picks up on his deceit; however, she allows him the chance to prove her wrong. They set off to find the alleged warehouse. The short walk lasts five minutes.

"Here we are," Samiri says. He reaches for Aspasia's hand fumbling inside her jacket pocket. She allows his firm grasp to dissolve into a gentle touch, once forgotten. The clasp of fingers sends a tingle to her chest, reminding her they are a set of three, joined by the simple hand-hold.

He pulls her to a corner at the warehouse's side entrance., then opens the door revealing a dark cavity.

The rushing scent of cinnamon, barley, and dried meats bombard Aspasia's heightened senses. Her stomach churns with hunger – as if a switch is flipped to bring on a voracious need to consume. She hurries in to indulge. Samiri closes the door, thrusting the warehouse into complete darkness. There is no need for lighting – some Watchers can see in the dark.

He butts up next to Aspasia. His hand carefully slides towards her jacket pocket. Between bites on an aromatic loaf of bread, Aspasia locks her hand on Samiri's. Her firm grip tightens. "You think I'm a fool?" She releases his hand to retrieve the communicator. "Here."

"It's not like you would not have done the same," Samiri says with a hint of sarcasm.

She gives him half her loaf. "That is why I knew you would attempt."

He looks at the screen. "How long do we have?"

Aspasia tilts her head slightly, chews her dried meat, smirks devilishly, and shakes her head. "The sun will be up soon. Before you go, allow me one more embrace."

The past month proves loyalty to one's master overshadows commitment to each other – Samiri ponders this in the seconds before wrapping his arm around Aspasia. He waits for a cold blade to gut him without remorse, yet it does not come.

The woman he knew eighteen-years ago possessed the vile reputation to accomplish such a betrayal. The new version of her seems subdued by a single degree, but that was enough to spark an outbreak of violence detrimental to his child.

To avert any complicated fighting, he pulls her tight. She stares into his beautiful eyes. Her skin becomes flush with anticipation. Her loaf falls without care. Both Watchers engage in a deep passionate kiss that transforms into an unrelenting need to copulate. The cold winter's air is forgotten; the impending arrival of Prince Vali's forces ignored.

Before sunrise, Cappadocians start their movement around town, engaging in miscellaneous tasks relative to baking, building, and farming. The community is a collective of souls supporting one another in maintaining an atmosphere of harmony unheard of in all the realms. 'The past is the past,' the town folks say to newcomers. Everyone is expected to repay the hospitality they are afforded. Transients who stay more than a week are integrated into the communal living without judgment or suspicion.

Food is free here. All one has to do is ask. The kind folks of this 'backward utopia' enthrall Queen Farah as she walks about the dusty streets in her dirty, yet regal travel clothes. Maya waves her into a tea shop with genuine enthusiasm. The Queen walks alone into the welcoming two-level building, absent of any worry for safety.

When she woke an hour ago, Persephone and Koray were fast asleep from a restless night watching over her. Samiri's treatment did wonders for her speedy recovery, although her purging of toxins in the woods proved to be very un-Royal-like. Her body gained strength, but her mind regressed. In a confused state she opted to search for food; basic memories occupy her fragile mind – her name is Demeter, and she has two daughters.

"You look hungry, love," Maya purrs. "Some hot breakfast will do you well. Here, eat."

Warm bread, smoldering tea, running eggs with bubbling goat-cheese on the side; Farah smiles and picks at the offering in controlled movements.

"You come in the big ship by the river?" Maya asks.

"I don't know. No. My daughters brought me."

"Best rest here until they find you then; you don't look well." Maya's eyes open as she remembers the girl Cora said she was here with family.

Outside footsteps approaching startle Farah. Maya's kind nature demands she open the door. She welcomes a frustrated stranger. "Some breakfast son?"

Markus looks around the empty area. His eyes fall on a woman crouching with her face hidden behind a mess of hair. There is no need to guess who it is. He immediately rushes towards her, drops on his knees and bows his head. "Majesty."

"No, I'm Demeter," Farah says, with genuine dismay at his behavior.

He smiles at her questioning stare. "Yes, and I am your servant," he says, glancing at Maya. "Where is your daughter?"

"Cora and Koray?"

The last name plunges Markus' heart into his stomach. It ignites into rapid beats, outracing any Illyrian engine on a deserted speedway. Anxiety builds to a crescendo of ugly thoughts, ready to erupt in unbridled anger. He imagines the worst things inflicted on his daughter at the hands of uncivilized tribesmen. "Where is she…they?"

"I don't know. I left them but know not where."

He helps her up with as much reverence as he can spare from the storm consuming him. Maya helps him. "Thank you, miss. If her daughters come looking for her, tell them we are at the big ship by the river; a blonde girl and a redhead."

Maya agrees and walks them out.

The sun is rising slowly, bringing life to main street. Villagers move about in their casual manner, hugging coats tight. Some are walking horses, others moving bison. No one pays attention to two girls in tattered clothing searching the crowd.

"Mother!" Persephone screams. Koray meets up with her after a fruitless search. They jump to a designated sidewalk to avoid an incoming herd of goats.

A hand grabs Koray and spins her around. "Osiris!" she screams with relief and a tight embrace.

Osiris peers out at the crowd for a face. "Your father is here, somewhere."

Koray breaks down into tears. It is two years since she briefly saw Markus at a secret reunion – a promise of a swift death still looms over his head if ever caught in Greater Illyria. Yearning for her father's shoulders and vengeful tendencies overcomes her.

Persephone joins in the intense hugging and crying with Koray on the uncomfortable Prince.

"Where is your mother?" he asks.

"I don't know. She disappeared from us this morning. She can be anywhere."

Osiris breaks their grasp. "Koray, follow that road straight to the river, to a tanker – you can't miss it." He looks at her bloodstained rags and bruises darkening on her face. "No one will hurt you…hurry."

Persephone gives her an approving nod. She takes off running with hopeful thoughts; each stride overcoming physical and mental pain.

Osiris grabs Persephone's shoulders. "We don't have much time. We have to find the Queen and return to Hyperboria immediately."

Panic-stricken, Persephone looks at Osiris with failing resolve. "Do you know anything about my father?"

"Yes, he is recovering from a treacherous affliction. Not to worry, Thoth and my father are with him."

Hearing the King is in the hands of Thoth and Odin relieves Persephone's tense body. She grabs Osiris' inviting hand. They run up the street desperate to find Queen Farah.

Samiri's clenched teeth match balled up fists, tense with self-deprecation inside the empty cave. His late arrival to administer a balancing elixir to Farah fuels his anger. He notices the careless heap of blankets near the dying fire. *They left in a hurry.* Lazy footprints with a dragging tail indicate a slow departure by the Queen; erratic indentations tell of panic by the two girls. *She is wandering about in a haze. Time is crucial – without treatment, her mind may be permanently damaged.* A change in the wind's howl alerts him to a figure standing at the entrance.

"You're slipping," Aspasia says in a winded voice. "You can't lose me that easily."

"Doesn't matter now." He looks at her with regret falling off his face. "I suspect your master has charged you with murderous intentions towards our Queen."

"Yes. Her execution is brought on by her own actions. My master would have let her live if she did not insist on betraying him."

He makes a quick calculation for a favorable outcome of tackling Aspasia without bringing harm to his child. His nostrils flare as his stance sinks low, ready to strike. She picks up on his tensing body, making ready for an attack. Suddenly, a crack of thunder interrupts their exchange.

Appearing in the sky beyond the village are four large vessels in a tight formation. The crafts drop to the surface, heading for the river.

"Stay your hand, Aspasia; a compromise for our son's sake."

"What are your thoughts?"

"Those aren't your master's ships – instead of forming a perimeter, they descend to one location; tribesmen by my guess."

"I must complete my mission, or I fear our baby will pay the price for failure, along with me."

"The Queen is more or less dead if I don't give her a tonic. Your obligation to find the Princess is satisfied, as evident by the tribesmen's arrival – surely your master is to follow. Give me but a moment and I will find a release for you."

Aspasia exhales the tension holding her body in a defensive posture. She considers Samiri's words carefully. She knows his skills at potion-making are unmatched by anyone in a thousand years. *If anyone can find a remedy to my oath, it's him.* "We should announce ourselves to the pirates."

No further words pass between them. They begin a rapid descent down the mountain, heading to the clearing where the pirates landed.

Panicking people make a desperate dash into the tanker humming to a start. Engines grumble with mighty roars, shooting out blue flame as the igniters run in the proper sequence. Minutes ago, four ships descended a quarter-mile away. Fate is on Markus' side as the tanker remains unseen behind a thick tree-line.

He has one additional passenger, yet lacking three. "Tim, get in here!" he screams into an intercom. Strong hands grip the throttle impatiently. Footsteps pounding on metal stairs ring out amongst the rumbling in the cockpit.

"We picked up a straggler," Tim says wryly. "Says you're her daddy."

The world goes blank. Enveloping silence takes hold of everything around Markus. His senses zone in on the figure behind Tim, peeking out to verify his identity.

His heart leaps out in desperate clamor to reach his daughter. She steps in front of Tim; her eyes overflowing with abundant tears. She lunges for Markus with arms outstretched but is yanked back into Tim's grasp, pistol drawn.

"Do right by yours and shut it down. Now!"

"Please don't hurt her," Markus whispers. Under any other circumstance, he would consider charging Tim without regard for his safety – not this time. Rattling bulkheads ease their tremors. The engines die down to a whisper. "You're with them?"

Tim's lanky body animates with frustration at Markus' belief he would be anything but a pirate. "Of course, I'm with them. You should know better...Erich. Oh, and just for your information, we know you work for those fat cats in Rekam. Switch on the comms."

Markus pretends to comply at first. His blood boils at the nasty man pressing his body against Koray's.

Her trembling body screams out for rescue. The bruises on her face do nothing to dissuade her captor from licking her skin, then running his hands across her chest. The pistol's aim is on the bulkhead.

A common man possesses minimal speed and coordination; a common Anuk achieves ten-times that of any man. With calculated precision, Markus whips out of his seat and wrenches Tim's pistol, snapping his wrist in two. With Koray safely two paces behind, he pierces the screaming man's abdomen with his bare hand, curling upward and back to reach his spine. He wiggles his fingers around sensitive nerve endings to illicit maximum pain. The shock on Tim's face turns into a gurgling fight for air. Markus smiles with malice, then pulls hard on the bone, snapping it with demented pleasure.

The carcass falls into a bloody pile. Koray ignores the hot blood spewing in random directions to curl into her father's arms. She holds on tight, unwilling to let go, for fear some other terrible demand may call on him. As fate plays it, heavy boots slam on the stairs, echoing over the silence, making ready to take away the small victory.

"What the bloody hell," Ruia screams. "You done killed the best man in me crew." She points her pistol at Koray. More footsteps bring Bal and three tribesmen. "See, told ya I'd get the fuel back," she says with pleasure to her brother.

Bal's presence sends terrible upheavals in Koray's soul.

Her trembling body and fear burning in her eyes bring joy to the formidable pirate. "Worthless girl," he says. "No longer fresh."

Markus grinds his teeth with rage. He inches forward, but Koray's gentle hands hold him back with enough intensity to subdue hateful intentions.

"Where is the other one?" Bal grumbles.

Markus spits at Bal's feet; the tribesman chuckles. A buzz on his communicator breaks his intense glare.

A blurry image of Princess Octavia appears above the device – only her head covered with a cloak is visible. "Well?"

"We have the mother… mistress."

"Not good enough!" Octavia screams with frightening ferocity. "You think I am blind as to what your real prize is? I should gut you and your sloppy sister like the shit-filled sea creatures you are." Her glare turns to Markus. "And you! You were contracted to oversee a fuel transfer; not have my merchandise stolen by pirates! If I had known it was you on the docket – Markus, former General of House ENki, your spleen would've been laid bare on those pompous halls in Rekam!"

Confusion besets the simple minds of the pirates. They look at each other with concern brewing for their mistress' dismay. Bal swallows hard, feeling his mortality shudder by the threat of an uncertain future. "What shall you have us do, Highness?"

"Do what you do best. Plunder, pillage, and take slaves. Find the girl. Bring her and the mother back in one piece, or you will meet the morning on a cross! Oh, one more thing…get rid of that degenerate, Markus. Make it look like an accident – the Creator knows anything suspicious will bring doubtful eyes on us." Octavia's image fizzles out in a shimmer of blue light.

"This was all your stupid plan," Bal growls at Ruia. "Now see what you caused?"

"All is not lost," she says with optimism ringing in her voice. "Get rid of those two, park this monster at the edge of the canyon five miles out, and let's do what her Highness commands."

Bal grimaces at Markus. "I've always wondered if you people can fly."

He points to the exit with his pistol. Markus holds Koray tight, striding with her to meet their escorts.

Frightened people resign themselves to a corner, mourning in silence for the hope ripped away. Amongst them, Farah sits confused against a bulkhead. Two brutes marshal Markus and Koray in a corner, paying a courtesy grunt to two tribesmen escorting a pair on board.

Relief strips Samiri of any immediate thoughts when he spots Farah. With potion in hand, he breaks off from Aspasia to administer the medicine; no one stops him. He gently supports her head before touching her chapped lips with the rim of a bottle. Slowly, he allows a bright blue liquid to flow into her mouth, which encourages a coughing fit from the Queen. She looks at Samiri with accusative eyes, then slumps down into a deep sleep. He settles next to her, leaving Aspasia to converse with the criminals in the cockpit.

"If either of you harms a hair on their heads, my master will make it his divine prerogative to destroy every fiber of your being…slowly, painfully." Aspasia's presence and tone drive the point deep into Bal's black heart. "Your poison has done untold damage to…do you even know who she is?"

Empty stares answer the question.

"I thought not. Carry out your tasking. My counterpart and I will remain to oversee your actions."

Bal nods, then snatches a communicator from Ruia. He dispatches his tribesmen from the other ships to carry out Octavia's orders.

Soon jubilant swarms of menacing tribesmen rush into the village, with roars of conquest spilling out their foul mouths. Weapons raise high, firing off shots of intimidation. Anyone caught in their path is met with violent blows; not even horses are safe from the rampage.

Narrow streets erupt with panic at the approaching wild-men. Women are captured – some are pulled into alley-ways to endure unthinkable crimes. Men are bashed in the head with maces and clubs; others are hit by careless rifle-fire. The mayhem is spreading. Persephone and Osiris get caught in a swarm of bodies rushing to escape the plague of tribesmen descending on them.

A large ginger-bearded tribesman swings a war-hammer at Persephone's head. Like lightning, she flickers away to his surprise and lands a mighty fist on his chest. The impact sends him hurling into a mass of fleeing residents.

Osiris knocks two attackers to the ground; a third fires off a barrage of shots at his back. His body absorbs the painful streams of light peppering his shirt – scorching holes expose reddened flesh in their wake, instead of severe wounds. He rushes his attacker, seething with rage.

Desperate screams are becoming unbearable. The swarming horde is too much to take on. Osiris reaches Persephone, grabs her hand, and pulls her away to a cross street. Within seconds, they reach an opening near a door. They burst through the thick barrier, encountering Maya with a dangerous rifle begging to be used.

"Please, we mean you no harm," Osiris promises with his hand in the air.

"Tell it to the door," Maya says. "Go on then, get out before they show up."

Persephone braves the threat of the rifle to get close to the woman. "Maya, it's me, Cora. Remember?"

Maya squints her eyes, then smiles.

"You should hide," says Osiris.

"Ah, they will be done when they are tired. Not the first raid, won't be the last. They never come inside."

"Not this time, old woman," Osiris says, as he secures the door. Persephone drops to her knees in front of the standing rifle. "They are searching for us, I'm afraid. Can you help us?"

"You say your name is Cora, eh?"

Persephone hesitates, "Yes my Lady."

"Your mother, Demeter, was here." Maya regards the Princess' face, touching it with a gentle hand. "A fellow came in, called her 'Majesty,' he did." She moves to a closet and retrieves a thick dark-blue shirt and matching pants for Persephone; old Hyperborian fashion, yet rich in color. "Put that on before you catch a cold. They're my granddaughter's – she won't be needing them anymore."

She allows the Princess some discretion inside the ample closet. Once Persephone switches clothing, the old woman shuffles off to a darkened hallway, gesturing at the pair to follow. They climb shaky wooden stairs leading to the roof. "He picked your mother up like a cherished doll and said they would be at the big ship by the river."

"Markus," Osiris mumbles.

They push through a flimsy door to the rooftop above the second floor. In front, the view of the attacking horde swarms a half-mile away; to the rear is a rising conical stack, which the buildings on this side of the street are jammed against. Maya hustles them into an enclave, leading through a cavern dug into a soft hill. Streaming light from the opposite end shimmers off a silhouette of a compact two-seater craft.

Out of breath, Maya stops to let the pair pass her. "I looked at old picture slides from my youth, when I graced the halls of the healing temple in Northern Illyria. And there it was, clear as day – an image of her Royal Highness Queen Farah. There is no mistake in my mind, she and Demeter are one and the same. That makes you…" Maya drops on her knees. "The blessed Princess Persephone."

"Thank you, My Lady," Persephone interrupts the reverence. She clasps Maya's old hands. "Your kindness shall not be forgotten."

"Where will you hide?" Osiris asks.

She answers him with a coy smile. "There's safety above, as is below. Go now, Highnesses." She waves them off before making a hurried retreat.

The pair climb into the cramped craft. Persephone struggles with her restraints but gets assistance from Osiris. "This should be easy to fly," he says with sarcasm, pointing at the outdated screens and switches.

"I hate being me; I want to be Cora." Persephone stares at her panel in a daze.

Osiris nudges her shoulder to interrupt her pouting. "Switch on the pumps – they're on your side. Whatever is going on is not your fault."

"You sure about that?" Her head hangs, staring at her dirtied hands resting on her lap.

He doesn't answer. A toggle on a starter and a push on the throttle propel the craft out the cavity.

Chapter 16: Friends in Old Places

The western sky is clear heading away from Cappadocia. Osiris struggles with the small ship's controls. More than once, he burst out with complaints about the lack of maintenance. They skirt an altitude of 500-feet; any higher brings on wild chirping from instruments, warning of possible engine failure. One-mile on the right, the hulking mass of the captured tanker comes into view. It rumbles in the air, moving slowly, 100-feet over a narrow canyon.

In the tanker's hold, everyone is in quiet contemplation. Samiri watches over the Queen with Aspasia. They regard one another in silence. For Samiri, half a problem is solved with Farah immersed in a deep rehabilitating sleep. Aspasia settles her conscience with new orders from Vali to let the Queen live. Neither worry about Bal's intentions for Markus jammed up against the exit door, nor Koray in the clutches of the vile Ruia.

A blast of wind assaults everyone near the opening door. The howling makes sinister promises to Markus. He sends Koray an endearing look which shatters her. "I love you, daughter. Remember me as I was?"

He gets no mercy from Bal. Instead, he receives a short blade piercing his side. The tribesman looks at him with delight twinkling in his eyes.

Nothing escapes Koray's lips. She watches her father's face sour with the nasty wound; beyond the wind at his back waits a deadly drop to the surface. Her weak limbs find a sturdy resolve. Ruia's firm grasp no longer brings mind-numbing fear of a dark and terrible future. The bright glare from outside softens with a tinge of blue from a shimmering lake. In the half-second that passes, she knows what she has to do.

A swift kick sends Markus plunging out the craft; Koray breaks away and jumps after her father. Both bodies fall fast, splashing with tremendous force on the shallow waters. Ruia sticks her head next to Bal's to catch sight of the crumpled bodies before they sink to a watery grave. The narrow lake's shores return the view to dry dirt with patches of snow. From the corner of Bal's eye, he spots the tiny speck of a ship following high on the left.

Persephone sees the falling bodies tumble out the tanker – it is too far to see who fell. "Quick, over there."

Osiris sends their craft in a dive towards the miniature lake.

A low hum grows intensely from the rear of the tiny craft. Shots ring out. Two trails of blue light shoot past them. Another hits their ship with the screech of twisted metal. The inevitable happens when six shots find their target on the main intake housing. Exploding metal gives way to black smoke erupting from the damage. The craft spirals out of control. It slams on an unstable surface at the foot of a hill. In seconds, the smoldering wreck begins sinking.

Persephone's side sticks up, with the surface barely visible. Osiris is unconscious, pinned between his seat and the crumpled instrument paneling; above his left chest, a jagged piece of material sticks out with blood oozing. A choking fog of gray smoke jolts Persephone awake. She looks around in a daze. Screaming alarms switch from a mild annoyance to an unbearable torment. She struggles to remove her restraints, catching a glimpse of Osiris as she breaks free.

Broken metal sticks out Persephone's side, yet she feels no pain. Expecting a sharp sting, she scowls and pulls the projectile hard, spilling blood as it comes out. Still, no pain.

She smashes the side window with her boot. There is a good chance she can reach an exposed rock to make an active climb out of the hole. *Maybe he will wake up.* The craft plunges two feet without warning, jerking everything in the cockpit. Persephone's body slams into Osiris. She panics in the darkness. Then the pain comes.

Gripping the crumpled dashboard, she pushes with all her strength. Metal stretching, bending into its near original shape makes an agonizing sound. She pushes hard; partially hoping Osiris will wake, and surprised how much pressure she is exerting on the frame. *You're the destroyer of worlds,* she reminds herself.

She gives voice to her body's stress, letting out a steady yell to aid the power coursing through her veins. Osiris is free. She breaks his restraints off and grabs his arm, ready to jump through the narrow opening she kicked off seconds ago. Her foot drops on the pilot seat. She heaves the body up. An unnerving sound from beneath encourages her to hurry. The Earth swallowing up unwilling prey flashes through her imagination. In a powerful leap, she drags Osiris up on to the surface.

The imploding ground breaks open to a large hole penetrating deep below. The wreckage is gone, consumed by darkness and an echo. Persephone looks at Osiris. His cold skin brings panic. She presses her lips to his, blowing the breath of life to his lungs, repeating the steps she learned long ago. This is the first time she is using the resuscitative technique. After minutes of trying, nothing happens.

Her heart squeezes out a familiar melancholy to her throat. Broken with despair, her eyes erupt with tears streaming on Osiris' face. His skin is clammy, devoid of any warmth, lips a deathly shade of blue. Gentle winds wash across the body, bringing with it the sounds of foreign footsteps struggling to keep moving. Persephone darts forward to confront the intruder.

Moving with noticeable pain, Markus grasps Koray tightly in his arms and pushes on. Their soaked bodies shiver with each whip of the wind. Persephone doesn't leave her spot. She flings her arms high for them to see; at the same time keeping a watchful eye at the disappearing tanker and the single escort craft that brought her down. "Here!" she screams.

Markus drops on the hard ground with Koray.

Persephone wants to break down at the sight of her savior from years ago; she has not seen him since. She falls to her knees to place her hands on his sobbing face.

He struggles with words, fighting to overcome joy and sadness, to manage a proper greeting for his better. "Highness," he whispers.

"Markus," Persephone says, with emotion bubbling in her chest. She kisses his forehead. "Is my mother safe?" She takes Koray's hand and squeezes it.

"She is in your watcher's care," Markus says. "There is another Watcher with them, whom I suspect is with the tribesmen."

"We don't have time to ponder motives," Persephone says, in a forceful tone which surprises her. *Why am I talking in this way?* She looks over to Osiris' body behind a hedge. Her face sours at the brink of tears. Markus notices the body and stumbles over to it. She looks back at Markus. "I think he's-"

"Not yet," Markus says with desperation. "He's on the brink. Come help me." Persephone and Koray crowd over the body. Markus grabs the protrusion in Osiris' chest. He instructs the girls to hold the body down as he pulls the metal out in a controlled, steady fashion. Blood rolls on over the entry point when the object is removed. Markus wastes no time in delivering life-saving breaths to the Prince. "Light a fire, girls, quickly."

Koray throws dry twigs into a pile. Persephone gathers dry bush. Markus keeps on trying to revive Osiris. They huddle next to the cavity where the craft sunk into earlier. Persephone spots a utility bag from the doomed ship – it remains secured to the window she broke out earlier. Fate smiles on them – the kit contains a fusion torch.

The fire is lit, and Markus has ceased his pushing on Osiris' chest. The Prince's eyes open. His weak hand reaches for Markus', taking it into his and clasping his gratitude.

"You're welcome," Markus says with a genuine smile. Persephone and Koray make room around the fire for them.

"He has to sleep," Markus tells the girls. "Highness, see the area above the chest?"

"I know, it's vulnerable…please Markus, call me Persephone."

"A bit too informal for me."

Koray smiles at her father. "Call her 'Sephie."

"Alright." Markus nods reluctantly. "Koray and I can survive a 100-foot drop; you two can overcome much more than that. The chest wound is what put him in that state. Once removed, the healing can begin, but only when the body shuts down, and the mind along with it."

"A lesson more effectively taught compared to all the tutors that have tried," Persephone says softly. She looks at the cavity, overcome with curiosity. "I wonder what's down-."

Markus screams as though dying; Persephone jolts. She looks back and sees the cherry red ember leave his wound. He throws the burning twig with a scowl.

"There are always secret underground tunnels and caves in places like this," he strains in a mix of pain and instruction. He huddles closer, as the wind bites with freezing fangs. "There's no telling where they all lead."

"Maya said there are places high and places low. Maybe she was talking about under everything." A strange thunderclap echoes across the sky, startling Persephone and the rest. They strain to see the ship hiding in the afternoon sun. "I think we should find out what's down there...keep out of sight."

The others agree.

At a sizable gap before the narrow canyon leading into Cappadocia, the behemoth of a tanker sits on the flat rocky floor. It dwarfs the smaller transport and larger military cruiser next to it. Troops wearing the colors of Octavia crowd around their vessel, keeping vigil, watching over the terrain.

Inside the military cruiser, Aspasia and her Watchers, along with Samiri, Princess Octavia and Queen Farah assemble in a holding quarters. A generous serving of food is on display for her Grace, along with a flustered medical doctor buzzing around the Queen. Farah's mental state remains questionable.

"Oh, for heaven's sake, let her be," Octavia scolds the wiry man with his scanning equipment. "Off with you. And take him, too…find out what foul elixir he forced down our dear Farah's throat." Two Watchers urge Samiri and the good doctor through a narrow passageway.

"My dear cousin, what have they done to you?"

"I…I don't know. Where am I?" The haggard Queen cringes with fear at Octavia's approach. "What do you want?"

Octavia picks up a hairbrush. "Remember when we were children? I used to brush your silky locks like this; see how good it feels? I was always jealous of your flowing blonde strands whipping carelessly in the wind, only to fall neatly back into place. Then you grew up into a vision, didn't you?"

"We are family?"

"Yes, dear, do keep up. You caught the eye of the King, the mighty Shuru, while I had to endure marriage to that deviant Sisyphus. You were much younger than me of course, and Shuru couldn't keep his twig in his pants long enough to appreciate my delicate offerings. It didn't matter anyway – you are of House ENlil. The most I could hope for was becoming the Primary of ENki…soon enough I suppose."

"Where is my daughter?" Octavia stops her brushing. She drops to her knees and gazes deeply into Farah's eyes.

"Yes, where is your daughter indeed? We need to find her. What good news can you offer to aid our search?"

"She's in the cave," Farah whispers. "I left her there."

Octavia snaps her fingers at Aspasia standing beyond the doorway. "Add a squad to your Watchers. Sweep the caves and find her. And please do not hesitate to kill every creature you encounter. Don't look at me like that; your master will have some sport left when he arrives. Now, do as I command!"

"Vali," Farah says with a mask of inquiry. "I owe him an errand, yet I can't remember. Where is he?"

"Like all manner of creatures suffering his gender, he will arrive when the work is done."

"The King...I'm married to the King. How is he?"

"Yes, you twat. No one knows where Shuru is; dead possibly. Your silly mind probably won't process that his absence is what stayed your execution."

Farah's face sours into that of a child fearing an imminent scolding. She relaxes with Octavia's gentle, reassuring caresses. Her demeanor mimics a simpleton lacking a grasp on reality. Octavia provides a kiss before departing.

The room is quiet. Farah hugs her knees wearing an innocent look. With as much discretion as she can muster, her eyes travel upwards to a corner. A black globe hangs through the metal ceiling with a faint red blinking dot. She returns her gaze to a blank stare.

Aspasia stops in front of the medical room. Her hand stops short of twisting the doorknob. She gazes at her boots, waiting for a slight kick to erupt from within – nothing happens. She takes a deep breath in place of a fetal reminder. *When the poison is subdued, I can make things right.* She steps inside in a brisk, determined fashion.

She looks up at the room's surveillance camera, then Samiri. He draws attention with a careful finger touching his lips.

They both exit the space and head for a crude corner, stacked with remnants of repair parts and supplies, less traveled by the crew.

Samiri offers Aspasia a thin vial with a bright blue liquid, "A corruption for your oath. It will subdue the affliction, not separate."

"Will it hurt our child?"

"No. I can administer a proper solution once in Hyperboria. I have requested sanctuary for you."

Aspasia's shoulders slouch down as her head drops. "I'm afraid."

Samiri clasps her shoulders with a calming grip.

She drinks the liquid. "What now?"

"Pretend to sweep the caves – we both know Persephone is not there. Buy me time to find her. When Vali arrives, I will have her out of harm's way." He reads Aspasia's questioning glance at the upper level. "Queen Farah dug herself into a hole in this affair, besides, her mind is that of a child. It may prove to work in her and our favor." He is surprised by Aspasia's goodbye kiss. The world drops away for a few seconds in the passionate exchange.

With a heavy heart and longing eyes, he watches her leave up a narrow stairway. The receding sound of her boots slamming on metal brings him back to the realities ahead. He returns to the medical room to prepare a placebo for Farah, with any luck to force her out of her malingering illness.

Chapter 17: Secrets from the Third Age

"'Sephie, stop!" Koray begs the Princess climbing halfway down the pitch-black hole.

After a winding descent through the cavity created by the crashed shuttle, they stopped a half-mile underground. The exhaustive walk through carved tunnels took them to a third level where Persephone stumbled into a cracked wall. Ancient writings fueled her curiosity, much to Koray's dismay.

"Don't go anywhere," Persephone urges the group. She wiggles her body through the shaft until it disappears; Koray huffs.

Markus tears open a wrapper on a protein bar. The crumpling sound brings Koray close. "Good thing we stopped for dinner," he says, and breaks off half the meal for his daughter. Pain from his wound sours his face.

"Good thing we stopped for supplies," says Koray. She touches the bandage on Markus' side. Her handiwork is proving useful, which shows in her proud smile. "Look, he's waking."

Osiris raises his body a few inches off the rocky ground. The burning fire hurts his eyes, adding to the confused state showing on his face.

Markus lumbers over with his lips pursed, offering the Prince his meal.

Osiris looks up. "You saved my life," he whispers, pushing away the offer

"We all did. Don't waste the effort then…eat."

"We need to leave this place." Osiris looks down at the crimson stains covering his shirt and shakes his head. "That's embarrassing."

Koray smiles coyly "'Sephie thinks it is."

Osiris looks at her cockeyed. "What are you going on about, Koray? Where is the miserable brat, anyway?"

"Don't deflect. I see how you two look at each other."

He shakes his head. "You're imagining things."

"Shut it you two," Markus interrupts. "Back to more important things? There's a heavily armed battlecruiser at the gap."

"How can you tell?" Koray asks.

"The way it came in, the rumble in the exhaust and the beacon patterns."

Osiris looks at Markus with a smile. "You miss it, don't you?"

"Of course I miss it. I'm a warrior, not a spy for the trade emporium. But those days are gone…destroyed by my own hand."

"Stop feeling sorry for yourself old man" Osiris lifts his shirt, pressing around his fresh wound. "Let's figure out our next move."

Koray's eyes widen. "What about the shuttle we hid behind the mountains?"

The others look at her like a fool.

She shrugs with a pout. "There's a small shuttle behind the cave we spent the night in. We can escape in it."

Osiris throws Markus a sour look. "It's your fault if they were anywhere near us." He looks past them at the darkness consuming the tunnel. "Where's 'Sephie?"

Koray huddles up to the men to point down the black void. "In there."

They look at the ominous crevice swallowing their fire's brilliance.

The cavity ends a tenth of a mile down. Persephone's descent is rapid, which her torn clothing and sore backside attest to. The room she stands in was constructed eons ago, when her ancestors brought on the third destruction of the world. When it was abandoned, the inhabitants cared not to retrieve the machines they cohabited with for a thousand years.

Wind gusts whistle with ferocity in a far-off corner. Its presence whips across displays, lighting up in tight arrangements. The ground matches the wall's gray color, with tiny silver dots ingrained into the material. Lighting fixtures recessed into the rock ceiling ignite in a fury. The space is no smaller than 100-feet long and 40-feet wide, with a ceiling 11-foot high.

Symbols jump out at Persephone. A rush of lighted words stream through her, stopping abruptly past her body;

there's no sensation, but the multi-layered colors make her smile. Her hand stimulates a corner into a frenzy of light, followed by images – recordings made by the long-dead sages who roam these hallowed halls.

A memory intrudes. A distinct thought, or rather a feeling - how to manipulate the complex system of ancient technology. *How could this be?* The fading memory of her dream encounter with Lords ENlil and ENki induces a cold shudder rolling down her back. Without thought, she plunges her hand on a dark panel. A twist of her wrist settles the swirling light into a single stream. A gesture resets the chaos into a manageable symphony of consoles fighting to come alive.

She plants her wary body on a dusty chair. A nagging desire to slide her hand across a panel brings pause to her curiosity. A few seconds go by before her impetuous nature wins. A glow envelops her long fingers, buzzing, snaking around like a creature. Unsure of its nature, malevolent or benign, she panics and springs off her seat in desperation, trying to fling the creature to the ground. The buzzing settles as a display explodes above her console. Her fist balls up with the coiling light.

Her thoughts jump to her companions. Instantly their faint images flood the display. She smiles with victory, realizing the basic operating concept. "Where is Samiri?" Nothing happens. She lets her shoulders fall limp and eyes droop shut. Her hands rise up to the sky as if in prayer,– still nothing. She focuses her thoughts on Maya. A dusty underground chamber with 100 frightened people fills the screen.

She walks further down the line of consoles until another dark panel catches her eye. Without thinking, she places the creature of light on the receptacle, which it dissolves into without hesitation. Ahead of her is a stockpile of weapons, left unused for countless millennia. A wicked smile erupts on her lips with thoughts of turning the tides on Bal and his gang of rapists. *How do I get out of here?*

Without thinking, she selects a sequence of switches. A display materializes on a wall. She recognizes a symbol noting 'Point of origin.'. She drops her palm on a now-familiar dark panel, resurrecting the tame apparition into her welcoming arm. A smile and a touch of a symbol send her body into a shimmering state. A moment later she disappears.

Persephone appears in a dark tunnel. Her latest arm accessory casts an eerie blue and white glow on smooth round-cut passageways. Muffled grumblings are faint, yet Osiris' distinct complaints ring out among subtle laughter. The elation for her discovery sends a rush of warm blood coursing through her skin, encouraging hurried steps to announce her arrival. With a broad smile, she stops in front of her companions. They stare in horror at the creature slithering around her forearm.

"Where did you come from?" Osiris cocks his head in surprise. "And what's that?"

"It's my friend, Adonis."

Markus carefully moves next to her to caress the creature's eel-like body, glittering in multicolored light. "It's a Wandaluz." He grimaces at the questioning stares. "A Wandaluz – an ancient conduit to access…well, I don't know what, but it's referred to in lore. Don't you children read?"

Persephone's eyes widen with her smile, as she strokes her artificial pet. "I know what it does, and I have a plan. There are a lot of frightened people somewhere in the tunnels. We will enlist their help."

Markus clasps her hands. "I hate to break it to you, Princess, but we don't have a single pistol between us."

A wicked smile covers Persephone's lips. She urges them to gather around. Still smiling, she shuts her eyes. In a blinding blast of light, they disappear.

Seconds pass before a flash disrupts the quiet of the ancient data center. Persephone and her companions arrive next to the cache of weapons stacked in a glass vault. An awestruck Markus and Osiris waste no time in examining the dusty rifles, pistols, and strange sticks with threatening points. Koray is whisked away by Persephone to a console where images of the hiding souls erupt in the air.

Persephone looks at Koray's wide eyes. "There are hundreds. Surely there are enough weapons to arm them all, and any we can free from captivity."

Markus breaks away from the gawking to study the huddling figures. "Highness…'Sephie, those are frightened people. They are not trying to get in a fight."

"Never underestimate the resolve of an abused or threatened soul." She looks at Koray, takes her hand, and squeezes with solidarity. "With Adonis we can monitor the tribesmen's movement. Attack where they least expect it."

"What is its' range?" Osiris yells across the room.

"I'm not sure. Markus, can you help me figure it out?"

Osiris finds a staff he likes and twirls it with skillful fervor, showing off for an audience who pays him no attention. "Right… I think if we lure them to the gap, we'll have a better chance of picking them off."

Markus frowns his concern borne from experience. "That cruiser is too close. They can box us in with troops."

"Let them come," Persephone says. Everyone turns to her, as though she were in the lead. Overwhelming discomfort makes her swallow hard, encouraging the swarms of butterflies in her stomach to go silent. "We will get as many from the town in here as we can, arm them, and then spread out in the gap. Markus and I will break into the cruiser. You'll take a few into the center-"

"Are you insane?" Osiris looks up at Markus for support.

"She's right." He looks at the Prince with a smirk. "While their focus is on you, we'll rescue the Queen."

Persephone relinquishes her Adonis to Koray. "You'll have to use him; I'll show you how."

A sprawling map of the terrain and sky fills a nearby wall with pristine three-dimensional accuracy. Live data is streamed from unknown sources, providing a vivid picture of all movement from the tanker to the town. The horde of tribesmen pursuing their prey is represented by faint red dots assaulting yellow ones. Streaks of green tracks show tunnels traversing vast distances beneath the Earth, spreading across a 25-mile radius. More yellow points gather below Maya's home.

Markus yelps with excitement. "I found it!" He rushes over with a handful of white pellets. They look at him with questioning faces. "Transmitters. Enough for the villagers."

Persephone spends the next three-hours instructing Koray how to use Adonis, guessing most of what she teaches; hoping fate intervenes to ensure success. Markus and Osiris unwillingly volunteered to be transported with crates of weapons to Maya. Their main objective is to rally as many people to that point before managing an extraction.

At the end of the exercise, any Cappadocian not captured or slaughtered found themselves in the secure chambers, which until previously were known to a select few. They were given the plan – free their fellow citizens during a prisoner march down the five-mile narrow gap.

Bal's slave raid accounts for 50-percent of people his tribesmen did not kill, the other 50-percent escaped. The tanker is the destination. The attackers' transports are parked alongside each other at the end of the gap, with the protection offered by Octavia's battle cruiser nestled out of view.

Yellow dots show off the movement of people. A new color emerges on the map; Persephone designates purple for the armed citizenry. Koray is currently transporting them to various exit points, from the tunnels to the gap. She gives her faithful handmaiden a warm embrace. "I wanted us to see the world, have an adventure; I never thought it would be like this."

A mask of strength and hate covers Koray's face. "Make them pay."

"I am sorry Koray, for everything that happened. You have always been my protector, my loyal friend, my sister. By the Creator, I swear, Bal and his band will meet a death worthy of song to last the generations. Blood will flow for the violation inflicted on you...on us."

Osiris slaps Markus' shoulder. "You ready old man?"

"If I fall today...tell your father I did so in penance for my crimes against him and your family. I journey to the cities of the underworld to be with my kin – let the citizenry in the afterlife..."

"Shut up!"

Markus rolls his eyes. "They had their moment...I thought I would have mine." He ignores Osiris in favor of his daughter's loving gaze. His eyes glaze over; his throat tightens. He sends a nod of admiration and love.

Persephone sandwiches herself between the men. She gives them a quick once-over, smiles then nods to Koray.

The space around them becomes heavy. Blue dots swirl around in a frenzy. Serpents of light latch around the three bodies, coiling without mercy until the very fabric of space and time is bent. They disappear with a flash into a collapsing vortex.

Koray slumps down on her chair, ready to begin the onslaught.

Chapter 18: Break the Broken

The gap between the village of Cappadocia and the outskirts runs through a narrow winding rock canyon. Winter winds lash out at 300 souls migrating to the broad plain at the end of the restrictive pathway. They stumble with fatigue at the perimeter of a small lake – tired, hungry; their reward is a fresh serving of random lashes delivered by Ruia and her gang of watchful tribesmen.

At the cold water's edge, everyone stops for rest. The new slaves are allowed to slake their thirst before marching on. Old, young, babies, all take comfort in the minutes they are afforded. Many cup their hands with a silent prayer for deliverance. Others resign themselves to a fate they ran away from long ago.

"It's just like me brother to drop the hard work on us, eh?" Ruia snatches a meat-pie from her fellow tribesman. "He hides with his mistress while we carry on like fish waiting for a hungry bear."

"Would you shut your hole…all you do is complain," one tribesman snaps.

"Better watch yourself. You might catch a stray shot when it begins." She looks at the ground with regret slipping through her voice. "This is a big catch, you know. Fetch a good price, it would have."

"Where do we do it?" he asks

"Right here is just as good a place. Nowhere to go but in the water." She gestures to 12 approaching watchers. "What they doing here?"

Dark uniforms stand out in the distance. Each walk in unison, widening the space between them with each stride. Aspasia is in the center, wearing a look of disappointment. They stop 30-feet from the closest tribesman.

A crackle on Aspasia's communicator breaks her thoughts. The pit in her stomach grows with each passing second, the device demands attention; this is a call she cannot ignore. "Highness, we are near the end. There have been some complications."

Vali's angry voice breaks through the howling wind. "Where is the Princess? This will be all for naught if you don't have her."

"She remains hidden. Perhaps with additional troops, we can scour the area for-"

"You disappoint me Aspasia. It's not in your nature to bring failure. If the creature in your belly has sway over my mission, I should tell you of a warrant I hold for its execution. A fair trade to ensure success. Your child for that insufferable wench."

Her stomach churns with disgust – more for herself than Vali. *Samiri will understand; he will.* "By your command, Master."

The communicator dies with all hope to escape the nightmare. She keeps her gaze fixed on Ruia, chomping away. A nod left and right readies her watchers. They wait in silence for the tribesmen to complete their part in the plan. Ruia's communicator echoes Bal's voice.

"Execute the prisoners," Bal orders with reluctance.

Ruia does not respond. She tosses her unfinished pie, wipes her mouth then picks up a thick rifle. "You heard 'im. Clear 'em out, lads."

Reluctant fingers begin a determined squeeze on triggers. Distant shots ring out, startling both tribesmen and Watchers. The unarmed mob rush for cover in a frenzied panic; the tribesmen duck behind anything resembling shelter; a thunderous rain of light descends on them. The Watchers dart on either side of the rock face 37-feet from where they stand. The Tribesmen return rapid-fire at heads bobbing behind ledges.

One Watcher reaches a cave with a dagger raised high, ready to inflict death on a slave. Before the blade reaches its mark, a blinding light erupts. In a flash, the man disappears. Similar results meet the others determined to stop the attack. The assault ends.

Seconds pass. Ruia sweats with panic, wiping her brow with clammy hands. She grips her rifle waiting for the barrage to resume. She grimaces at a whisper reaching her worried ear, 'Its ghosts." Her comrade cowers in frightful dismay.

Watchers wait for another wave of attack; they know the nature of the technology employed. It begins as expected from a bend in the rock 60-feet away. The Watchers run off with blurring speed to intercept.

Before they reach the second wave, a volley of light fires off from the original position. Bolts of death streak toward cowering enemies. In the chaos, prisoners sprint off into crevices within the rock face. Several Cappadocians provide their comrades cover fire as they scramble on to ledges. Secured in groups of five, the space turns into a violent vortex sucking in the uninitiated to a location far away.

The angry tribesmen catch on to the rouse. Merciless shots pierce fleeing prisoners on their way to freedom. A band of fighters sees the slaughter. They hurl their bodies off perches on to softer dirt mixed with snow, ignoring Persephone's warning of 'Do not leave the safety of rock – it's the only way to keep you in the stream.' Hate cuts through reason and safety for a chance to lash out at the invaders.

A half-mile west of the fighting, Osiris arrives with 20 armed villagers near Octavia's perimeter guards. The soldiers are startled at the sight of the approaching mob; they point weapons at the group, ready to fire.

"Tell your regent Prince Osiris is at her door!"

The claim is met with confusion; rifles promptly point to the ground; rigid postures are relaxed. A lead soldier makes a call to the ship. The returning instructions screamed into his ear prompts his response, "Hold your ground!" Rifles return to their original aim. Alert eyes stare at Osiris – all trying to determine the reason for his presence; none have ever seen the heir to House ENki.

Osiris smiles at the 12 ignorant troopers. His heart ignites into a steady beat, increasing in speed with every shift of his footing. His hand gestures his frightened companions at the rear to stand their ground. His nostrils flare; bruised skin heats up with the blaze of the ancestors. Between human heartbeats, he disappears.

One by one, the soldiers receive damaging blows to fragile body parts. Screams mixed with the snap of bone and fevered shots ring out in random patterns, trying to hit the violent wraith. All fall without catching a glimpse of their attacker.

Satisfied with the small victory, Osiris waves the villagers forward. His hand shoots up to stop the advance. The ground rumbles with the thunder of boots rushing their way. "Damn it," he mutters at the two hundred armed soldiers coming into view. *Our job is done I suppose.* "Take cover!"

They scatter into the canyon wall whence they came. Shots fire at the villagers without mercy. A barrage of concentrated fire hit their intended rallying point, bringing down a cave's entrance and any immediate hope of escape. All duck behind boulders and return fire at the troops.

Away from the fighting, Octavia's ship remains unguarded. In haste, the soldiers rush off to secure Bal's prisoners, as commanded. Two of Bal's shuttles whisk away reinforcements to join the assault on the villagers; the anxious pirate joining the troops himself.

One inconspicuous entry point is the best, according to Markus. He leads Persephone through a cavity near a landing strut while complaining all the while about not having proper tools to break in. They manage to clear a panel blocking access to a narrow exhaust shaft, snaking below the lowest level.

A screen lights up at Markus' touch. "Octavia is here; there's a straight shot next to the medical bay."

Persephone shrugs. "Seems easy enough."

"Has the Royal evacuation-code changed?"

"What? I don't know." She looks at him sideways. "I never thought I'd have to use it. What are you doing?"

"You are the worst Princess ever; did you know this? Give me what you remember."

Persephone sends him a sarcastic sneer. She provides the last evac-code given to her at age 15; each year royals in the Greater Houses are provided a distinct transmission sequence with the sole purpose of calling for help.

The current code has changed several times from the one Markus hurriedly enters on a communications box. A small shower of sparks fly from a box he converted into a wide-area-transmitter. "There, that should seal my death warrant."

"Wouldn't they know you rerouted a signal?"

"Relax, I know what I'm doing," he says with a cocky smirk. An alarm blares above, joining flashing red lights and a tirade of movement, the crunching of boots running along the ground. "Move!"

The way ahead narrows into an uncomfortable squeeze into a towering shaft, howling with recycled air. Pounding boots beyond the crimson frame diminish into a retreating patter. Fierce gusts of wind kill the silence around the two infiltrators as they continue the short climb upward. A sign posted on the wall promises to lead them into the medical bay.

Samiri delivers vials of a concoction to treat Queen Farah. Two armed guards observe his every move; Octavia is adamant on securing Farah's recovery before Vali's arrival. They notice a corner hatch crack open. As the bulky floor plate rises, one soldier strides up with his weapon, ready to confront the intruder; the other points his muzzle at Samiri's head.

Markus smiles at the determined face glaring at him. He pushes the door up, nearly locking it into its securing latch. "Hello boys, we seemed to have made a wrong turn."

The rifle's muzzle draws close to his face. He slams the door hard against the bulkhead, the latch engages with a loud metallic 'ting.'

Startled, the soldier snaps his head to the noise.

Markus yanks the weapon to the floor, along with the soldier. The man's head smashes on raised metal near the hatch.

Before the second guard can react, Samiri opens his throat with a scalpel.

Persephone climbs out after Markus. She rushes to Samiri and embraces him. Her emotions threaten to break out of the impenetrable fortress created in the damaged part of her soul. Despite her best effort, a tear escapes. The intense urge to give up control to her Watcher flows back into the protective mental box, breaking at the seams.

"Highness, are you hurt?"

She composes herself. "No. My mother?"

"Right above us." He shakes his head. "I'm afraid her mind is...far gone."

Markus slips closer. "Talk later...escape now. Is there a way out?"

"Also above us. There are 12 guards stationed-"

"Childs play for you and I," Markus interrupts. "'Sephie, get your mother."

Samiri grabs his vials before following Markus out the door, with Persephone trailing.

Octavia's soldiers hover around Queen Farah's compartment. They are evenly spread with weapons clutched in anticipation of trouble.

Markus makes his presence known with a whistle and hands raised. "Excuse me, I'm here to see the Queen."

All rifles aim at his head. He moves to the closest gun with a steady heart. With both hands, he shoves the barrel off to the side. His powerful grip wrenches the weapon from the man before slamming the butt on his forehead. A quick shot at the closest target opens the way for the rest.

Samiri engages two with deadly accuracy, sending the bodies slumping on the metal ground, broken and twisted. The rest fall at the hands of the two, allowing Persephone to rush into her mother's holding room.

Lights flicker on. Farah sits on a comfortable sofa, dazed and incoherent. She looks past her daughter as if she sees an apparition stumbling into the meeting. "You've come to visit. The servants will bring tea at once." With a subtle glance, she looks at the surveillance camera.

"Mother, snap out of it." She tugs at Farah's arm, to no avail. "We have to go, quickly!"

"Have you brought news of my shaggy bird? I was told the cat ate him. The cat is coming...best do as the cat says."

"Stop your babbling. Come on."

Farah locks Persephone's arm in an intense grip.

The crazy talk makes sense to Persephone, alone. "Shaggy bird is safe." she whispers. "We have to go." She stares deep into her mother's eyes, which travel once more to the camera. Persephone lets go. A surge of heat courses through her veins, her focus shifts to the tiny object embedded in the wall. She grasps the intrusive spy, her feet are four-feet off the floor, and Octavia's peek into their reunion is over.

"For the good of all, stand down. Don't resist." Farah grabs Persephone's arms in a desperate plight.

"What? Mother, people are dying so we can get you out."

"I was weak, Persephone. Vali offered help. Years would pass until I learned of the awful truth of his motive. I swear I did everything I could to prevent it."

"You're not making any sense, Mother. What did Vali do?"

Farah drops her gaze. "He engineered your birth. It was the only way to produce an heir. You must understand, those were desperate times – your father does not know."

Persephone pulls away. A rot develops in her stomach, a guilty torment souring her resolve to avoid a truth clawing up her back. Uncomfortable memories swarm around her in a violent symphony – Vali's doting, his tales of divinity, the fat priestess in Aryavan. Her thoughts crack with the flash of a strange man in a field, then a dark cave, a violated body, Koray's rape, her rape, those dead outside. Her lips tremble to push words out. "Why was I…made? What am I meant for, with Vali?"

"Marriage." A hateful glare cuts her soul. "Listen to me, do as I say. It's our only chance to survive."

Shouts from Marcus urge them to come out. Persephone ignores his intrusion. "All this is because of you…because of me? The attacks, the dead?"

"No, child, it's my fault. I have a plan. All will end; you just have to trust me."

"Trust you?" She starts towards the door. "Goodbye, mother. May your confederates deliver you home safely." She storms out.

Farah drops on the cold floor in shame. She remains crumpled in a corner until Octavia rushes to her.

"Where is she?" Octavia's hand strikes Farah's face, hard.

"I don't know. A strange girl came. She tried to take me away, but I didn't let her."

Octavia grunts her frustration. "Look, you crazy bitch, when we find her, I will beat you like a runaway slave…you hear me!" She pushes Farah back to the floor then marches out.

Nineteen soldiers continue to assault Osiris and his party behind a rocky outcropping. They push forward without mercy, ordered to kill everyone in their path.

Of the 20 in the Prince's group, two remain. A disturbing thought crosses Osiris' mind. He peers out to his companions pressed against the rock wall. He looks behind him at 10 soldiers flanking their position – their comrades are moments away from a frontal assault. *I could take the back, but those two will die for sure.* He hesitates.

Sudden screams erupt from the 19 soldiers. Osiris opens fire on the 10; his companions find renewed strength to join in. Osiris drops his weapon and braves the cross-fire to reach the attackers. Shots sting his torso, but he doesn't slow down. With a dagger in hand, he swings at exposed necks, plunges in stomachs and plows his body through any in his way. The two men rush to him with gratitude for the dead that lies before them.

They drop near the corpses, waiting for the other troops to near. The men tremble with the terrible shrieks sounding in the distance. All goes quiet. They look at their Anuk patron with furrowed brows and questions begging to be voiced.

Osiris signals them to be calm.

He peers over a bush to confirm his suspicion –
Persephone, Samiri, and Markus are covered in blood and scorch
marks. "Over here!" In the blink of an eye, they arrive. "What's
wrong with her?"

Persephone stares at the short grass as if it is a terrible
reminder of things long forgotten. She bites on her favorite
fingernail, mimicking the demeanor of a child to the others.

Samiri helps Osiris up. He maneuvers his body in front
of the Prince's questioning glance at the Princess. "She hasn't
said a word since the cruiser. Best not to ask about the Queen."

"We should get to a cave and call Koray," Markus yells.
Persephone hurries off to meet him. He wraps his arm around
her. She stops her nail-biting comforted by his protective smile.

Most of Ruia's prisoners lie around the small lake in
motionless piles of dead flesh. Attacks dwindle to random fire
coming from a small group attempting to reach the safety of
rock. The Watchers regrouped with the tribesmen and Bal's
contingent of reinforcements. Fleeing villagers are now mere
sport and target practice for trigger happy soldiers.

Thunder echoes in the valley. Aspasia peers up to the
clouds at Prince Vali's cruisers – three in all, bringing 450 troops
eager to tie up loose ends. The knot in her stomach constricts
with nausea coming up to her throat. She can't decide whether
it's from mental anguish or Samiri's potion. It doesn't matter
now; all soothing effects subduing physical pain return at the

slightest thought of disobedience. She breaks off from her group to head to a dead body.

Bal grumbles to Ruia before hurrying to Aspasia. He catches a glimpse of her palming a white pellet no bigger than a fingernail. "What are you doing? What is that?"

"Get back, tribesman. My affairs are my own." She sprints off in a blur towards the cave the villagers are trying to reach. The moment she ducks into a darkened corner, her body is sucked into a vortex of light.

The journey to the control center lasts seconds. Pain disrupts Aspasia's nervous system, reminding her of her master's invisible hand. She spots a gathering of numerous villagers, cramped in a cavern 12-feet below her. *Where is she?* A solitary figure glows off in the distance. She darts towards Koray.

Oblivious to the approaching Watcher, Koray taps lighted switches on a control board, scrolling through images on the giant display, trying to find Persephone. Adonis' multicolored glow on her arm turns to solid red. She gasps as Aspasia rushes up to her.

"Where is the Princess?" she growls with dangerous intent, then drops her gaze to the coiling creature on Koray's forearm. "Give it to me."

Koray grabs a nearby pistol and fires off two rounds at Aspasia's head, then darts off to the safety of a stone column. Her chest tightens and body tenses. She hears the Watcher's light footsteps approaching. The pistol shakes, as fear overcomes her. She swallows hard then fires off more rounds into the shadows.

A flutter in the wind brings Aspasia three-feet in front of her. Before she can fire another shot, a violent hand grasps her throat, squeezing, lifting; her feet are dangling off the ground.

"I said, give it to me!"

Koray tenses her body before delivering a powerful kick to Aspasia's stomach. She drops on the ground as her attacker falls backward, stunned. She runs off towards a high ledge.

Aspasia goes into a panicked state for her child. The moment passes. Her blood boils at the outrage. She spots Koray pulling herself up on to a rocky ledge.

In a heated dash, she reaches the girl, and slams an angry fist on Koray's jaw, breaking bone on impact. She grabs her arm, then flings her to an adjacent wall.

The impact knocks the wind out of Koray. Pain grips her senses, but she ignores it and tries to flee from the angry Watcher, charging with a murderous glare. *'Sephie!* Before she can stand, Aspasia's foot lands hard on her stomach.

Fifty-feet away Persephone appears with her companions. She nods to Osiris as he and Markus walk down a ramp heading for the gathering. A faint sound alerts her to trouble. She glances around with worry creeping up her spine. She spots Koray in the distance.

Blow after blow on the poor girl does not weaken Aspasia's resolve. She grabs Adonis, but the creature constricts on Koray's arm. *Maybe death will relinquish it.* Without mercy, she pulls her dagger and plunges deep into Koray's chest. She pulls the blade out and readies for another plunge. An agonizing scream thunders through the space.

Blind rage propels Persephone faster than she has ever gone. Aspasia's hand drops; Persephone lowers her shoulder and levels her. Aspasia's fist fires towards her at breakneck speed. Persephone shifts her body and the blow smashes into the rock wall. Aspasia draws back, then kicks, her foot connecting violently with Persephone's face.

The commotion draws Samiri's attention. He darts off to the fight, fearing for his child's life. Markus sees him disappear and follows.

Aspasia delivers several blows, but holds back her attack, as she recognizes the Princess. In the moment of hesitation, Persephone removes her hidden dagger. Samiri arrives behind the pair, and Markus kneels beside his dying daughter.

Persephone plunges the dagger deep into Aspasia's stomach. She withdraws the blade for another strike. Samiri holds Persephone back with as much strength as he can muster. With incredible power she slams her elbow on his face, sending him reeling on the floor. She recoils then strikes hard into Aspasia's heart. Satisfied with the deadly blow she hurries to Koray.

Markus' heart shatters. He clutches his baby tightly, staring into her fading eyes. She smiles at him, with his gentle sway soothing her approach into the unknown. He kisses her. Her dying touch on his face breaks him. Tears flow freely down his face. Persephone kneels beside him and takes Koray's cold hand into hers.

Aspasia slumps down in a pool of her own blood. She pushes out her last breath with pain and sorrow for the loss inside her.

Samiri holds her. He is lost in her gaze, remembering her smile, her touch, and their baby's moving inside her. He fights back the tears, knowing any break in his resolve will betray his affections, yet he plunges into a terrible despair. He leans down to receive Aspasia's last words, and hears "Revenge," replacing her true whisper, "Forgive." He ignores his instincts and kisses her lips. Her final breath flows into his lungs as her body goes limp.

Osiris reaches his friends, and chokes back his own sorrow for Koray. He rests his hand on Markus' shoulder, squeezing with empathy.

Koray coughs up blood. Her eyes dim; Adonis' faint glow matches her life force it seems, fading rapidly with his host. Her grip on Persephone weakens. She smiles at them all before slipping into the abyss of eternal sleep.

Her body goes limp in her father's arms. The tears stop, giving way to rage. He throws his hateful gaze at Aspasia's body; Samiri stands in silence, observing them – he shakes his head calmly to indicate Aspasia is dead. Markus' storm calms, only regretting he did not inflict the killing blow.

Persephone gives Koray a goodbye kiss, then hugs Osiris tightly. "Forgive me. If I had listened to you, maybe-"

"There's nothing to forgive. Hush. There will be time for mourning – we have pressing concerns." He releases her to pick up the dormant Adonis. A quick wrapping on his arm revives the creature of light, with its color turning into a somber gray.

He leaves the group and heads for the main screens. The sector by the lake appears. He gasps with surprise at what he sees. Prince Vali's ground forces are firing upon both Octavia and Bal's people.

The carnage ends as suddenly as it started. Several tribesmen are left standing; Bal and Ruia are among them. They are restrained and marched off to a waiting shuttle. Suddenly, the screen turns to static. It normalizes with a distorted image of Prince Vali.

"Persephone, my darling, don't be afraid. All is well now. You can come out. The heathens are subdued and in custody. I know you can hear me. Come on, let's put an end to this affair."

Momentary caution disappears in Persephone's thoughts. Her past affections for Vali emerge, blinding her to everything she experienced in the recent days. *Uncle Vali.* Her mother's words intrude, bringing back a disruptive feeling of self-loathing. Her eyes travel to Koray. The haze of lies dissipates.

A rush of blood warms her cold heart, balancing her mental turmoil. She hurries to Osiris and stares intently into his eyes. Her slow smile and outstretched hand touch his.

He stares back, sensing an unknown feeling between them. "I don't know how to work it." He relinquishes Adonis.

She dons the creature with ease. Her finger points to a dark-gray panel pulsing on the console. Without explanation, she smiles, then disappears.

Chapter 19: A Union of Convenience

A whirling shimmer of blue light explodes above a ledge on rose-colored rock near Prince Vali's soldiers. The stunned troops formed up next to their shuttle assume a defensive posture to greet the unknown enigma. Princess Persephone appears inside the shimmer.

She remains silent. Peering at the rifles pointed her way, she makes no effort to command or be commanded. A casual glance at Adonis' fading color prompts her to shake the creature off her arm, and into a protective crevice. It drops on a shaded patch of ground, turning into a thin black silk shard upon impact.

A soldier breaks ranks, tears streaming down his eyes with reverence. He drops to his knees with devotion and bows down to the Royal Anuk they know is Persephone – this man's religious inclinations remind the rest of the Princess' divine status. In humble solidarity, the rest drop on their knees, followed with outstretched hands, and foreheads bowed to the dusty ground. The first soldier to offer respect screams out, "Blessed be art thou our god, for she is above all mortal flesh and binding!"

Outrage burns Persephone's very being. The blasphemous words threaten her calm demeanor as she inches near the rocky ledge; a whip of panic strikes her at the 30-foot fall to the ground – she has never attempted a jump from this high. *Don't react; use it to your advantage.* A gust of wind howls through the cave kicking up dust in its wake. She swallows hard, inhales, then steps off.

She lands hard on her feet. The impact sends a shock through her legs. Stunned, she drops to one knee, her hands drop to the ground. Her insides hurt, her diaphragm struggling to draw breath. A moment passes as she rises slowly, keeping her gaze fixed on the worshipping troops. Welcomed air rejuvenates her strength. She steps gracefully to the lead soldier.

Staring down, she waits for the humble man to rise before stepping lightly between the others. The shuttle's ramp promises an end to her ordeal. Each step forward sends a shiver of doubt up her spine, slashing away the trust and love she afforded Uncle Vali. Her scheming mother's words linger, *I have a plan; you just have to trust me.* Only twenty feet remaining to the ramp's edge.

Faint rumbling overhead grows louder. Warm air washes beneath the stationary shuttle, from another on a quick descent. The stink of exhaust assaults everyone on the ground. Persephone turns on her heels to the Captain. "Protect me."

Dust settles once engines wind down. As the shuttle's ramp drops, the troops behind Persephone swarm around her in a protective pattern. The fast approach of Prince Vali does not receive the expected courtesy soldiers always offer. Apart from being the highest-ranking Royal between the two, Persephone is also a god.

Vali bites his corner lip and shrugs. *I've created a monster – now it's time to control it.* "My sweet child, my prayer has been answered. You're safe at last."

The sea of black uniforms parts for the Princess to view her uncle. "Where is my mother?" Her stern tone surprises her, but she does not let anyone see it. Her fists clench tightly – fingernails dig into her palms. "Where is Octavia?"

"Oh, her? Not to worry, she is in custody, and Her Grace is resting comfortably on my cruiser. Rest assured Octavia's treachery will not go unpunished."

"I want your word, Vali – all in hiding will have safe passage back to their homes."

"Come now, little girl, I am here to rescue you, not to kill the innocent."

"Your word!"

The Princess' protection detail raise their weapons together in a ready position. One by one, they look on Persephone, their fists placed upon their heart, announcing their shift in allegiance. Vali fights back words he knows will inflame already souring conditions; he opts for a warm smile and kind words. "Persephone, my dear, why don't you give the order?"

Persephone nods. "Captain, no harm must be done to anyone gathering beyond the ridge, am I clear?"

The Captain's fist draws on his chest once more, as he exclaims his compliance.

"Offer any help necessary and spread the word to the other squadrons." Satisfied, she strides towards Vali with her false courage solidifying into a firmer resolve.

Thunderclaps echo above – five battlecruisers appear. Smaller fighter crafts swarm out of the host, spreading out in formation above the canyon. Vali's surprised expression indicates to Persephone the identity of the new arrivals.

"Prince Odin?" she asks in a cold tone.

"It's the only logical conclusion. Best we join our beloved Regent." Vali throws his former soldiers a disappointing glare before marching off to his shuttle.

Several minutes pass before a mob of Cappadocians emerge beyond a ridge. A massive transport craft lands between their path and Persephone. In droves, the people gather near the hulking ramp. Figures dressed in white uniforms rush down with slim cases, eager to find Prince Osiris. They find him walking solemnly behind Markus. Koray's body rests in her father's grieving arms.

Rushing through the crowd, Prince Odin ignores any decorum afforded him on the way to his son. He slows his pace at the sight of Markus. His heart races, pushing warm blood and adrenaline to clenching fists. Promises of a painful death to Markus ring in his mind, then his gaze drops to Koray; his tense fingers remain curled, his eyes are turning red.

"Father, stop! Save your anger for the conspirators in this affair."

Markus drops to one knee, balancing Koray and fighting back the pain seeping into his voice. "Highness."

Odin's relaxes. His trembling hand hovers over Markus' head. Eyes fall on the girl he knew before she took her first steps, before her first word. Past betrayals dissipate into a whisper, begging to be forgotten. His hand makes contact with Markus' head, bringing the grief-stricken parent to tears. "Go, Markus. Seek shelter and rest on board."

Hovering jets rumble overhead, as Vali's shuttle squeezes into a small space in front of a rock wall. Osiris moves closer to his father. "Has His Grace recovered?"

"He is safe in Thoth's temple, fully recovered. I convinced him to remain there until the orchestrator of this treachery can be revealed."

"Father, grant me a shuttle. No questions."

"Take any you wish." They move away from the approaching crowd to receive Prince Vali and Persephone. "Now, get ready for the lies, son."

The Princess' resolve cracks when she nears the pair. She embraces Odin, breaking down without care of who sees the careless display of humanity. Vali's crooked smile comes with a slight nod of acknowledgment to the Regent of Hyperboria. "Odin, your arrival is very fortuitous, but as you can see, we have subdued the perpetrators. I was not aware that your son had joined the search."

"It was a task he took on himself," Odin says. "I think the fortunes are with you, cousin – if it weren't for your interventions, many more would have been slaughtered."

"Yes, the tribesmen seemed determined to kill off the villagers, without any thought of retribution."

"Tell me, Prince Vali, what does a horde of slavers gain by killing their catch?"

An awkward silence overcomes Vali. He shrugs his shoulders and offers a smile. "Who knows the mind of the wild man? We did capture the leaders. Rest assured I will interrogate them in Illyria."

Odin glares at Vali in a visual interrogation; making the lesser of the two men tremble. "They will join us in Hyperboria. Be certain they do not end up dead before arriving."

Vali nods. "Of course."

"And what is Octavia's part in all this?"

Persephone releases her embrace. "Her efforts were instrumental in rescuing my mother, Uncle."

Vali gets closer, "Come now, Princess, we shall depart for Hyperboria immediately. Odin has to return for counsel's end-of-week deliberations."

She ignores the request and instead gives Odin a look which screams of heartbreak. "My father?" Her face sours from Odin's sorrowful look; Vali can't help but let a smirk escape.

"Uncle Vali, I will return with uncle Odin, please."

Vali begins to protest but is startled by Osiris moving between him and Persephone. "You heard her, Prince Vali," he says with noticeable anger in his voice.

"Very well. I will deliver the Queen promptly to the palace. I will be sure to attend tomorrow's council session." With his last word, Vali strides off.

The last of the villagers are safely onboard the transport. Odin puts his hand on Osiris and Persephone's shoulders. "Don't be long." He leaves up the ramp.

Persephone hugs Osiris. She gets lost in his comforting arms, returning a sliver of feeling throughout her numb body and soul. "Thank you for coming for me."

He smiles at her. "You've been making my life miserable since before we left the cradle. Why stop now?"

She closes her eyes and rests her tired head on his shoulder. Her eyes spring open with a desperate thought. "Where's Samiri?"

"He asked me to send him to the riverbank. 'Sephie…he took the Watcher's body with him."

"I suppose they have their rituals to attend to." She shakes her head. "I'm not sorry I killed her."

"Nor should you be. What happened back there, since Octavia's ship? Why did you lie to my father? You know Octavia is deep in this conspiracy – she's probably the one who composed it."

"Don't ask me to explain, because I can't. Even though she doesn't deserve it, I trust my mother's words. We should get inside."

She walks off to the ramp, realizing Osiris is not following when she reaches the steel edge. He smiles at her. "It's your fault you know."

"What's that?" she asks.

"You asked me what I am doing to help the people. No better place to start than here, won't you say?" The ship's engines begin their hum, drowning out his voice. "Go! I'll see you in the village."

She watches him run to a small medical shuttle. The ramp begins its slow lift towards the bulkhead, forcing her to move inside. The multitude of faces staring back at her brings pause to her thoughts. Everyone bows reverently at the girl they knew as Cora, sister of Koray.

Pacing in the manner of an irate peacock, Octavia mumbles questions to herself without pausing to think about the answers. An air pocket hits the craft, sending her rocking back on the bulkhead. Her scowling face snaps to Farah, smiling as if she is feeling the bumps in the sky for the first time. Octavia huffs without a glimpse being afforded to her by the crazy monarch. Approaching footsteps brings a scowl for whom she suspects is coming.

"Where did your pilots learn to fly, Vali? They're causing my stomach to churn. I demand I return to my ship."

"Compose yourself and be quiet, woman. Guilt is not a good look on you."

"Must be nice to stand there all innocent," Octavia says. "Odin will see right past your deceptions."

Vali looks at her with disdain. "He's as clueless as you are right now. Everything is working in our favor."

Octavia points at Farah. "Is that in our favor? Not sure what you people call it in the north, but in Corinth that is bat-shit crazy!"

"Calm down, you pathetic windbag." Vali resists the urge to slap her. "She is crazy, yes, and more than likely will say what we need her to say. I learned of a most generous fact Odin let slip – Shuru is in severe decline, possibly at the cusp of eternal sleep."

"He said that?"

"Not in words, no. Without the King, the Queen's word is final. Move aside, let me talk to her." Farah's gaze flows to Vali when he snaps his fingers at her several times. "My sweet girl," Vali whispers. "I have an important job for you. If you promise to help me with it, you'll be in a nice warm bed in no time. Tomorrow, when we go to the special gathering of cousins, all you have to do is say you give your blessings…you hear me? Say, 'I give my blessing.'"

Farah repeats the words, smiling with each rendition. Octavia smiles briefly but quickly turns her anger back on Vali.

"Why didn't that tramp give me up?" Octavia asks. "She was on my ship, then fled. I saw it myself."

"She is a simpleton who got scared when your goons attacked her. Now, be a dear and bring Farah some cake for her good behavior." He reaches for a communications panel. "Find me Aspasia!"

)●(

With a heavy heart, Samiri covers the openings of a pyre with dry branches. Behind the six-foot-high platform, the river Hayles roars; soon funeral ashes will be swept down its raging current. Aspasia's body lies on the top of the pyre, in eternal slumber. The sky is already dark with a tinge of light streaming on the horizon. A small fire flickers with the mild breeze.

Dry-twigs snaps, alerting the Watcher to an intruder's cautious approach. His eyes turn vicious, hands make ready to break bones and tear flesh. His body shifts to deliver a deadly blow.

"Calm yourself," Osiris says with hands in the air. "I'm here to help."

"Highness, my apologies; recent events have left me… perturbed."

"I've been sweeping the area for survivors. My task is finished, so I thought it prudent to tend to one more."

"I assure you, I am in no need of assistance."

Osiris rests his hand on Samiri's shoulder. "Please, allow me to lend an ear to your struggle."

Vile contempt swells in Samiri's chest; the numbness encasing his emotions cracks with every consoling look the Prince sends his way. *How could he begin to understand my loss? How dare he try to empathize?* "My struggle is only to honor the dead in the way I was taught, Highness."

"Then allow me to pay respects with you."

The offer unhinges Samiri's rage. "I do not understand. This is the Watcher who tried to assassinate the Princess. Why would you honor her?"

"You have been Persephone's Watcher since her birth. Putting that aside, I've known you all my life, albeit not as well as her. If you find it necessary to do this, then I see no harm in standing beside you."

Samiri's storm subsides quicker than anticipated. He gathers a handful of twigs in silence, moving in the manner of a cautious cat. *Does he know something? Is he baiting me?* Suddenly, Lord Thoth enters his mind, re-tasking his mental fog to patch a crumbling wall of emotion. "Highness, you need not dirty yourself on my account – please, I will finish building-"

"You clearly have not heard of my less than regal nature, Samiri."

"I've heard of the disregard you have for your station. I think a ruler should be among the people and not above them. Your behavior would shake the very foundations your ancestors built."

"House ENki needs a bit of shaking up, won't you say? My brother mentioned you joined his order."

Samiri nods. "A privilege I am most grateful for."

"Doesn't that create conflict – you're a servant of House ENlil, and now ENki?"

Warning bells ring out. "Watchers are not bound by the stringent rules of the Royal Anuk. Just as the common Anuk can mingle between Houses, so too can we. I fear the Prince has not been educated properly by his Watcher."

"I got rid of her years ago – too many rules. You know this one, don't you?"

"Aspasia." Samiri tries desperately to maintain a calm demeanor. "She was my teacher a long time ago."

A curious look creeps across Osiris' face. "And dual alliances can account for her serving Prince Vali and Octavia?"

"I cannot speak of things I know nothing about, Highness." *He is trying to trap me; foolish boy.* "She has paid for her crimes. We must be thankful the balance has been restored, and the guilty will soon be revealed. Highness, there is a subject I meant to enlighten you with."

"It's hardly the time for school, wouldn't you agree?"

"This bit of education will rock the very foundation of the Forefathers themselves – all for the better. You will come to see, after I place the facts before you."

"Ahhhhh." Osiris nods. "Any topic breaching the realm of the Forefathers is one knocking on the doors of blasphemy. Besides, religion is not my strong suit."

"My Prince, this is where I beg your indulgence, and at the risk of incriminating myself in the turbulent affair, my aim is partially to restore Aspasia's good name." Osiris remains silent. Samiri looks up at the corpse with a respectful gaze, masking his cunning trickery.

"Highness, you must first understand I bear witness only to what I know. Aspasia's actions brought on her own demise. Yet her intentions were genuine in her aim to rescue Persephone. I too was on that road, although separate from hers. She learned of a terrible truth, most of which was not imparted to me. I did make a request to Lord Thoth on her behalf, requesting asylum. First, tell me, do you harbor affections for the Princess?"

Osiris' blushes at the candid question. "What? That is very bold of you, Samiri."

"Please, Highness, indulge me in the presence of the Creator and the dead; I am trying to help you, and Persephone."

"Alright…" Osiris shakes his head, embarrassed in the admission he's about to make." Ever since childhood, she has been a mean spoiled brat; a pain in my ass. Rude, obnoxious; thinks the world should love her just because she's Persephone."

"And now?"

"Now? Now… she is waking up to the realities of the world. Something she should have done a long time ago. When I look at her, I feel…" Fear of the truth creeps up his spine. "Respect."

"Yes. The shroud over her eyes has been lifted. The blinding shield is no longer held by those conspiring to an evil end. Your aversion to one another is nothing but the result of an unnourished hunger. Search your soul, Osiris…see the connection you share."

He shakes his head. "Even if I liked her, we're forbidden to pursue any formal relationship."

"This is the rock which shall bring down the fallacy the forefathers built."

"How does anything you're saying help Persephone? Spare me the riddles, Samiri!"

"Information has come to light, verifiable by the Queen and record-keepers alike. Swear you will keep this secret." Samiri stops his forage for kindling.

"I'm not sure I want to hear this."

"You must," Samiri pleads. "or I fear the world will change overnight – making a quick descent into oblivion."

Osiris shakes his head. "Alright...I swear it."

"Persephone carries both bloodlines of ENlil and ENki. Made so by conspiring forces before her birth."

Osiris rocks back in disbelief. His eyes cringe at the blasphemy, the outrage, the violation. Sadness replaces the storm.

Samiri's plight shows on his face. His desperate gaze begs to be believed. "According to the law, she is an abomination, doomed - not of either House, but potentially of both. Have you ever wondered why others bearing this stain have met their demise?"

Osiris' anger glows in his eyes. "This is impossible. Do you even know what you suggest, Watcher?"

"Casual joining of the bloodlines through procreation alone is not enough to bridge the divide. Insurance devised by the forefathers, so the accused never survives trial. An effective means to keep the status quo."

"The King will not condemn his own daughter...his heir."

"This is why you must protect the secret, and her. Consolidation of power rests in her reign. She may never see that power if determined forces forge a claim through a union. It may have been their plan all along to expose the Princess' forced heritage."

Clarity washes over Osiris. "And the conspirators shall make themselves known in efforts to facilitate a union."

Samiri nods. "Now, you understand."

"What can we do?"

Samiri lets a smirk slip. "Seek the counsel of the Amon-I, through your brother. You are the heir to House ENki - in line to become Regent over all banners of both Houses. Command him...he must comply." His smirk turns into a smile. "I will help you. The council convenes tomorrow. You must act before it is too late."

Osiris ignites a long branch in the crackling flame. He nods with respect, prompting Samiri to climb the pyre to offer his last words.

Aspasia's body lies in wait for her send off to the Hereafter. Her hands are crossed on her chest, and thin vines bind her legs tight.

Samiri draws close for a whisper. "Your death and that of our son will not go unpunished. As I still draw breath my promise to you shall extend beyond this life and into the next. The seed is planted, and bloom it must. We shall wade in the ashes of the Anuk when they destroy themselves. Sleep Aspasia, sleep my son. Into the Creator's hands, I commit your souls for divine protection. Travel now into the dark and be resurrected with those held in esteem. Goodbye, trusted Watcher...your service is remembered."

Chapter 20: To the End of Things – How Quickly It Comes.

An unusual cold season has gripped Hyperboria. Ice forms quick on the giant window panes, around the royal palace's central kitchen. This is the largest of 12 such kitchens spread around the complex, similar in build, and identical in tyranny.

Giant furnaces are ablaze with fire, pushing heat to generous compartments above it and out the sides. Metal shelves stacked above one another hold platters of raw-dishes in wait of the oven. Trolleys travel around the room; hurried feet push with determination. Seven cooks converse with others in an adjacent room about their extra frustration today.

Everyone flutters about in food-stained uniforms, busy mixing, packing, and complaining about conditions. On an average day, the atmosphere is playful and full of innocent mischief. Not today. The head chef is irate with a bumbling crew, working hard to finish a lavish spread of cheese and bread, complemented by scrumptious pastries. "Quick, quick, quick!" he screams at the fools. His white chef jacket is bursting at the midriff; his angry hands fire off over his head with insults targeted at deserving victims.

Chatter goes quiet in an instant. The chef's demeanor changes from kitchen tyrant to obedient slave. Prince Vali strolls in a magnanimous way, toward the group charged with Queen Farah's platter of deserts. He wears a cape today – waist length and matching his tight black clothing. His finger runs along a counter, searching for accumulating dust and filth daring to warrant an outburst.

He studies Chef's worried look, infecting his posture. "You." Vali points to the chef. "Come here."

"Highness." The chef steps forward cautiously with his head lowered.

"Why hasn't her Majesty's request been delivered? Don't speak, it was rhetorical. I'll tell you why." He makes a broad gesture at the silent cooks locked in reverent stare at the floor tiles. "You are a collection of buffoonery, charged with simple tasks beyond your comprehension! You forget you are slaves, not revelers at a party. Do your jobs or I'll have you whipped!"

Vali dismisses the group to their affairs. He strolls out like a king, smiling at the seeds of fear he planted. *My servants shall learn manners.* He exits the kitchen at the opposite end, pushing through a high door with a scowl. *It appears manners are severely lacking throughout.* His hand shakes off imaginary grime.

A contingent of soldiers meets him in the wing's foyer. Octavia strolls up from the rear. "Vali, is it vital to have me escorted like a commoner? And how do you people bare this cold?"

"Do shut up, Octavia, for your own good. What do you want?"

"Thoth is here. He is on his way to see Farah!"

"Keep your voice down," Vali whispers. "You forget where we are?" He pulls her to a windy balcony, much to her dismay. "All of you, leave us."

"She may be crazy as a baboon, but Thoth is no fool. While you were inspecting the kitchen as if you own the place, our doom was being knitted in the bosom of your-"

"Now now, dear Octavia... you're coming undone. Insist you remain with our demented Queen for her protection and comfort. Thoth may simply be bringing unfortunate news of Shuru's demise – he has not been seen for a week, has he? The council meets in three hours. Farah will agree to the union, no matter who talks to her."

"And me?" Desperation shows in Octavia's eyes. "Persephone remains under Odin's watchful eyes. What happens when she implicates me?"

"Where is the necklace I gave you?"

Octavia gives him a confused look. His pleading smile convinces her to peel back her coat to reveal the oval gift hanging around her neck.

Vali pulls the pendant close along with Octavia. He flips the flat back to face his lips. "Remember our childish promise? A gesture of our bond and fulfillment of affairs?" He presses his lips on the stone, afterward pulling back with eyes fixed on the moistened surface. "Now your turn."

Octavia renders her kiss on the front. She pulls her coat tight as a palace guard approaches. "Every time one of them comes I feel as if it's for my soul."

Vali's eyes remains fixed on Octavia. "What is it, guardsman?"

"Lord Thoth demands an audience with your Highness in the Queen's chambers."

"Very well. Princess Octavia will greet him. Tell the Keeper I will be in Counsel with his father. Now, go away." He pulls Octavia close, leaving an intimate space between them. "Play your part and this shall be over in three hours."

Persephone sits in her vast chamber, surrounded by a plethora of childish things. Her empty gaze on meaningless trinkets incites a weighty feeling of loss bearing down on her chest. An untouched food platter catches her gaze – a cup of wine still filled to the brim invites her need for escape. She ignores it in favor of her toy bunny. She sniffs the coat in her usual way. The doors open but her adoration for the rabbit does not stop.

"You still have that stupid thing?" Osiris' voice calls out. He strolls on to a flight of descending stairs from the entrance, with Samiri following several paces behind. Peki slips in after to lock the door.

Persephone's heart leaps out. The dam holding back a flood of tears breaks. She rushes to the Prince, wraps her arms around him and breaks down into uncontrollable weeping.

It is uncomfortable at first, holding the girl whom he considered an irrefutable menace. He feels her tight embrace constricting, pleading for understanding of her vast sorrow unable to be subdued. His arms match her squeeze, and without thinking he presses his lips on her forehead, delivering a kiss full of genuine emotion.

Her shaking body settles. Her sobs trail off into unabashed awareness. She gazes deep into his eyes with an acceptance of a new-found affection buzzing within. *You're the only one left of my childhood friends. If you leave me now, I'll break beyond repair.* Realization of her uncomfortable thoughts force her eyes to drift away, yet his touch electrifies her skin into awkward yearning.

Samiri steps closer. Before he utters a word, Persephone hugs him tight. "Thank the Creator you are safe. I fear danger is still lurking."

"Peki," Osiris says. "We're going to my brother's temple. Refer all inquiries for the princess to my father. No one must know that she has left the palace."

"Of course, Highness." Peki shuffles off to a communications panel to converse with the guards outside.

"Why are we going to the temple?" Persephone asks. She allows Osiris to take her hand. His touch brings back the tingles under her fingers she first felt in the muddy Aryan village.

"There's someone you need to see," Osiris whispers.

Samiri nods his agreement. "I'll remain here. There are things I need to discuss with Lord Thoth."

Osiris leads Persephone to her bedchamber. He closes the door without a word of protest from her. "I believe you know what this is?" From his pocket, he brings forth a thin coil of dark silk. He wraps the fabric around both their arms, smiling at her wide-eyed gaze.

"Adonis," she says with excitement in her voice. The creature lights up to a familiar brilliance. "How?"

"Samiri re-calibrated it to work within five miles of any clean portal. Lucky the Keeper's temple is not far. Now, you know what to do."

They close their eyes. A stream of light swarms around their bodies. A serpentine coil wraps them in fluorescent blue brilliance. It brightens the moment the air goes heavy. The space in front and behind collapses into a vortex of black. In an instant, they disappear.

The drumming of boots marching along polished stone approach Queen Farah's chambers with rapid precision. Six armed guards lead the march with Lord Thoth following close. Samiri inches around a corner with care not to upset Prince Vali's soldiers. He raises a cautious hand to catch Thoth's eye, then slides back on his wall when Thoth breaks off from the escort.

"Samiri, I received your note. What is the status?" Thoth turns his back to the waiting soldiers' steely gaze.

"I'm afraid the Watcher Aspasia, and her offspring are dead." He swallows hard, trying to contain his anguish. "A full report shall be presented to you at a more convenient time; however, I assure you matters are linked by a common thread of deceit. I wish to stress the need for privacy during your interrogation of the Queen."

"This is not an interrogation. It is an inquiry about events and solidifying culpability with the tribesmen." He keeps his demeanor as neutral as possible.

"My Lord, the tribesmen are but pawns in a much larger ploy. You see it; you feel it."

Thoth breathes silent relief. *It doesn't matter if he is a part of this, I need him.* "Knowing who to trust has been daunting. Come with me."

A ripple reverberates through Samiri's heart. His words of gratitude fail to escape trembling lips. Elation overcomes him, but not for the trust Thoth affords him. Instead, it belongs to the shortening journey to the elusive Amon-I. He hurries behind his Anuk Lord.

Thoth enters Queen Farah's chambers with a cold gaze and a sour mood. His composure remains respectful with a smile for Princess Octavia. He fakes warm affection at her embrace. Farah sits on a comfortable chair to a far end, facing a veranda overlooking majestic mountains.

"Nephew, it is good you are here during these troubling times, but is it necessary to have a 'Doh-fan-ae' present?" She steps back to regard Samiri with a sharp stare. "This is a private family affair. If word got out, the scandal would be outrageous."

Thoth keeps his eyes fixed on Farah. He waves Samiri towards the Queen, then returns his attention to Octavia's outrage. "Watchers aren't in the business of gossip, Thia. As for scandal, I'm afraid the world already knows of unfolding events. In case you did not know, the Primaries from all the Greater and Lower Houses shall be in assembly today."

"How gracious of them to show their support." Octavia smiles bordering on sarcasm. "And where is the King?"

"As you know King Shuru was at death's door. This is a matter I will speak with Her Grace about in absolute privacy. No exceptions."

"I will not leave her side." Octavia edges toward the Queen. "She has been through enough, poor dove. Look at her; she can't even keep a straight thought together." *Shuru is dead, has to be. I must inform Vali.*

They gather around Farah. Samiri attempts to move away but is held in place by Thoth's steady hand. "Faithful Samiri, I require your indulgence in prayer for our Queen."

"My Lord, I offer it willingly."

"What foolishness is this? Explain yourself." Octavia blocks their path.

"Thia, it is a simple Anuk prayer I am certain you are familiar with. One to seek a calm return of Her Grace's faculties; you do understand, don't you? Trust me, I will ask questions afterward, but first, let us pay our respects."

Octavia slides out of their path. She strains her memory to recall any such occurrence, then remembers prayer is sometimes offered for those in mourning. Relief washes over her. She removes herself to a nearby seat next to a vibrant fountain. *So Shuru is dead.* She gets lost in her thoughts of her days spent with the promiscuous monarch. The falling water captures her attention. *I need one of these.* She removes herself in search of a communications panel.

With a firm yet respectful grip, Thoth situates Farah near a darkened corner. He leans over to whisper to Samiri. "Clear your mind. I am about to draw on your strength, adding to mine to breach Her Grace's soul. Once inside, all you hear and experience must be held in secrecy. Do you understand?"

"I am bound by it. How is this possible my Lord?"

Thoth opens his palm to reveal a red ruby-like gem. It dazzles Samiri's eyes, forcing him to look deep into the lighted center. His heart plunges with immediate reverence. "Is this…the Amon-I?"

"No." Thoth clasps his hand quickly to keep from inviting Octavia's prying eyes. "It draws power from the Amon-I. It is a conduit you can say."

"Is it close?" Samiri realizes his enthusiasm is threatening to undermine his true intentions. He swallows hard to combat irresistible questions from betraying him. "I mean only to understand, Lord."

"It is, yet beyond the reach of the unworthy. Come now, Samiri, clear your mind."

They sit on the ground around Farah with eyes closed and hands on their thighs. Samiri is silent, eager to feel the rapture he has yearned to experience for so long. Thoughts of Aspasia, his son, conspiracies new and old, swarm in a violent storm inside his mind. He inhales deeply, clearing each thought as if it were a block of wood on a sturdy table. He exhales, letting the tension from his body flow out through his toes. By the next breath, an invisible force grips his being into a frightening funnel of black.

A torturous feeling grips him, like falling into the unknown; he is overcome with fear. Indiscernible surfaces are foreboding, shooting upwards at speeds he dare not contemplate. An abrupt end to his fall appears miles below. He calls on all his training to reconcile his mind's interpretation of what he feels, against what is occurring. Relief calms him, yet it is short-lived. Cold air envelops his senses. Every fiber explodes in orgasmic euphoria, electrifying the very essence of his soul. His feet touchdown on a gray metallic surface without injury; Thoth appears in a shimmer next to him, alongside Farah.

"Don't be afraid," Thoth whispers. "Deep controlled breaths. Keep your focus on the here and now."

"Master, where are we?" Samiri's pride falls away. His longing for things he could not understand dissipates in the fog that lives in the world he left. *I called him Master.*

"We are in the realm of the soul, crafted in haste to contain our essence, or a mere sliver of it." He looks over at Farah. "Majesty, are you alright?"

Farah locks on to Thoth's hand. Her fear of the circular environment disappears. Her face fills with plight, "Shuru...where is the King?"

Thoth nods. "He is safe. The Princess will be with him shortly."

"Surely Samiri relayed some of the conspiracies."

"He has alerted me to it, yes."

Samiri regains some lost anxiety. His memory flashes to the data tube the Queen imparted to him for delivery. He focuses on the same tube he later left for the Keeper, containing a vital request on Aspasia's behalf. Fear creeps in for the unknown capabilities Thoth has in this enclosure. *Can he read my thoughts?*

"Look at me, my Queen. Pour out your thoughts into mine. Relinquish control. Allow me to peer through your soul."

Farah hesitates, pulling back with fear in her eyes and sorrow in her voice. "Thoth, you must understand, you must forgive. I can't..."

"You must," Thoth says. "Time is precious. We must proceed for the sake of all."

She nods with a slight aversion to what will be revealed. Her thoughts dwell on Persephone. It begins with a single memory – the image of Persephone as an innocent child, then Farah's memories are seized. She feels the burden of her time spent with Vali, at his medical facilities in Illyria. A thin stream of images pours out in front of her, displaying her hand in the tragedy inflicted upon Shuru's consorts, marital betrayals, Vali's threats; the images solidify into a bright floating orb.

Thoth clasps the small ball. He closes his eyes, feeling the sting of energy coursing through his veins. His eyes roll back to show the whites. Samiri drops hard, with a sudden sickness overcoming him as if drained of life.

As suddenly as it started, Thoth's episode ends. He folds over at the waist and grabs on to weak knees. He fires a sharp gaze on Farah. "Persephone?" he asks with a mask of curiosity.

She nods with embarrassment.

He straightens up. His hands tightens, jaw clenches, facial muscles go tense. "Abomination," he growls. "This changes everything."

Farah drops on her knees, holds out her hands in plight, trembling with tears. "Shuru was desperate for an heir. I was unaware of Vali's sinister motives. The use of the Forefathers' to achieve the pregnancy was not known to me until after she was born. Please…spare her…she is innocent."

Thoth grips her with firm hands. She weeps in his arms without fear of judgment or consequences.

"Majesty, I am bound to take action. I am sorry, I do not have a choice."

"Then may Shuru sway your blind cruelty." Farah resumes a regal pose. "The deception ends then. May the Creator's will be done."

"My Lord, Majesty," Samiri interrupts. "With regards to the conspirators, is it wise to move on such powerful members of the aristocracies without a plan? The tribesmen are in custody, the culprits are known. What gains shall be realized without solid evidence to bring accusations?"

"Villainy," Farah yells. "I want the rabid creatures to tumble for all to see."

Thoth resumes his calm demeanor. "Villainy it is. We must go. In less than three hours it will all be over." He nods to Samiri and Farah.

Faster than the rush of conscious thought, the supernatural world disappears. Samiri opens his eyes to see Thoth staring at him. Farah resumes her royal demeanor. "How long were we gone?"

"Thirty seconds, or less." Thoth helps the Queen to her feet. He whispers something in her ear before looking Octavia's way. "Thia!"

Octavia ends her daydreaming at the fountain. She huffs on her way to the group. "Done already? Is that all the praying you need?"

No one answers her.

"Well, what are your questions?" She notices Farah's intense stare. A bead of sweat forms on her brow. Her skin becomes flush with heat rushing through her guilty soul. "What trickery is this?"

Farah pushes past her and heads for a communications panel. "Guards!" Within seconds, Octavia's armed troopers rush in. "Restrain Princess Octavia and secure her in the dungeon…the lowest one."

"You can't do that! I am your regent!" Octavia's protests fall on deaf ears. The soldiers grab her with force.

"I am their Queen," Farah says with an uncaring look on her face.

Lord Thoth's assistant, the young Watcher Amaya, stands quietly in the corner of a hidden chamber, deep below the Keeper's Temple. She keeps vigil at a panel where Persephone's Adonis recharges itself. The curious creature slithers inside a fixed space of light, moving in a docile motion.

Across the room near a roaring fire, King Shuru holds Persephone and Osiris in a tight embrace. A minute has passed, and the hug is becoming uncomfortable.

Shuru has not regained his full strength, and his thoughts are still wandering. Amaya informed them his faculties will return, but his mind is in a delicate state of repair.

"Papa," Persephone whispers. She pushes his hand away.

"Daughter, Osiris…always getting into mischief. What have you done now?"

Osiris puts his hand on the king's shoulder. "Uncle, focus."

Persephone nudges the happy King to his chair. "You and mother are safe. That's all that matters."

"My little bird is out of her cage?" Shuru's eyes open wide to match his brilliant smile and drunken demeanor.

She grimaces at him. "That's his pet name for mother – his 'Little-bird.' He's her 'Shaggy-bird.'" She drops her head in despair. "She's faking it, and he's really crazy."

"Throw you in, and it's a riot." Osiris' joke wins him a nasty sneer from Persephone.

She softens her glare. "No matter how rotten I think you are…you're still alright."

He smiles back. "No matter how much of a brat I know you are…you impress me." His face sours in disbelief for the words spewing out. *What is wrong with me?*

Amaya brings a cup of steaming tea. "Drink, Majesty. This will have you right in moments." She lets Persephone help her father drink the mixture of herbs, wine, and a drop of extract from a sacred plant.

Intoxicating steam drums up a calm euphoria, filled with a mist of fragrant tropical flowers caught under gentle raindrops. Osiris' catches the disturbing scent. He stops Amaya's exit with a concerned hand grasping her arm. "Is it safe? I smell Lotai."

"Of course, Highness. His Majesty will sleep for a few minutes. When he wakes, his mind will be intact." She quietly retreats to her previous station.

"When papa wakes, what happens next?"

Discomfort creeps into Osiris. A glance at Amaya conjures thoughts of Aspasia's burning pyre. He begins a slow, thoughtful pace behind the King. "'Sephie, I learned an awful truth, one I am struggling to believe."

"He's asleep," Persephone says to Amaya. Her heart leaps into rapid thunder. "I can't, Osiris. I can't handle anymore. Papa will wake shortly; we will tell him of Vali and Octavia's treachery. Mother is safe…" Her voice trails off to a precipice of tears. "Koray…"

Osiris' rough hands caress her face. He lifts her chin to bring her eyes to his. "Did you know?" His face begs for an answer. "Is it true…you carry the bloodline of ENlil and ENki?"

Her face cringes with horror. Her stomach plunges into a dark void. Everything goes numb. "That's impossible. Where did you hear this?" The powerful memory of the forefathers holding her hand dispels her anxiety. Her expression keeps its worried appearance, embolden by disbelief, fighting off a ringing truth.

Osiris grips her trembling shoulders. "If it is true, no one can find out, understand? Remember what happens to any who claim such union, or is afflicted by it...trial, abomination."

Persephone's reddening face tells Osiris all he needs to know. He holds her tight, as her tears erupt. His stomach plunges, sending his feelings spiraling down with hers. Their silent sobs block out sounds of hurried footsteps rushing towards them.

Lord Thoth's rigid expression screams his thoughts.

Osiris faces him. "You can't. Not after everything. Brother, please, I command you to let this be!"

"My hands are tied, Osiris. I am bound to a greater task, beyond ties of blood or affection." Thoth slides over to Shuru. He drops close to the King's forehead with his red gem. Within moments a joining light bursts over both bodies.

Persephone hangs on to Osiris hard, fearing the conversation transpiring in celestial silence, knowing her fate is set. Her heart leaps when the shimmer above the Keeper vanishes.

Shuru locks eyes with Persephone. His face crumples into a mess of despair. Thoth helps him over, to gaze upon his frightened daughter. "I am sorry, my child." He forces out his trembling lips and breaking heart. "I renounce the world, and give it in trade for your life."

Still holding on to Osiris, she looks at Thoth seeking validity to the offer - he very subtly shakes his head and looks at her with sad eyes. She rolls on her father and breaks down with hopelessness in her soul.

Chapter 21: The Loss of Everything

Noise and clamor infect the majestic gathering hall of the Royal Council. Each sitting Primary of the Great and Lower Houses are present - a first in almost six-thousand-years. Old rivalries erupt, tempers flare; an Aryan street market has a better display of decorum than this collection of rulers who claim dominion over the world.

Chief among the agitators are Prince Vali and his older brother Atlas. They stand together near the King's center seat, spewing insults at their opposition's wretched accusations. Two rings of a bell subdue the tempest, if only for a moment. The heavy chamber doors swing open, allowing Prince Odin to stride in amongst the chaos. Raised voices erupt once more.

"Silence!" Odin shouts on a device; his order booms in a thunderous wave. The members reduce themselves to compliant listeners. "You're a collection of children!" Odin calls for the traditional supplication to the Creator to sanctify the proceedings.

Vali leans over to Atlas to whisper, "Where is Octavia?"

"I thought you knew," Atlas whispers back. "Farah had her arrested."

Sourness shrouds Vali's face. He discreetly reaches for a device in his pocket. With a heavy heart, he initiates a silent command. He stares at the floor pretending to be in humble observance of Anuk ceremony, but his despondent voice within cries out for mercy.

He imagines the catastrophic destruction of Octavia's office in Corinth. *The lovely servant boy, a real tragedy.* He grimaces, knowing Octavia will succumb to a lethal dose of poison from the Lotai, administered in a thin mist via his charming gift around her neck. He cranes his neck towards Odin as the prayer finishes.

He collects his wailing thoughts and offers the Regent a cocky grin. "Prince Odin, I must protest the secrecy you have allotted for yourself in matters which affect us all. And where is the Princess?"

"Yes, dear cousin," Odin says with accusation heavy in his voice. "Where indeed. She is broken, tormented, alone."

Prince Atlas pushes himself in front of Vali. "If it weren't for my brother's valor, she would be in the bed of a tribesman!" The floor erupts in outrage, yet showing solidarity for Vali.

Vali calms the crowd with outstretched hands. "Cousins, respected Lords and Ladies, please give the chair a moment to receive my address." All eyes fall on him. "As you are aware, I have loved and cherished our dear Persephone since her first breath. We share an inseparable bond, made strong over the years through difficult and trying times. From the tragedies at Persepolis to this nightmare, she has always looked to me for comfort and guidance. I will reach across the realms to keep her safe, as exemplified in this recent affair. Because of this! Because of this…King Shuru extends his blessings, as delivered by Queen Farah, for my union by marriage with Princess Persephone."

Widespread outrage erupts again, with voices roaring over each other. The bell rings twice; the doors open. The gathering goes quiet.

Vali gestures to the entrance. "Here is Her Majesty now, to bestow warm blessings."

Farah remains stationary at the doors. She sends a smile Vali's way, but she does not move. A single bell rings out; everyone gasps, holding in an imaginary breath.

The chambers are quiet. Everyone peers past the Queen to reconcile the single bell with a recipient. Hearts race, waiting for a figure to give a face to the patter of feet. The crowd bows with humility; Vali chokes as his head lowers.

Shuru and Farah stride into the center, hand in hand. Shuru waits for Farah to take her seat next to Odin. He glares at the gathering in the manner of a parent about to render harsh discipline to the wayward children. The moment he sits the crowd slides silently into their respective chairs.

"Prince Vali!" the King yells with divine authority. Vali steps forward with reluctance. He remains silent, staring at Shuru, waiting for praise or punishment.

"You have been instrumental in the events preceding this momentous gathering." Shuru's delightful grin breaks Vali's tense poise. "The Queen informs me if it weren't for you, she would be in the vile clutches of Octavia, a known criminal in this tragedy. If it weren't for you, the Tribesmen would not be in custody. If it weren't for you, my heir would…" He pauses to recoil from the sting entering his heart. "Well, Persephone waits at the Temple for her occasion to join the ranks of legends."

Shuru steps off his platform cautiously, reminded of his weakened state. He gestures Vali to drop on his knees.

The Prince complies with an expecting heart and joyous fervor.

"Prince Vali of ENlil, Primary of House ENlil and all banners in the bloodline, I hereby strip you of your titles, all lands under your domain, the military under your control, and the safety of Hyperboria!"

The gathering gasps silently.

Vali's soul shatters into dust. Invisible hands grasp his throat with murderous strength, wrenching his thoughts into despair. He dares not look at His Majesty. He remains on the ground trembling, waiting for the guillotine to drop.

"Prince Atlas!"

Without delay, Atlas drops next to his brother with fear showing through his face. "Henceforth you shall inherit all titles and responsibilities of Primary for House ENlil. You are innocent in this affair, thus spared of the stain it brings. The law prevents me from punishing Vali in the manner he deserves, and in the wretched fashion I desire. You are bound by the law and your oath to Hyperboria; therefore, I commit Vali to you for sentencing. I urge you to make it a quick one. Get him out of my sight!"

Guards rush in and drag Vali away with as much respect they would afford a common criminal. Shuru returns to his seat. The council is still silent, afraid to get caught in a whisper. Shuru keeps his stern gaze fixed on the gathering.

"All lands, wealth and concerns held by Princess Octavia of ENki, shall be bestowed on Prince Osiris of ENki. Upon his union, he shall inherit all the lands of pTah, irrespective of which House it belongs to; compensation to aggrieved parties shall be made.

"Markus, former General of House ENki, will inherit all Aryan lands bordering those of House Moira of ENlil, up to 100-miles past the 'Mount of Mercy.' He shall be known as the 'Protector of the Princess' and Regent of Persepolis in her stead.

He is reinstated as a General of Hyperboria and my personal military adviser.

"The Watcher's counsel shall be dismantled. The 'Doh-fan-ae' Samiri, will be chief adviser for all matters previously held by the council. He will be the sole instrument of Lord Thoth for the affairs of the 'Keeper-of-Forbidden-Knowledge' and Hyperboria. This is my will, so recorded for judgment by the Creator. May my rulings find favor with the forefathers upon their return."

Shuru looks at Odin, softening his gaze to the point of tears. His eyes drift over to Farah. They glaze over, screaming desperately for his baby.

Chapter 22: Trial of the Innocent

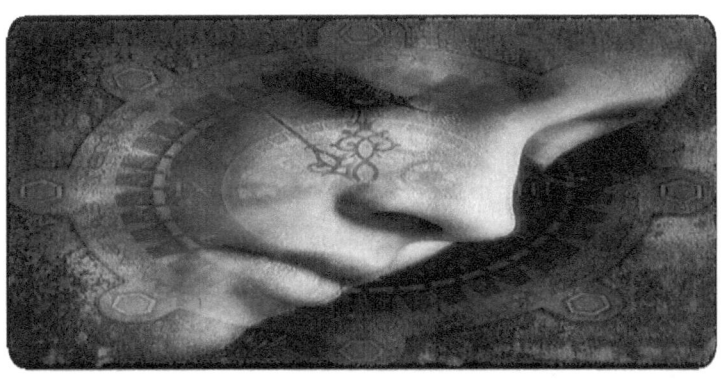

Fire urns flicker with subdued brilliance in the halls of the Keeper's temple. 'Doh-fan-ae' assigned to witness Persephone's trial make their way to the catacombs in silence. Samiri leads the slow procession of 12 robed Watchers. His face projects utter despair, eyes slightly glazed, hands placed one over the other inside wide brown sleeves. His heart races with delight for the victory within his grasp. *I am the supreme Watcher. The Amon-I...the Amon-I. Soon I shall know your secrets.*

Stone stairs wind down to an ancient chamber lit with brilliant torches, each held to the wall with an archaic sconce. High vaulted ceilings match black granite floors shining with a sporadic dusting of silver particulates ingrained into the materials. At the furthest end, a gathering of seven stands in solidarity for Princess Persephone.

General Markus, still in his rugged attire, towers over a heartbroken Peki. Prince Odin stares at the polished floor in silence. King Shuru struggles to contain his emotion next to a stoic Lord Thoth. Prince Osiris props his head on a wall with his back turned to the group. Queen Farah is slumped on the floor, locked in an emotional embrace with her daughter. Samiri ends his chain of Watchers behind Markus.

Osiris looks at Persephone. The tears streaming on her mother's bosom tug at his heart: her soft cries rob her of steady breath, yet assaults his ears..

Female Watchers lift the Princess with strong hands. She inhales deep, accepting her fate. One Watcher removes Persephone's boots, another removes clothing. Any embarrassment for her nakedness is stifled with thoughts of Koray. A line of tears run down her bruised skin, collecting at an open wound on her side. Her shame is covered in a thick gown similar to Thoth's.

The display of her abuse, old and new, floods the minds of all present. Markus drops his head into his hands, feeling his heart burst with thoughts of his daughter.

Samiri takes his position next to Thoth, behind Persephone. His breaths run shallow; tongue numbs at the tip. Toes curl inside boots with increased anticipation for the addictive nirvana he felt from the Amon-I's power. His eagerness is rewarded with the presentation of the red-gem in his hands.

"This is the key to the Amon-I," Thoth says. "Hold it close, for it shall drain you. If you release it without me, you shall die."

Samiri cocks his head. "I'm not going, my Lord?"

"No," Thoth says, devoid of emotion.

The dismissal stings. Samiri struggles with rage gnawing inside. A deep inhale calms him. *Patience. The road is long, but it ends.* "I am here to serve my Lord."

Osiris' blood boils over. "You're condemning her to death!"

He marches to Thoth, stopping face to face, an inch apart. His nostrils flare, fists clench into a ball, muscles tense in wait for the Keeper's response. Welled up tears roll down his clenched jaw. Then, he notices the wet reflection of flames dancing on Thoth's tear-glazed eyes.

Thoth grabs Osiris' tunic and forces him on the ground. "You think I want this?!" He drops to meet his brother's gaze. His face crumples with profound sadness. "The universe is cruel, little brother. I am bound to carry out the law. If I do not, what sort of Keeper shall I be? If she does not survive, her death is on my soul. If she does not endure this, she will lose everything."

Soft, warm hands roll over Osiris' shoulders. Persephone looks into his eyes, then at Thoth's. She caresses the Keeper's face, offering a forgiving smile in place of words. She receives a kiss in her palm.

Her attention returns to the emotional Osiris with a whisper. "My sweet friend. I would reach the stars with you if I could. Each moment has brought me to a singular reality. A truth long ignored. A secret never spoken. My heart bursts with its joy for I know it is shared. Stay strong like our sister, stay strong for me."

Persephone presses her trembling lips to Osiris'. They are lost in a forbidden moment, locked in an eternal fever. Time loses meaning in the passionate goodbye kiss.

"I have only now. Remember me, Osiris. I love you."

Her words cut deep into his resolve. Before he utters a reply, Watchers pull her away. "No, not yet." He strains against them. "Give her more time!" His words fall on deaf ears. His father's arms pull him into a tight formation with Shuru and Farah. "'Sephie, I love you! I love you!"

Thoth clasps Samiri's small hands and begins a low chant. His voice reverberates through all present, rumbling in thick tones given form by a fast-moving energy wave. Faster and faster he chants. With each syllable, the wave strikes out into open space. At the height of the rising crescendo, a thin blue field of light strikes down on the granite floor. Samiri's body is encapsulated in a red-light field. Thoth releases Samiri. He takes Persephone's hand, leading her into the stream.

Swarms of blinding light attack Persephone and Thoth in a void of black. Their bodies are clothed in strange dark fabrics with glowing bands around the collar. The assault ends. The soles of their feet touch soft, yet solid formations, like walking on a cloud. Two rows of dotted lights ignite on a path towards a brilliant tumbling sphere. Loud slicing sounds emanate on either side, stirring up images of a guillotine - sharpening its blades for a willing victim. They begin the short walk to the path's end.

"I cannot go with you," says Thoth. He squeezes Persephone's trembling hands. "Do not be afraid, for death is not the end."

She casts a defeated look on her destination. "Is that where I must go?"

Thoth hesitates with a deep breath. He stares into her eyes. "At the end of the journey await the Forefathers, their souls. You are Anuk, Persephone, which equips you to traverse this plane. Hold strong on the way there. Stay strong."

"What will it be like?" she whispers.

"Your body will be torn into pieces, your mind fractured. Phantoms will promise relief, and relief it is. An eternal one."

"I'm afraid." She turns away from the sphere. Nausea seeps into her stomach. "Thoth, must this be?"

"All who have gone in perish within moments, for their blood is not strong. Their connection to the Forefathers is frail in its makeup. You have the raw genes of ENlil and ENki themselves, making you better equipped to survive."

A terrible shudder overcomes Persephone. "Are they gods?"

"No. The Amon-I was created on their world, connected to them through their own unique bloodline. When you make it, and I pray you do, they will judge you."

For the first time since learning of her fate, she feels a spark of hope enter her soul. She kisses Thoth's hand. "Protect our family." She takes a deep breath, then jumps into the light.

Intense hues of green spark fire off in a wild frenzy inside the void. Invisible hands grip Persephone's body with fingers, ripping her flesh. Low droning sounds turn into high pitched whirling phantoms; as promised, each tease at instant relief. Smoke condenses into long malicious tentacles, reaching for her body, coiling in a slow, foreboding fashion, caressing flesh as they constrict.

Her body shoots off in a rapid descent. Walls of blue fire stream close, searing flesh on contact. Her eyes burn, bones threaten to shatter from the pressure. Nerve endings explode with unforgivable pain. Still falling, she pierces the rushing void. Hot air whips across exposed flesh.

Phantoms hover near her bleeding chest. Chunks fly off with crimson droplets following. Bones give in to pressure, snapping, crunching. She cries out in her mind for it to end. An apparition answers the call. It seduces her with a soothing touch, gliding close with a promise of rest, relief. *No! I cannot.*

She relaxes her mind, forgetting the pain, the torment. Blaring sounds fall off to a faint whistle. Thoughts of mangled body parts dissipate with imagined breaths escaping her bruised mouth. The phantom's embrace is gone. Warm light touches new skin with delicate regard. Fear disappears. Cooling relief of the present washes over her. Slow at first, her eyes open to incredible brightness.

Surrounding light softens to a manageable level. Her bare feet touch a solid white floor. She looks at her body, marveling at the renewed flesh dressed in an off-white gown. The air is cold, yet pleasing. A prominent lavender scent circulates in the air. Ahead is a semi-circular platform, raised three feet off the ground. Seven bodies sit in Congress, each behind an identifying symbol; she smiles.

From the left sits Dragoi, Odin, Shiva, Sakhmet, Xi-Wang-Mu, ENki, and ENlil. Persephone drops on her knees and bows with reverence. Her anxious heart thumps hard against her ribs, fueling a paralyzing fear manifesting in her trembling limbs. She squeezes her eyes shut, forcing her mind to clear curious thoughts about the faces she does not recognize. *Will they condemn me?*

"Rise, child," Lord Shiva commands. "Why are you here? Why do you disturb our rest?"

Persephone keeps her eyes shut as she rises in a slow, non-threatening manner.

Lord Sakhmet's strong female voice echoes, "I do not recognize this one."

Lord Dragoi asks Lord Xi, "Is she one of yours?" She confirms her ignorance in unison with Lord Odin.

A familiar voice soothes Persephone's fears. "She is of my brother and me," says Lord ENlil.

Persephone musters up building courage to open her eyes and gaze upon those not seen in 33,000 years.

Lord Dragoi is built with fierce muscles befitting warriors worthy of battling mythical creatures. Pale skin and long shaggy blonde hair match his short beard and square face. Lord Odin is similar in appearance, but leaner with short dark hair and olive skin. Lord Shiva is less intimidating with a softer body, light brown skin and long black hair tied in a neat ponytail. Lord Sekhmet has piercing hazel eyes that appear haunting with her vibrant dark skin and well-shaped body. Lord Xi's dark brown hair is long and flowing, matching her light-beige complexion. Lord ENlil and ENki resemble Dragoi, with ENki wearing a deep tan.

Persephone's heart leaps out of her chest. Words form but cannot be expressed. ENlil's questioning gaze prompts her to stop fidgeting with her soft robe. "Forefathers," she stammers. "I am Persephone, sent here for judgment."

All eyes snap to ENlil. In a shimmer, the sacred seven form a circle around Persephone. Each tower above her and are more significant than they previously looked. Dragoi closes his eyes. "Abomination," he growls, igniting Persephone's fear.

Xi rests her large palm on the girl's head. "Yet she is not. I feel the power of ANu resonating within her."

Odin meets her gaze. "You have been touched by the Amon-I before?"

Sekhmet locks her mighty hands on Persephone's waist, lifts her and smells her skin. "She's innocent. Formed by the hands of deceit."

Shiva throws Sakhmet an annoyed look. He peels Persephone off her with care, cradling her in his arms the way a father holds a newborn. "This beautiful child will bridge the divide humanity seems desperate to cling to." He points an accusatory finger at ENlil. "Your doing. Setting up laws to keep the bloodlines apart encourages the divide."

ENki takes Persephone from Shiva in a similar fashion. "Our father's rules, not his. What is your decision brother?"

ENlil regards Persephone, smiles then takes her from ENki. "Tell me little one, what is the state of humanity?"

Persephone chokes. *If I tell the truth it will anger them, yet a lie will seal my condemnation.* With courage she looks into ENlil's eyes. "It carries on, flawed, inhumane, unjust. But there are those who see solutions to problems, protectors aiding the weak, and heralds of justice for the down-trodden. There is an uncomfortable balance, yet there always has been such."

"The child speaks the truth," Dragoi says. "Nothing has changed."

"Yet she is a product of wickedness, designed to tip the scales," Sakhmet says.

Odin steps closer to ENlil's arms. "Tell me, how fares our bloodlines?"

"They fare unwell, my Lord. The Anuk are dwindling. Offspring hard to achieve, Royal or commoner. The Houses are in constant opposition, seeking wealth and power above all else."

Shiva steps in. "Man cannot rule man, but they may have to if the Anuk are the instruments of their own destruction."

"When is the awakening?" Lord Enki asks. He helps Persephone off his brother's arms. "What period in the Sar is this?"

Persephone's mind races to recall the calculation of a Sar. "We no longer measure time in Sars, but the awakening is due at the end of the age of Virgo. That age starts in 847-years, so 3,007."

"Less than a drop in the ocean of time," says ENlil. "You are of my brother and I. Simple human words would say you are our daughter."

ENki touches her hand. "Because of this we will spare you our verdict; you shall remain with us."

Persephone's heart drops. "But I can't. I have to-"

"Your light burns dim, little one," ENlil says with a smile. "Your years are short, 1,000 by your glow. Why suffer when you can rest here where time is irrelevant?"

Her mind spirals down with despair. Her thoughts linger on parents, friends, Osiris. *Could everything have been for nothing?*

Lord Xi slides next to her. "Perhaps the time she has may allow her to shape things for the better? If it is the Creator's will to bring unfavorable judgment, then so be it. Maybe she can stay their annihilation through her deeds?"

"You have already passed judgment on the world?" Persephone asks, with disbelief souring her face.

ENlil's pleasant demeanor changes to a stern parent. "Since before our departure it was clear, humanity on Earth was a mistake. A social experiment held to heart by our father, ANu. We have given them time to change; they have not. This realm of the Amon-I is a plane within a vessel. Don't you see? Our essence is trapped here until the awakening. Our mortal flesh trapped on the Earth until judgment."

"I beg you, Forefather," Persephone pleads. "See the world as I want to see it. Time is nothing for you, for any of you. It is a precious commodity for me. Condemn me if you will, but I see the truth of it…you want to go home. Here you're trapped in a non-corporeal construct. You're trapped there in bodies absent a soul. You're trapped in the world for reasons I cannot comprehend. You simply want to go home." Persephone lets her tears run free. "I want to go home."

Lord Shiva drops to his knees. He takes her tiny hands into his and looks at ENlil with sympathy covering his face. "She is of your blood, making her part of us."

"What harm could it do to let her return?" Xi asks.

"I urge you, brother," Sakhmet says. "Give her a chance."

ENlil looks to Dragoi, the obvious nay-sayer in the group.

"Let her go, brother," says Dragoi. Odin agrees. ENki nods.

"Very well. Humanity has 3,007 years to change. If they do not, we shall end them."

Persephone looks at Lord ENki. "Forefather, you called me 'The Destroyer-of-Worlds.' What does that mean?"

ENki closes his eyes and tilts his head upwards. Persephone feels a warming sensation flood the back of her neck. It drops to her stomach, causing mild nausea to erupt. It dissipates into a swarm of butterflies traveling up her spine.

"Our language is complicated. Destroyer of worlds, bringer of destruction, the herald of the end…so many meanings." He offers her a devilish smile. "It all depends on the role you play."

"Enough," ENlil orders. "You shall return. The knowledge fresh in your mind, but it will fade with time. Be warned, Persephone of my name, you have taken charge of humanity; the burden rests on your shoulders. You will answer to the Creator when the time comes."

She inhales deep, forcing away the sick feeling in her stomach. She bows humbly, ready to undertake the horrifying journey to the beginning. She shuts her eyes tight, waiting for the agonizing phantoms to begin an assault. Nothing happens.

Whooshing sounds from rotating bars on the sphere drop heavy behind her. Droning from above becomes clear. Thoth's voice welcomes her. She opens calm eyes to see him staring with a smile and tears streaming down his face.

Elation drops him to his knees. Persephone hugs him tight, crying tears of relief. "It's over," she says with joy.

Chapter 23: Beginning of the End

Three days have passed since King Shuru made his proclamations to the Royals and Aristocracies. Three days since Persephone defied expectations and merged with the essence of the Forefathers. For three days the Princess has been dreading this day, her birthday.

Patient citizens of Hyperboria collect together in the capital's Grand-Square. Over 100,000 souls stand shoulder to shoulder to witness the day's main event. Royal Anuk mingle with commoner in the dense crowd, ending at the edge of a ten-foot-high platform. It is acceptable in Hyperboria for the upper classes to mix with the lower ones. Unlike the rest of the world, here the most inferior servant is the richest somewhere else.

Giant screens hover above restless heads at strategic points, streaming live images from the front. Skilled broadcasters pan cameras back and forth at the stage, capturing the patient Royal family. Grim faces are locked in a cold stare; not the usual smiles and joy beaming out to the masses.

King Shuru holds Queen Farah's hand, Persephone sits in awkward silence next to Prince Osiris. Prince Odin is sandwiched between him and Lord Thoth; his two wives at his back. Prince Atlas and his family are at the opposite end of Shuru. Samiri walks out with a procession of Watchers.

Former Watcher High-Priest Gaius wriggles with discomfort between two of his contemporaries in the dense sea of armpits. He sneers at Samiri, hoping his old comrade takes notice. "Look at him, cocky bastard. I am certain his hand played a part in Aspasia's death."

"The accounting says different," the Watcher on his left says. "What's done is done. We should concentrate on the future by using what we have learned to benefit 'Doh-fan-ae' instead of dwelling on things past."

"Quite right," Gaius says. "It will be wise to keep Samiri out of affairs. Work in secret. Trust no one outside our ranks."

The Watcher on the right huddles closer. "Is it true? Did the Princess commune with the Forefathers?"

Gaius' rolls his eyes and grimaces in disgust. "Lies told by that wretch, Samiri. Whatever transpired in the Keeper's presence, one fact is clear; the dividing line between Watchers has been drawn."

"Do you believe the rumors about...uprising?"

"Not the place to discuss such matters," Gaius whispers in a harsh tone. "Whatever support Vali has is best left in the shadows...for now. It is doubtful Atlas will give up title as Primary in favor of his brother's desire for vengeance."

"But we need Vali's science to continue our work."

Gaius shakes his head. "If the need arises to weigh options, we shall lean towards those inclined to further our cause. It is about bloody time; they are bringing out the prisoners."

General Markus leads a procession of soldiers; Bal, Ruia, and their tribesmen march alongside, as captives. He stops in front of ten metal poles arranged on the ground, brought in for today's spectacle. His face is cold, angry, hateful. Satisfied with the columns, he hurries to the King, drops on one knee and bows. "Majesty."

Persephone cringes at Bal's atrocious stare. She grabs Osiris' hand and twitches in her seat. The hairs on her neck stand, her eyes darken. Parts of her body ache.

"He can't hurt you anymore," Osiris whispers. "No one can." He places a reassuring hand on hers.

She stares into his eyes, finding the comfort she needs before facing her tormentor. "Despite my childish behavior in the past few days, I need you. I was ashamed of my reaction to... you know. Forgive me?"

"There's nothing to forgive. I will admit, it was a shock. I do love you, Persephone. Don't know when it happened, but I do."

"I wish your mother could be here when-"

"I like to think she looks in from time to time." Osiris looks at Odin, staring blankly at the crowd. "It's good that father made peace with Markus."

Persephone stares at Odin with love pouring out her heart. She feels her spirit soar, bringing on a warm smile. "I can't believe this is happening. It's history, you know."

"Hush, children," Odin interrupts. "The King is about to speak."

Shuru steps forward near a floating sphere. He stares into it and shivers at the thought of showing off a wispy beard. A quick touch of a circle pinned to his lapel sends a shrieking sound through the screens below. He clears his throat, peers back at his family, then begins a short Anuk prayer in the old tongue. Everyone bows their heads in silence. The supplication ends with a resounding repetition of sacred words booming from the gathering. Once settled, Shuru casts a stern gaze on all.

"Evil, anarchy, tumult, discord, treachery…treason; a few words to describe a lifetime's indifference to history. We are all guilty; we turn a blind eye to horrors being committed in the name of blind devotion. The strong take from the weak. Allies support plans they do not understand. Justice is cast aside in favor of opinion. We fail to learn from the past.

"Assembled are representatives of humanity. Anuk, man, and Watchers. Blood rules Anuk tradition. Houses are determined by lineage. Power is bestowed on Anuk and nobleman with blood ties to the Great Houses, yet they can never ascend higher than a lower station. The commoner accepts their fate, and those finding favor welcome it. The scales are tipped into a pit of evil, anarchy, tumult, discord, treachery, and treason.

"In light of recent events, I have pondered a remedial course for civilization. Many will not like it. More will disapprove. Within my own household I received strong opposition to my proposal. With a heavy heart I gave in to some concerns, and with others, I stood firm.

"The condemned behind me conspired with my own kin to facilitate an evil design. A father was robbed of his daughter. A mother robbed of her dignity. A girl stripped of innocence. Horrors done to my family!

"To set humanity right, to prepare for the return of the Forefathers, Princess Persephone will be married to Prince Osiris, three years from now."

The crowd erupts in thunderous cheers and applause. Those disheartened with the declaration are lost in the storm of elation. Similar reactions sweep throughout the world wherever the news is broadcast. A full minute passes until the crowd settles.

"Starting today, a three-year plan will be enacted to open all Lower Houses to everyone from all classes of humanity. A person's merit will afford them the right to govern the people to whom they are responsible. The Greater Houses shall remain in the control of Anuk Primaries, but their deputies shall be from the Lower Houses.

"Now, these criminals shall meet the fate their souls sought when they joined a foul task. The Tribesmen Bal and Ruia will not be nailed to posts. No, such players will be crucified on the old trees at the capital gates. They will bare their souls in their ancient pagan way, to honor the crossing of the heavenly bodies. For three days they will be kept alive, drunk with phantoms, bodies split open, starved, tortured. May it be a painful sacrifice." Shuru returns to his seat and nods at Persephone.

She strides with a purpose to Markus. His approving gaze gives her strength. She accepts a dagger from him, and together they confront Bal.

The Tribesman sits on the ground with his confederates, all bound with rope. Persephone and Markus hover over him, while the rest, except Ruia, are strung up on the poles with frightening efficiency.

Hammers pound nails into soft fleshy palms, then hard bony feet. With each strike, blood-curdling screams spew out from the condemned. First, the left palm is secured as high as it can reach on the pole. The ball of the right foot is aligned so that it's touching a short platform. Then, when screams for the mutilated palm drop in tempo, the jailer smashes a heavy iron mallet on the dorsal part of the foot; it's easier to drive a nail through shattered bone - this lesson learned from years of practice. A rope is wrapped around the waist. The process is repeated for the right hand and left foot combination. The pole is hoisted.

"Mercy," Bal pleads to Persephone. He looks at Markus. "Mercy." The throbbing vein on Markus' forehead tells him none will be granted.

Markus cuts Bal's ropes then grips his neck, yanks him off the ground and props him on the wall. Ruia's frantic crying encourages the General to look at her with a crooked smile. "You reap what you sow," he shouts at her; her bladder opens, flooding her legs with urine. He nods at Persephone.

She gets close to the whimpering criminal. In a vile tone, she asks, "Who am I?"

"Princess Persephone," Bal cries with fear pouring out his lips.

"I promised if you touch me you will lose a hand...this hand." She slams his right wrist against the wall, brandishes the blade in front of his eyes, then slices slowly at the soft flesh. She reaches bone, then eases the pressure on the hilt. The blade pushes subtly against the bone, ensuring each crack is felt, each shatter assaults his senses. The blade butts up on the wall, ending the slow cut. The condemned hand drops unceremoniously on the blood-spattered ground. Markus lets him fall hard.

Bal wails. Blood spurts in a wild spray with each beat of Bal's blackened heart. Persephone positions herself on Markus' side, nods, then clasps Bal's neck. Without any effort, she lifts him over her head and smashes him on the wall.

Markus cuts his trousers off, allowing his genitals to hang in full view of the floating cameras. "Remember me?" he whispers. "I'm the Princess' protector. I'm Koray's father!" He cuts off Bal's manhood, root and stem. Medics rush to administer aid to Bal. "Let him bleed long enough to remember the pain," Markus tells the medics. "If he dies before tomorrow, I'll cut you too."

The commotion from the crowd does not reach Markus or Persephone's ears. The Princess looks at the General with tears glazing over her eyes. Her emotions threaten to break until Markus wraps his arms around her to block intruding eyes. "It is over," he whispers.

She stares blankly at the crowd chanting support with their raised arms; they show blatant disregard for personal tragedies fueled by an ancient insatiable desire for blood. Her hands clutch Markus' tightly. Her blood burns. Sadness, closure, and contentment disappear. Her face tightens into a growl, as she stares ahead. "No, it is just beginning."

PART III

Mother of Destruction

"Blessed is our Queen whose voice shall echo through the ages" - Peki, beloved friend of Persephone (circa 1,320-age of Libra)

Six years have passed since the late King Shuru proclaimed his vision for the future. A concept which destroyed eons of Anuk tradition; an unacceptable path for those unwilling to relinquish their power. Queen Persephone held ultimate dominion over Hyperboria, giving her and any offspring absolute control over all Principalities of the world; a dangerous concept for the disenfranchised.

Prince Vali gained support from Watchers loyal to Gaius, in exchange for banned science allowing procreation. Soon an unstoppable wave of assassinations forced a significant number of Houses to rally to Vali's cause - usurp the throne. Prince Atlas fell victim to his brother's designs, afterward being relegated to a puppet Primary, executing disturbing campaigns against his Queen.

The unthinkable happened, Vali captured Hyperboria. Six months of heavy fighting brought on incalculable losses. Cities were reduced to rubble, populations purged. In most realms, the dead outnumbered the living. A ceasefire was sought, promising an end to the horrors. Queen Persephone was encouraged to travel to Thoth's stronghold in pTah for the duration of her pregnancy - at this point, she had completed six-months out of a ten-month term.

In the year 1320 of Libra, Queen Persephone's transport, en-route to pTah from Persepolis, was attacked by Vali's agents. The loss of her newborn Koray fueled unbridled rage, which decimated the forces of Moira. Her last thoughts were for Osiris, trapped half a world away.

Days before Persephone's exodus, King Osiris, Lord Thoth, and Samiri, journeyed to the Western Continent to secure destructive weapons at the ancient Citadel. They did not calculate the inevitable arrival of an armada bent on annihilation. The ceasefire was violated, and their mission remained incomplete.

Liviana Badur

Chapter 24: The World in Chaos

WESTERN CONTINENT

Explosions rock sacred walls of the ancient Anuk Citadel. Forty-thousand-year-old towers crumble into piles of sacrilegious rubble, folding over with continuous bombardment from above. Older fortifications prove challenging to subdue, yet military cruisers blast their ordinance to show it can be done.

Surrounding cities loyal to Queen Persephone fall victim to a coordinated attack during pre-dawn hours. Through foreboding clouds, the ravenous crafts came. In groups of four, they hovered over skyscrapers, waiting to light up dark skies.

Sabotaged infrastructure, disabled defenses, subdued military, all carried the stink of Watcher interference. Once the board was set, the attack commenced in a violent fury. Yellow fire rained down on buildings, without regard for the innocents dwelling within. The slaughter mimics previous ones carried out in the other continent across the sea.

Wave after wave of attack craft push through red canyon walls in search of high-value targets to demolish. They descend on fleeing people heading to a grand-canyon, firing at those seeking escape to an underground refuge. Many fall as thick streaks of intense light cut down everything in their path.

North of a granite gorge, the Temple of Isis remains untouched atop a high bluff. Constructed 100,000-years ago, it is a shell of its former self - a repository of ancient knowledge. It is the site chosen by Osiris to negotiate another ceasefire with the self-proclaimed King Vali.

Thoth paces under a shaded cavity. His frustration catches Samiri's eye. He leaves Osiris on a wide landing platform to attend to his master. *Maybe he will let me hold it again. Oh, the shiver it brings my soul. The release of built-up yearning for its sweet embrace.* He bites his trembling lips and wipes his sweaty palms. "Lord, what troubles you?"

"There is a disturbance in the ethereal plane. I fear the Amon-I is collapsing within itself."

Horror washes over Samiri's face. Not at a possible loss of the Forefathers' souls and the repository of knowledge from the stars, but for his addictive euphoria gained at each exposure to the relic.

Six years he traveled with his master to an otherworldly construct contained within the Amon-I, learned basic forbidden knowledge bestowed on a Keeper, and felt electrifying ecstasy infect every cell in his conniving body. Despite the privilege he enjoyed, he has never once cast a reverent gaze on the holy object.

War prevented the Keeper from storing the volatile artifact in any random place. Samiri hoped this predicament would either bring him within its grasp or warrant a trip to the forbidden Lumeria. No matter how hard he tried, failure met him at every turn.

He has tried, after all. In the early days after Persephone and Osiris' coronation, innocent whispers left his lips, destined for the ear of the aristocracies. Bold outrage at the decimation of tradition festered in the hearts of the most loyal, after proper prompting by this unscrupulous fellow. Each incitement to rebellion failed to capture the Amon-I. He almost gave up until Vali took control of Hyperboria. Thoth removed the Amon-I from his Temple, but still, it has never been seen.

"Please Lord, I beg you, let us secure the holy Amon-I in Lumeria. It may be the only hope."

"Samiri!" Thoth yells down at him. "Lumeria is forbidden, as you know."

"Forgive me, Master. These are indeed trying times."

"You show less restraint than Amaya."

Samiri's eyes widen, his hands go cold. The sting of betrayal induces a stammer, "Amaya, Lord?"

"An oversight on my ancestor's part was to entrust the title of Keeper to a single individual. I will not repeat that mistake." He cuts Samiri's heartache with an intimidating stare. Distant rumbling shifts his attention. He points to the horizon. "A craft approaches. Stay in the shadows."

Thin trails of black smoke spew from a shuttle angling towards the stone platform. Osiris smiles at severe scorch marks blackening the craft's side. Engines kick up gusts of hot air, stinking of exhaust. "Brother, I have a bad feeling about this."

"Majesty, I agree. We should be alert."

"Damn it, Thoth. Today I need my big brother, not a compliant subject." He softens his harsh tone after noticing

Thoth's scowl. "I am sorry. It's been a hectic day, won't you say?"

"It is quite understandable. No apology necessary. What is really bothering you?"

"I haven't heard from Persephone." Osiris drops his head. "It's been two days; she should have arrived in pTah by now."

Thoth looks at his little brother. He smiles with pride infecting his heart. "She is the most stubborn, headstrong, determined Anuk I've ever known. Nothing prevents her from achieving any goal, including reaching pTah. She is the most endearing in my family."

"Four months of safety, that's all I ask, and you shall have another."

Shuttle engines whine down, encouraging Thoth to lower his voice. "I received the latest health scans from Persepolis two days ago. I only just reviewed them."

Osiris' face pales with worry. "What's wrong?" Thoth's smile pulls him back from the edge of panic.

"Baby Koray has a brother." He pauses to allow Osiris to process the revelation. "His development was hampered by Koray's dominance. Turns out your wife has two wombs. The fetus is only three months, but healthy."

Osiris' eyes shift up towards the sky. "Even in the heat of chaos, the Creator sends joy. Thank you, brother."

Vali strolls up casually, removing his flight gloves and smiling at the brothers. "Do share the good news, I am sure it can't be better than mine."

Osiris straightens up. He struggles to subdue the rage boiling in his blood. "Prince Vali-"

"King Vali. Get it right."

"Shall we proceed?" Osiris contains his anger. He gestures to the covered area with a smile.

They sit around a small stone table across from Samiri. Vali throws the Watcher a disappointed smirk. "You, 'Doh-fan-ae,' I'm thirsty. Hurry now, bring your King wine." Samiri complies after receiving a nod from Osiris.

"How is that wretched wife of yours?"

Thoth drops his hand on Osiris' shoulder. "Brother, don't."

"We're here to discuss a ceasefire, not my wife."

"Oh?" Vali purses his lips and turns his gaze to the horizon. "You are only Primary of ENki, nothing more. She is the real power. I should be speaking with her."

"For once you are absolutely correct," Osiris says. "She is the Queen…who are you? A worthless usurper."

"Osiris!" Thoth says. Vali dismisses the insult with a wave of his well-manicured hand. "We are here for a purpose, Vali. Get on with it."

"By all means, Keeper. Here are my terms. Surrender immediately…" Osiris chuckles, eliciting a scowl from Vali. "All hostilities shall end. Multitudes of lives will be saved, and things shall return to the way it should be. You resume your seat in Hyperboria as the Primary of ENki, and your wife…well, this is the tricky part."

Thoth sees the deceit in Vali's caviler smile. *He's sweating on his brow, eyes tense, ear lobes red. He's trying to antagonize us. Does he truly want peace?*

"It will be hard to swallow, I'm afraid, but it's what's best for all. Queen Persephone shall renounce her union with you and join me in holy matrimony. Oh, and the thing she's carrying in her belly has to be put down."

Osiris jumps off his seat and grabs the table's edge. His tight grip cracks the polished stone. "Never!"

Rattling cups shifts Vali's attention to Samiri carrying a wine tray. "Ah, refreshments. I'm parched, be a dear and pour me first."

"He's not your slave," Thoth says with uncharacteristic harshness.

"No, but he is yours, isn't he?"

The brothers are engrossed in their stare down of Vali, causing them to miss Samiri's soft nod and lazy blink to Vali.

Vali gulps his wine before addressing the vile glances coming from Osiris and Thoth. "Did I mention I had good news? You see, while you are sitting here, refusing delicious wine…goodness I must have a cask…my forces are securing the Citadel stores."

Shock overcomes Thoth. "That's impossible. Even if you knew where it was, you can't breach the barrier."

"Oh, but I can," Vali says calmly. Hurried footsteps echoing up hidden stairs put a smile on his face. Twelve soldiers in gray uniforms brandishing heavy rifles assemble behind Osiris and Thoth. "Wipe that stupid look off your faces. They're Anuk soldiers. You can't fight all of them."

Osiris ignores Vali's taunt. He swings the table away to clear a path to the villain. Thoth attacks those closest to him.

Vali avoids Osiris' hand reaching for his neck, then lands a fist on his jaw. Thoth and Samiri tackle the soldiers but have little success subduing them.

In the small space, shots ring out. Intense red beams hit Osiris' shoulder. He ignores the pain to counter Vali's weak blows. He catches hold of him and swings the thin body hard on the ground. The wind is knocked out of Vali. He raises his hands to fain surrender. Osiris shoots a quick glance to his brother. Thoth drops one soldier but falls victim to another's blade piercing his gut.

The distraction provides Vali a short opportunity to stab Osiris's leg with a small syringe. Instantly the poison courses through his bloodstream, finding its way to the central nervous system. Osiris tumbles over, paralyzed.

"Don't worry." Vali hovers over him. "You will die." He looks at Thoth stunned on the ground. "You, I need. We can't carry on without a Keeper now, can we?" He points to Samiri. "Take that away." He relishes in Osiris' panicked glare and kneels down close. "Did you know your whore of a wife was supposed to be mine? Where was that place she liked to go? Cappadocia, her own personal haven for criminals, slaves, and other wicked sorts. I wonder what she did there. I know…she would spread her legs for a troop of tribesmen, entering her in turns, sometimes in pairs. Is the creature in her belly yours? I'll find out when I cut her open and spill its guts. Now, be a good boy and die, will you?"

Thoth heaves his body against a wall. The wound stings. His muscles collapse into numbness from poison. "You will not win. The Forefathers will destroy you."

"Really?" Vali drops halfway to the ground, angling his head to sneer at Thoth. "Hurts doesn't it? This will sting even better. From the Citadel I will launch a strike on every continent, wiping out my enemies, including the Forefathers. Mark my words, Thoth, Keeper, the time of the ancients is over."

"Please, spare my brother," Thoth says between violent spasms. "I will serve-"

"Save your breath." Vali lets out a chuckle. "He's on his last breath. You will serve me anyway. Your first act is delivering the Amon-I. Defy me and you'll join your brother. Did I mention that I'm going to cut him into pieces, then deliver a slice to each House? I didn't? Where are my manners?"

"Animal," Thoth whispers.

"Do shut up. To show you how merciful I am, you can have the last moment with this wretched filth!" He kicks Osiris' in the side, then gestures to two soldiers on his way out.

Thoth falls on the ground to begin his painful crawl to his brother. A pair of strong hands help him along the way. The soldiers drop him and step back.

"Breathe slower. Slow your heartbeat, remember how I showed you." Thoth's face crumples with sadness. "This is not the end, I promise."

He caresses Osiris' face with his bloodied hand and delivers a kiss on his forehead. He conceals a red-gem. With care, he rolls on Osiris' chest then touches his heart. "You will live on. I will see to it. Fear not, brother, for the journey is quick. I promise Persephone will be safe. Your children will be safe. Close your eyes. Drift off into the waiting abyss. I love you brother."

Thoth's clenched palm glows red. He closes his eyes at the start of a sacred chant. The soldiers share a worried look between them. Osiris' body convulses. Seconds pass; a lifeless corpse remains. Thoth stares at the frightened soldiers. "If I were you, I'd run. You're Anuk; your kin warned you about me."

They sprint out of the room with haste. Thoth wraps a smoke-colored silk strap around his arm; Persephone's Adonis. The creature lights up with its brilliance. A large void opens; Thoth disappears.

~Forbidden Desert to pTah~

Racing along the desert floor, three armored troop transports kick up dust in their wake. Sunbaked terrain radiates waves of hot air, shimmering with a promise of death. Nothing exists in this expanse; aircraft avoid the hot airflow in a 100-mile radius. Ground vehicles go around to the longer perimeter road. Demons may brave the desolation, but the travelers aren't demons.

Under cover of darkness, General Markus ordered a quick escape in vehicles provided by the dead from House Moira of ENlil. Their smoldering airship offered no escape, but it served as a proper decoy for any who ventured in search of the missing battalion.

At the break of dawn, a miracle happened. As the sun pierced night's veil, faint signs of life begged to be heard from the dead Queen. For a brief moment her eyes opened, weak fingers clung to Peki's tear-soaked scarf, skin warmed beyond its Hyperborian chill. Her revival lasted seconds, but it rejuvenated lost hope in the hopeless.

Green hills beckon Markus' lead vehicle; signs of pTah are in sight. They race for the border marked off by a narrow river. Desperate tires dig through elevated mounds on a riverbank. One by one they make the crossing, sloshing past startled animals.

Rolling along the sweet grounds of pTah, they push hard towards Giza, waiting 300-miles off. Without warning a blanket of blue light envelopes them. In a flash, the three vehicles disappear.

Seconds pass before Markus' convoy materializes deep underground, in a glorious chamber adorned with towering columns. Tires grab murky sandstone floors, screeching, struggling to end their slide before crashing into giant walls. The abrupt stop jars the passengers into a state of panic.

Limping with a hand on his side, Thoth beckons the group to an entrance. Desperate eyes search for Persephone. Peki climbs out cradling a cotton shroud; Markus appears holding the Queen in his arms. Thoth's heart plunges to the floor. His legs give out.

He forgets his bleeding wound as Markus runs towards him. The General's words are muffled, distorted in a haze. Everything appears in slow-motion. Peki's shouting carries no volume. Frantic soldiers tearing out transponders have no meaning. Memories of Osiris' face incites nausea, choking, erupting spasms coursing through his weakened body. He peers at Markus running to an enclave exploding with brilliant light. *Amaya.*

Frantic, Markus rushes the startled Watcher. "Please, help Her Majesty," he pleads. Amaya grabs Persephone's wrist.

Worry creeps over her face. "There's no pulse."

"She's alive. I know she is. Please help her," he pleads.

"Lord Thoth is the only one who…" Before she can finish Markus runs off to Thoth.

"Please, she's alive. Please help her."

His words tug at Thoth's heart. The Keeper looks at Markus, then Persephone. With his empty stare, tears break out. Markus' voice clears in his head. *She's alive he says. But how? The child…the second child!* Blood returns to his face. His eyes widen, the race is on. "Come, hurry!"

They crowd into a small chamber. Markus places the body on a slab in the center. Amaya brings a short staff. Peki lights hanging torches. Three women drop on their knees to pray. Thoth enters with a leather-bound book.

Without delay, he begins to chant in a low tone. It rises in pitch, inciting a soft golden glow on archaic symbols etched in the walls.

Amaya's staff explodes with blue light at the tip. A soft thread shoots out to Persephone's body, enveloping it with a dull glow. Blinding light floods the chamber.

Thoth holds his red gem over the body, chanting with intense fervor. His hands shake, the gem glows, Amaya's staff rattles violently. Walls shake with an ominous thunder. Everyone drops on their knees, then the clamor dissipates with the fading light.

Persephone's eyes open slowly. Her hands flicker. Dazed and confused, she forces a smile at the tearful gathering before her.

Thoth hovers close. His face washes over with sadness, and he falls on her chest to weep without end. Words aren't needed to explain his grief. She feels it from his racing heart and tightening hands. She does not cry. She stifles grief with rage. It warms her, fuels her resolve.

Weeks pass without incident from above. PTah is a recognized territory of Osiris and Persephone. When they fled here after Vali captured Hyperboria, none of the breakaway Houses ventured into the sovereign state. The Royal Anuk knew Lord Thoth moved his Library here years ago, with an unknown arsenal they dared not challenge.

Persephone recovered at a rapid pace, due mostly to her exposure to the Amon-I's power. She grieves for her deceased daughter and husband, but finds solace in the miracle she still carries; Thoth informed her it was the child who kept her alive, her unborn savior.

She spends her days in the underground metropolis roaming dingy halls, hoping to encounter an apparition. She yearns for her parents, murdered by agents of Vali. She calls for the spirit of Prince Odin, also killed at the hands of her enemies. Most of all she dies each night in want of Osiris. On many occasions, Peki would peel her off cold floors after hours of wailing, crying for an end to the pain.

One day she stopped crying. Her focus shifted to finding safety for those loyal to her. Her main concern is the awakening and her promise to save humanity. At first, it seemed an impossible task, but her son makes her embrace life over the comforts of death.

"Majesty," a voice calls out; Markus' voice. He approaches his Queen with his wife holding their one-year-old son.

"Come, my beloved Markus." She opens her arms to receive the child. Her heart explodes with love, warming her cheeks and lifting her spirit. "Little Calis. An elegant name. I wish him and his progeny gracious blessings from the Creator."

"Are you sure you won't change your mind?"

"I wait for Lord Thoth. I will rest easier if I know my loved ones are safe." She shoots Peki an annoyed glance. "Some are giving me grief with their defiance."

"Don't mind her, Markus," Peki yells from the entrance. "She still can't make her bed or dinner without assistance."

"Pay him no mind." She kisses little Calis and passes the child to his mother.

Markus locks her in a tight embrace. His emotions crumble with hers. "Come find us quickly, understand? The Western Continent is just a portal away." He barely contains his tears and trembling voice. "May the light of Orion shine on you. May the Creator keep you safe, and the strength of Lyra burns in your soul."

She releases Markus. He bows then takes his leave. Persephone watches him stride away. A deep breath chases away a meltdown.

His departure prompts the beginning of an exodus to the Continent across the sea. Refuge will be sought under the grand-canyon surrounding the Citadel. Anyone from pTah who wished to make the journey can do so. However, few remain of the citizenry. Similar efforts are made in Western Illyria, Cappadocia and Aryavan.

Persephone wipes her tears and lets out a deep sigh. "Peki, I'm ready to visit my temple."

Chapter 25: The Key to Lumeria

An elegant sandstone temple sits in the shadow of the Great Pyramid. It is not as ancient as the shimmering structure, but old enough to show years of weathering. Generous heaps of moss creep through stone tiles, bathing walls with green strands hanging on to ornate carvings. Outside the perimeter, a magnificent stone lion peers at the horizon, waiting for a visitor to descend from the heavens. On the eastern side, a massive river flows with calm reverence.

In a private chamber, Persephone sits in solitude, hunched over a small console shimmering in a dark corner. Fresh fruit collected in a cream-colored ceramic bowl catches her eye. She gets lost in its golden depictions of a Hyperborian procession - an illustration of a time of innocence, lost. *It's just sitting there, waiting. It's so easy to fall... do it.* Her better senses restrain a tantrum.

Rhythmic beeping blares from the console. She throws an expectant look at the screen, cringing as information streaks in a rapid outpour. Her face changes to a mask of worry.

Droning from a floating light pod near the ceiling disrupts her senses. She grabs the bowl and lashes out at the artificial creature. Dates tumble alongside grapes and pomegranates, but the perfect aim makes up for the spill as the device crashes to the floor.

The irrational behavior does nothing to appease Persephone. She is still angry. A click on the chamber's door pulls her from the brink. Her tension melts and spirit soar at the sight of Thoth.

He hurries along polished floors, with welcoming arms begging for an embrace. "My Queen." He hugs her tight. His hand rests on her bulging stomach. "He's taking his time to grow. No matter, he will be safe in the days to come."

"It's been a long wait. Please tell me we are at the end."

"Cappadocia is secure; citizens are underground. So too is Markus and his migrants. I could not reach all at Persepolis, but a great number fled to safety."

Her face sours. "The eastern settlements are destroyed. Much of Aryavan, transformed to scorched sand. Those were innocent people."

Thoth grabs her shoulders. Worried eyes stare into hers. "That's not all, the Southern continent is frozen. Hyperboria launched a preemptive strike with weapons stolen from the Citadel. Lumeria is under miles of ice."

Shock washes over Persephone. Her trembling lips barely voice her words. "The Forefathers, are they alive?"

"They are for now," Thoth whispers. "They won't be for long if this onslaught continues."

"They won't dare kill the Forefathers." A sudden chill overcomes Persephone.

They slump down on a couch. Thoth's anger seeps out in his voice. "Won't they? What better way to prevent judgment day?" He rests his large hand on her slender shoulder.

Her stoic demeanor melts into sadness at his touch. "Is this the end? Are we the last of our house?"

"Attacking Lumeria changes everything. Hiding like humanity did eons ago will not stave off its end." A glimmer of hope shines in his eyes. He looks at her, smiling subtly to melt the despair. "We must go to Lumeria. From there, we can end this conflict."

His confident demeanor does not influence Persephone. Hopelessness chokes her resolve. "Virgo ends in three-thousand-years. That's a long time before the awakening, before the Forefathers can help."

"We can't trust or wait for the Forefathers. We must end this ourselves."

"And what prevents them from finding us? Shall we trade a grave for a tomb?" she protests. Thoth dismisses her frustration with a smile.

"I am still the Keeper-of-Forbidden-Knowledge. All routes through the network have been corrupted. The portals are down, 'Sephie. Lumeria is our sanctuary. Your son should be born in the presence of our ancestors." He hesitates with words forming on his lips. "I made the arrangements days ago."

She sighs and holds her stomach with a worried look. Her eyes glaze over with thoughts of what Thoth has planned. She looks at him with a plight washing over her face. "We will be killing so many. They are our family, our blood."

"And when they kill us, who remains from House ENki? Shall we leave a murderous line of ENlil to reign?"

There is no defeating his argument. She resigns herself to accept it. Her curiosity is peaked as Thoth removes a small amulet around his neck. About a third the size of a palm, it is made of gold and silver cased in a Gray colored ore. It falls apart into three pieces. Engraved symbols cut in the inner surface glow with a yellow brilliance then fade out in flowing ember.

"A key I created at the Citadel, years ago."

"For what purpose?" she asks.

"Lumeria itself," he says while putting the two larger pieces together. He holds up the third. It is similar to a cartouche with sacred Anuk symbols keeping a steady glow on the face. "This is the heart. It powers the key. Together it gives us full control of the complex. Weapons of old and the ability to take the long sleep."

Persephone feels compelled to protest. The thought of joining the ancients scares her. *What happens when they wake and find us? What will they do?* She throws him a stern look. "That is forbidden. Only the Forefathers can sleep."

"I am not suggesting we must, only that we shall, if events prove to not be in our favor."

A brief silence passes. Persephone stands. A sudden ache in her stomach encourages her hand into a protective grasp. She caresses Thoth's tired face and offers a compliant smile.

She hurries to a counter with an empty bag next to miscellaneous articles deemed necessary for any journey.

Amongst clothing in a drawer, a stuffed bunny beckons for her affections. She holds it close as if she were a small child. Warm memories of innocent days flood her thoughts - the day King Shuru presented the toy, the moment Osiris held her close in her chambers, and the day Thoth secured a path to the Amon-I within its body. She tosses it into the bag on top of three sacred leather-bound books.

On the wall, she taps a silver symbol. A drawer extends, presenting a small red gem. With reverence, she kisses it then breaks down with inconsolable sorrow. Her heart shatters and hands tremble.

Thoth explained what he had to do before Osiris' body died; he transferred his essence into the relic. There it remained, hidden from the clutches of death. This prize kept Persephone on the path of life after so much had been taken away.

Doors burst open. Peki rushes in. Beads of sweat cling to his face. He regains his composure with hands on tired knees. "Majesty, Hyperborian forces have entered the perimeter. Two armed ships in the river, twenty more in the air. Ground forces are swarming through the eastern gates."

Persephone forgets her pain. In the blink of an eye, she reaches Peki and pulls him into an emotional embrace. She presses her lips on his forehead. "My heart is with you, now and forever. I love you, old man. Your friendship has kept me alive, and I am grateful to have you in my life. Go now, may God watch over and protect you. Get everyone out. Protect them."

Peki bows with reverence. Before retreating, he looks at his queen one last time. Love and heartache pour out from his eyes. Alarms blare, prompting him to rush off to execute a pre-planned evacuation.

With haste, Persephone begins filling her bag. "Our family is intent on destroying us, and now themselves."

"Hurry, we have to go," Thoth says.

At that moment when the bombardment started, when the temple walls shook, Persephone made up her mind, *my enemies have to die. Maybe the time of the Anuk is over.*

Temple walls shake with a promise to come tumbling down. Crashing stone at higher levels drowns out screeching alarms and rumblings on the ground. A mist of dust clouds tell on intruders, with helmet lights blazing through the fog.

Thoth breaks off from Persephone when they encounter a dozen troops blocking their path to a portal. He insists she use another route and avoid the fight.

Two levels below the ground, Persephone reaches a wide chamber with a shimmering pool. Columns rise to a low ceiling, sparkling from the water's lighted reflection. It is menacing and cold; from above she can hear the muffled sounds of carnage. She spots the portal's arch at the far end. Boots crunching pebbles from behind stops her advance.

Fear is a condition she chooses to ignore, yet the hairs on her neck tingle with suspicion. She grinds her teeth, knowing any soldier would promptly demand she turn around, or shoot her. Thoth would not stand in silence. *There can be only one.* She clenches her fist and faces Vali.

"My Queen," Vali whispers. No weapons, his hands are empty; wearing black clothing dusty from the rubble. A golden perversion of House ENlil's emblem stands out above his left breast. He notices her aggravation. "Do you like it?" he asks. "I like tridents. It's the new banner."

"My eagle suits me just fine," she says.

"Why not have both? End all this, come with me and it stops. A new world awaits."

Her nostrils flare and chest heaves. "Never! You die today, traitor."

He counters with a sneer. "That thing in your belly dies, not me." He lets out a blood-curdling scream and lunges at her.

She blocks his fist and grabs his arm, twists, then throws him against a wall.

Vali hits the ground hard. He coughs up dust, then looks up at her. Another lunge connects with her stomach. He lets her slide across the room and crash on a wall. *Now that you know the stakes let's see you protect it.* He charges.

She darts away. He intercepts her retreat. Another smash to the face sends her reeling. Vali fires at her stomach but receives a swift kick in the midsection.

Pain shoots through his body. His eyes blur. He shakes off the hurt and lets a smile escape his lips. "You wicked little girl." He ducks an incoming brass urn, jumps high, lands behind her. Before she reacts, his hand swings her head into a column, breaking off marble on impact.

Blood spews from Persephone's mouth. Her shaky legs find quick footing. Blurry eyes regain focus. She blocks Vali's punch but receives a knee in the gut. Fear mixes with pain, as she screams and falls face down.

Vali drags her to the pool's edge and slams the side of her face on floor tiles. He drags her forward, so her face is hovering over the water. His knee presses into her back. "You could have had everything!" His hand shoves her head underwater, holding firm against her wriggling body and resistant head. He pulls up to tease a gasp of air. "But you'd rather be Queen of the underworld!" He submerges it again.

With a powerful throw, he sends Persephone's body sliding across the room. In a blink, he's on top of her with an iron rod held high. His gaze falls on her upper torso - the vulnerable soft spot fatal to all Anuk. Hesitation disappears when Persephone opens her eyes. He rams the rod deep inside.

Persephone screams. Her face fills with fear, pain, rage; breaths quicken. "You've condemned humanity!"

"Be a sweet, sweet niece and die. I don't want you anymore," he says in a childish manner, then climbs off and begins a stroll towards a column where his cape lies in a heap.

Enormous pressure bears down on Persephone's chest. Blood burns near the wound. Her head spins, body is being drained of strength. Pain overcomes her, squeezing vital organs, inducing fear for only one thing, her child. Her eyes close, breaths disappear, yet she is not dead.

She falls quick into a meditative state, ignoring sensations from her flesh, replacing it with memories of light within light inside the Amon-I, where the souls of the Forefather's dwell. At first, it's warm, comforting. Whispers of ancient prayers are soothing.

In an instant, a violent roar washes over her, pressing her thoughts into an overbearing tremor. Her eyes open, hands yank the rod free; the pain is unbearable, but she does not scream.

Vali shakes the dust off his cape. His nose twitches with a change in the air. Eyes open wide, but he doesn't have time to react. A strong hand throws him near the pool.

In a heartbeat Persephone is on him, her dark eyes glaring down with fire. One hand keeps Vali subdued with the force of a thousand Anuk. The other grasps the bloody rod. Her chest heaves back with a deep inhale, drops with a controlled exhale. Eyes dark with strands of red where the white should be.

Vali's eyes fix on the iron rod. "You stupid girl, you think you've won? It will take three lifetimes for you to regain a semblance of power." Droplets of red fall on his face. Panic infects his resolve. He can't move. "Alright," he says, finally realizing his dire circumstance. "I'll be good, promise. We can negotiate."

"Unlike you, uncle, I don't murder my enemies." The rod goes flying off to the side. She sits on his waist and stares into his eyes. "This world is beyond saving, for now. It needs a cleansing hand to clear the path for the Forefathers. I am that hand."

She presses her soft lips to his forehead. His heart takes off in rapid thunder at the goodbye kiss. His lips tremble. "I'll give it back. Everything, it's yours."

"Then what?" Persephone positions her face close to his with an intimate stare. Her stiff fingers wrap behind his neck where his spine meets his head. "I wait for another villain to challenge me? Where's my husband, Vali? Where's my daughter?" Her menacing gaze intensifies.

"If I die, it will not end. Only I can stop it." His voice breaks into full plight. "You said you won't kill me."

"No, I won't murder you." Her fingers tighten. "I'll wreak vengeance upon you."

Her fingertips pierce Vali's skin, pushing hard to his spine. She grips the base of his skull and pulls.

Bone snaps, blood spurts out. Vali's face remains frozen in terror. His body thrashes but soon ebbs into the lifeless shell of disgust that it is.

Thoth's presence is near. "Our struggle is not over," she whispers. "Let's finish this."

~ *THE TOMB OF OSIRIS* ~

The tomb is deep underground; dark, damp, with light emanating from pods secured into the rock. A robust gray platform is in the center. Four-foot-wide granite forms a catwalk-like perimeter around a moat. In the middle, another platform sits with a cavity filled by blue water. Four tall obelisks stand at each corner, with Anuk symbols carved in deep. At the top, the capstones are polished to a smooth white finish.

Muffled explosions vibrate through rock. They come from the surface. With no obvious way into the chamber, enemy soldiers are attempting to blast their way through.

A nearby arch cut into the earth begins to glow blue. The light reveals a smooth depression cut into the surface. The cut goes four feet into the wall, standing eight feet high. A flash of light brightens the space. In an instant, Persephone appears with Thoth.

They leap high into the air, aiming for a landing on the platform. They clear the six-foot-wide moat, casting a haunting blue glow within the space. With feet planted firm, Persephone wastes no time in breaking open a panel at the base of an obelisk. She removes a box with pistols inside. *Never thought I would have to use these so soon.* It was not two weeks ago she hid the weapons there.

"How long before they find us, you think?"

Thoth holds out his hand. He appears calm, yet panicking inside. "Any moment now. The gem."

He takes the red gem and a pistol from Persephone, examining both items. Satisfied, he hurries to the center. "This will take a moment."

Blue light ignites in a stream across the symbols on the obelisks. A low hum sounds, adding bass to the explosions above. Blue light emanates from the capstones, pulsating with lightning bolts. In a dazzling display, they connect. Sparks lash out in wild brilliance.

"Hurry!" Persephone screams. She drops to her knees, grabbing her stomach, then cries out with momentary pain.

Thoth does his best to manipulate symbols materializing in the air. A sarcophagus rises in the center cavity, sloshing blue water on their feet.

"Remember, as soon as you arrive, put the key in the main console," he says. "The countermeasures are pre-programmed. It is all automated after that."

Explosions reverberate around the cavern. Rubble falls from the ceiling. A far wall explodes with a thunder. Enemy intruders brandish heavy weapons as they climb through a small hole.

Persephone and Thoth fire their pistols. Concentrated light crisscrosses incoming enemy fire.

Three soldiers fall in the wave of dozens scrambling to attack the Anuk. Thicker beams hit the sarcophagus, breaking pieces of the stone. The soldiers blast away at the obelisks.

A well-aimed shot hits Persephone in the chest, inflaming her wound. Scorched garment mix with burnt blood smoldering above her golden-eagle crest. Another blast hits her hard, opening the injury as much as it burns the area around it. She falls.

Thoth blasts the shooters. He slams a lighted symbol on the floor. Without delay, searing lightning streaks through the air, striking the men. Bolts intensify, forming a chain of death, piercing flesh as it travels through the soldiers. They all fall screaming, dying.

Blood oozes out of Persephone's wound. Thoth panics. He picks her up with one sweep, taking her to the waiting sarcophagus. "Easy, try not to move."

A panel opens up on the side. A small screen materializes. Thoth puts the gem into a slot while trying to hide his frown from Persephone.

"What, what is it?" she asks with worry in her voice. Thoth doesn't answer.

Fearing death will find her, she struggles to remove the Key to Lumeria hanging around her neck. Thoth reaches over. His gentle hand pushes her down with a solemn look giving away his intentions. He grabs her bag, examines the contents and sighs relief. "You will need the key."

Persephone's heart shatters once more, inducing panic for the answer she already knows. "You're not coming, are you?"

"There's power for only one." Thoth forces a comforting smile, yet inside he feels the same sting she feels.

"Then you go. I can't do this. I thought I could, but I can't."

"No, you must." He pushes her back down. His stomach sours with thoughts of defeat. *If I don't survive the child will not. There is another way.* He rushes through countless calculations in his mind. Within seconds he finds strength in a silent decision. "I promise your son will live at the time of the awakening. End this in Lumeria. Find a med-station and sleep. I will find you. Now, be still."

"No." A look of fear grips her. "He's all I have left." She breaks into desperation. "Thoth, don't take my baby!"

"'Sephie!" Thoth's compelling tone shocks her into silence. He softens his gaze. "Sister…it is the only way. Let him sleep with his father while we prepare the world."

Her hands fall on her belly, eyes fill with tears.

Thoth selects a pair of symbols. A droning hum intensifies. Light envelops Persephone. She screams in agony, cringing in pain, trying not to move. Muscles tense up with electricity traversing through her atoms. The weight in her stomach latches on to an invisible hand.

She remembers the abyss on the path to the Forefathers, expecting a phantom to coil its smoke-filled tentacles around her child. Her mental anguish shifts from pain to her unborn; another life snatched from her.

Her toes curl, fingers shrivel into a ball. Eyes roll back. Her body dances with violence. The hum decreases, and the light diminishes with her muffled screams.

She catches her breath. Beads of sweat roll off her forehead. "Is it done?" she asks.

Thoth looks at the screen. He gasps. A smile breaks the uncertainty. He moves closer to gaze upon her with relief. "This has never been attempted before. He is alive…sleeping."

"Where will you go?" Persephone asks. "The fallout… nowhere will be safe."

"Atlantis. It should be safe. I'm at less risk as Markus and the others. Besides, we have enough antibodies to weather the storm."

She struggles to get her words out. "There's nothing there but wild tribes of man. Nothing but pagan barbarians." Thoth caresses her soaked forehead, bringing her some calm.

"It's a perfect place to start over. When the air clears, I will find you in Lumeria, I promise. But first, you must automate the complex."

"By the ancestors and the Lord of heaven, we will meet again. Thoth, I-"

He cuts her off with a kiss. She smiles with a nod, then stares at him, making a second last a lifetime. Her hands rest on her flat stomach, but she does not grieve. She nods once more and closes her eyes.

Thoth taps a symbol on the lid; it rumbles loudly as it slides shut. He grabs the gem before the blue waters flood the island, then jumps clear, landing close to the arch. When the sarcophagus drops below the surface, he looks on solemnly.

"Goodbye Persephone, until we meet again." A blue light flashes. He disappears.

Chapter 26: Kill Them All

EDGE OF HYPERBORIA

Dark chamber walls shudder with rumbling seeping up from metal floors. The space illuminates with scattered screens lighting up. Symbols materialize in the air at various points. Instruments hum. Overhead fixtures fill the space with gradual light, dim at first, then illuminating to a comfortable level.

A raised platform in the chamber's center houses a standing sarcophagus atop a flight of stairs. Blue light forms under the metal box. In pulses around the platform, creating an ionized barrier. Dull droning sounds match spinning light, increasing in pitch with every second. Plumes of smoke emanate from beneath the platform. An explosion of colors burst into the air. The sound winds down with the brightness, calming the rumble as it goes.

The sarcophagus' lid peels off to the side, revealing Queen Persephone. She climbs out, struggling to make it on to the platform's edge. Her blood-filled hand smears red on the metal. Her cauterized wounds open up - made fresh from the journey by light. She falls down the short metal stairs, then chides herself for not using the railings.

There are several panels on a sizable table-like console with warning symbols flashing. Persephone looks for any vacant part with a crevice to match Thoth's key. Her pain intensifies, bringing on concern for her survival in the coming hours. An empty slot catches her eye. She snatches the key from her neck. A moment of hesitation overcomes her. A deep breath washes away doubt. She slams it in. Red lights flash, alarms blare.

Persephone bows her head. "I seek forgiveness with the Lord of heaven, the Creator and Cherisher of the worlds." She taps several switches before rotating the key ten degrees clockwise, sixty degrees, and back to ten.

The key secures itself to the panel as it glows gold. The chamber rumbles with violent thunder. Distinct roars of rockets igniting rattle the bulkhead. Shaking intensifies, deep below at first, then throbbing booms. Wave after wave of departing missiles disrupts everything in the room.

Two displays materialize over the console. One shows a globe with targets, spread all through the realms, the other provides live data. Persephone looks at the information, fighting overwhelming panic invading her resolve. The noise and clamor dissipate, leaving a symphony of electronics to join the sounds of the sobbing Queen. *I did this!* Her stomach drops on the floor. Everything appears in a haze.

She limps away, holding her mouth with one hand while grabbing the wall with the other; she wants to scream, to wale, to let her emotions pour forth, but won't because this is a sacred place. She makes her way to a catwalk with an endless abyss below.

Stopping midway on the metal corridor, she peers down at the darkness, inviting her to descend into the unknown. *No!* Her head snaps to a circular room at the end of the corridor. Her boots drop heavily on the metal, creating a frightening echo reverberating through the cold air. The 30-foot journey appears impossible, but she hobbles the best she can.

The doors slide open, lights brighten. A single medical bed is in the center, with a glass covering suspended in the air. Persephone limps over to the bed exhausted, ready to lie there, to fade away into oblivion. She strips off her bloody clothing, cringing from the effort and Vali's blood, mixed in with hers. She tosses it all into a heap with disgust.

A sink catches her eye with a stack of small towels. *They really were just like us,* she thinks. She wastes no time in cleaning off the remnants of Vali from her skin. Midway in her washing, she breaks down. Her flat stomach chokes her soul. She forces herself to focus on Thoth's promise to keep her son safe.

Sensation returns to her limbs. The sterile bed invites her aching body to rest. She slides on the flat surface. It promptly inclines, folding her at the waist and disrupting the wound. She cries out in anguish, wishing someone would hear. Feeling alone in a void where death may find her.

She slams her palm on the bed's sides, searching for a compartment with anything to stop the wound's fresh round of bleeding. A chamber-door slides open, providing a medical kit. She finds a pad and presses it to her skin. Green gel forms. It fizzles into a white powder, bringing intense relief.

The glass covering descends, stopping three feet away from her face. She selects a sequence on the bed frame. A screen materializes. She clears her throat, wipes her tears. She is many things, and vain is one of them. She straightens out her hair while looking at a mirrored image on the screen. Satisfied, she selects another button.

"I am Persephone, Isis of pTah, daughter to House ENlil. The true heir to all the lands of the east, the west, and

Hyperboria. Wife to Osiris of House ENki. I commit myself to the long seep, though I fear I shall be dead before judgment day, at the time of the awakening. The world is in ruin. I am afraid I played no small part in this."

She pauses, ready to confess her crime.

"I launched devastating weapons on the planet. Outposts of ENlil shall be destroyed, including Hyperboria. Lands will be frozen, while others will be burnt; a combination of devastation engineered by my ancestors, your ancestors. But they did not unleash it on the world. It was I, Persephone, who did.

"I also unleashed a biological weapon, a plague for all Anuk, and those with our blood. I know not whether any of my kind or the watchers will survive. If shelter and care are sought in time, then maybe.

"You exist only in essence now. With the help of my cousin Thoth, you shall be preserved through the annals of time, hidden away for your safety. When you are born, know that you are from me and your father, King Osiris."

Tears roll down her face.

"Treachery and betrayal destroyed my house, your house. You are the heir to the world, little one. I pray you are born into a generation free from the failures of our kin. If not, you must fulfill your destiny. Bring order to chaos before the awakening.

"Judgment day is at the end of Virgo when the forefathers will rise. Destroy the house of ENlil if they exist, before they bring on the destruction of humankind. Vengeance must rain down on them if they live.

"I love you my child, more than I will ever be able to share. Rise above our nature. Become a beacon of hope. Rise above the winds of time, let the light of Orion flow through you. Until we meet, in this life or the next, I love you."

She taps a switch, the screen dissolves. As she closes her eyes the glass descends, sealing her in. The lighting in the room goes out, with only lights from under her enclosure illuminating the darkness.

PROPHECY

"In the beginning, we came to a lush and fertile planet, blessed with abundant life and resources. Now, the failings of us all have seen our brothers and sisters in humanity consumed by war and pestilence. The impunity by which death regards the living is but the will of the Creator.

To you my progeny, I leave the world in a state of peace and prosperity; may we meet its likeness upon our return. A departure from harmony will usher in retribution as commanded by the Creator. Know this, the awakening shall bring your judgment. Seek a Golden-age, or the slates shall be wiped clean, and our journey here will end with a cleansing wind." - Lord ENki, Lord of the wind, King of the foreign lands, son of ANu (circa last year of 3rd Sar)

Three-thousand-years passed since Persephone's disappearance. Humanity emerged from the ashes of conflict, with the progeny of man dominating the planet. Prince Atlas and cousins from Aryavan survived a terrible plague designed to wipe out all with Anuk blood. Watchers dwindled into a handful of survivors at first, trickling down to two in this age.

Persephone's heir has emerged, but more important, he is awake. Samiri has allied himself with the powers of Atlantis to achieve his miserable ends.

Conflict is brewing. War is on the lips of warriors. The Forefathers' return is near.

- *Liviana Badur*

Chapter 27: The Awakening

Myth surrounding Lumeria relegated it to a forbidden land of the forefathers - the gods of old. A handful of souls knew it to be the enormous craft that first brought the Anuk and their wonders to the Earth.

When the seven Forefathers set off to establish themselves in the world, their giant mother ship descended to the Southern continent at the bottom of the planet. It nestled itself in a vast lake to remain hidden. The onslaught of weapons launched into the continent, 3,000-years ago, set off instant freezing of this land. The ship was frozen under miles of ice and snow, never to be seen again.

Since the great Anuk Thoth traveled to the craft, no one has managed to infiltrate the structure. In this age, fate would deem otherwise. First, it was the High Priest Remus and his doomed expedition. Then the Watcher Samiri, who arrived via a forgotten portal not but one hour ago.

On he trots, in his aged body, long grease-filled hair, pale curdled skin, mangled limbs.

In pure ecstasy for his achievement, the villain roams forgotten corridors of sealed-off chambers. His portal dropped him close to a sacred hallway leading to the resting place of the forefathers. His triumph further serves to embolden a sense of power fueling his wretched plans.

For all he has caused and become, Samiri remains one of two with enough old knowledge allowing him to safely navigate Lumeria. If it weren't for his evil ways, he could be a Watcher to behold, comparable to the Keeper-of-Secrets. Revenge on Thoth consumes him in these halls.

He knew Thoth and the one Anuk he hated the most, Persephone, slept amongst the sacred seven. Although he lacked the Amon-I and the Key to Lumeria to properly execute his revenge, he took solace in a more primal approach. *I'll bash their heads to a bloody pulp.*

With every step he takes his heartbeat grows. He slows his pace to a crawl as he approaches a narrow catwalk. Darkness lies ahead with specks of light shining high in the air, mimicking starlight. He looks at the 29-foot bridge crossing ahead of him. Hesitation overcomes his feet. Caution demands to tread with care. The metal grate is sturdy. Cold air washes over him, cooling his panicked sweating.

There are many traps in Lumeria set for unwelcome visitors; even though he disabled many on this level, he remains wary of sudden pitfalls. Inhaling a calming breath, he proceeds to the massive circular enclosure waiting ahead.

Twenty-foot high doors slide open without cause, giving him much grief. The chamber comes to life with dim light, throwing an ominous glow on a path. Fear fills Samiri, for this is, after all, a sacred place; not even he can denounce it. He steps inside and waits for the doors to close, but they remain open.

To his left is darkness; same on the right. Gray floors in front of him are obscured by blue light from above. There is no discernible ceiling or walls.

A muffled droning sound becomes pronounced. It is not a rumbling or anything sinister; there is a subtle rhythm to it, much like a giant fan spinning slowly. Further in, he spots dim lighting over two rows of sarcophagi. His heart picks up speed like an Illyrian super-train. He hurries forward.

Undisturbed black granite makes up the sleep station of the ancient Anuk. Each of the nineteen 80-ton enclosures rises 10.5-feet high, 13-feet long, and 7.25-feet wide. A clear electronic field makes a faint hum forming the lid. Light from above streams on each sleeper, giving them a golden glow.

With his short stature, Samiri is unable to peer in at the residents, but a symbol carved into the granite presents their identity. He is familiar with the names and shows his respect by lowering his gaze. He passes the five, sounding off the names in his head; Dragoi, Odin, Shiva, Xi, Sakhmet. The final two jolts his heart - the resting place of ENlil and ENki.

Samiri bows down with reverence. He utters a prayer, repeating it three times, then sits on his heels and looks ahead, nervous about finding the pair he came to see. At the end of the darkness are two illuminated sarcophagi. *Thoth and Persephone.*

He takes off running; the anticipation of causing their demise fills his heart. He musters all his strength and jumps to the top of the granite's edge. He peers in with malicious delight at the sight of Persephone. He sweats in a cold swell of hatred. Crawling on the side he makes his way to the head of the box. He looks in at the sleeping Queen.

A metallic object from his jacket slides into his hand. He flips a switch igniting a short stream of light on a jagged edge. With hate in his heart, he slams the weapon on the ionized field.

Over and over Samiri strikes the invisible shield to no effect. His frustration sends him to the center for another attempt at bashing away. Cries of failure leave his lips. A mild disruption is visible by ripples of static coursing over the area. He looks over to Thoth's enclosure and leaps to it. Again, he does the same without success.

A hiss reveals a lighted panel materializing on the edge. The ancient Anuk display begins to spew information at rapid speed. Samiri reads as much as he can with intense concentration.

Thoth and Persephone were the only two in stasis with their essence, their souls, contained within their bodies. Anuk technology allowed a limited transference of consciousness beyond their bodies, without the help of the Amon-I; the sacred relic could carry a soul indefinitely. There is an apparent interaction between Thoth and an unknown interface. Samiri frowns at what he reads.

"So, you have been conversing with Lord Arias at the Citadel?" He asks, then reads on. "The conduit was made empty, renamed the Gem of Persephone; blasphemy!" He hurls a mouthful of spittle.

"Where is the Amon-I, Thoth? What have done to it?" His oatmeal complexion turns red with rage. He manipulates the display to rush through many logs of Thoth and Arias' interaction. Then, Samiri drops his weapon. His expression turns to one of realization mixed with rage. "The boy!" He repeats his words, each time rising in pitch and anguish, unafraid of disturbing the sleepers. He jumps to the ground and runs out of the chamber. The giant doors shut as he exits.

Weeks remain before the end of the age of Virgo; weeks before the awakening begins. Without the essence of the seven ancient Anuk, they will rise up in an unknown state. The destructive power of Lumeria will be at their disposal, to do with the world as they see fit, or as commanded.

Prince Timon, a descendant of Prince Atlas has the Key to control that power, along with the sacred Amon-I texts to facilitate the returning of the forefather's souls, and the Gem of Persephone - the holy vessel once channeling the essence of the seven and untold power.

The console on Thoth's sarcophagus disappears; the field on Persephone's flickers. It's not noticeable from the ground, but the light over her brightens. If you were near her enclosure, you would hear the hiss of alien machinery pumping a mist inside her space. Then, you would see the elegant fingers grasp at the edge.

The end of Virgo is near. Judgment day is at hand; are you ready?

The Journey continues.

Thank You

If you enjoyed this novel, please help us out by leaving a review on Goodreads, amazon, and any other review sites you are inclined to use.

Your patronage is appreciated, and may all your pursuits be blessed.

www.goodreads.com

https://www.amazon.com/dp/B07SJ9G2XC

Please visit

demarowriter.com

www.theanukchronicles.com

www.jennamoreci.com

www.iwriterly.com

www.vivienreis.com